DYING TO STAY YOUNG

A DCI Caron Dell Story

Glynis Drew

Amazon KDP

Copyright © 2025 Glynis Drew

All rights reserved

The characters and events portrayed in this book are fictitious. Any similarity to real persons, living or dead, is coincidental and not intended by the author.

No part of this book may be reproduced, stored in a retrieval system, or transmitted in any form or by any means, electronic, mechanical, photocopying, recording, or otherwise, without the express written permission of the publisher.

ISBN-13: 9798285676973

For my parents, Gladys and Bill, with love, always xx

DYING TO STAY YOUNG

Glynis Drew

1

Caron Dell – Aged Eighteen

24th February 2006

A perfect day. A horrific night.

I watch the North Sea's icy waters ebb and flow against its familiar English seashore as the plush bridal limousine passes along the bay's long, curved road overlooking the beach. Bitterly cold temperatures cause me to tighten my faux fur stole around my dark green bridesmaid dress, as a tingle of excitement runs through me.

A lone dog walker struggles against the wind, not daring to venture onto the sand below. Winter's uncaring snowstorm would challenge their return up the steep ramps at the end of the beach. Ice-white particles dance with fine blonde sand as the expansive coastline shows its wild beauty. Flashbacks provide happy childhood memories with my older sister, Beryl, swimming in the blue sea during the warmer summer months–different times.

We arrive at the sandstone steps of the Parlour Hotel, a five-storey Victorian building overlooking the sea, which was originally used as a summer residence by the Duchess of Northumberland. Fully refurbished at the turn of the twenty-first century, it is now a popular, sophisticated venue. In years to come, Jack and I will look back on today with hilarity at our clever plans to escape the wedding. No one suspects a thing.

A cold blast of salty sea air catches my breath, and hungry seagulls squawk above us as I watch Mam gingerly make her way up the gritted steps to the enormous doorway. The hotel attendant holds an emblazoned Parlour Hotel umbrella over me as I move my long, slim legs over the car's footplate and onto the powder-white pavement. I see dependable Jack waiting for me at the foyer's entrance, my excitement goes up another level. A romantic winter wedding was a perfect setting for the next step in our relationship. Jack had booked a single room at the rear of the hotel, which was deadly quiet. Perfect.

Beryl's Vintage Rolls-Royce stopped alongside the snowy curb. The raging sea and graphite sky provided a dramatic backdrop, complementing my sister's striking looks. Her cream bridal gown with an intricate lace stole enriched the image. Our proud Dad took her arm as they walked through the enormous, ornate foyer. Deep black and gold carpeting silenced their footsteps as they made their way to the grand hall from the marble-tiled entrance. Cold and excitement prompted goosebumps as I watched Beryl stand alongside Keith, her future husband. Grandma Peg said you'd never find a better match. A happy day, 150 smiling guests demonstrated that.

High ceilings within the generous reception room presented a comfortable formality to accommodate the happy day, and deep-pile carpet would be removed later for dancing. Tall Victorian arched windows framed the dark seasonal storm roaring outside, very much in contrast to the brightly lit room, with white linen on the tables, shiny cutlery and sparkling crystal glasses. A subtle scent of spring was promised by the peony rose and jasmine posies placed on each tabletop. Spring seemed a long way off.

Mr Terence Kimmage officiated the marriage, and we all cheered as the married couple kissed. Dad and Keith's speeches brought sentimental tears.

Danny, Keith's best man, was well known for his potty

mouth, which caused Mam some concern. We needn't have worried; his tales of Keith's childish shenanigans had the party crying with laughter.

Richard, the spoilt brat son of mam and dad's snobby friends, always kept me close. He was watching me every time I glanced around the room. I hadn't seen him for a number of years and felt uneasy at his attention, did he want to chat, or more? Whatever his reasons, he made my flesh crawl, and for the umpteenth time, I turned away from the stare of his dark, haunting eyes. Richard was a creepy man.

I kept an eye on Dad as much as he infuriatingly kept Jack close. It was like he knew what we had planned later that evening.

The day was perfect, with lots of laughter. Beryl and Keith's friends were hilarious. I could imagine happy festival weekends with that lot during the summer; their merriment was infectious and I wished someone could bottle the atmosphere to use another time.

An evening buffet was served, and after a respectable afternoon celebration, all formalities were now out the window. Harmless, drunk dancing was in full flow. I made my way to Jack's room. He would manage to get away from Dad, of that, I had no worries. Smiling photographs were constantly being taken by the spectacular, highly scented floral backdrop as I walked past the happy crowd waiting for their picture to be taken.

I collected my evening outfit from my room and walked to the rear of the hotel. I carefully hung up my bridesmaid dress and laid out my black outfit and shoes for later. Switching off the light, I left the door ajar and waited.

The creaking door said Jack was here. We had agreed on no lights in case someone came a-knocking.

A heavy, cigar-smelling bulk was on me in seconds. Forcing my hands behind my head, he stuffed a handkerchief in my mouth. It wasn't Jack. I kicked, tried to scream, bit and continued to fight like a lunatic. He was much too strong as he ripped my underwear from me.

Seconds later, I heard the tear of my body as he raped me.

The bastard took more time fastening his trousers and taking his handkerchief before he left. Leaving nothing to suggest what had happened. He didn't make a sound.

Silence.

Numb.

I struggled to process the horror. My virginity was taken in a few terrifying minutes. Had it happened? Blood and bruising between my legs were evidence enough that it had. I'd fought like a wildcat. My whole body ached, my wrists and arms were bruised, but the physical hurt didn't concern me. My body would repair. Would my mind?

Everything started to spin. I sat up and flicked on the bedside light as I looked around the small, depressing room. Unlike the rest of the building, it appeared unloved. I knew the feeling.

Who would believe me? My clothes had been carefully arranged, and the door to my discreet hotel room was open. I was lying on the bed, waiting. Fucks sake I was gift-wrapped!

He had ripped apart my feelings of devotion to Jack in minutes, I would never be the same again.

My mind whirled. Blood, bruising? Stupidity and the humiliation that a courtroom interrogation would bring. 'Rough sex,' no doubt, would form their defence against my physical injuries. I couldn't put myself or my family through it. Shame overwhelmed my judgment.

Apart from my wild thoughts, would he ever be caught? One of Beryl's friends? A wedding guest or a hotel employee? Did he follow me to the room? Had he watched me all day? Richard! Cigars, the smell of cigars. And something else, another scent. My recall is already starting to fail me, my mind trying to protect me from my trauma, and I couldn't remember. What was that smell?

Then, from nowhere, a rage I had never experienced in

girls make themselves comfortable in the luxurious living room of the Cartwrights' impeccably designed rambling property. The deep seats of the leather sofa hug the youngster's small frame, accentuating their vulnerability further.

Greg is talking into his mobile phone, relaying information from the screen of his company's laptop to an associate. Mary can hear some of Greg's business speak, 'I am prepared to consider further business with your company, and if you ping over some figures, I will see where we go…' She is mortified at how relaxed her husband is and how quickly his young guests have made themselves comfortable. Greg continues to waffle on, unfazed by the fact that his visitors are children. The situation is sickening to watch.

Mary clenches her fists as she sees Tony Boulter strut his authority across her navy-blue Persian rug before placing his laptop on the marble coffee table. Heavy curtains are drawn across the floor-to-ceiling windows, blocking out the inky sky and intermittent grey clouds as the moon softly pokes its winter beams through the darkness.

Boulter is Cartwright Construction's business manager, who Greg has employed to do the hiring, firing and much more since the company's inception fifteen years earlier. Tony Boulter is charming and easy to trust, whilst being highly respected in the local community. Mary has never heard a bad word said against him, but as the situation unfolds, she thinks those of sound mind probably detest him just as much as she does. His broad, fit frame, pale grey eyes and sharp facial features make him instantly attractive. His confidence and good looks have captivated many new clients, and the believability side of his conman personality benefits Cartwright's business deals and negotiations. Some women even fall at his feet. He makes Mary shudder.

Mary has often confronted Greg regarding his manager's involvement in their business and private lives. Her husband constantly dismisses her concerns as pathetic accusations with no proof. There is no doubt that Greg unreservedly

3

The Cartwright's Home – Leeds

13th December 2024

Winter's icy wind continues its haunting wail outside the Cartwright's overstated stone-built summerhouse. Inside the rear of the bespoke structure, oil heaters warm its dark, windowless storage room. There is a stylish sofa bed in one corner, jarring against the messy myriads of wires crisscrossing the floor, snaking up the legs of the solid oak picnic table. Digital gadgets are placed at one end, with a kettle and microwave on the other. It is now eight pm, and the weather is turning colder. Mary Cartwright turns up the heaters and zips her black fleece jacket to its highest point under her chin.

Holed up and well out of sight, she studies the laptop in front of her as she watches her husband, Greg, cheat on her yet again.

This time it's different. A horrendous, sickening sight is being played out in her own home, only a hundred metres away from her current hiding place. Leaving enough room for a football pitch between both buildings. Watching Greg now, it seems that football is the last thing on his mind. Her porcelain coffee mug shatters on the solid wooden floor as she automatically covers her mouth to stop her screams, even though they won't be heard.

Plumping up sumptuous velvet cushions, three young teenage

2

Detective Chief Inspector Caron Dell

13ᵗʰ December 2024

Now, aged thirty-six, with a solid police background, I hope my chosen vocation continues to be just as rewarding. My recent appointment to DCI within Northumberland's Force is what I have worked for.

Holding my hot tea, I look out of my bedroom window across the bay, just five miles north of the hotel where my attack took place. I think about the decision I made all those years ago, and wonder what would have happened had I reported my assault. No doubt a 'rape kit' would have been used and logged, valid for any future attacks.

Did he rape again? Had he done it before? Is it too late to do anything now, eighteen years later? Shame, guilt, and the hatred I feel towards him, whoever he is, never leaves me.

That night changed my life in every possible way. It shifted my focus to securing justice for every victim, regardless of gender or age.

If the courts don't deliver, I will.

my life took over. I threw bloodied sheets into the bath whilst pulling my dirty, abused body under the full force of the shower.

What would the housekeeper think – what would Jack think?

Shame constantly overrode my intelligence. I couldn't report him, my attacker. No one's parents should go through that – neither should I. Every male in the building would be suspected. DNA taken, processed, eliminated. NO! I couldn't do it! Besides the fact that he could have already left. He has tarred Beryl and Keith's friends with his evil attack.

I dressed, plaited my hair and reapplied makeup by memory. I couldn't bear to look at my puffy, tear-streaked face, nor could I behold the shameful image that would be reflected.

I wondered should I return to the party?

Of course I did - I had to try and find my bastard rapist. Think logically: what would I have done had our plans worked out? I return to my room with my bridesmaid dress, now rolled up into a ball, before I face the party. How can I do this? I begin to shake; I have to go.

Catching a glimpse of myself in one of the many ornate, full-length mirrors takes my breath away. What a mess. Mam bumped into me as I stepped back into the dimly lit party room; the dance floor was full, with laughter and singing saturating the air. 'What the hell happened to you? It might be a good idea for you to go to bed, darling. It has been a long day for everyone.'

Richard raised his brandy glass to me and slugged it back, and Jack mouthed, 'Sorry.' It took all my strength to stay upright. After a minute or so, I steadied myself and left.

trusts Boulter. What a sucker her once strong and thoughtful husband has turned into. Unlike Boulter, Greg is shorter and carries too much weight around his middle. His loyalty demonstrates his sloth-like brain.

Boulter's coercive behaviour is becoming more obvious. Without a doubt, the Cartwright's have unwittingly been pulled into his vile world as he continues to manipulate their business, and it seems he has done so for years. His controlling way has empowered him to expand his illegal activity: drug supply and money laundering. It looks like child exploitation is now added to his CV. Mary continues to watch and record what she is witnessing, realising her own life will be in grave danger if she is discovered. Instinctively, she picks up her phone and sends a message to her father: *'URGENT young girls in danger.'*

Frightened, as she sits in her lavish summerhouse, Mary is at a loss as to what else she can do. She wonders if their home represents a picture-perfect snapshot of a happy one, because today, inside, it shows a different story. Those three girls will be subjected to nightmarish abuse over the next few hours; something will need to be done before it's too late.

Mary backs up her camera evidence to USBs, never doubting her laptop will vanish at some point once it is handed over to Yorkshire Police. What she has witnessed is way beyond her original theories, and the evidence she has for her divorce proceedings is exceptional. Now, though, she can trust no one, thanks to Boulter. The enormity of what is being played out in her home contributes to her fear. It's essential she stays focused and considers what must be done to protect herself. Boulter cannot locate her. For Mary's safety, their summerhouse must appear vacant as it usually would be during winter. The window shutters are closed, with undisturbed ice-white particles providing a forlorn, eerie scene.

The Cartwrights' property is purposefully set back from

the quiet roads in the affluent village, shielding their home and gardens from nosy neighbours. Single-lane tracks crisscross the rear of their garden; at this point in time, apart from her father, no one knows she is there.

Mary pulls a large hessian rug over the coffee stain and puts her broken porcelain mug inside a rubbish bag. With the flick of a switch, the corner bed clicks back to its sofa setting. She quickly folds the bedding and returns the oil heaters to their original location. Wires are unplugged and packed. If she were to be discovered, Boulter would know what she has witnessed; it doesn't take a genius to recognise that Mary will be a problem for Boulter.

All that Mary has left to do before she leaves is pick up her laptop. Her camera feed continues to provide proof of Tony Boulter and her husband's horrific crime. Her shivers are not totally due to the icy cold air weaving its aroma into the building.

Mary's father, Judge Phillip Hicks, knows his daughter is in danger. She must protect herself and get out before that evil bastard, Boulter, finds her. Mary's phone pings with a message from her father, '*W safe house.*'

The longer she continues to watch events unfold in her home, the higher the risk of being caught. Contacting the police is also out of the question. Some of Boulter's closest associates work for Yorkshire's force – undeniably, they are well-paid. Any of those involved would trip over themselves to inform Boulter of her whereabouts. Within minutes, she would be found.

Sitting in his solicitor's office, Judge Hicks makes an anonymous emergency call to the police, stating a robbery is currently underway at the Cartwrights' address. He ditches the pay-as-you-go SIM card after he hangs up the call; more aware than ever of the danger Mary is in. Implicating himself will cause her more damage. As strong and determined as Mary is, he hopes his daughter can escape her home without leaving any trace. A nervous wait ensues as he watches his mobile phone for her update.

Back at the house, Greg's young guests are bemused but not frightened. Their actions demonstrate a familiarity with their hosts. During the last six months, Mary has never seen youngsters in her home. Nausea overwhelms her at the thought of what lies ahead.

Boulter is wearing medical gloves as he passes gift bags around. 'Unbelievable,' she says, under her breath, 'Party bags.'

Each bag has twenty-pound notes peering from the top. One of the girls begins to giggle as bottles of what looks like spirits - gin, vodka, it could be anything - are also distributed. Unscrewing the bottle tops, the two younger girls immediately begin to drink the contents. Both girls are wearing oversized clothes and instantly become woozy. The third girl looks towards the dining room and screws the top of her bottle back into place. She then watches her friends' reactions. Recognising what is happening, she begins to fake her drunken stupor.

Clever, thinks Mary, but this is a million miles away from observing the usual escorts her husband has lusted over during the last few months - if you can call such perverted behaviour towards anyone lust.

Mary watches Tony as he carries one of the young girls, who has seemingly passed out, from the living room to the rear of her property. She cannot see where he is taking her, the dining room, the orangery or their soundproofed games room; ironically, that door tends to slam shut! But no slamming door could be heard.

Her bile continues to rise. Mary's restricted view prevents her from seeing where the girl has been taken.

At the same time, Greg opens the front door, and another unknown male enters the living room. He wears a beanie pulled down as far as possible over his forehead, with a dark scarf covering his nose and mouth. He, too, is wearing protective gloves. Mary doesn't recognise him. He nods at Tony as he returns to the living room from the rear of the house.

Boulter approaches the third man and steers him out of Greg's earshot. They stand facing each other beside a tall bookcase.

Mary holds her breath. If either man were to turn their head towards the shelving, they would see her surveillance camera, it is tiny but not invisible.

Tony speaks to the visitor with urgency, 'Petra knows about Hock. I had to bury his last one. He had him so shot up that the boy was blue when I arrived. The lad has been on the streets for years; no one will miss him. Hock's a liability, get rid of the thick bastard and deal with these kids tonight.' He glances over to Petra, happy to see her in a daze. 'Don't let on to Cartwright. He is taking the rap for it. My use for the dozy fucka is done.'

Mary clasps her hand over her mouth. *The boy won't be missed, the girls are next, and clueless Greg has been completely set up.* Her microphone has not picked up much conversation in the past, but this! It couldn't have been clearer: gold dust evidence. Boulter's silver-grey ponytail, chiselled face and soulless pale grey eyes are easily recognisable. Towering over his ally and built like a ripped machine, no one could match him in sheer power and strength. Under five feet tall and as thin as a pencil, Mary wouldn't stand a chance of fighting any of them off. If Boulter notices her camera between her hard-backed books, she's as good as dead.

Mary needs to escape quickly. Her safety and evidence are her main concerns, but she is conflicted about leaving the girls, feeling helpless as she decides what to do. Boulter makes her sick. No one would believe it of the magnetic Tony or Greg. Both have been caught red-handed, and both could go down for this.

Furiously, Mary can't ignore that Tony is nothing if not well turned out. She lets out her breath as he removes his dark grey cashmere overcoat whilst walking away from her camera. His god-awful, evil eyes stare into the void of the rear hallway. Has he paled under his tan? Or is she just imagining it? From her limited view, Mary can't see if anyone else is lurking. Boulter appears to be staring at something or someone. Muttering something under his breath, he shrugs his coat back on. She knows his father would be furious if he were still alive to see how his son has turned out.

Mary observes the shorter man as he walks towards the dining room. She can't see his movements clearly, and she wonders what vile act he will carry out. Mary's stomach contents are emptied into the bin bag at her feet.

Tony Boulter collects his laptop from the table. Is he going to set up some sick recording? She turns her focus back onto the oldest girl, Petra, who is watching her keeper. The young girl wraps her coat closer around her. Is she looking for a way out? Mary observes her as she, too, stares towards the rear of the house from beneath her greasy mousy-brown fringe.

The girl stands and feigns a drunken apathy. Mary guesses she heard Boulter's discussion with the shorter man. Petra flicks her eyes towards the rear hallway. She seems to panic slightly. Did she nod? Is someone there who Mary cannot see? Not for the first time, Mary acknowledges that the girls certainly appear to know the Cartwrights' home. She gingerly takes a sip of water, hoping it stays down.

Boulter walks out of the living room and into the rear of the property for the second time. The contemporary kitchen, dining room and orangery are to the left of the rear corridor, taking full advantage of the summer sun and garden. The enormous open space has a large bespoke dining table, more sofas and a splendid reading corner.

However, Boulter turns right from the passageway and enters their vast entertainment room. Mary hears the familiar sound of the heavy door slamming behind him. Her blood begins to boil. Boulter is swanning around her home like he owns it; nowhere seems out of bounds.

Greg's desire for a "boys' club" games room included a full-size snooker table and bar; both are well used. Their party room provides enough space to accommodate at least thirty guests, with occasional tables strategically placed for ease. Greg's snooker table is positioned on the right side of the room, alongside cue racks and a dart board, surrounded by Banksy's art prints. "Boys and their toys" has often been quoted. Mary scoffs at Greg's inability to play either of the two games very well. The Cartwrights' private, fireproof office is out of sight behind the impressive walnut bar. Mary thinks only she and her husband have access, but after watching Boulter these last few months, he, too, might use their private room.

In the living room, Mary watches as Greg closes his laptop and goes to pour a drink. He seems oblivious to what is taking place under his nose.

The third man glances towards Greg, standing at the drinks cabinet, as he lifts the second unconscious girl from the large sofa, then turns to take her to the rear of the property. Mary is livid and can't see where he is taking her; clearly, she is unable to put up a fight. After a couple of minutes, Mary hears the slam of her entertainment room door a second time. Has the third man followed Boulter, or is Boulter returning? Silence, no footsteps could be heard.

Mary watches Petra stumble towards her husband. With her party bottle in hand, she offers to help. Her back is to the camera, blocking Mary's view. Could Petra be filling his glass from her bottle? With a slur, she shouts, 'Bottoms up!'

Greg turns to Petra and says, 'You know the drill: drink before the fun starts.' He necks his tipple, and she pours him another. Before he gets a chance to drink it, he stumbles and falls with a thud. Petra quickly makes her way towards the rear corridor.

4

Mary And Petra

Mary imagines the girl is terrified as she disappears from view.

'What are you doing? Oh God, she's looking for her friends?' Mary shouts to herself in frustration as she paces up and down the summerhouse, grabbing at her long, curly red hair. She despairs as to what to do. 'Get out. Go out the front door.' Boulter will easily find her; she is running directly towards him.

Mary's panic heightens. She can't see where the girl is going; she hopes and prays the third man went into her party room, and Boulter was not on his way out.

Petra trips and falls as she walks across the dining room floor, looking for her friends. She can't find them. Terrified that her life is in danger, she knows she has to leave. Quickening her progress as she heads toward the orangery, she unlocks the outside door and runs quietly into the enormous garden. She slips and slides down the frozen patio steps until she finds her footing.

Running down the icy landscaped garden, her heightened adrenaline pumps through her body. Petra doesn't think of the bitterly cold temperatures engulfing her thin frame; fear drives her on.

Mary packs up her laptop, tucks her hair under her woollen hat and pulls on her gloves. Remaining in the shadows of her summerhouse, she places her bin bag into their garden waste bin, which is not ideal, but at least it's out of sight. Mary quietly locks the door, carefully wraps the chains across the handles, and padlocks them together. She only has minutes and is amazed at how quickly she has secured the building without a sound. Listening for any movement, she goes towards the side of her summer house and watches for Petra to come into view.

Mary remains out of sight as security lights stream across the garden's side patio. She spots Petra panicking. In different circumstances, the Cartwrights' park-like garden would be chocolate-box perfect as it poses in its shroud of winter.

The chilling wind cuts through Petra's clothes as she runs across the vast garden, lost.

Mary has turned off the remaining security lights in the garden, for fear of being spotted, but now raised voices can be heard from the house. Doors slam. Mary can only assume Greg and the two other girls are rendered useless.

The storm is being blown towards the east, allowing December's full moon to peek through patchy dark clouds. Its muted silver beams assist Mary's vision as the night air freezes the land.

Petra hurriedly looks around the grounds for help from a neighbour or anyone who might be about and realises Cartwright's safe space is now her prison. It always was. Surrounding the garden is a tall, thick hedge and a six-foot wall. She is very aware that no one will look for her, even if her screams are carried far and wide. In an exquisite, well-to-do area, who would be crazy enough to be walking on a freezing night such as this? And who would be crazier to follow the screams of a young girl? Petra knows she is on her own.

A barn owl hoots and throws her further into nightmare territory as it watches her from its familiar hunting post, waiting for the season's meagre pantry to open its doors. Petra continues to remain upright despite the slippery, frosted lawn. She can hear the crunch of feet running over icy grass; they're too close for comfort, and she realises her pursuer can easily hear her. Now in full panic mode she looks for somewhere she can hide. Why didn't she leave through the front door? Too late for that now. Petra takes off her shoes and silently crouch-runs towards the generously tall laurel hedge entwined with holly. She races alongside it, praying her shadow cannot be seen. Ignoring scratches from sharp, spikey leaves piercing her arms through her thinly padded coat. Sheer determination drives Petra to escape the clutches of her terrifying ordeal, as she continues to distance herself from the sickening situation back at the Carwright's home.

Another stone building in the middle of the never-ending garden comes into view. Terror encourages her to look for what she hopes is a place to hide. It's her only plan. She hears a man's voice, cursing. Has he slipped and fallen? She turns to look but sees no one. Petra tries to keep the sound of her footsteps low, knowing she's almost there: just a few more steps.

Mary is just as terrified as she watches and waits, alert to the horror unfolding.

Petra groans as she sees the shutters and doors of the garden building are bolted and locked, with their chains and padlocks in clear view. She runs behind the summerhouse, hoping to find an open doorway or a window.

Mary grabs the girl, covers her mouth, and whispers in her ear, 'You're safe. Keep quiet.' Petra nods, and Mary takes her hand.

They move quickly to the snow-covered evergreen border on the ground's outskirts, skidding as they go. Is escape still possible? They weave through the arches cut out of the tall, dense green hedging. Mary stops and listens to the noise of sirens in the distance, leaving only minutes to get out safely, as far away from her home as possible. Boulter must never know Mary is involved: he'd kill her in a heartbeat, or one of his minions will.

Mary and her father know some of Yorkshire's officers cannot be trusted. Corrupt police officers, controlled by Boulter, will score many brownie points if they hand her over to him. Staying put while they wait for the police to arrive is too much of a risk. Boulter will find out sooner or later that Mary was a witness to tonight's events.

Gasping for breath, the pair eventually reach the garden's sandstone boundary, running along its border until they come to a break in the wall. Mary keys in the heavy iron gate's security code and quietly pulls it open. They pass through, and Mary softly clicks it closed. She lifts her finger to her lips to ensure Petra remains quiet as she watches her slip her freezing feet back into her shoes. Gasping for air shows their determination to escape Boulter's clutches, while their white breath is a reminder of the cold night.

Petrified, they move quickly downhill into the dip of the short, unlit track which leads to arable farmland. Dense copses edge acres of fields, marking landowner boundaries. A little further on, the outline of a humped stone bridge is easily identified as it spans the River Wharfe. Like many country access roads, the bridge was initially built to accommodate horses and carts hundreds of years earlier; it is now used for much larger, single-file traffic. In the distance, pale yellow streetlights outline a small town marking their safety. Petra moans, realising her escape is still not guaranteed.

Mary knows the area and town well; local landowners and farmers regularly drive their tractors and machinery along the designated track. The next hundred meters of the gravelled road are open to the elements and sparkle with ice as the moonlight peeks in and out of the patchy clouds, while winds constantly change the night sky. Slipping and sliding, Mary and Petra continue to move as fast as they possibly can to reach the small pitch-black woodland beside the narrow road; ebony shadows beneath the trees offer somewhere to hide if necessary. Mary's hired car will take them both to safety, but only if they make it across the bridge and into the town. Will they reach it?

After running along the track for a few minutes, Mary stops. She recognises the noise tyres make as they rumble across the gravel; the approaching vehicle makes her blood run cold. Looking back over her shoulder, she sees the glow of headlights pulling up from the dip in the track a short distance away. If she can see them, it won't be long before they drive up onto the flat track and spot the pair of them running for their lives. Mary is silently thankful for the eerie-looking, thick undergrowth beneath swaying evergreen pines. For the second time that night, Mary grabs Petra's hand and they launch into a dark, wet trench to the left of them, hoping the gloomy woodland conceals their hiding place.

Mary whispers, 'Stay down, keep quiet.' After a few seconds, car tyres slowly crunch across frosted stones. Mary freezes as the vehicle stops less than ten feet away from their ditch. Someone climbs out. Terrified, the pair don't move a muscle. Petra is trembling with fear. The man stands with his back to them as they remain out of sight in the darkness. He speaks into his mobile.

'No one here, boss. She wouldn't have got this far, and there are no footprints on the track. She'll have headed for the road, not knowing where she is.' He turns around and walks a few paces closer to the runaways, leaving just a few feet between them. Mary can guess who he is talking to. Boulter. The man stops and looks back down the track. 'Hold on, boss, there's something here.' Petra's heart stops. She, too, has heard a sound coming from behind them.

Mary is petrified but needs to know what is causing the crunching sound of the icy land. She turns as more twigs snap under the weight of someone or something not far from their current place of safety.

Petra, trembling with fear, also takes a brief look over her shoulder.

A pair of bright amber eyes stare at the two frightened humans. Mary's heart sinks as she considers what to do if the inquisitive fox gives them away. The animal moves closer to the pair, curious as to why they are in his domain. Mary is thankful the mating season is still a few weeks away. All the same, she prays there are no cubs around.

The fox creeps forward, sniffing the air. Petra shakes with fear as the animal runs past them onto the track.

Then silence.

Mary turns to look at the man still standing a few feet away.

He speaks again into his mobile. 'It's nothing, just a fox. Yeah, let's leave. See you tomorrow. I'm outta here.'

He returns to his car and continues driving towards the town, Mary's escape route. They wait for his car lights to disappear before starting their freestyle, slipping and sliding as they make their way over the bridge.

After a nerve-wracking twenty minutes, they both climb into her rented SUV, purposefully parked on an affluent avenue. Petra lies across the back seats. Mary's phone pings: '*W safehouse asap.*' Mary messages back, '*One girl with me.*' She can only imagine her father's reaction. She changes SIMs and ditches the used one down the drain. Her heart skips a beat as Tony Boulter's matt black Range Rover slowly turns onto the long avenue. Not once has Mary given Boulter a thought about him executing his plans to find Petra.

The bitterly cold weather has frosted every vehicle, and Mary can make out Boulter's facial profile as he slowly scans each car. His car crawls along looking for his enemy. Mary moves her seat back and slides into the footwell, the pedals dig into her knees. She whispers to Petra to keep still. Locking the car would draw his attention to them as Boulter pulls up alongside her vehicle. Thankfully, her car windows have not defrosted, making it difficult for him to look inside. Heart racing, Mary holds her breath, anxious that he will spot white fumes as she exhales. Hearing the soft purr of his Range Rover as he drives off, Mary slowly moves back into the driving seat and watches through the rear window as the enormous car moves further away at a snail's pace before turning left.

Mary starts the engine and heads in the opposite direction. The main roads in town are gritted, then, carefully, she drives to their safe house.

Boulter
Petra fucking Gould is as good as dead and buried. That's a certainty. Ches Blain will have already issued my death warrant if he knows about my sideline, and it'll be me six feet under – no one double crosses Blain! But who the fuck is going to grass me up to one of Europe's most wanted? No one.

5

The Viaduct

Winter's chill doesn't deter the hardy ivy as it creeps up the archways of Yorkshire's Arthington Viaduct, spanning the valley and River Wharfe below. Each of the twenty-one arches will have many a story to tell, if only sandstone could talk.

A homeless community meets every Friday and Saturday around midnight below one of the semicircles. The damp moss and green lichen reach up from the cold ground, they're not a discouragement; the group are safer here than sleeping on the streets each weekend, getting pissed on as folk hurl abuse or being attacked by scummy toerags.

Sweeping hail and snow focus the crowd's attention on the brazier, where foraged combustibles contribute to the dry kiln that Bart supplies. No one bothers their diverse group as long as fires are put out and they move on before the next day's trains run overhead. Johnathan Wilbur Barton, "Bart" as he prefers, makes sure of that. He knows from his experience as an ex-army captain that the warmth will prevent the freezing night air from crawling into their bones. The viaduct has been their safe spot for months.

Jessie and Emily, two fourteen-year-old friends, left home six months earlier to escape the disciplines of school, social popularity contests and their home life. Bart suspects Emily left home due to abuse – he has never voiced his thoughts.

Fifteen-year-old Petra makes up the young trio, and all have one thing in common: they search for excitement outside of their suffocating routine and look to enjoy life while they are young. They can choose which doorway to sleep in, but the freedom they are searching for is not what they've found. Together, they feel safe, huddled beneath the viaduct with a larger group. The girls won't be there tonight though. Tony Boulter has made sure of that.

As usual, Bart works the burning brazier underneath the viaduct's western arches. For the first time in many months, he is alone this Friday. His homeless friends will not shelter here on this particular night. The group generally shuffle along after the last train of the day heading for Harrogate, has travelled overhead. Now approaching midnight, no one has arrived.

Bart was born into wealth with the privileges his Hampshire-based family name carries. Now, he has chosen to stay away from his descendant's country mansion at this stage in his life. After completing twenty-four years of military service, he has decided not to return to a life of luxury after witnessing the horror and death his company saw. How could anyone think his return home would resemble his life before the Army? He will never be the same again.

Bart's mother accepts his decision, but his father, a retired Lieutenant Colonel, struggles with the fact that his son chooses to be homeless when he has a perfectly formed pile to live in. Bart can't think of anything worse.

To keep the peace, and with no ill will toward his family, he returns home for a couple of days each Christmas and speaks to his mother on her birthday. His sister Bernadette relishes any time with him. Now, with her own family, Bart enjoys the excitement of Christmas morning with his two young nephews.

They will grow to become military men themselves if their Grandfather has anything to do with it. Despite the difficulties Bart faced during his time in the army, he has no regrets, the deaths of his fallen colleagues being the exception. Bart will also encourage the two youngsters to consider a military career when the time is right.

A move north is good for him; he's far enough away from home, which gives him peace. Putting some form of discipline into his routine adds to the attraction. Bathing every morning in the cold River Wharfe, focuses Bart's mind on helping others worse off than himself.

He is a familiar face in the aptly named The Arches pub, a few minutes away, where he drinks a pint of Yorkshire's finest ale every afternoon. The landlord hired him to unload barrels and other deliveries twice weekly, and the work is welcome. His reward is a few quid in his pocket and a free pint every day.

The Arches is a popular local, with farmers and landowners frequenting the friendly atmosphere. Friday nights aren't always as pleasant; it can get a bit raucous. By Saturday morning, all disputes are forgotten. Their Sunday roast is exceptional and attracts many locals and gastropub enthusiasts.

Christopher Walker is a well-to-do landowner who has taken a shine to Bart. He also provides him with work as an assistant to his elderly gamekeeper. Mr Walker is no fool; Bart is one of his poaching problems, but Walker keeps his enemies close, a mantra that has never let him down. Bart jumps at the chance, only if he can continue to work at The Arches; giving up a free pint each day is a ridiculous sacrifice.

In return, Bart is provided with a shelter of sorts if he wants to use it, and was pleased to learn the run-down original gamekeeper's hut has external walls, but that's about it. This gave him another reason to spend time here, repairing the building and providing a base for as long as he works for Walker. His working arrangement has been in place for over three years.

Bart's cottage is now watertight and has a living/kitchen area, a shower room, and sleeping quarters. Although the bedroom is tight, he places four camp beds in the small but perfectly square room. A broad canopy has been erected to the side of the property. The quaint stone building has a generator to supply electricity. Bart prefers to bathe in the river and likes to sleep outside. His landlord is more than happy with his choices.

His homeless friends stay in his single-storey cottage or sleep under the canopy if they choose to seek shelter. There are rules, however: they supply their own sleeping bags and clean up before leaving, and only on a Friday or Saturday night. The majority remain beside the brazier below the viaduct.

Bart expects an unwanted visitor tonight. A few regulars from The Arches have made him aware of the trouble at the Cartwright's, and he isn't shocked. He has suspected that young girls from the crowd have been used and abused regularly by Cartwright and his cronies, but, like everything Boulter is involved in, there is no proof, nor are there any witnesses.

After receiving many underlying threats from the local constabulary and direct threats from Boulter, Bart's hands are tied. In reality, he knows nothing of what goes on but fears for the girls and others all the same.

He is aware of his surroundings and alert to any noises while he stokes the fire's flames as the cold sleet threatens to dampen them.

As anticipated, a large dark shape storms towards Bart, and he braces himself for a full-on challenge. He is probably the only man who could come anywhere near to defeating Boulter - if the fight were fair.

'Where's Petra?' Barks Tony Boulter in the howling wind as he approaches the homeless man.

'Do you think I know Petra's every move?'

'Yes, you do. Where is she?' Boulter persists.

'You know, Boulter?' Replies Bart as he picks up a heavy piece of wood. 'I don't, but I would guess she has run for the hills to escape your evil clutches. Where are Emily and Jessie?

Where are your concerns for them?' He moves from behind the brazier with his shovel-sized hand tightening around the solid oak branch. Given half a chance, he'd break this bastard's neck.

Boulter looks at Bart's hand and steps forward. 'Think you can take me on you fucking posh halfwit?'

'Pick your weapon of choice, Boulter. You won't stand a fucking chance. I'd be doing everyone a favour.'

Boulter pulls out his reliable handgun and asks again: 'Where is Petra?'

Bart looks at him and guffaws. 'You've not checked in with your whore then? You need to work on your own lack of thought before you call anyone a halfwit.'

Boulter turns and walks away, smug. He takes no heed of the wind as it whips up his cashmere coat above his head. Striding back to his car, he knew this day would come.

Bart hopes Boulter's whore survives the beating she's in for. He would have preferred for her to be arrested.

During the bleak winter's night, the small white single cottage looks warm and welcoming against tall evergreens laden with white dots of snow and ice. Over a century old, it had been left derelict for years before Boulter purchased it for his mother's last days at a knockdown price.

Boulter
Little did my mother know that her days were numbered. I fucking amaze myself sometimes. Her unmarked grave is deep, alongside my father's do-gooder skeletal remains. Their deaths have been and will continue to be a smokescreen for me. If they were alive, they'd be stunned to learn how much property they own.

My well-paid, emotionally damaged accountant keeps the taxman at bay. Impressive really, how easy it has been for me to manipulate so many thick bastards – they always had a choice: do as I ask or die.

I'm not an unreasonable man.

6

Alina

As he drives towards the isolated cottage, the icy wind seems to endorse Boulter's cold heart. The freezing trail is treacherous, but his determination keeps him focused. He can see the faint glow of the cottage lights in the distance, a beacon of warmth in the bitter night.

As he approaches, his thoughts turn to Petra. Where could she have gone? He clenches the steering wheel tighter as he drives slowly, his mind races with possibilities. The idea of her betrayal is simmering, ready to boil over.

Finally, the cottage comes into full view. It stands there, pristine and untouched by time, much like the memories of his mother. He parks his car and steps out into the biting cold and crunches his way along the frosty path. With a deep breath, he approaches the door, the weight of his thoughts pressing down on him as he prepares to face Alina.

Alina opens the door to her man, just as Boulter reaches the secluded cottage less than half a mile from the viaduct. Cold air swirls inside the cosy room, bringing a bone-chilling welcome with it. He grins as he walks over the threshold, which leads him directly to the small living area. Boulter dips his head below the original beams before sitting in a comfortable chair beside the open fire.

Alina pours her man his favourite tipple and then lays across his lap as she gently encourages a more sensual attraction. Boulter smiles, like the cottage she has lived in for the past fifteen years; he owns her outright, too.

With the building registered in his mother's name, Boulter knows it won't be long before some bright spark joins the dots. Yorkshire hasn't come looking for him. They wouldn't dare.

'Have you seen Petra?' He asks as he begins to remove her clothes.

'Petra? No, I have not seen her for a while.' Her English is excellent but her Polish accent remains as she begins to breathe heavily.

Boulter studies Alina's eyes. He knows she won't lie to him. She'd be a fool to.

'What has that girl done to run off?' She uses her best seduction techniques, but her man has his mind elsewhere.

'Ah, you know that girl is so flighty, I just need to speak to her.' He looks again at Alina. In different circumstances, they wouldn't be sitting in an armchair. She is undoubtedly beautiful.

Aged twenty-five, Alina's young body was altered to meet Boulter's requirements, giving her the perfect figure. Many years later, no one has touched her but her keeper. Alina is more than happy with his arrangements. She works hard to keep in shape and takes the best care of her looks. Alina would never say how thankful she is that he left her beautiful face alone. That would sound very ungrateful.

Alina is eternally in debt to Boulter. He took her from the streets in her late teens, and she does not doubt for one minute that they will marry and have a family in time. But for now, her current role is to look after the younger homeless group, and she is more than happy to be referred to as the leader of Tony's Tribe: a real accolade.

Alina takes care of the girls and ensures they are well, especially after a heavy night. She reminds them that everyone has to earn their keep by whatever means, and nothing in life is free. Keeping her man safe is her number one priority.

Boulter knows her eyes are mesmerising, and Alina's clear skin is perfect. It's a shame she is in her mid-thirties; she's too old for him.

'Here I have a gift for you. It means a lot to me.' He pulls out a gold locket. 'I want you to have it. We can replace the broken chain.' Gold necklace wire is threaded to hold the locket in place.

'I can't accept that, Tony, it is your mother's - will she not miss it?'

'Not at all. She wants you to have it. She doesn't like to wear it in the heat.' Tony keeps up the pretence that his mother and father are still alive and living somewhere in Spain. Not once has anyone questioned his parents' choice of location. They have absolutely no reason to.

'Lift your hair.' He wants to look into her eyes.

Alina turns to face him, her eyes shining with love and gratitude. He will know how grateful she is later.

He tightens each end of the locket wire. Alina is dead within minutes. Her mesmerising sparkle is extinguished forever. He can't ever remember being so excited in his entire life.

Boulter leaves her naked body on the floor. Never before has he considered necrophilia, but is tempted for a moment. He chooses to walk away. He needs to find Petra. Taking a spade from the shed and plastic sheeting from the boot of his Range Rover, Tony Boulter heads into the vast wooded garden behind the cottage and digs.

After a while, he places Alina's wrapped-up body into the cold ground. Boulter smiles and says, 'You can look after your flock now, Alina. A few of your young friends are deep in the ground beside you.'

He picks up the spade, wipes it clean and returns to the cottage to collect his belongings, placing his mother's gold locket in his inside coat pocket.

Boulter walks out the front door, locks it and never looks

back.

Bart watches from afar with fists clenched. There are bastards, and then there is Tony Boulter.

Boulter
My future is with an untouched, sixteen-year-old waiting for me in Mexico, young, fit and obedient. Her father was happy to trade his offspring at the age of twelve. But I've waited. She is too beautiful to force into anything, and she will worship me for not coercing her too early. In a couple of years, she will have a few tweaks to keep her young. Perfect.

With Blain on my case, I'm glad I decided on Mexico - he won't look for me there, he has a history with drug lords who are far worse than he is! For me, there's nowhere safer.

I need to dispose of Petra Gould, she heard me at Cartwright's, and I need my laptop. Deleting my personal files via other means won't prevent some smart-arse from discovering my plans.

No one has come looking for me at my home, and not for one minute do I think the coppers will – to be safe, though, it's time to move out. I contact one of my trusted employees to collect me and bring a hired car. Then they can drive my car back to my home.

7

Wakefield Safe House

13th December 2024

Their safe house is not far away, but Mary realises she could easily be noticed as very few cars are on the roads, and the weather is adding to her anxiety. She thinks of Petra, shaking with cold and fear as she lies across the back seat, hidden under a warm throw; her young life has seen far too much. Mary's anxiety can wait.

Ensuring the car's temperature is warming up, she concentrates on Petra. She must keep her hidden. 'Let's not talk until we get to our safe house. It's only a few miles away. We should be there around half past nine.' It is not that Petra will think time is essential, but Mary is trying to keep a log of events, as tricky as it may be.

Mary pulls her sun visor down, not wishing to be identified by any CCTV, and one thing is sure: if someone finds her, he will know her whereabouts too.

Fortunately, the roads outside the small town have been treated with grit, preventing the snow from freezing. Mary focuses on the road ahead. No one is to know Petra is with her in the aftermath of their escape, for both of their sakes.

Glancing at the hidden shape on the back seat for the hundredth time, she wonders how on earth Petra will process tonight's events. Mary's guilt at leaving her two young friends plays on her mind; who knows what despicable acts they face? How could she leave them to Boulter's lot, wondering if they are repeatedly drugged before they're raped? Mary hopes and prays they come out of their drugged state and get out, neither girl should fall into the hands of corrupt officers.

They arrive at their two-up and two-down end of the terrace house just after 9.30 pm. Mary looks around before she steps out of the car; the streets are silent. Several vehicles can be seen parked up, with icy windscreens confirming none are currently being used. Mary watches as Petra walks up the three steps to the front door, still wrapped in her blanket from the car. Their safe house is warm and welcoming. Remote heating and lighting control grants the pair a temporary home with a lived-in appearance. Mary closes the kitchen and living room blinds in silence without turning on any other lights.

Mary suspects Boulter will be scouring the area looking for Petra. If he thinks she is involved, he will never give up the search for either of them. At least they are away from her home and out of his reach – for now.

Mary has stored non-perishable goods in her temporary kitchen, knowing this moment would come. There is enough tinned and frozen food for a couple of days, allowing them to keep a low profile. She also brings in a small case of clothing from her car boot to cover all bases in the spirit of self-preservation. Her spa break story gives her an excuse for her ready-to-go suitcase, which she never took into her summerhouse.

Petra looks exhausted as she pulls out a chrome-framed dining chair and sits at the small kitchen table. She should see a doctor. Mary does not doubt that her father will bring their GP to see them tomorrow.

Mary continues to control their terrifying ordeal; she can't help but look at Petra's feet, which have a purplish hue from the cold. She walks upstairs, draws the curtains across each bedroom window, runs a hot bath, then places clean, warm clothes and socks on Petra's bed. With everything in place, she returns to the kitchen and relays her thoughts to Petra.

'Petra, please be careful when getting into the hot water; you are still very cold. I will be in the next bedroom, just let me know if you need me.' Petra nods and walks upstairs to the bathroom. She locks the door behind her.

Mary keeps busy by fussing around the already made beds, too worried to leave the young girl alone. After a few minutes Petra is bathed and dried and sitting on her bed looking much warmer. She still has a long way to go.

'Let me put some antiseptic cream on those cuts.'

Petra lets Mary help with her painful feet, before following her downstairs to the kitchen after putting on clean, warm socks. She sits in the same kitchen chair as earlier and watches as tins of soup are heated. Mary takes thick-sliced bread from the freezer and toasts four slices under the grill. She doesn't expect Petra to eat, but some hot food, as basic as it is, will make both of them feel better in the long run.

Petra does eat, has a second bowl of soup, and devours another round of toast. Mary sees how ravenous and slim the young girl is, almost skin and bone. She has dark circles under her eyes, making her seem much older than her fifteen years. Mary plays around with her food, unable to face it, knowing she will have to process what she witnessed earlier and what she is part of now. Her own life and the girl's safety take priority.

Hail pounds off the windows, a reminder of the bleak weather and their situation. Petra begins to shake from shock and exhaustion.

Mary knows she will be in the same predicament soon enough. Both need to rest and give their exhausted bodies and minds time to recover. She wraps a blanket around the young child and, in silence, they walk upstairs to the bedrooms.

Their short-term residence is on a traditional row of terraced houses, which is small and cosy, especially after the last few hours. Petra falls into bed while Mary rechecks her room temperature, ensuring it's warm. Petra is asleep in seconds. Overwhelmed with sadness, and looking at her worn-down shoes peeking out from under the bed, Mary pulls the warm bedding up to Petra's chin. It takes all of her strength not to break down. She places Petra's shoes underneath the hot radiator, then turns back to look at the small girl, a child, she is just a child. What has her husband done?

Mary returns to the kitchen and clears the dishes away, leaving her own bowl of soup to reheat in case she feels like eating later. Her mind flits back to earlier in the evening, where flashes of the traumatic scene seem far worse than she could have imagined. She suspected her husband was having an affair, her father Judge Hicks, indicated it could be much worse. Not once has she ever suspected such horror.

Now, she realises her digital evidence is vital, more than she first thought, and many will want that to disappear. Judge Hicks is not being cruel, he wants his daughter to see who the man she married is really like. Her dad is just being his usual down-to-earth, realistic self.

Mary is thankful she has him in her corner as she downloads the last of her video evidence onto her USB. Once complete, she places her proof in the pocket of her overnight bag.

Mary doesn't know if Greg is dead or alive; she doesn't care. She must focus on her priorities inside this house right now. It seems a lifetime ago when, together with her father, they devised her spa-break cover story to provide her with some time to investigate her husband's vile undertakings, knowing how vitally important evidence is for her divorce, if Greg makes it out alive.

Mary's parents bankrolled their business. Judge Phillip Hicks never took to Greg. With their pre-arrangement in place, Mary would be entitled to more of their business if they divorce. Greg was more than pleased to agree to the terms proposed, and Mary could see now that her husband would never think she would leave him. What a fool she's been.

Not once did she anticipate such disgusting atrocities

happening in her own home. Her breathing is coming short and fast as her fear increases. Mary finds a paper bag and begins to inhale and exhale slowly into the void until her breathing returns to normal. Her first-ever panic attack, she silently wonders how many more she will endure before her nightmare is over. Giving in to her sorrow, she sobs uncontrollably.

Mary agreed to her father's ridiculous idea to watch her husband's moves closely, more to prove him wrong about Greg's behaviour, she couldn't have misjudged it more.

Discovering he is a cheat, liar and thief, with plenty more to be added to his vile personality. She sobs, wishing the world to stop. Desperate to hide and forget all that she has witnessed, Mary has no option but to carry on, and although it makes her physically sick, she must cease her self-pity.

Their discoveries were never shared. Even her mother was shielded from Greg's mortifying undertakings, for her own safety. Last night was completely unexpected, and Mary can't help but wonder if this was what Greg had gotten up to during the past few months. God, she couldn't think straight.

Sitting in the living room of an unfamiliar house in Wakefield, she can only hope and pray that none of her husband's associates find her. Staring through closed blinds, she can see flickering Christmas tree lights through the thin fabric. Mary wonders what will happen to her Christmas tree delivery, as she absentmindedly pulls the lined curtains across the window.

At eight am the next morning, Petra sits at the kitchen table in her clothes from the night before, her vulnerability is evident. Shadows under her eyes show an exhausted child, even though the previous night's gentle snoring indicated she was asleep within minutes of her head hitting the pillow. Mary ponders how long it has been since that poor child had a full night of restful sleep.

Petra's fingernails are bitten down to the quicks, and some show blood spots. Mary hands her a fresh change of clothes.

'Put your clothes from yesterday in this bag, please, Petra. The police might need them, and I don't know if we will be separated, but we should be ready to leave quickly.'

Petra takes the bag from Mary and does as she is asked. Remembering her coat is still in the hallway. She changes into her fresh clothes upstairs, and bags last night's make-shift pyjamas into a bin liner – she might need them later, or they might be binned. She is bright enough to know she cannot be linked to Mary.

'What about my shoes? My feet are smaller than yours. Should I keep them?'

'Yes, until we can get new ones, Petra. They are dry now, put your feet into them; it will help keep you warm.'

Mary busies herself by making scrambled eggs and buttering hot toast. Petra looks and smells much fresher as she sits down at the table. Mary carries her coffee and toast into the living room to give Petra some privacy.

Petra washes her breakfast dishes and Mary's soup bowl from the previous night and places them back into the cupboard.

Mary switches on the TV. The default setting is BBC News. The channel is running a breaking news update. A freezing reporter conveys his take on last night's activities as the broadcaster's headline runs along the foot of the screen: *'Two bodies discovered at millionaire's country house.'*

'Police are keeping tight-lipped about their findings today with one exception: they have confirmed two bodies have been found,' says the reporter as he stands in the bitterly cold hail and sleet. 'Property owner Greg Cartwright is currently under police protection in intensive care. There has been no confirmation from the police whether he has been attacked, nor is there any information on other aspects of what happened here. Still, strong indications lead to Greg

Cartwright being injured during a break-in at his expansive property. Our earlier BBC drone footage of the garden shows markers placed across the lawn supporting this theory. Unfortunately, we cannot show our actual footage due to reporting restrictions. However, we expect a further update on the situation sometime today.' He pauses before continuing his update. 'As expected, there is no sign of Mrs Cartwright.'

A wedding day photo of Mary and Greg flashes onto the screen. Mary realises she will have to change her appearance; her long, red, curly hair will be spotted a mile off.

The newsreader carries on with his report. 'It has also been confirmed that Mrs Carwright was out of the country when this tragedy took place last night. It is now believed she has returned to her parents' home and is being looked after by her family. Other than that, we will wait to see how this unfortunate event unravels. What I can state at this point is that Mary Cartwright is the daughter of Judge Phillip Hicks, so there is speculation around a theory of revenge by high-profile criminals who have been on the receiving end of his judgment. But I must state nothing has been confirmed or ruled out at this stage.'

December's winter season is obvious in the reporter's white breath. A tepid orange dawn sun indicates a cold, bright morning ahead. But not for Mary or Petra, that's for sure. Not knowing what comes next is chilling.

Petra is standing in the doorway and hears the report. 'Are they dead? Jessie and Emily.'

Mary goes to Petra and hugs her. Petra doesn't respond.

'Are they dead, Mary?'

'I don't know. Those bodies could be anyone. They haven't stated who they are, their age or their gender, nothing to say they are your friends, Petra. Don't give up hope; you escaped. They might have left the house, we don't know what happened after we ran, do we?'

Petra was silent for a few minutes. Mary looks into her

eyes and sees pure sadness. She continues to question her husband's actions. Their nightmare is horrific. Mary tries to remain positive in front of the child before her, she knows deep down those bodies are this girl's friends. She has to hold it together.

'Why were you there?' asks Petra. 'In that garden building? It is twice the size of my parents' home?'

'It's a long story, and you've had an awful shock; a doctor is on his way to check us both out. We need time to process what happened. Petra, we've both been through so much. You've been through a lot more.'

'Who was the builder, Mary?'

'Who do you mean, who built our home?'

'No. He looked like he was working on your house, wearing work overalls. He was blue with cold, standing there, and he led me out of your home.'

'I didn't see anyone like that, Petra.'

Petra looks at Mary, 'He only appeared near the dining room. I hadn't seen him before. No idea who he was. I didn't see him once I started running, too scared to look for him.'

Mary's phone pinged, distracting her from Petra and a description of a man she couldn't place: *'Keep her hidden police with me don't let them know she is there keep away from windows, doors. Living room lights to be off, I will let myself in five minutes away.'*

Mary switches off the light.

8

Family Support

Mary enters the pantry and flattens the skirting to the ground before opening a brick-clad door on the wall of the small storage space. She shines her phone torch down the stone steps to the cellar.

'Petra, my father has asked me to keep you hidden. The police are with him, and we don't know who we can trust. Can you please wait down in the cellar? We can't use the light in case it shines through.' Mary passes Petra a couple of throws and a bottle of water.

'There is no way I am going down there and you can't make me,' shouts Petra as she points her blood-spotted finger at Mary.

'Don't worry, there's an oil heater already switched on. No one must know you are with me; this is way bigger than I can handle. Please trust me. The basement is clean. There is nothing in there but a table and a few chairs under the stairs.'

'NO! It'll be full of spiders. Wait, a heater is already on. Did you plan this?'

'Spiders!' says Mary in absolute astonishment.

'Yes, spiders! Have you seen how many long legs they have? Absolutely no chance, nope!'

'So,' utters Mary very calmly, even though she can feel her sweat and panic increase. 'A heater has been on all night. Our safehouse has been chosen for its access to the cellar; unless you know it is there, you won't find it. It is no exaggeration to say your life is in danger, and so is mine, but for now, they're looking for you, Tony Boulter, and his crew. You've been through enough already, and everything we've done since last night has been done to protect you and me. I am being brutally honest; you are a wanted girl by the wrong people. Besides that, a tiny little detail to note, there are no spiders in December, as winter kills them off. Seriously, none at all.' Mary is on the verge of throwing Petra into the cellar.

They both look at the front door, hearing footsteps approaching.

Petra walks into the pantry and pushes the imitation solid wall open further. 'My coat! It's in the hallway!'

Mary has never moved so quickly. She picks up the thin padded coat and throws it into the pantry, hoping Petra will catch it before securing the door behind her.

Petra softly closes the brick door just in time as she hears their visitors begin to chatter. She silently walks down the solid steps, terrified she will draw attention to herself. Petra feels her way around until she finds the table and chairs Mary told her about. She doesn't notice DCI Dell sitting in a dark corner, partly shielded by a load-bearing support column. Caron Dell's eyes are well adjusted to the darkness as she watches the girl's every move.

The teenager quietly lifts a chair and places it close to the table, sitting with her back to her company. Petra peels her ears back, straining to hear the conversation that is taking place upstairs. Her basement partner puts her earbuds in position and listens clearly to the discussion above.

Mary's relief at seeing her father, family solicitor, and doctor walk into the living room is palpable. Two officials follow the group into the house: Detective Inspector Eric Rustler and Detective Sergeant Tim Mosley are both from the Yorkshire division. Their partnership could easily be mistaken for Laurel and Hardy: short and slim DS Mosley wears a sharp suit under his quilted coat. His older and much wider DI wears a brown suit with a shirt and tie, all covered with a dependable trench coat. Standing alone, he reminds Mary of a 1970s TV detective whose name slips her mind.

Mary makes hot drinks for everyone, and the coffee's aroma is more than welcoming. Without saying much to her guests, she directs the party to help themselves to milk and sugar. She discreetly clicks the pantry door closed just as the toaster pops.

DS Mosley doesn't need to be asked twice as he piles three spoons of sugar into his mug and butters a couple of slices of toast, showing no etiquette whatsoever. The judge wonders where they got him from, and DI Rustler wonders the same. Mary is pleased he likes attention.

Everyone stands around the small kitchen table, and their poker faces are 100 per cent set, except for Mosley.

Dr Rhumer, in his most professional and authoritative voice, states, 'Nothing will happen until I examine Mary. Do you all understand? No questions, not one. Is that clear?'

The two officers look across at each other, hoping their irritation doesn't show. DS Mosley shrugs to his superior and takes another bite of his toast while removing his padded coat all at once. His DI cringes.

Dr Rhumer, all five feet of him, asks again to fend off any questions, 'Do you understand?'

Without waiting for an answer, he places his coat on the back of a vacant kitchen chair, gently takes Mary's elbow, and leads her away from her visitors. She is about to say, 'The living room is fine,' but one sharp squeeze to her arm tells her to keep quiet.

Dr Rhumer leads Mary upstairs and closes the door behind him. With his entire focus now on his patient with voices heard from below, he speaks to her with a seriousness she hasn't witnessed before. 'Don't mention the girl at all. I cannot go into all of the details here. Mary, this is a clear instruction from your father. He will provide more information later.'

'Petra; her name is Petra,' Mary responds. The doctor takes no notice.

'You are only to confirm what you have stored on your laptop, nothing else. There is no doubt DI Rustler will ask you where Petra ran to when she left your house; you say you don't know because you didn't see her. You hadn't focused any cameras on the garden, and your father said you had disabled the lights across the back of your property while you were staying in your summer house. There is no way you could have seen her.'

He pauses, seeking reassurance that no one from downstairs is listening to their conversation. He carries on, content that they are in a safe place by the mumbled drivel he can hear. 'No one is to know about Petra. Her statement is crucial to her key witness evidence, including who and what she was involved in. Numerous bounties will have been put on her head by Boulter, and if they know she is with you, that will place you in just as much danger. He will have a price on your head, too. Only speak about what you have recorded and why. You know what I am referring to: your divorce because you thought Greg was cheating on you.' He winces. 'Confirm only what you have seen, and do not add your opinion on anything else you saw which has not been recorded. Mary, it's a lot to take in, but do you understand?'

Mary looks at the doctor in a daze and says, 'Yes, of course I can do that. What about the USBs I have? Do I hand those over?'

'USBs?'

'Yes, these are what I backed up my evidence onto.'

'No, they must not be disclosed at all. If asked, say everything is saved on your laptop. Knowing there is evidence saved elsewhere will possibly place you in more danger. Is that clear?'

'Yes, yes, of course,' Mary begins to think straight, 'But why?'

'Your father will tell you. So then, how do you feel?'

For the first time in two days, Mary wants to laugh.

'I'm OK. Greg's colleagues do not interest or bother me at all to be honest. You've known me for years: you should know better than to ask.' Mary is trying to convince herself more than her trusted doctor.

'That's as maybe, but you will be suffering from trauma, shock.'

'I am shocked at what I witnessed, that is an understatement. But regarding trauma health-wise, nothing except confusion. Petra seems to be suffering, from what I saw of her last night.'

Dr Rhumer thinks Petra has more sense than you on this one, Mary, but he keeps that thought to himself. 'Can Petra be trusted? I mean, how well do you know her?'

'Not very well at all, but we must all trust her. Goodness knows what she has seen.'

Fifteen minutes later, they both return downstairs to the awaiting group.

The judge asks his daughter, 'How are you? Do you understand the scale of what has happened and what anguish might be in front of you?'

'Yes, I'm OK, but the extent of my husband cheating on me has knocked me sideways, not to mention the fact that his life is hanging in the balance.' Mary's response is more for the two officers than anyone else. 'I cannot honestly be expected to think straight, but I will do all I can to help.' Mary rubs her eyes, appearing upset and worried about her husband. Biting her bottom lip adds to her pretence.

The judge nods, pleased to see his daughter has taken the lead provided by Dr Rhumer. Mary understands how the conversation should go when she is interviewed.

To avoid making eye contact with anyone, Mary busies herself by toasting more bread. Whilst she is not afraid of the party in her temporary home, she fully understands the need for secrecy and self-preservation.

'Why are you spying on your husband?' asks DS Mosley

from his chrome kitchen chair. The rest of the group remains standing. His superior turns to look at him with disbelief. Mosley slurps his umpteenth coffee.

A tense, highly charged emotional atmosphere ensues, which prompts Judge Hicks to step in. 'All right. Everyone, let's take a calm, pragmatic approach to this situation. There are strict parameters we need to agree on here and now. What is discussed or uncovered is not to be repeated or recorded by any of you.' He looks across at Mary, knowing she understands the need for secrecy, and then he continues.

'Before anything further is said, I need you to understand that absolutely nothing about the present situation, of our location or the fact that Mary is even here should be disclosed outside this unit.'

DI Rustler looks at the judge in disbelief. 'Now you know that's just not possible, Judge. I need to capture all information for evidence. Surely you must see that.'

'Indeed, I do, but having spoken to your very own Chief Constable Gallows here in Yorkshire, our joined-up focus sits squarely on witness protection. This has been agreed.' He waits and lets his words sink in. The atmosphere does not improve.

'Have you not wondered why your CC's office selected you?' He let the silence build the atmosphere.

'You have been chosen for your integrity and professionalism, I understand. Nothing further shall be discussed until my requests are agreed upon; it is as simple as that.'

'I need to make a call to confirm this is the case before I can agree to anything of the sort,' said DI Rustler.

Judge Hicks takes the phone out of the DI's hand and places it on the table.

'No phones.'

'What is going on here?' asks DI Rustler. 'Am I being kept in the dark on purpose? How can we pursue this case with no records?'

Judge Hicks stares at DI Rustler. His irritation begins to increase as his bow tie tightens its hold. His own family is in danger, and the usually level-headed judge struggles to remain calm. Silently, he counts to ten, then continues. 'Besides your ignorance of the importance of your attendance, are you saying you have never worked a case to protect a witness? A more significant witness would be hard to find in this instance.' The judge takes a deep breath and walks around the table to face the DI.

'Chief Constable Gallows is involved in this case, as you are both well aware. He is to be updated by you. The point here is that no one, I mean no one in Yorkshire's Police force, or any force, should be informed of any further details. Does that help clarify the situation, DI Rustler?'

The family solicitor, Stanley Brassington, clears his throat as he stands between the two men. 'Your complete trust and agreement are required before another word is spoken.' The unease continues.

'The only record going out of here is on that laptop and a preliminary statement. No details of the location, nor any confirmation of Mary's well-being or my presence. That should more than satisfy your needs, DI Rustler.' The judge has returned to his professional self.

Mary begins looking from one to the other. 'Sit down and act like grown-ups; people have died. If you don't start agreeing, others are more likely to follow the same outcome. Christ's sake.' The warmth in the kitchen intensifies.

'What's your solution, then?' asks DS Mosley.

Stanley Brassington produces a document which requires everyone's signature. One by one, they sign, and the friction in the room starts to lift.

'This will protect Mary's statement and everyone here. When we get to court, it will be an honest first account of what happened, even though Mary is in shock.' Stanley puts the signed document in his briefcase.

Mary turns away and wonders how soft do people think

she is. Greg would see straight through this charade. The judge also believes it is a waste of time, but everyone knows that he is in charge. That is enough for him.

'We have a family laptop on which Mary has saved her findings.' The judge says as he nods to Mary, and she hands her laptop to her father. 'All Mary's evidence should now be stored securely. DI Rustler, DS Mosley, myself, my solicitor, and Mary are the only people with access to the information collected here. No one apart from the investigation team should see this footage.' He pauses to give DS Mosley a chance to catch up.

'Chief Constable Gallows is not to be shown any data. Is that clear? We need an independent team to lead this investigation, which CC Gallows is appointing. Only when the selected team is briefed and has knowledge of the facts will we push your investigation forward. As the case builds, some information will be released in due course. You two are the only people with access to Mary's laptop. If any details make the press or social platforms, it will be down to you.' He let the silence drip with the threat. 'It is in your interest to ensure the security of this information. Do you understand?'

DI Eric Rustler nods.

After the "essential preliminary investigation" spectacle is complete. Mary, Stanley Brassington, DI Rustler, and DS Mosley re-read her statement. Dr Rhumer confirms the following caveat, which was added: *'Mary Cartwright is suffering from trauma due to current investigations whilst continuing to process life-changing events regarding her husband, Greg Cartwright, who is currently in critical condition.'*

'Has anyone spoken to the girls' parents?' Mary deflects the room's attention from her.

'Family liaison officers are with them,' replies Mosley absent-mindedly.

'Is that a good thing?' Mary persists.

'Yes, it is. We don't know any more, but all the parents have enough support with them.' Rustler is red with rage at Mosley's disrespect for the dead.

No one is with any of the girls' parents - the two dead bodies have not been officially identified. There is speculation as to who the deceased are, but nothing has been confirmed. Why the hell did Mosely say that?

Mary's clothing from the day before and laptop are bagged, labelled, and handed to DS Mosley. Her statement is also given to the officers. After a gruelling ninety minutes, the police delegation leaves.

Mary looks at her father and thinks: Where is Boulter?

Boulter

Text message received: *Mary is not with her mother she's with her father Judge Hicks is at a Wakefield address with officers - no sign of PG.*

It won't be long before Mary is out of the way. Mini-me will see to her. It's better to be safe than sorry - no information on Petra Gould. Excellent news.

9

Northumberland Police

Recently promoted DCI Caron Dell's first case within Northumberland's constabulary would test the tenacity of the best of them. Chief Superintendent Kelvin Krubb has commissioned Caron to lead the Cartwright's challenging investigation. Krubb will make sure the defiant bitch will not succeed. Clever or not, her popularity will soon dim when he trashes her reputation. Krubb wanted an alternative DCI to be appointed, instead of Dell. His request was ignored.

Adding insult to injury, Caron Dell brought her DS from Cumbria to work alongside her. There was a vacancy, but that was not the point. How dare a woman dictate to him! Krubb looks forward to removing her from the force as soon as possible, comforting himself that she will be gone before the new year.

Chief Superintendent Krubb has made the same mistake as other senior police personnel: underestimating his force's newest DCI. He does not know Caron Dell, no, not at all.

14th December 2024
Caron
I don't rate my superior, Chief Superintendent Krubb, who, according to my research, climbed to his position through his overinflated ego, confidence and discrimination. He tries to

keep a lid on his vile personality, but if you watch his body language, you will see his loathing for some of his squad members, especially the women. Krubb, however, has proven to be popular in the higher ranks; he can work an audience.

He relishes dishing out orders, and if you were to slice him open, "delegation" would run straight through him. That's his skill set in a nutshell. Krubb certainly didn't gain his position on merit, and it hasn't taken me long to discover what colleagues deal with on a daily basis: his despicable personality. Bigot.

My opinion will not interest him in the slightest; he's far too wrapped up in himself, and I am yet to meet a co-worker with any charitable words for Kel Krubb, which says a lot for a force the size of Northumberland's. Nevertheless, we both have one thing in common: neither of us trusts anyone.

Krubb's call last night captured my interest; Judge Hicks has personally requested my help.

I should mention at this point that I hold Judge Phillip Hicks in the highest regard. He's a consummate professional dismissing any criminal-turned-victim crap in an instant. As a witness in his court, I have seen his exemplary skills first-hand.

Following Krubb's instructions, I keep a low profile and use a hired car instead of driving my reliable second-hand Volvo. Why am I driving to Wakefield at 4.30 am on a cold December morning? I don't know the full details exactly, but one thing has been made crystal clear: Yorkshire Police is not to be informed of my assignment yet, and I can understand why.

By my own confession, I used Cumbria's constabulary to progress my career over the past two years under the control of Chief Constable Debra Petal. My choice provided me with career opportunities to reach my DCI appointment.

As a DI within Cumbria, I was appointed to collaborate with Yorkshire Police colleagues a handful of times. A couple of caseloads left a sour taste. Threads were left to unravel by one or two senior officers, and some cases were not handled correctly: that's my view. My attempts to intervene were rebuked. However, some officers were moved out of the force; divide and conquer is not always the solution. Investigation and dismissal should have been the only port of call.

Something evil lurks in that force, and it is buried deep. Now, though, I can't help but wonder if this is my chance to get below the surface and not just scratch at it. However, my main priority tonight is to concentrate on the task at hand.

Krubb has begrudgingly agreed to one of my requests as long as I keep all activity under the radar: senior forensic pathologist Léa Cochran will be available to assist me if needed. Although not employed directly by Northumberland Police, their arranged contract means she does spend a lot of her working hours supporting our investigations. She is well respected in her field, hence Krubb's approval - he will arse-lick to anyone who can enhance his reputation. Léa has been and remains my most reliable friend since we met at university years ago. Our friendship has never wavered.

Tonight, I am travelling alone at this ridiculous hour, with my regulatory winter weather survivor's kit in the boot, along with a couple of warm throws - I have been stuck in bad weather too many times to overlook the risks of it happening again.

The weather is a typical example of our British winter: snow, hail, wind, and sleet. I've no doubt there will be sun at some point in the coming days as well.

I have clear instructions on how and where to collect two key witnesses from, an address in Wakefield. Renting a vehicle and driving through the night to safeguard vulnerable witnesses is all a bit cloak-and-dagger, but necessary.

Before Krubb abruptly ended our call earlier, he stated unidentified Yorkshire police personnel were suspected of being on Tony Boulter's payroll. Reflecting on my time at Cumbria, Krubb's information is no surprise. I have probably met a few and even worked alongside them. It only takes one or two bad coppers to give any force a bad name. But who the hell is Tony Boulter?

My interest is more than piqued.

Boulter

Text message received: *Your laptop was not found; it's still at Cartwright's. Your home is not on the radar yet.*

I can bide my time; my puppet in the force is keeping me informed and they will ensure my home is not looked at until I have everything I need. Apart from that, the clueless fucking prats' have no idea where I am.

10

Witness Protection

Once the officers drive off, Mary calls Petra back to the kitchen.

Petra still does not notice the figure sitting in the corner of the basement. DCI Dell watches her as the party upstairs carries out their business.

Dr Rhumer intervenes again. 'I must ensure this girl is well before anything else happens. Is that clear?'

Judge Hicks responds, 'Yes, of course. Mary, we will use the room upstairs, which you used earlier, to check the girl out.'

Petra opens her mouth to voice her opinion, but Mary steps in quickly. 'Petra has her own room. And that is her name, Dad. I want to be with her for any examination, but only if Petra agrees.'

Petra nods, and the two adults accompany the child to the bedroom.

Judge Hicks rings a number from his phone and hangs up without speaking.

A tall, slender woman in her thirties, with a platinum pixie haircut tucked under a black woollen hat, steps into the kitchen. She closes the pantry door behind her and clicks the skirting board back into place.

The woman walks directly to the tall fridge-freezer, picks up her phone and unplugs it. 'Rookie error,' she tells the room as she waves her phone in front of the remaining group, 'I have heard your conversation and pretty much everything Petra and Mary said this morning. You all need to be vigilant. Your offices, cars, and homes may be tapped. Remember, we don't know what we're dealing with, according to Chief Superintendent Krubb, so just a gentle reminder to keep you safe. This house is clear of anything out of the ordinary. I checked when I arrived.' Caron Dell knows the difference between her paranoid mind and her gut instinct. She will take notice of each of her attributes until she fully understands what she is dealing with.

Her audience of two share a sheepish glance. 'Yes, you're right, of course,' the solicitor says. 'In the rush to get here this morning, we should have been more vigilant, Phillip; we still don't know which officers are part of Boulter's close circle.'

Judge Hicks nods his agreement as he turns his full attention to their visitor.

'Caron, you have no idea how good it is to see you. I cannot thank you enough.' The judge extends a warm hand, which turns into a hug and a clap on the back. 'Fortunately, no one has entered the building apart from those who are here now and the two police officers who have recently left. But I take your point; we do need to be on our guard.'

Though dressed in black, Caron lights up the room. Her warm and genuine smile immediately gains Stanley Brassington's trust. He thinks whatever personality trait it takes to make someone this engaging; DCI Caron Dell has "it."

'Glad to help in any way I can is thanks enough for me, even if it's your son-in-law. Or should I say especially if it's your son-in-law,' she grins, already knowing Greg Cartwright's fate. After what she has heard during the early hours of the morning, if he survives and is guilty, she will track him down. He won't touch another child or adult in his life.

Caron remains standing with her hands firmly in her black leather gloves and her backpack on her shoulders. She absorbed some elements of forensic science as her partner in crime, Léa Cochran, progressed her career. Being identified is a risk to her and everyone else, so Caron avoids touching anything. Her distrust is absolutely on point.

'Is the house being watched?' Caron asks the two men.

'Yes, unfortunately for us,' replies Judge Hicks. 'I spotted the black Range Rover just after leaving Stan's office. Whoever it is, they're desperate to find Mary. No doubt expecting to find her here once we leave, which leads me to ask if you managed to sort everything. Off the record, of course.'

'Yes, house and transport are all arranged, and the sooner we move, the safer it will be for everyone.'

'Any travel implications impacting your journey?'

'Just the weather. It looks like the sleet has stopped. Let us hope it stays that way.' Caron can still smell winter's cold temperature from a couple of hours earlier when she walked the bleak, chilly streets from her car, which is parked a short distance away. Judge Hicks had given her the key safe code enabling her to enter the property from the basement.

'Another word of warning,' DCI Dell continues, 'Key safes can be smashed open. Especially when it is placed in a quiet outbuilding, they are sometimes safer seen from the street. If Boulter knows Mary is here, and on her own, he'd have just smashed the door in, so don't beat yourself up.'

'Understood,' replies Stanley Brassington, blushing; he thought his idea was genius.

Caron turns to the judge. 'Tell me about Boulter.'

'Lowest scum I have ever encountered, Caron. Greg is wrapped around his little finger for his money laundering scams. It seems he is not aware of what is going on with regard to Boulter, but their collaboration has now developed into something much worse. I suspect children and trafficking are of his own making as a personal money spinner. I have seen many heinous criminals in my courtroom, but few have been as despicable as Tony Boulter.' He is extremely worried for his daughter as he holds back his frustration. He continues.

'He is a dangerous man who is unfeeling, clever... and

has escaped justice for years. No one will go after him. Boulter's disgusting actions are now on my doorstep, literally. I will nail him, Caron. It won't be easy with my family in the firing line. I cannot state enough that he needs to be stopped soon and brought to justice. If he discovers what evidence Mary holds, she'll be killed without a second thought. It would also interest him if she knew of his plans. Mary has not said anything about his next move, but she may have some knowledge of this without realising it. She and Petra are to have the highest protection, but must remain in this country, Caron. I need to reach her if necessary. And a final warning, do not underestimate Boulter and never turn your back on him.'

Judge Hicks is one of the strongest, most resilient men Caron has ever encountered, and she can see his worry. His fury is evident. Boulter is a bastard, plain and simple, and Caron needs to wipe him off the face of the earth. With police in his pocket, he always has someone looking out for him. Caron knows he is a dead man walking. Unless that is, he kills her first. One thing is for certain: she will never give up.

'Everything will be done to protect Mary and Petra,' she says.

'I have every confidence in you, Caron, which is why I requested your help to protect Mary. The girl must also be hidden. We are certain Boulter is unaware of whether Petra made it out of the area. You can understand why we need to keep this information within our circle.' For a few minutes, the silent room provides a calmness, providing space to digest Judge Hicks's words.

Caron recognises the enormous challenge ahead of her. Police corruption and the names of Boulter's clients will show her a bigger picture of child exploitation and a burning rage to bring Boulter down. Outwardly, she is the most professional, level-headed person in the room. Inwardly, she wants to rip Boulter's head off.

Mary, Petra and Dr Rhumer are shocked to see Caron. The Judge provides a quick update and overview of what will happen next. 'Of course, Chief Superintendent Krubb is aware and agrees this is the only way to keep you both safe.'

'Who is he?' asks Petra.

Caron explains. 'He is my boss, Petra, but not as high a rank as Chief Constable Gallows. My Chief Super is in Northumberland Police. We have his full backing, so no need to be concerned about him, and I can answer any questions you have over the next few days. Right now, though, we must get moving.'

Mary looks at her father. 'What? Moving again? I thought this was our safe house?'

The judge is about to speak, but DCI Dell has taken over. It's her show now.

'This address is far too close to yesterday's incident. You will be travelling with me to a different locality this morning, and your new address is not registered within the police database. It is also outside of Yorkshire. You will need to change your appearance, which I have planned to accommodate on the way. Gather your things; we're leaving in five minutes.' She squeezes Mary's shoulder and gives her a reassuring look. 'Don't worry, our plans are secure.' They get the small party ready to leave. Caron wonders how Mary will react to a change of hair colour. Hers is the most striking red she has ever seen.

DCI Dell, Petra and Mary make their way to the rear door. Dr Rhumer removes his coat, tie, and glasses and ruffles his hair as he complains to one of the bin men about the state of the lane. He remains upright despite the sparkling tarmac threatening his balance.

The trio stand in the backyard waiting for the refuse truck to draw alongside the back gate before leaving. Judge Hicks ensures the driver is distracted before he places a couple of full rubbish bags into the back of the bin cart. Mary had given them to him to destroy, one of which includes the clothes Petra slept in. It was far too risky to keep them for evidence. DCI Dell has

Petra's clothes bagged and labelled from the Cartwrights; these will not leave Northumberland HQ.

Caron, Mary and Petra walk down the lane in the opposite direction of the bin wagon. Before they turn the corner, Caron instructs Mary to take a different route from her and Petra, appearing as if she's alone. If anyone recognises her, Boulter will soon learn she is with Petra.

After a brisk five-minute walk, Caron unlocks her hired Kuga. Petra takes the winter rug from the boot and hunkers down on the rear seat to conceal her presence further. It's too risky to rely on the car's tinted windows. Her hair is tied up, and she tucks it under her woollen hat. Caron drives to a different car park.

Mary crosses the street towards a supermarket a little further down the road. She walks through the lane behind the back of the store towards the car park. Seeing Caron's rental, she climbs into the rear seat. She, too, hides under the throw.

Caron knows how easy it is to track someone's phone, so she instructs Mary to ditch her mobile. Any contact with her mother or father must be made via Caron, with no exception. Petra was not permitted to have a phone – Boulter's orders.

After a few minutes of driving, Caron gently builds a rapport with her two passengers. She avoids conversation regarding the danger that undoubtedly lies ahead, together with an almost guaranteed harrowing court case in which they will both be key witnesses.

They hope Tony Boulter will assume Petra is well away from last night's events. His only interest is finding Mary, probably suspecting she knows something about his plans.

Sensing their anxiety, Caron selects Classical FM, which usually helps her relax; she hopes it has the same effect on her passengers.

Petra and Mary ask about heading north and what they should expect.

As light as any conversation can be under the

circumstances, Caron divulges her plans for today to keep them both safe. Their next step is to briefly visit York and pose as a family.

Mary scoffs. 'Yes, of course, we look like family. Your platinum, Petra's mousy-brown and, well, my red hair couldn't be redder if you tried. We'll never get away with it!'

Caron smiles. 'Great point, Mary. That's why we are stopping off at York; you're both going to change your hair. I think some shade of blonde, don't you?'

Petra screeched from the back seat. 'Yes, I always wanted to be blonde, I am up for that. You bloody beauty.' It was good to hear Petra being positive.

'Well, I've made someone happy. You will also try to change your usual style of clothes. Mary, you like your designer gear. What would be the opposite of your chosen look?'

Mary sat there, furious, 'Blonde!' She knew she had to change her appearance, but that didn't mean she had to be happy about it, and she certainly was not going to be blonde! 'This is ridiculous and over the top! Should I find a suitable charity shop and buy a new wardrobe? Surely, using my cards is risky. What is your solution to that?'

'That's the spirit, Mary. Hand me your credit cards, please, I will destroy them.'

Reluctantly, Mary hands over her cards, all eight of them.

Caron gives them a wallet of used notes, provided by Mary's father; the force wouldn't stretch to a new wardrobe.

'Your father is a generous man, Mary. I am to let him know if you need anything further.'

Petra screeched - again!

The homeless child and the millionaire business owner are poles apart.

Snow starts to fall, and Caron is tired. Further eye strain could be dangerous. She slows down again for Mother Nature's winter weather.

Caron
Both witnesses are more relaxed as I glance at the rear-view mirror. Petra is all hunched up on the back seat, hidden from sight, which makes me wonder how she will cope with the trauma of the last few months. Witness protection is not easy, and giving evidence is far worse. Their future task is enormous. Petra, Mary - or anyone, for that matter - will find it a challenge to recall every detail accurately after such a traumatic experience. I remember how my life changed beyond recognition at eighteen. I couldn't have reported my nightmare at that age. With Petra being such an important witness, she will need to dig deep. Petra is far too young to comprehend what lies ahead; she seems streetwise, but her vulnerability is transparent.

Vulnerable is such an understated word when I look back at my ordeal. Assaulted by a trusted guest at my sister's wedding, my life turned on its head. I sometimes wonder how accurately I remember specific details of that night. One thing was certain: I would never be the same, nor would I ever be a victim or a statistic.

After all this time, I still think of Jack occasionally, my lovely Jack. He was so patient and kind. We knew our relationship had become serious. It still shocks me how innocent our lives were back then; eighteen is not that young in the grand scheme of things. Totally loved up with our future at our feet, we were captivated by the romance of such a special wedding. That time of my life was naïvely wonderful. Growing closer to each other, we were incredibly happy. We had plans to travel the world together during our gap year, knowing our studies had to be completed on our return. We were ready to take responsibility for our lives and grow up. That was a guaranteed outcome by the end of that fateful night.

Whoever my attacker is, I will continue to look for him. After so many years, I am no further forward, and sometimes wonder if I want to identify him. I am ninety-nine per cent certain it is Richard, the son of Ken and Pamela Hartford. But I need to be 100 per cent sure. He changed my life.

It wouldn't do to kill the wrong man now, would it? Nor would it do to get caught.

Boulter

Text message received: *MC is alone in Wakefield.*

With two bitches dead, I have been guaranteed the other will turn up in a body of water somewhere and Mary fucking Cartwright is on her own. That'll do nicely.

11

Leaving Yorkshire

Judge Phillip Hicks, Stanley Brassington and Dr Rhumer sit tight at their Wakefield safe house. Watching the Range Rover, Phillip Hicks declares, 'He, must be freezing sitting there all this time, I am assuming is it not Tony Boulter?'

'It won't be Boulter; he will have gone to ground if he hasn't already left the country.' Stanley pipes up. 'The grapevine confirms Boulter is still at large and no one has been apprehended. He'll want to protect his reputation as well as Carwright's. They followed you here to locate Mary. Mind you, they could have followed me as well. It made no difference if you came along or not.'

A worrying silence lingers whilst the three men ponder their thoughts. The lawyer pipes up again. 'Do we have any clear view of the driver? It could be one of his henchmen. Our problem is getting out of here without whoever it is in that car seeing us. Impossible, I'd say.'

'Absolutely impossible,' says the judge. 'I think whoever it is waiting to pounce should see us leave. Knowing the police have been here, they will think Mary is still in the house. No one knows Petra is with her. We have to ensure the cellar cannot be found. It would be remiss of us if we were to give away any further details. Caron has removed any trace of her presence on the property; of that, I have no doubt. Give whoever is sitting in that car false hope. Mary and the girl need more time to get out of Yorkshire, and an anonymous call to the police once we've gone will do the trick. He will be in here as soon as we leave.'

The three men work together to protect the two witnesses. Hiding all evidence of the cellar's existence. Beds are made with no trace of Petra at all. They leave the main bedroom as it is, with a towel, some of Mary's clothing on the bed and her weekend case beside the wardrobe. That is more down to luck than good management, they agree.

An hour or so later, Judge Hicks's phone rings once, and he checks the number. 'Time to leave. They're well away from here now.'

They quickly leave the house and drive off without a glance towards the parked Range Rover.

Tony Boulter is not watching the house. Josh Holder, aka 'Box,' one of Tony's minions, has been ordered to obliterate Mary. Box had followed the judge to Stanley Brassington's home address, then onto Wakefield. Bingo! He will soon have Mary six feet under.

Box admires Boulter to the point of emulating his style and personality whenever possible. He has the same bodybuilder image; however, Box is a lot shorter, and his body shape is as wide as he is tall, which automatically leads to his nickname.

Finally, the property is clear of the bizzies and suits, and he is now able to access the car parked at the side of the terraced house.

Nothing, not even a sniff of perfume or a receipt - zero. Box is undeterred; he assumes Mary is resting after the previous night's events, even though it is late morning. No sound or lights are coming from the property. Armed with an array of tools, together with nylon ties to bind his victim's hands and feet for torture, Box forces the front door and lets himself into the house. He loves violence, and if the opportunity presents itself, he will be straight in and straight back out to prevent detection. It has worked for him so far. The police know him well as a city nightclub bouncer; he has never been arrested in his life.

Box doesn't care for snobby Mary, and he has everything crossed that she keeps silent, relishing the idea of torture. Laughing to himself, she has no idea as to what's happening in her own home. Drugs, prostitutes and now kids. It has gone on for years. The posh bitch has no inkling of what her sucker of a husband, was up to.

The front door doesn't make much noise as he breaks in; he wants to surprise Mary. Creeping into the downstairs rooms, he finds each one empty. Slowly, he walks up the stairs and silently turns every bedroom's doorknob, resulting in more empty rooms.

'You've gotta be joking me,' he shouts in frustration at finding nothing, nothing at all. He returns to the kitchen and checks the fridge and kettle to see if they are switched on. The fridge has some basics, the central heating is on, and there are clothes and toiletries in one of the bedrooms. Mary will be back. Box sits down and makes himself comfortable while he waits for her to return.

Boulter gave him a job to do last night, and he is sure no one has seen him today, as he waited in his blacked-out car, watching the house. He didn't even turn the engine on. Greg's condition is still critical; he has to die. No use for him any longer, Box has no worries about killing him, nor Mary for that matter – there is far too much to lose if they testify. Even Greg doesn't know the scale of Tony's operation. He laughs again as he imagines Greg's tiny mindset, thinking he is in charge. What an absolute wanker.

An anonymous call from the neighbourhood watch has alerted the police.

Two officers arrive at the property, unbeknownst to Box. They open the damaged front door quietly. Box has been too hasty in his hunt for Mary and didn't secure the external door after demolishing the lever. Finding the door to be forced open gave the attending officers more reason to suspect breaking and entering.

Once inside, they make their presence known. Recognising Box, they instinctively change their initial approach.

Box reaches for the nearest tool lying next to him. His hammer misses its target each time. Obviously, he wasn't expecting a visit from the bizzies.

After a few attempts to calm him down without any success, Box is blindsided when a taser is produced and the go-ahead for its use is given. He feels its wrath. Arrested for breaking and entering, Box is taken to Wakefield Police Station. He knows further charges could be raised against him; his mouth will remain shut.

Keeping himself under the radar, Boulter has sent his mini-me to eradicate Mary Cartwright this morning. Within minutes of arriving at the police station, Boulter is told of Box's arrest, and he is raging. He was initially unsure if Mary has any evidence of his money laundering and paedophile ring until his sidekick followed Judge Hicks. Now he knows for certain she has proof of some kind. Why else would she be holed up in a terraced house in Wakefield?

Box is furious that he has been detained. Consoling himself into thinking he will catch Mary soon enough. He is sure his boss will see to his release without charge. Boulter will deal with Greg, the pathetic arsehole who doesn't know what is happening in his business or home. Now on life support, Box knows Greg Cartwright won't survive. He will be wiped off the face of the earth along with everyone else.

Those street rats are ungrateful bitches. Not one of them ever complained about Boulter providing them all with alcohol, and the three teenagers were happy with what they were paid. Now, they're surplus to requirements. Box told his boss to take one down at a time or get them out of the country, but Tony's arrogant persona made him think no one would miss them. Their drinks laced with morphine prompted an immediate reaction: unconsciousness, and the volume of morphine ensured death soon after. Box does not doubt that Petra Gould is lying dead somewhere; she did drink some vodka. She likes alcohol; after all, she has drank plenty of it at Cartwrights' in the past without complaining.

Boulter

As that bitch Petra ran from the Cartwrights' home, I heard the sirens and decided to stage a robbery gone wrong. As Box chased Petra, I collected the plastic sheeting from the dining room and rolled the two bodies off it before scrunching it up and placing it in the boot of my car—genius, as my fingerprints would have been all over it.

I had no choice but to leave quickly, not before I collected the bottles of spirit laced with morphine before pulling out and emptying a couple of drawers. Driving around the streets without any luck in finding Petra Gould made me a happy man. She would have heard the sirens and legged it. Dead in a ditch is my thinking. No copper has set eyes on her, nor has any of my lot.

I must silence Mary; I'm not sure she knows anything about Mexico. Her thick husband doesn't. My laptop also needs to be in my hands; too much information is stored on it. Encrypted or not, some smart-arse will be able to get into my data: Mexico. Banks. Fuck.

My high-ranking protection faction will tell me where Mary and my laptop are. As soon as they do, it'll be another murder on their books.

12

Yorkshire Police

The intermittent snow and ice cause DI Eric Rustler's car windscreen wipers to squeak against the glass as the officers head back to the station. Had they spoken to each other regarding this morning's events, they would have discovered their recollections were surprisingly different.

After some time, DS Mosley presents several questions: 'Right, how did the CC get involved?' He continues to build a picture of what happened in his mind. Mosley thinks of CC Gallows as a superhero without a cape. 'Greg Cartwright's wife has legged it, and he is nearly dead. Why the secrecy? Did she try to kill him, and why? Why would anyone want to get rid of a top bloke like Greg Cartwright?'

Eric Rustler looks straight ahead, deliberating what he has done to deserve such a fool. 'That's an excellent question. I'd say something is way off here. Is Greg Cartwright a paedophile? I never saw that coming.' Rustler feels sick to his stomach, seeing how far Cartwright and Boulter have taken their criminality. 'The CC is involved because the crime happened in Wakefield, our area, our community.' He tries to remain professional, but needing to point out the basics is worrying. Nevertheless, Rustler tries to support Mosley's understanding, 'It appears they were young teenagers; PC Rawdon identified the fourteen-year-old girls. Apparently, they'd been homeless for months, and how they ended up dead in a millionaire's mansion is anyone's guess.' Rustler wants to understand what Mosley knows. 'I have a question for you, Tim. Why did you tell Mrs Cartwright we had family liaison officers with the victim's parents? We know who they are, but they have not been officially identified.'

'Telling her we have everything in hand would stop her asking questions.'

DI Rustler despairs, 'You do know that you have confirmed who the deceased are without formal identification taking place, do you realise that?' Rustler thinks of his own family and the anxiety social media causes his wife. 'As there are many details across a number of social platforms, hopefully Mrs Cartwright will not follow up on what you said. Tim, you must be careful what you say, and don't be so flippant in the future.' Rustler hopes his DS understands, but doubts it. 'It is vital we keep Mary Cartwright's location and initial statement behind closed doors. Something is way off here, Tim, much more than I originally thought; surely you realise that?' Mosley hadn't, not at all.

They both return to their bleak thoughts.

Rustler heads for the rear car park to avoid the press outside the station. Their car crawls through a mix of sleet and snow, making it a sad, depressing sight before they find a vacant parking bay. The last thing they need is for the reporters to see them together and start asking questions. Rustler does not want to be identified as a key investigator until he knows what he is dealing with. Mosley wonders how the journalists keep warm in such conditions.

Approaching their office, Chief Constable Gallows summons both officers.

'Tell me, what happened this morning?'

Rustler relays the morning's events.

Mosley hands over the laptop. 'This is what we have recovered, sir. Whatever Mary Cartwright has witnessed is stored within this device. Her statement confirms this.' He wonders if his CC would suit red pants.

DI Rustler looks at Tim Mosley in disbelief. This

morning, it was clear that no one should have access to the content of Mary Cartwright's laptop. The first thing Mosley has done is the exact opposite of that agreement. Jeez how can someone be so dense?

CC Gallows nods. 'So, nothing more than what you have stored on this laptop and a statement which cannot be used? Is that correct?' He picks up the device.

'Yes, sir. You are aware of the situation, I understand?' Rustler asks, now feeling uncomfortable. Mosley has stopped breathing. Rustler gently nudges him, and his lips make a high-pitched noise as he exhales.

'That is correct,' the Chief Constable confirms. 'I can see you're both trepidatious about what has transpired. Make no mistake, this will be one of the biggest cases you will ever work on.'

Beads of sweat form on Rustler's brow. 'Can I ask for more information, sir?' he says as he takes the laptop from his superior.

'You can, but I have very little information myself. I know Mr Cartwright has been on our radar for some time. I understand his trading activities will bring his business into disrepute. What his recent personal activities are, I am not sure. With at least two forces interested in this case, you can guarantee it will not be resolved easily.' Gallows is silent for a few seconds. 'Do you know where Mrs Cartwright is?' He turns to look out his window, not really seeing the picturesque winter scene before him.

'She is remaining at the safe house.' Pipes up Mosley. Rustler despairs.

'Was she alone?'

'How do you mean, sir? Judge Hicks, her father, was with her as were a doctor and solicitor - so, not alone.'

The CC turns to face them both. 'There was a third girl. I have no doubt you have witnessed that fact when you viewed the Cartwright's laptop?'

'Well, we haven't viewed the footage yet, sir.'

'You mean you are unaware of what evidence you have?'

'No... yes, but we were assured everything Mrs Cartwright witnessed is held on this laptop,' said Mosley, grovelingly.

Gallows shakes his almost bald head as he looks at his DI and DS. His pale blue eyes flick from one to the other incredulously. Very quietly, he speaks to his two men as if they were teenagers themselves. 'Then I suggest you both find yourselves a safe room, a secure, safe room to view and listen to what has been provided. Do I have to stress the sensitivity of this case and the need for your information to be absolutely secure? There may be numerous people impacted by what is held on there.' He pauses.

'We have an appointed DCI leading our investigation, who will have her support team working alongside the task force she selects.'

'She!' exclaims Mosley, unable to disguise his prejudice. Realising what he has said, he apologises immediately: 'Sorry, sir. I just thought well, erm, thought DI Rustler would be given that task.'

Gallows looks at Mosley with the same despairing look Rustler gave him a minute earlier. 'You would do better if you put your brain in gear before you express your opinions, Detective Sergeant! DCI Caron Dell from Northumberland will lead. She will be in contact with you both tomorrow morning. Keep your ears open and keep your mouths shut. You report directly to DCI Dell. And most importantly, you must keep me informed of all activities. To make it crystal clear to you both, no discussions with anyone but me on this, and that laptop will be wanted by a few people.' He realises his voice has risen in volume. Gallows tones it down before speaking again. 'Ensure it is securely stored. DI Rustler, you know what to do. Once I have your preliminary views, you may be invited to join DCI Dell's task force. Anything else you wish to ask?'

'One thing,' says Rustler. 'Is Greg Cartwright under armed guard?'

'He is, Mr Cartwright's hospital location has not been shared with anyone other than Northumberland's CC, Chief Superintendent Krubb, myself and the armed guard. Our press office has confirmed Greg Cartwright was blue-lighted to the nearest Emergency Care Hospital, St. James in Leeds. For your benefit, Mosley, this is Leeds's local hospital, known as *"Jimmy's."* It is safe to say he is not actually there. Unfortunately, I cannot disclose that classified information. Now, is that clear to you both?'

Together, they respond, 'Yes, sir.'

'I will ask you both again: was there another girl with Mary Cartwright?' He looks down at his desk whilst he waits for an answer.

'No, just Mrs Cartwright,' answers Rustler. 'We were all in one room. Dr Rhumer examined Mary in her room upstairs. There was no evidence at all of another person being in the building. One cup and a plate on the drainer with a single glass on the table. I noticed one coat with a single pair of shoes in the hallway as I entered.'

CC Gallows' jaw relaxes as he looks directly at DI Rustler. 'Get on with it, and do not let me down.'

Mosley carries the laptop under his padded coat as Rustler locates a secure office away from their colleagues' hub. Selected for their professionalism and integrity, they understand the enormity of the task ahead, but Rustler is not sure those attributes describe Mosley. Rustler has serious reservations about him. After today's display, he will keep him close.

Boulter

Text message received: *Mary Cartwright had evidence on a laptop. All evidence now wiped and destroyed.*

I text back: *Then, the same obliteration must apply to her.*

Box has fucked right up.

13

Travelling To Safety

Petra arrives at The Fox and Hound on Tadcaster Road wholly transformed, with wavy blonde locks under the hood of her new winter coat. With a touch of makeup and a new outfit, she looks way older than her fifteen years. Her sad eyes remain unchanged. No one can change her memories of the horror she has been through. Caron knows she needs careful treatment and handling. Allowing her to go shopping alone was risky, but Petra couldn't be seen with anyone yet. After purchasing a new coat for her, Caron dropped her off outside her hairdresser's salon and watched her walk directly through the door. Still risky, but thankfully, she is OK.

Caron bought herself a bottle of sparkling water and a soft drink for Petra as they waited for Mary. It will take much longer to change her Titian hair colour, that's for sure. They order food and make small talk; anyone would think they are mother and daughter.

The lunchtime rush is now over, and the pub is quieter. Caron gently probes for answers about Petra's two friends. It is clear to Caron that the two bodies found at the Cartwrights' home were her friends. She isn't sure Petra has made the same assumption.

Just as Caron gets somewhere, Mary breezes through the door, bringing a swish of cold air with her. She is unrecognisable with her much shorter black hair. Mary removes her hood to reveal her stunning, shiny, bobbed haircut. Her face shows her dislike.

'I'm not impressed; this just isn't me.' She put her hand up to stop any further comments. 'But you look stunning, Petra. I take it you're happy?'

'Hell yeah,' says Petra, running her fingers through her waves for the hundredth time. Caron can see she is trying to be upbeat.

'Well, it will take some time for me to get used to my new look.'

Caron smiles at her. 'You know it does suit you. More Pulp Fiction than Doris Day.'

'Who the hell is Doris Day?' snaps Petra. Caron and Mary both grin.

Caron notices Mary has taken her wedding band and other jewellery off. Mary catches her looking. 'I couldn't continue to wear any of it. The fact of what my husband has done turns my stomach. Most of my jewellery was commissioned and is easily identified by anyone who knows me.' Mary sees the briefest of concern pass across Caron's face. 'Don't panic, DCI Dell, I can't sell it. Well, not yet anyway. Have you both eaten? Do I have time to order something? Just a sandwich of sorts. I'm not sure I will be able to eat anything though.'

Glad all the same that she has taken steps to protect her identity, Caron wonders if Mary has grasped the danger she is in. Tony Boulter is less than a hundred miles away. He could be closer than they think, for all they know. Caron needs Léa Cochran by her side; another pair of eyes is necessary.

'Yep, we have about an hour before the next leg of our journey,' replies Caron as she looks Mary up and down. Her flat patent loafers with wide woollen trousers pair nicely with chunky knitwear. Everything looks good on her, no doubt about that. 'It must have been a challenge to buy a quilted coat, Mary?' she smiles.

At the same time, her witnesses are gobsmacked as they both gawp at Caron.

'Never mind her clothes - are we not staying in York?' asks Petra.

'No, we have a couple of hours of travel yet. I did say we weren't staying in Yorkshire, and someone is joining us.' Caron sees their startled look, 'She is a very good friend. I trust her completely. Now might be a good time for me to tell you that your observation skills need to improve, and I mean really need to improve.'

Mary and Petra look at each other. 'What do you mean by that?' asks Mary defensively. She considers herself an armchair detective and is always alert to what is happening, except when it's right under her nose and in her own home.

Caron stares at her silently. Mary has to agree with the DCI.

'Well, neither one of you knew I was in the cellar with Petra. Mary, you didn't check to see if it was safe or if anyone else was there, either, as you practically forced her through the door. Anyone could have been down there. I arrived just after six this morning and walked through the house when you slept. Neither of you has asked me how I entered the property. It is vital to your safety that you are aware of your surroundings all the time, no matter what. You need to question everything. So, here's a bit of a test for you. Who was sitting at the table alongside us, Petra, just now whilst we were eating?'

'How should I know? I was starving!'

'Have either of you noticed anyone taking any interest in us? Since we've been here?'

'Well, I've only been here five minutes...'

'Not good enough. You need to be aware of everyone and everything, with no exceptions. Are you aware of the possibility of others recognising either of you? Boulter could have been in here waiting; how would you know? Keep alert!' Caron has not decided whether to listen to her paranoia completely, but she probably will for now.

A Black woman of medium height wearing a navy raincoat joins their table just then. 'Hi ladies, lovely to see you all again.' She blows a kiss to each of them.

Mary and Petra are gobsmacked!

Caron speaks up. 'Lovely to see you too.' She kicks Mary and Petra under the table.

'My gosh,' said Mary. 'I didn't recognise you; you're looking fabulous.'

'You didn't recognise me? Are you kidding? Is it because my hair is now very natural?' She replies in her French accent.

The four of them burst out laughing.

'That's better,' says Caron encouragingly. 'This is Léa, one of the finest senior forensic pathologists in her field, and we go way back, about twenty years. Léa will assist us on our next leg of the journey and will help get us to your safe house. Remember, this house is off the books. No one in the force knows of it.'

'One question, Caron, before we leave, if you don't mind,' says Mary. 'Are either of you going to change your appearance? I mean, let's face it: you both could be on the catwalk, to be honest. You cannot miss that fact, surely? Léa, when you walked in just now, everyone turned and watched you as you walked to our table. It is no doubt the same everywhere you go, Caron. Six feet tall, I would guess, slender, impeccably dressed, your hair and cheekbones are to die for. And you, Léa, have the same attraction, only you're a bit shorter than Caron. I should also say my observation skills are already improving.' She is enjoying her moment.

Caron glances at Léa before answering. 'I am sure there's a compliment in there somewhere, albeit your comments are extremely shallow, and I have no intention to insult the modelling business. Would you have said that to any of my male colleagues? Men look after themselves, too. So, a question for you both: do either of us look like we are police or forensics?' Caron waits as Petra and Mary sit uncomfortably.

'No, job done then. To address your concerns, no one is looking for either of us. If cameras are used to track us down, they absolutely won't recognise either of you. You will recall we had never been seen together in public before your radical transformation. I hope that satisfies you. I look after myself, as does Léa. There is nothing wrong with taking care of yourself. You do, Mary – why should there be any difference?'

Caron stands up and pays their bill in cash. As friendly as she can muster, she says, 'Come on, ladies, we'll miss the party.'

Léa squeezes Mary's arm in assurance as they leave the pub.

Petra and Mary fall asleep, still hidden under the rug in the back seat; you can never be too careful. Mary's soft snoring is a godsend to Caron, giving her time to think without the witness watching her every move. Caron is also pleased that the weather has changed in her favour.

'How is it going?' Léa asks Caron quietly.

Caron slightly turns up the rear car speakers just in case one of them is listening.

'Well, all things considered, not too bad. Mary and Petra are vitally important, Léa. We must handle this right; evidence and witnesses are paramount in securing sentencing. Up to now, no one is onto us, but Boulter's reputation is alarming to say the least. Two young girls dead that we know of, probably more. I cannot comprehend how Petra must be coping with events. Her mind must be all over the place. Laughing one minute and deep in thought the next.'

'Who knows about Petra from our end?'

'Well, you, of course, and Krubb as well. Which is unavoidable. He will make sure he gets something out of this for his career, the selfish buffoon that he is. Lastly, undercover protection detective Callum Brown - I'm assuming that is not his real name. He's just back from a three-year operation abroad, so I hope he is fit and well. I haven't told Mary or Petra that bit yet.'

It has been a long day, physically and emotionally. Caron is making mental notes for her next steps, and how to protect both witnesses is a significant factor in her thinking. Her investigation will be touch-and-go, with quick, sound decisions being made. Every movement and piece of factual evidence is to be recorded. There is no way Boulter is getting out of this, especially not on a technicality. She will ensure he never sees the light of day again if he does.

Caron glances at the back seat. Mary's life won't be the same either; she is another victim who will be haunted by Boulter all her life. Caron knows Greg Cartwright won't make it. Boulter will guarantee his demise.

Mary can't hear what Caron and Léa are saying in the front of the car, but she is glad DCI Dell is on her side. She can see a formidable woman right before her with an uncompromising resolve, just the kind of person you want walking beside you. Mary hopes Caron wipes the floor with Boulter.

Boulter

Text message received: *DCI Caron Dell has been transferred to Yorkshire to investigate.*

I await for further information on her; she won't stand a chance, which means Mary isn't far away. I need to be patient. Cartwright is not being treated at Jimmy's. I'll get to him soon enough. Even though he knows nothing of my plans, he knows too much about me and will need to take the rap for the girls.

14

Last Leg

Arriving at Newcastle upon Tyne's central train station enables Caron to return her rental vehicle as arranged. Her taxi journey in the early hours will make anyone assume she picked up a train to wherever. She has no doubt Boulter will locate her at some point - the more time and space she can put between them for now, the better.

Together, the group of four enter the station pub in pairs, orders drinks and sits at one of the round tables. Caron waits quietly, contemplating what lies ahead. Ten minutes later, a well-dressed man walks in with two suitcases. She immediately knows it is Callum. She tells Mary to smile and wave to the man at the bar. He waves back with a big grin.

'Who is that?'

'That is Callum Brown, your protection officer,' replies Caron.

'Christ's sake,' says Petra. 'Should I expect any more surprises? I feel like I've been hit by a friggin' bus.'

'One thing at a time, Petra. You will need protection, and he is one of the best.'

'Does my father know?' demands Mary.

'He insisted,' smiles Caron.

Callum walks across the bar to meet them, and Caron discreetly points to Mary.

'Hello, darling. I have missed you these last three months. I am glad I have some decent leave after my accident to spend with you and our darling daughter.' He kisses her on both cheeks and sweeps Petra up from her seat.

'Well, I must say I have missed you too,' Petra giggles.

Caron is aware of Mary staring at her and chooses to ignore her.

After some back-clapping and excitement, Caron turns to Léa. 'Is everything ready to move on now, or do you want to do another sweep?'

Léa hands Caron her car keys. 'Go to the car. It's in the hotel car park behind the station.' Petra and Mary are a bit giddy. 'I'll be there as soon as I can.' Léa clips on a London North Eastern Railway employee badge and places a lanyard around her neck, which fits well with her navy coat. At a glance, she could be taken as an employee of the railway. One thing Caron learnt as a police officer is that the public mainly notices the uniform, not the person.

Léa says, 'I will check the platforms once more.' She also walks outside the station in case they have been followed, but sees nothing suspicious.

Caron picks up Léa's keys, scans the near-empty pub, and then moves. She feels much safer now that they are in Newcastle. The final leg of their journey by car will only take another thirty minutes, and they will be at their safe house.

Once on the road, Caron breaks the news of her witness's new identities, which goes down like a ton of bricks.

'Hang on just a minute, Caron, let me get this straight,' says Mary. 'Now I need to get used to being an artist with my "husband" recovering from what exactly?' Also, she stops Caron from responding. 'A new partner, great.'

Petra puts her two pennies' worth in, 'Well, I think this is great. How exciting is it being someone else?'

'Right, ladies, a reality check.' Caron is furious but hopes her authority will come across more than her frustration. 'I cannot stress enough the severity of what you will be put through, the danger you are both in and the absolute need for you to be protected from numerous people. People who want you dead, is that clear enough for you?' Caron maintains eye contact with Mary. 'Don't worry about me, Léa or Callum, and never mind everyone else working in the background to protect you. Just think of yourselves. Have an adventure, twist and moan as much as you like. But from here on in, take some responsibility for your own actions. Your next few weeks, months or however long this takes will be difficult enough. That's it, no more warnings. Now get over it.'

Mary looks at Caron while she concentrates on holding back the tears. She realises the enormity of the impossible situation she has found herself in. 'Yes, of course,' she says meekly. The adrenaline from the last couple of days is beginning to ebb away as she begins to feel the weight of what is ahead of them all.

Six months ago, she had what she thought was a happy marriage; now, her husband may die. Worse still, he is a paedophile and so much more.

Callum waits for Caron's deliberations to sink in before he presents them both with new identities.

'Mary. You are now Janey Brown. Petra. You are now Cerys Brown. Use your new identities from now on. Cerys, call us Mum and Dad. I will give you more details when we arrive at our temporary home, including driving licences and passports.'

Janey is speechless.

Boulter

Text message received: *Mary Cartwright has moved from Wakefield but is still in Yorkshire. Unable to access the Cartwrights yet. Your laptop has not been found or logged as evidence. No PG.*

Dozy bastards are still investigating. I can wait, but not for much longer.

Good news: Petra Gould has vanished.

15

Safe House #2 – Artists Retreat

Arriving on the north-east coast of England just after seven pm, icy blankets of hail and sleet wrap themselves around the party of five, as the wind drives the freezing snow into their bodies.

Artists Retreat is located in the south-eastern part of Northumberland. The lonely, double-fronted building provides a haunting focal point against the dark, gloomy sky where it meets the invisible horizon of the treacherous North Sea. Clouds give way now and then to the odd flash of silvery moonlight over dark waters as hail showers sting the group's exposed hands and faces.

Artists Retreat uses *The Seafarers Inn's* private car park, less than a minute's walk from the tiny island via an iron-railed wooden foot bridge. It is not wide or strong enough to support any vehicle. Freezing temperatures force them to move quickly across the narrow tidal estuary cut into the cliffs hundreds of years earlier, showing perilous rocks below.

Cerys appreciates the safety of the waist-high solid stone boundary of the hundred-year-old building surrounding the garden. In stronger light, they will find the wall is some fifty metres away from the cliff edge, giving way to white foamy waves crashing against the rocks below. Darkness reduces the impact of the wild water, as the island's cliff edge cannot be seen. The wind whips up the sea's salty aroma, jolting Janey to the present as she realises how different her life has become.

The last twenty-four hours have been sickening. She shudders from cold and fear as she tightens the belt of her full-length coat and pulls her scarf up to her nose.

Caron informs her company that the lighthouse-looking building standing before them will be their home for the foreseeable future. It is a blessing that they cannot fully appreciate how high they are suspended above the bitterly cold estuary.

Their temporary home was used as a coastguard's watch house until the late twentieth century. A square glass tower rises above the whitewashed building, providing evidence of its historic past.

DCI Dell's tired group battles against Mother Nature's seasonal weather to reach the other side of the walkway, which takes them less than fifty steps to cross. Caron leads the group up the short stone path to the door and unlocks the deadlock first. She then uses a Yale key to gain access. It takes them less than two minutes to get from the car to their new home. It feels much longer.

Walking through the entrance carrying various-sized bags, the company stand in a stone-flagged hallway. A strong, dependable, solid oak door shuts out the cold behind them, and silence prevails, apart from what Caron thinks are some teeth chattering.

'Wow, not used to the freezing weather,' Janey comments, switching on lights around the house. 'But it is incredibly warm inside.'

'You can't see just now how beautiful a spot this is,' Caron replies, walking into the living room. 'There is a beach north of this little island, about ten minutes away on the main coastal path. It does seem to go on for miles. Walking along the dunes in any weather helps blow the cobwebs away and puts things into perspective. Make sure you're wrapped up, though it can get extremely cold. You might even catch the Northern Lights at some point.'

'Walking in this, you've got to be joking,' replies Janey in complete astonishment.

'I've slept in colder weather, "Mum," don't knock it until you try.' Cerys looks sad as she removes her hat. Her blonde locks tumble across her shoulders. She looks at Caron. 'Jeez, no one will find us here, surely?'

'It didn't take us that long to get here. It's not so far away, so don't become complacent. You must work together to keep each other safe and under the radar.' Caron needs to keep the focus on their own safety.

'On the south side of this tiny island is a more habitable community. A natural curved bay has a promenade and a crescent of houses, one of which is my home, so I am not too far away. There are a couple of local shops around, which will provide most things you may need. There are more pubs than shops offering incredible food. Since the pandemic, they have continued to meet the takeaway demand. But order your food early.'

'On the second floor are three small bedrooms and a shower room. Callum, there is a room past the kitchen which you can use.'

'No chance of that, I'm afraid, I'll be sleeping in the living room. I don't need much sleep. I dare say any animals walking around at night will trip the camera sensors.'

'Animals!' exclaims Janey. 'Christ, where have you brought us?'

'Same as some of the animals found in Yorkshire, I'd expect - foxes, rats and the like, but they're a bit tougher here, being further north and all that.'

Léa smiles. 'We should be making tracks, Caron.'

Caron nods to her friend. 'We'll be on our way in a few minutes. I have a couple of things to go through.'

'The glass tower upstairs is used for art, obviously, and you can't miss it. A couple of easels are set up, but if you don't use any of the items provided, please move the easels and chairs around. If anyone wanders by, they will think it is being utilised.'

'Doesn't this pose a significant risk to our safety, being in the tower, DCI Dell?' Callum's face is etched with concern, underlining the gravity of the situation.

'Well, yes, it can. In all honesty, though, looking at us standing here, I don't think the tower will be used often. The glass in the tower is apparently 'tornado-proof,' and it will offer some protection if shots are fired. Nevertheless, it is a risk.'

'OK, well, that's out of bounds. I will move chairs around to make it appear as if they are being used. Neither of you should be up there. Is that clear, Janey, Cerys?'

'Well, I don't think we'd have much use for it,' replies Janey sarcastically. 'If you're talking about shots being taken, I will definitely give it a miss.'

Callum bends forward as he places his suitcases on the living room floor. Cerys spots a gun under his left arm as his wool coat falls open. He catches her watching him.

'I am working, Cerys; this is what I do. I will kill if needed, so a gun or two is required.' Callum nods to his smaller case. 'Don't think for one minute that I would hesitate to shoot. I will protect you both at all costs, even with my own life. We may even have Uncle to stay if things get hairy.' His grin, though forced, is a testament to his determination to survive.

Cerys freezes.

'Not that kind of uncle, Cerys. He's a colleague of mine who goes by the name of Uncle. Do you understand? I am not interested in you or Janey, no offence. I am here with one sole aim: to ensure you both remain alive.' Callum begins setting up his surveillance cameras, linking them to his PC and other digital devices. This will take some time. Even so, it has to be done as soon as possible. He will ensure no one will see his high-end tech equipment easily unless someone is specifically looking for Janey or Cerys; they would know in an instant they were here. If they are as good as Callum thinks they are.

'Callum, the tidal system gives way to rocky access on

the north and east of the island,' says Caron. 'You would need to set up surveillance on those spots. The island can be accessed by the iron steps fastened to the rock, which are dotted around the cliff face from the estuary and used by locals for access from their small fishing vessels and sailboats. It's not ideal. Remember, no one knows about this place from a police perspective, only us.'

Callum considers what he has been told about the island, which throws up more issues than solutions. 'I will complete a full survey in daylight when the tide is out. I have enough equipment, so it shouldn't be a problem.'

'We should leave you to it,' says Caron, 'Some ground rules first. You each have a pay-as-you-go phone; use it only when absolutely necessary. Start each text with the word "beach," then delete your message once you have sent it, so that I will know that it has been sent from you. It is quite straightforward. Please don't write it down, Cerys, you must remember. Caron removes the note from Cerys's hand.

'Someone needs to let Bart know.'

'Who is Bart, Cerys?' Mary keeps her voice level and kind.

'Bart lives by Arthington Viaduct in Otley and knows a bit about me, Emily and Jessie. Boulter will probably think he is protecting me.' Cerys pales.

'Give me his number. I assume Otley is in Yorkshire?'

'Yes, it is, Yorkshire is massive!'

Caron steps out of the room and dials Bart's number.

'I am DCI Caron Dell of Northumberland Police. Are you Bart?'

Silence.

After a long pause, a well-spoken man's voice answers. 'Yes, this is Bart. Is she with you?'

Caron has made a mistake; how else would she have his number? Fuck, fuck, fuck! She replies immediately. 'Who are you talking about?'

'I will come and find you.' He ends the call.

Caron walks back to the group and tells them she will

speak to Bart in more depth as soon as possible.

'Janey, you will have time on your hands, you all will, Take the time to study a little bit about art; some smart arse will test you, no doubt, especially as you are staying in Artists Retreat. And I am serious. Plenty of books are here for you to study. I recommend specialising in one area. It is a complex topic, I've been told.'

'Christ's sake, it's like bloody James Bond.' Janey is trying to keep calm.

'You've had a tough time during the last couple of days. Take this time to recover. Unwind, go for walks together, and never go out alone, not even for a minute. You'll have to keep an eye on your hair colour, Janey: sorry to have to point that out. No one knows you are here, not even Krubb. He will be told in due course, and so will some of my team and support workers. Callum, who knows from your end?'

'I can't give names, but only one of my seniors and my location is saved within a complex security system that only allows access by two others, let's say top brass. Your Ch -Supt Krubb has a contact number if he needs to contact my seniors. Does that reassure you?' He continues linking his camera software to their remote devices.

'Never doubted it.' Caron will confirm Callum's information with Krubb.

'OK, everyone. I will see you both tomorrow. DS Denny Winston and I will take formal statements from you, Janey, and Cerys. Now rest.'

16

Cerys

Cerys is quiet. The talk of 'shots' being fired has added another layer of fear to her vulnerable state. Out of the blue, she begins to talk about what she and her friends have been through. Caron sees her fear creeping back in.

Callum automatically presses 'record' on his laptop following DCI Dell's instructions to take notes or make actual recordings of any details or conversations where possible. Cerys is opening up, and Caron needs to hear what she says. She cannot risk missing any names in relation to Boulter. Everything from here on in will be recorded and immediately sent to her secure email address.

'I became friends with Jessie and Emily while living on the streets.' Cerys looks down at her feet. Caron doesn't want her to clam up now.

'Just take your time,' she coaxes.

'I don't know where to start.' Another pause. Everyone holds their breath before Cerys continues, 'I know we all left home for similar reasons. I was called a difficult child for as long as I can remember. The more I heard it, the more I believed it, in and out of different schools, bullied and alone. I was quite bright in most subjects but got ribbed for it. The snobs weren't the right group for me; my family wasn't in that league. Most of those girls were usually OK and kind. I would never have fitted in with the popular groups either; they hated me. My interest in classical music made me odd to others, so I left the choir and the orchestra. I had a good chance at sport as well, to be honest. After so many years of trying to please everyone, I just left the things I enjoyed doing.' Tears start to roll down her cheeks as she tells her story. 'I just couldn't be arsed to deal with the crap anymore. I need to get some of this off my chest. It's been building up for years.' Cerys pauses. She looks totally lost.

'Every comment wore me down, *"There she is showing off, teacher's pet, brought an apple in for Sir, or something else?"* I started to hit back. I'd fight anyone and anything, and I became your worst nightmare, the worst bully you'd ever meet in your life. I had plenty of cautions, warnings, punishments and friggin' tons of support from the right people. I didn't want to be part of a shitty world where I didn't fit in. I love my Mum and Dad. They hated what I turned into, but they never turned their backs on me or threw me out. I thought they'd be better off if I left. Desperate to get away from my piss-boring excuse of a life, I was. What I needed was to be free, a life where I didn't need anyone and no one needed me. All I have ever wanted is to fit in. Looking to enjoy my life with other people my age who wouldn't judge me no matter what I did. So, I left. Clueless with no idea where I would go. Fuck's sake, my family must be beside themselves. I've hurt many people, and I am far too sad about it to go back. What would happen if life were the same, and I still didn't fit in? I would hurt them all over again. I can't do it. Besides the fact that I don't even want to return, it's too dangerous for me. Ha, listen to my messed-up head, "My home is too dangerous," compared to what I am doing. What a fucking mess.' Cerys looks out at the storm. The black sky stares back.

Caron speaks softly to Cerys. She doesn't want her to stop talking as she tries to build up trust. 'Cerys, this,' Caron spreads her arms around the room, 'is more than just you. Your friends have died. You are a vital witness to the sadness surrounding our current situation.'

'I know you're confused and scared, but nothing will happen to you here. We could do this differently, have a doctor visiting daily, admit you to the hospital, or have a family liaison officer living in. For now, at least you have a support network that I think you trust to a certain degree. You're in the safest place we can provide. A police cell won't provide the security you need. The aim here is to give you both the best possible chance of space and privacy whilst being protected. Your past life is equally important as the present and future.'

Cerys nods, and she gives a half-smile, then continues. 'Jessie and Emily had run off together. Both had the same thoughts as me. We didn't want to grow up, so we said: stay young, have fun, and don't grow up. They were only thirteen and fourteen.' Janey couldn't stifle her sharp intake of breath. Cerys looks across at her, 'Do you know anything outside your world, your success, your commissioned jewellery, your money's no object, your stable life? There are thousands of homeless people, all suffering from something they cannot fix or they don't need or want to be fixed. You can afford to be confident, brave and fight the good fight from your friggin' ivory tower. I don't have a judge for a father or a life I love. You don't have a bloody clue, "*Mum*." Throwing money at noble causes is great. I bet it makes you feel like a right proper do-gooder. If you're not in the system or feel like you don't belong, it makes no difference to me or my street friends how much money is provided. Apart from the soup kitchens - I would have starved without them.'

Janey puts her head down. 'No, I don't know about the suffering and the reasons that caused the hurt to you and your families. I am sorry you've had such a difficult time during your young life.' Janey knows she is on the verge of patronising Cerys, so she nods for her to continue.

It takes a few minutes for Cerys to gather herself before she begins again.

'We would try to stay together. Meet up with a few others on Friday and Saturday nights. It suited us. Bart made sure we had somewhere safe at weekends. He works with a local gamekeeper and was given a rundown hut-type thing.

That is what the landed gentry provided - a shell of a building for him to do up. Christ, we don't stand a chance; there is always someone to take advantage of the homeless. Bart is happy with his lot, though. He is solid, a decent bloke.' Cerys looks almost whimsical as she reminds herself of her friend, Bart.

'We felt secure when we met under the viaduct each weekend. Bart would let us stay in his hut, a small building with a couple of rooms. It was heaven for us three. We slept on camp beds. Bart said he used similar sleeping benches when he was in the army. We were safe there, and no one ever interfered with us. We looked after the place and cleaned up before leaving on Sundays, but we couldn't stay with him every night or under the viaduct.' A crash of hailstones hits the window, making the party jump. Caron doesn't move a muscle.

Cerys begins again. 'A few of the group didn't want to be stuck indoors, so they stayed beside the fire under the viaduct; the arches were as safe as any place we could find. We moved around and kept out of sight as much as possible during the week, relying on food banks before Boulter recruited us. It's hard to believe we three girls came from the same part of Yorkshire, we didn't know each other.' Cerys looks at Janey. 'You know, we thought we'd hit the jackpot with your husband, he didn't want young girls, and we were OK. He never touched any of us. Tony, on the other hand, was a right bastard. He thought Greg was really into the young girl thing. Greg liked classy women, pretty women.' It was Cery's turn to apologise to her new mum. 'It's not what you expected to hear, I guess. I don't think he was interested in any of us. But Greg let it happen; he didn't stop it. He used his money, his house, and grand gestures. He's as bad as the rest of shitty twats, probably worse.'

'Boulter would go from Jessie to Emily. I got too old for him after a couple of months. He does like them young. His blue pills were never out of reach, friggin' pervert.'

'The rest?' asks Caron.

'Hell yes, there were all kinds of posh, rich blokes. We were often collected and taken to The House. We were allowed to use the back door, of course. We used to laugh using the complimentary toiletries - nothing expensive, but the laughing stopped as we were passed around the dirty bastards. Sometimes, three or four in one night. I never wanted to do any of it. Every time I fought, it turned them on more. I learnt that far too late. We were so thick during those first few weeks on the streets. I thought I knew everything and didn't think I'd be taken as a friggin' mug.' Cerys pauses to gather her thoughts. 'We hadn't been to your house for months, but then Tony told us where we were going last night. I knew we were in trouble somehow, but I didn't think I'd be in line for being bumped off.'

Cerys sat quietly for a moment, and Caron thought that was it for tonight. Then Cerys seemed to remember something.

'Tony's tribe, that's what they were called,' she looks directly at Caron. 'You know the older women who were under his spell? When Tony hooked us in, they were told to look after us, and Alina was the main one who used to check on us after we had been to The House. Alina was with me when I rang Mum and told her I was all right and needed to be alone. She still had the police look for me, but I was OK. I went to the local police station and told them I didn't want to go home and that I was safe. Alina came with me. Tony's tribe did the same for Jessie and Emily. We were idiots. There was no way we could have fought any of them off once we knew what was happening.'

Caron could feel the fire in her belly rising, knowing precisely what Cerys meant by trying to fight; it's impossible to win.

'It was always just us three at any one time, but others were abused as well. I heard Tony talking to someone. It wasn't Greg. It sounded like he was grovelling to a big shot, I don't know his name. Greg was never at The House and was more of an afterthought. Once the paying customers had their fun with us, Tony made sure Greg had a chance to do what he wanted. He never did. Jessie and Emily thought he was gay. I didn't think he was interested.'

'How did you know Greg preferred older women?' Janey asks.

'He was that drugged up one night lying on the bed just telling me to fuck off. He wanted a real woman, someone who was old enough and wanted to be with him, to appreciate him, Christ, what an ego. Greg wanted to be wanted, but not by teenage kids.'

'Most of the time, I would raid the fridge. Sorry, Mum. I can cook. That's one thing Mum and I have in common: we love to cook.' Cerys smiles. 'When the high wears off or the hangover kicks in, I'm usually starving, so I made whatever I could from your fridge, Mum.'

Tears were streaming down Janey's face out of relief that Greg hadn't raped this vulnerable fifteen-year-old girl. He was as guilty as the rest of them. Cerys was right, no exception; he should have stopped it. 'Don't ever apologise to me, Cerys, never.' Janey hugs the young girl standing in front of her. This time, Cerys hugs her back and sobs into her arms.

Caron and Léa move into the kitchen as Callum puts a couple of pizzas in the oven, knowing they'll be hungry soon enough. 'This is developing into something quite different,' says Caron. 'Trafficking? Paedophile ring? One thing is certain: Tony Boulter must be caught and put in custody immediately. I will notify Krubb. He'll be over the moon getting a call this time of night.'

'It had better be good, Dell!' says Krubb when he answers.

Caron repeats what she has been told.

'I will instruct Yorkshire to put out a nationwide alert for Boulter if they have not already done so. I will speak to you in the morning. Think about who you need on your task force; Yorkshire personnel will be limited. And Dell, this information is not to be shared with anyone else. Goodnight.'

'Prat,' says Caron aloud.

17

Heading Home

Caron and Léa walk back to the car. Once inside, Caron turns to her friend, 'We need to keep them safe and out of the way, Léa. And as always, thanks so much for everything you've done today. Time for home.'

'Anytime, Caron. What are your thoughts on Tony Boulter?'

'Well, it could be one for us to sort out. Justice will be served; there is no doubt about that. Before we do anything alone, let us see what we find. We need to have one hundred per cent certainty that he is guilty. At this stage in the proceedings, he is. And he's not the only one.'

Léa drives less than half a mile along the crescent of terraced houses, where Caron's home is located at the southern end of the bay. The expansive upper esplanade path leads to a grassy bank that runs downwards to the lower promenade before reaching the shingle cove, with access steps and a ramp at each end. High tides batter craggy rocks at the north and south sides of the shoreline, whilst snowy foam waves cover the beach.

Artists Retreat is located at the northern end of the small fishing village. Its prime position looks over the most easterly edge of the estuary directly above the North Sea. Caron's home is a three-bedroom, semi-detached with bay windows offering spectacular vistas. It also provides a clear view of the safe house from its southerly location.

Christmas tree lights are a welcome sight as they continue their drive: a stark contrast against the inky dark water on the left. Caron thinks the vista out to sea isn't so spectacular tonight.

Léa and Caron confirm their plans for the next day. With arrangements made, Caron climbs the three steps to her door and waves to Léa as she turns her key and walks into her home. She places her bag and coat in the hallway as usual, walks into the kitchen and switches the kettle on. As she waits for the water to boil, she sets the microwave to warm up black bean chilli leftovers. Caron takes a moment to reflect on the information from the last twenty-four hours, then drafts a list for herself to review in the morning: who she needs to speak to and where she needs to be. Once complete, she places her tasks on the hall table and leaves work right there in the hallway - no more thinking about tomorrow's challenges. DCI Dell needs to recharge and rest.

Feeling relaxed and warm, having devoured her food, she walks upstairs with her second cup of hot tea.

She turns the shower on full blast. The hot water eases her aching muscles. Twenty minutes later, she is lying on her bed as her winter throw hugs her bare skin, keeping her warm from the cold, wintry night air coming through the slightly open window. Caron looks at Artists Retreat standing alone at the other end of the bay, a forlorn building on the edge of the small peninsula. Some lights are still burning.

Caron's mind taps into the unmistakable sound of the dark waters crashing their salty-white foaming waves against the rocks. She sleeps like a baby.

Boulter

Updates keep coming. Cartwright is still critical: I need to reach him soon, in a day or so. Is Bart protecting fucking Petra in his brick shed? I'd love to smash that posh twat's face into a pulp.

And at last! My delivery has been made, new clothes -

shitty puffa coat and trainers. Fucking hell man, who wears this crap? Hair dye, razors, hats - fucking beanies! Different but necessary.

18

Mary Cartwright

15th December 2024

It is approaching four am, and Cerys' words run through my head repeatedly. A feeling of anguish engulfs my whole being.

I ponder my past. I have always been lucky and privileged, some might say. Boarding school was a good experience for me and I made friends for life, Tilly, Betty and Cora. We don't see as much of each other as we should. Tilly emigrated to Canada with her husband and two girls, who are delighted with their life. Betty lives in Norway as a finance director within a successful business. She has no family, but that's precisely the lifestyle she wants. Then Cora, lovely, cuddly, dependable Cora, whose soul is so sweet, she would do anything for anyone. Cora has the most fulfilling life; her vocation is to save the planet as a volunteer protecting endangered species, and she is happy with her contribution to the cause. She supports her vision by working as an English teacher with her partner in Peru. Clearly, we aren't close geographically, but I can pick up the phone and speak to any of them at any time - helpful, comforting, and supportive lifelong friends.

Greg and I have partied away our lives without a glance at the world around us. We still party and entertain many clients and our circle of friends, who are pretty much the same as us – spoilt. Even the games of one-upmanship have ceased;

we have everything money can buy.

Cerys's family live relatively near to me, and so do her friends. Young teenage girls have been abused, beaten, raped for months - and God knows what else. What goes on outside my financially secure world? I don't think I will ever know.

I studied hard to build our business and worked long hours to ensure Cartwright Construction was successful. Without family money or my parents' support, I couldn't have done it. Is that cheating? What have I achieved on my own? I got married in my twenties, but from a young age. I partied week in, week out. My lousy judgment resulted in marrying a spineless, vile criminal who promotes paedophilia.

My fiery temper once matched my red head, but that has long cooled. I take no crap though; Boulter was the exception - in the beginning. Now I am terrified of the man, but I would still stoke up the fire to have a go at him, verbally, of course; he would snap me in two otherwise.

With self-pity out of reach, I hang my head in despair when I think of Cerys and what she has been through. I enjoyed my adolescent years, rebellious, smoking, drinking, and staying out, not a care in the world, because I was fortunate to have wealthy parents to bail me out and take me on holiday anywhere at the drop of a hat. Different scenes meant a different mindset; for me, it worked. That approach didn't work for everyone I grew up with. My friends and I would now be classed as solid.

What a vile predicament for Cerys; her story is just the tip of the iceberg. After this, my life will change dramatically, not just with charity donations but also with hands-on involvement. God knows what that will look like!

One thing at a time. Cerys has to get through her witness protection, and so do I.

19

Caron

My alarm goes off at 6.30 am, as usual. Early mornings give me a chance to exercise for twenty minutes. My choice of workout is nearly always yoga. With earbuds firmly in place, I keep work at bay. After breakfast, I shower, change, and prepare for the day.

I inevitably wonder how Cerys is going to recover from her traumatic ordeal. What is also unavoidable is my need to reflect and analyse my nightmare for the umpteenth time.

Over the years, part of my recollection from that night has changed; to be honest with myself, do I really want to know who my attacker was? I don't know, but I am still betting on Richard.

Boulter
I know DCI Dell's in Leeds. I need to take my time with that. If I get to Mary first and get my laptop back, she'll be off the hook. For now, I need to be patient; I can do that.

No one has tried to access my offshore accounts, and there are no new emails regarding flights, bank details or Mexico. I have changed my passwords and my smart-arse IT expert setup, which will prevent anyone from locating my plans. But if my laptop falls into the wrong hands, I will have to change everything, including moving my woman out of Mexico. It's not a dealbreaker situation, but risky.

20

The Investigation

DCI Dell summons DS Denny Winston into her office. She was already instructed by Chief Superintendent Krubb earlier that morning to press on with her task force and get Boulter in custody. Krubb was far from impressed to have to work on this case on a weekend, so as soon as he could, he had technically passed it over; it is now off his desk, so to speak. Krubb can go and enjoy his golf – it'll be the 19th hole in this weather. He won't give the investigation a second thought.

'You OK, boss?' asks Denny.

'Yes, grand. I need to speak to you privately.'

They discreetly walk out of the office.

Caron has worked with Denny for almost five years. He is a committed DS, and they have a strong policing partnership. Although Caron cannot trust him totally, he's a bloke. That would be a mistake on her part.

Denny is a couple of years older than Caron and happily married with two daughters. He married young and had his children by the time he was twenty-one. Both daughters are now settled with families of their own. If his grandparents were here, they would be so proud. You wouldn't think it to look at Denny; he looks younger than his forty-two years.

Caron respects Denny's wish not to climb the career ladder, but it won't be long before he changes his mind. She has often told him that it would be a privilege to work for him, not alongside him, and that he should lead in a superior role; she will do anything to help his progress when he is ready.

Caron is not interested in further promotion; she wants to lock bastards up, regardless of their background. Seeing their eyes widen with fear as they realise they have nowhere to turn is the best feeling in the world.

Caron provides Denny with an update on the current case and a full explanation of their next steps. She has only been with Northumberland for a couple of weeks and has been supporting other cases; she now needs to pull back from them.

The pair spent a few hours reviewing the Cartwright case details, and Denny was instructed to liaise with the Youth Justice Services to appoint an appropriate adult. Due to a conflict of interest, Mary Cartwright cannot act as such.

'Why didn't you take me with you instead of Léa?'

'DS Winston, you must know the answer to that,' she teases. 'The fewer people who know, the better. Pulling you into this in the middle of the night would have raised far too many questions at the station. When Léa and I flit off, no one bats an eyelid. Also, honestly, I didn't know what lay ahead as the case hadn't been assigned. When Krubb said Judge Hicks had requested me personally, well, I thought it could be something big or had the potential to be. Especially as it involved his son-in-law.'

'This means what exactly, to our current investigations?'

'Well, I will update DI Plaiter and DS Carter with a cover stating we're working on something for Krubb. We cannot divulge Cartwright's case data across our HQ; this cannot be shared until my team is in place.' Caron ponders, 'What do you think of Jaz, Denny?'

'I've only been here the same length of time as you, but I see why you would ask. Punctual, dependent and from what I have seen, exceptional analytical skills.'

'Mm, yes, she collared me a few days ago regarding her evidence collation process. It went over my head, but I could utilise those skills on our case. When the time is right, Denny, bring her up to speed, and I will pull her on board. She already has clearance in place to update HOLMES. Right then, let's get going.'

Thirty minutes later, they arrive at Artists Retreat safe house.

Boulter

I need to put pressure on them to keep me updated with the bizzies' investigation. The latest is that Dell is still in Yorkshire, setting up her team. Fucking clueless the whole fucking lot of them.

21

Statement: Mary Cartwright

As promised, DS Winston, appropriate adult Connie Tate, and Caron arrive at Artists Retreat after calling ahead. Callum opens the door, allowing a whoosh of frosty air to blow into the building.

Caron introduces DS Denny Winston to the group and explains he has been brought up to speed. Connie Tate has also been introduced as Cerys' appropriate adult. Connie is provided with the time required to ensure she is fully briefed on her rights and obligations as a witness and victim.

Callum confirms Cerys and Janey have been relatively subdued overnight, but both appear to be coping, under the circumstances. It is not his remit to babysit, so to speak, but he has kept a watch on their behaviour. Callum feels that these next few days will be like the calm before the storm. Caron and Denny fully understand his intuition, and another specialist officer will be attending Artists Retreat.

Recording equipment is set up, and everyone is fully prepped. They start with Mary.

'Please confirm your full name, address and date of birth?'

'Mary Cartwright, No. 1, Fieldview, Leeds, ninth of May 1986.'

Denny continues, 'You are here voluntarily as a witness to a crime committed within your home, which has resulted in your husband's hospital admittance. Greg Cartwright is currently being treated in the critical care unit for a suspected drug overdose. He was found unconscious by police officers during a suspected robbery of your home. Two young females were found deceased on your property. The objective of our discussion today is to gather as much factual information as possible from you. Mary, you will be asked numerous questions specifically about your marriage to Greg Cartwright and your home life, together with recordings which you made of his activity during the last six months. You will have an opportunity to provide as much detail as possible. To be clear at this stage, we encourage you to be honest in your statement and to tell us everything you know. This may prove difficult; we can take a break as often as you wish.'

'I understand,' responds Mary.

'You have chosen not to have legal representation. That is your choice. For our records, can you please confirm this is still the case before we begin?'

'Yes, I don't require any legal representation. If I do, in the future, I will request a lawyer to be present.'

Caron thinks a solicitor should be supporting her, but she is grateful Stanley Brassington's services have not been requested. Boulter would have quickly picked him up.

Caron continues. 'It may be useful to know that we need to establish certain facts and issues. It is your opportunity to explain either your involvement or non-involvement in the incident under investigation. Tell us anything you feel is relevant. You will not be interrupted. So, take your time to consider any questions before you answer.' Caron left a minute for Mary to digest what she has just been told.

'Are you ready, Mary?' asks DI Winston.

Mary feels the world is on her shoulders, and then she thinks of Cerys and realises others are far worse off than she is. 'Yes, let's start.'

'My father, Judge Phillip Hicks, informed me last June

that he thought my husband Greg Cartwright was having an affair. He had been tipped off by one of my neighbours about some unusual activity happening at our home when I was away. Funnily enough, I don't have close contact with any of my neighbours. The nearest one is about a quarter of a mile away. Anyway, I didn't question my father; he always has my best interests at heart.'

Mary goes on, 'If Greg were having an affair, I need concrete evidence to prove my suspicions, before I can do anything official regarding a separation or divorce, as outlined in our pre-nuptial agreement. If I had any idea of what was taking place at my home, I would not have used hidden cameras to capture my husband's infidelity. If they had been discovered, I wouldn't be sitting here now.'

DCI Dell watches Mary shuffle in her seat. She has taken some risks to uncover her husband's extramarital affairs.

Mary carries on, 'Greg usually has a very shapely visitor, and I have learned she is an expensive escort. Paid handsomely in cash. But Greg likes her for more than just sex.' She pauses and takes a deep breath. 'He wanted her for keeps.'

DS Winston asks, 'Why do you think that?'

Mary squirms. 'We didn't have sex for weeks. He excused his behaviour stating he was working on a new project, but his manner had changed. It turns out his new project had nothing to do with our business.'

DCI Dell can see that the conversation is becoming difficult. She waits for Mary to continue.

'Together, we made the decision not to have children because we're both very selfish. You may think that strange, but I know couples who don't want to have children for various reasons. For us, it was plain selfishness. Before I witnessed his behaviour, I felt he might have changed his mind.' Mary laughs. 'God, I couldn't have mistaken his intentions more wrong if I tried.'

Mary went on to talk about the fantasy sex Greg had with his escort, which was something they'd never done: whips, role-play and much more besides. She earned her fee, and he always made sure he got his money's worth.

'I also noticed a different pattern of money deposits and withdrawals within our Cartwright Construction business account. Greg is our CEO, and I have access to our business finances. Money seemed to be pouring into our account. Even as a millionaire, you still worry about money.' She is extremely embarrassed.

'How much are we talking about?' asks DS Winston.

'About 800K came in on one Monday from a new buyer's account; a company I hadn't heard of. For a construction company of our size, 800K isn't a lot of money to be paid for goods or services, but there were red flags for me. I had no idea who this customer was. Then, a few days later, a further 1.2 million was deposited into the account in the same way. After a week or so, two million pounds was paid to a supplier for high-end products. This was also a new contact; I kept trying to convince myself that it was not a great amount of money for trading. In all honesty, I knew something was off.'

'I installed cameras with help from a security company my father had employed in the past.'

'We'll need their details,' says DS Winston.

'Yes, of course. Money was stashed all over the house, which I knew nothing about. Hidden in places throughout my home, places that I didn't even know existed. Secure drawers here and there with locked safety boxes under floorboards. I had no idea. Drawers were hidden inside drawers, and hundreds of thousands of pounds were handed over to Greg from Tony Boulter, and I don't know why. He is on the payroll and paid legitimately; there's no reason why he would be paying cash into the business. At first, I wondered if Greg was going to offer him a partnership or if he was considering starting another business, so I kept a close eye on all transactions from then on. Over the last couple of months, many similar transactions have taken place. It must be illegal. I can't think of any other reason.' Mary pauses: Caron can see the impact beginning to take its toll. Mary has a long road ahead of her.

'I began to collate evidence for my divorce. My father had other ideas and was in contact with Chief Constable Gallows of Yorkshire Police. He wants Greg arrested and imprisoned. I want out of our marriage.'

'Yes, we already have a statement from Judge Hicks. When did you first meet Petra Gould?' Caron watches Mary very closely and notices her eyes flick to the left, then she takes a drink of water. Caron immediately recognises her body language. Denny will have also clocked that she is lying.

'Er, that would have been the night of the thirteenth of December when she was running from my home through the back garden.'

'Not before?' persists DCI Dell.

'No, no, not that I can recall.'

Caron smiles her most reassuring smile. Mary looks away.

Mary's statement clarifies more details, including how long she has known Greg's colleagues. She didn't provide any further evidence of money, escorts or girls, nor did she refer to any 'rich bastards' in any hotel.

Mary confirms on tape that her recollections from the night of the thirteenth of December are correct to the best of her knowledge, and she will sign her name at the foot of her statement once printed and agreed upon, even though her recorded confirmation is enough. They wrap up her interview.

Her USB evidence is handed to DS Winston, and for security purposes, she reverts to Janey.

Caron leaves the room ahead of her witness, as they head into the kitchen; she doesn't want her two witnesses to collaborate now that Janey has provided her statement.

22

Statement: Petra Gould

Callum ensures both parties are kept apart until DCI Dell and DS Winston invite Petra, as she is to be referred to, into their interview room. Together, the officers have agreed on their approach. Connie Tate accompanies the teenager.

In addition to the freefall statement from the previous night, which she witnesses on record as an accurate account of her comments, she provides further information under her real name: Petra Gould. DCI Dell has also noted her reasons for no legal representation.

'Petra,' says DS Winston, 'how long have you known Mary Cartwright?' His first question yields a similar response to Mary's. Petra flicks her eyes, then stares at the wall when she answers.

'I can't think why you'd ask that. December thirteenth.'

'Just checking the facts, Petra,' responds Caron.

The interview continues, and Petra provides relevant information about other people she has met.

'I think one of the regulars was a judge or mayor, because he was referred to as "your honour." I'm not sure if that's true, though, because the rest of them laughed. I thought I had recognised him from somewhere, but I can't remember where. Laughter was something I didn't do much of in that room.' You cannot miss Petra's sadness; her face is etched with pain. 'How could I let it happen to any of us? And poor, bewitching Jessie had a vile time, because she was the youngest of us all. Jessie was incredibly pretty with a childish-looking, thin face and a tiny, freckled nose. She looked so delicate and innocent, and was forced to wear children's underwear. Her natural blonde hair had to be plaited.' Petra puts her head in her hands and weeps.

'Do you want to carry on, Petra?' Asks Connie.

'No, not really, it was so much worse. Do I have to go through this?' She asks.

'It is beneficial to know the details, Petra, but you can stop anytime. Do you want to stop now?'

Caron watches Petra and cries inside at the deprivation the girls have grappled with. It will be a lot worse on the stand for the child sitting in front of them today. If they ever get that far. 'Do you wish to continue, Petra?'

Petra wipes her eyes and blows her nose before she speaks again.

'I can't stop, can I? You should know what happened so you can get the bastards.' Petra tries to compose herself; everyone can see what a traumatic experience these three children and probably many more have been through. 'Emily used to make us laugh with the names she made up for some of those men. Wanker Banker,' Petra laughs. 'He always had a briefcase. Emily opened it once, and it had loads of paper with a bank's name on it. I can't remember the bank, though. Emily could make fun of anyone; she was so childish.'

That will be because she was a child, thinks Caron.

'Can you remember if Emily noticed anything else in the briefcase?' DS Winston probes.

'He had loads of cards, Emily said. I thought the cards that you played games with, but it could have been bank cards. I don't know if she saw anything else; we just laughed at the names she made.' Petra goes silent for a minute before sniffing and blowing her nose again.

A rattle of hailstones startles the young teenager. Caron worries about her future; can she ever recover?

'Was it the same men every time?'

'Yes, the usual five, but sometimes it was less than that. Wanker Banker, Fudge the Judge, he might have been something else only we liked to think he was a judge. We could tell him a pack of lies, so thick he was, he believed them, that's how he got his name: Fudge the Judge. We thought he was at least seventy – a skinny streak of loose skin and bones. Then there was Toot. He went like a train.' Petra burst out with a nervous laugh. 'We were glad if we got him because it was over in seconds. Mr Tremble was scared of his own shadow, a big, fat, pig of a man he was. Grey slicked-back hair, he seemed one of the youngest. I'm not good with ages, I'd guess about forty.' Petra shrugs.

'They were bastards, but Big Phil'er was the biggest bastard of the lot of them, worse than Boulter.'

'Can I clarify something here, Petra, please?' asks Caron. 'Did Tony Boulter abuse you and the girls?'

'Yes, I am sure I told you that?' Petra says.

Caron thinks for a moment. In general terms, yes, she did, but with no specifics. It is now caught within Petra's second statement. 'Sorry for interrupting you, Petra. Please go on.'

'Big Phil'er, he'd get sick of one of us and move on to another sometimes, he'd go for hours. He liked boys as well.' Petra stops for a drink. Caron can see her start to shiver. She isn't so sure it's from the cold, so she pauses the interview until Petra is ready.

'Petra, are you ready to start again?'

'Yes. He, you know, Big Phil'er, ripped Emily to bits once. Alina had to sort out tablets for her. Big Phil'er reeked of cigars and aftershave. He was slim, about thirty-five, I'm no good with ages as I've said.' Petra is trying to lighten the conversation with her quips and random laughter. There is nothing to laugh about here. Caron sees Denny clench his fists a few times under the table from anger.

Caron looks at Petra. 'Would you recognise these men

again?'

'Hell yeah, they're in my nightmares most nights. The easiest thing to do is to get CCTV of where they partied or the streets nearby. The House is five minutes from Wakefield train station. I can look through the CCTV?'

'Brilliant idea, Petra. Denny can arrange that for us.' It's no wonder Tony killed the girls and has gone on a rampage to find Mary. Thankfully, he doesn't know Petra is safe. She keeps her thoughts to herself, not wanting to worry the child further. Petra continues.

'We had another bath before we left. Each time we'd finished cleaning ourselves up, we'd come out of the bathroom, everyone had disappeared except Tony. Any leftover food was stuffed in our pockets before we were hurried down the back stairs again into his huge car and dropped off by the train station. Tony would give us money, forty quid each. We took it every time. He'd broken someone's hands once for not taking it.' Petra looks at her hands on her lap. 'I don't know how many people he's used, only I thought our time was up. No more dirty bastards, thank Christ. I expected Alina to be part of our next move, but she didn't show up. That's when I knew we were in trouble.' She pauses again and takes some time to gather herself. 'A couple of new faces had shown up, younger girls and boys – don't forget there were always boys around – they had been spotted on the streets. I thought we'd be taken abroad before I realised that wouldn't happen.' Petra glances up at DCI Dell with a haunting look on her face, startling DS Winston. She has aged again.

'We can take a break here, Petra. Let us have a few minutes to give you some time.' Caron wants to reflect on what she has just been told, and taking a breather will help.

Caron and Denny are silent as they grab a hot drink to take back to their makeshift interview room.

'I know it is hard not to get too involved, Denny, and

God knows what will happen to Petra after this. Our goal is to focus on Boulter and his group. Sensitivity is paramount to ensure Petra provides us with facts.'

Petra comes back into the room, fifteen minutes later. She looks fresh, but that's all; there is no escaping the horror she has been through.

'Just when you are ready, Petra, no rush,' encourages DS Winston.

'We started our plans to make a run for it.' Petra continues. 'Tony had different ideas for us.'

'How did you know the men were rich?' Denny again.

'We could tell by their clothes, how they spoke, how their posh stink got up my nostrils every time.' Petra takes a deep breath. 'We would walk into the room. And they would be waiting with their dicks out. *"How lovely your little bodies are."* They'd force us to do what they said. Ugly fuckwits. All the while, Boulter is standing, watching.' Caron's skin crawls whilst her blood boils.

The way they smelled, thinks Caron. Why does that strike a bell for her?

'Can we go back a minute? Who is Alina?'

'Alina is Boulter's property; she will do anything for him.'

'Has she been to the Cartwrights?' DS Winston makes a mental note regarding Mary, she never mentioned Alina.

'Not when I was there. She might have been, at some time. She would die for that man.'

'Can I ask you about the Cartwrights that night?' Caron wants to know more about Boulter. 'You ran out of the house from the dining room. Did you notice anything unusual as you left Greg Cartwright's home?'

Petra sits and thinks for a couple of minutes. 'There was another man, a builder, I think. I asked Mary about him; she didn't know who it was. He shook his head as I unscrewed the bottle in the bag that I was given when I got there. So, I just pretended to drink.'

Caron is astounded she hasn't been told of this other man. 'Can you give us more details?'

'He seemed older than Tony. I think he had seen him too, as he shook his head towards him. It went cold, I mean, really cold. Tony put his coat back on; he must have felt the chill as well. The man was just a bit shorter than Tony and had a little bit of grey hair, and he wore a kind of work overall with a bright scarf around his neck. That's all I remember of him.'

'Can you remember anything else unusual?' asks DS Winston.

Petra thinks, 'I remember slipping and falling on the dining room floor. It wasn't the usual hard wooden floor, I've been in there plenty of times to know.' Petra sits quietly and ponders. Streaming tears roll down her face.

'I touched something… something which felt like skin, I'd forgotten all about that. As I stood up, I reached out to grab a chair that would normally be there. But it wasn't. There was nothing there but what was lying on the floor. Something, I'm not sure, plastic?' Petra looks at Caron. 'Was Emily lying on the floor, already dead?'

'We don't know, Petra. That's why it is so important that you tell us everything you can remember.'

'I don't remember much more than what I've told you about the dining room. I've told you the rest.'

'I know this is difficult; we are almost finished for now. There are just a couple more questions. Is that OK?' DS Winston asks gently.

'Yeah, go on,' replies Petra with a newfound energy.

'Petra, is there anything more you can tell us about Greg Cartwright or Tony Boulter apart from what happened that night? Do you know anyone else who could be involved?'

Petra wipes her eyes and blows her nose. 'They always had loads of money. They'd hand over rolls of banknotes to pay, I mean, the men at The House would hand over bundles of money. Tony always had plenty of cash. He tried hiding the fact from us, but there was just so much he couldn't do anything about that. There were wads of it. Greedy Tony Boulter had everything he wanted: women, cars, drink, gambling and control over us kids. No one would ever stop him.'

Caron knows what Denny is thinking and vice versa: money laundering and trafficking were clear possibilities.

Caron looks at Petra and sees the slight frame of a worried child. As headstrong as she is, she could break down at any point. Caron needs to include further support. 'One last question,' she says, 'Were you aware of any other people, child or adult, being taken away by Tony or Greg?'

'You are joking? At least ten of us over the months, some didn't return. While on the streets, I saw many come and go. I heard some were on a rent-a-family move, but I don't know what that means. Tony promised us our own place, you know, just for the three of us. He bought us and promised us the world. Freedom and a place to come and go as we wanted, so we weren't tied down. We were so stupid; I believed him at first. In the state I was in, I would have believed anything anyone told me to get warm and some food.' Petra stops talking; her eyes give way to her hurt and sorrow.

'Is there anything else you want to add?'

'We three wanted to be free from the system, and definitely no school. We just wanted to be ourselves, with no hassle and have some laughs. That never happened; we were just about broken. My heart ached for Jessie. Do you know what I mean? She just wanted to be a child, never to grow up like. Even though we were all young, we saw too many terrible things. All three of us wanted to stay young, to be free and happy without worrying about anything. I think that has something to do with Jessie starving herself. She didn't want to get any older. Looks like she got her wish.'

Petra sobs into her hands. 'We saw tons of problems which I never even thought about.'

'DCI Dell, I think we should stop for now,' says Connie Tate. 'Petra is distraught. She should be under medical supervision.'

'No, no, please let me continue. I feel better talking, and I promise I will see a doctor if you think I should. I would rather get this over and done with.'

'Connie is right, Petra.' Caron says. 'We should stop now and give you a break. We can pick this up tomorrow after you see a GP.' For selfish reasons and with her duty of care, Caron is pleased Connie has highlighted her concerns for Petra's welfare on record. Petra's statement can be dismissed in court if she continues if she is unwell. Looking ahead, the defence may state that the witness was under duress. There is no way this case will be thrown out on a technical issue.

'No, I am fine. I would cry at any time reliving this nightmare, it is something I won't get over.' Her pleading eyes look at Connie.

'I may need to overrule you here, Petra. You are not in a good place.'

'Who would be? Just a few more minutes, then I will stop for today.' She then turns her pleading look to Caron and DS Winston.

'I am content for you to continue for a few minutes more, no longer. Only if Connie agrees that you should.'

'Petra, I must insist no longer than a few minutes. Then we must stop and consider medical treatment.'

Caron is content that she can continue, even for a few more minutes. 'Just for the record, Petra was examined by a private doctor on the fourteenth of December. She was given a clean bill of health physically and medication for her mental health. There was no evidence of confusion or misinterpretation; however, a medical expert will be called upon to ensure that Petra is well enough to act as a witness and provide evidence. Thank you for your intervention,

Connie.'

Without warning, Petra starts talking again. Connie nods to Caron and adds a footnote confirming this is acceptable.

'At the beginning, some of the others disappeared. We thought they'd been given their own place to live, wondering what their rooms would be like, how friggin' stupid is that.' Petra looks directly at Caron and says, 'After a few weeks, I knew they were either dead or trafficked. I couldn't tell Emily or Jessie; it would have broken them. That's when I started to keep some of the money back, putting as much as I could behind the bath panel in the room we used. We had the same room at The House every time. I saved a couple of hundred quid, but it wasn't enough for us to leave Yorkshire. With no plans for where we would go, I kept my thoughts to myself and played the game. Honestly, I didn't think our time was up yet. But running off was not the answer. Bart would have helped if I hadn't been too scared to bring it up, and I needed enough cash for all three of us.'

'Could you take us to The House?' asks DS Winston.

'I'll just give you the address; that'd be easier.'

DS Winston can't believe he'd asked such a foolish question.

Petra became agitated. 'They're all minted, why pick people off the street? Want to hear a laugh? I almost felt sorry for them. The five men, I mean. With all their money, and some have families of their own, so more lives will be ruined once they learn about their husbands or whatever they are. They were worse off than we were; they had everything at their feet, and it still wasn't enough. Some people shouldn't have money. They're bastards who get off on raping kids.'

Caron thinks Petra is wiser than a typical fifteen-year-old, even though she has acknowledged for the first time that she's a child. And, she has one thing absolutely right: there are many bastards, far too many, but she's wrong to pity any of these evil creatures.

Petra provides the address of The House and the location of her stashed money. The names of the women she knows are also provided. Now, though she is washed out, exhausted, angry and very frightened.

Petra agrees her statement, which will be signed alongside her recorded evidence. Caron confirms a support officer will be appointed to Petra, and an urgent medical examination will also be carried out. Callum is to recruit Uncle.

Connie Tate confirms her confidentiality and will act as the sole appropriate adult for the duration of the case and afterwards if necessary. Ch -Supt Krubb will liaise directly with her superior to underpin the importance of everyone's complete discretion.

Caron needs to ensure everyone living on their tiny island feels as well as they possibly can in such circumstances. 'Come on, let's look around this minute piece of rock and get some fresh air.'

Remember, you are to use Janey and Cerys for all conversations. I know it is frustrating, but your safety is paramount.

23

Fresh Air Clears The Mind

'You are joking,' says Janey. 'It's freezing.'

'Get your coats on,' instructs Caron, 'We're all going outside. Honestly, you'll feel better for some fresh air.'

A few minutes later, the sorry-looking group wander around the garden, wrapped up against the elements. Caron walks out of the gate, and the others follow.

'Christ, it's friggin' freezing out here,' Cerys forgets for a moment how many nights she had slept out under a cold winter's sky. 'The size of this place will take less than three minutes to look at.'

'That's right, but I want to show you how remote you are. Look to the east.' Everyone looked out across the North Sea. A few tankers could be seen way off the coast, bobbing on the horizon.

'Rather them than me on that water. What a way to earn a living,' observes Janey.

'Best keep your own company then, eh?' replies Cerys. Janey once again feels ashamed. She worked all hours building her company with Greg to earn her place within the construction world. Her guilty feelings because of her greedy husband and his atrocities will continue to haunt her.

'Below us, within the cliff face, are many nooks and crannies.' Caron informs the group, 'Some are accessible by the iron ladders fixed into the sides of the cliffs, you can see the handles poking above the edge. Many sets of these stairs circle this tiny spot, and I daresay they are a welcome sight for some. I've explored this rock a few times, in better weather. One or two caves can be found just around the north-east point, as you turn into the estuary.'

'I thought the inlet from the south-east was the estuary?' says Janey.

'There are two. One of which runs under the wooden bridge, the south-east, as you've rightly called it, Janey, is far too dangerous to use when the weather is up. Especially if you don't know the area well, locals wouldn't recommend that anyone use it after dark because of the protruding rocks and those that are hidden under the water. Either one of them could rip the bottom of any boat to shreds.' Caron pauses as she catches her breath in the wind. 'The inlet was purposefully created years ago to enable boats and their occupants to come into the estuary when the tide is low. It took many men to cut through the thick stone, but it was worth it.'

The group look around the lonely island, and Janey wonders if they will be safe here if Boulter finds them.

Caron continues, 'The estuary at the north of the island was naturally formed, but the waters are very shallow when the tide is out. So, the southern niche was created.'

'Don't get too close to the edge,' instructs Cerys. 'You'll get blown off.' Just then, a hungry seagull swoops over them looking for food. Cerys laughs, a reminder to everyone how young she is.

Callum is quiet as he takes in the surroundings again. The primary reason for his recce is to ensure Cerys and Janey can get off this odd piece of rock without using the bridge. He thinks he has a solution, but it could prove too dangerous as he looks over the edge again. However, it might be helpful in an emergency; he knows not to rule out any escape route.

The group go back to the house, now slightly fresher from the intensity of statements and formality.

'OK. Keep yourselves safe and look out for each other,' advises Caron. 'Talk to each other when you need to, try not to bottle things up.'

Janey makes tea and toast, all of which are eaten in minutes. Callum opts for a full English breakfast.

DCI Dell is content with Janey and Cerys's moods. Both seem calmer now compared to when they arrived. Both officers prepare to leave.

'Keep me updated with anything you remember, even if it seems trivial. Cerys, a medical professional, will contact you via Connie. She is a mental health practitioner whom our force employs regularly. She is well aware that confidentiality is key, so don't be concerned about security breaches; she has been specifically selected to support you during our case.' Cerys does not reply. DCI Dell continues, 'Let me know if you need anything and thank you all for today; it has been a difficult one.' Caron doesn't want to expand any further for now. Her witnesses seem more settled after those few minutes outside. The fresh air appears to have put some positive thoughts into their minds.

As Caron and Denny drive off, Caron says, 'We both know what rent-a-family means. We will need the National Crime Agency to assist. We will use their expertise to work alongside our task force. Money Laundering on a wide scale is a major factor here, Denny. I suspect people trafficking is also on the list. I am beginning to think the three girls were Tony Boulter's sideline, he is not the only one controlling money laundering on this scale. He's bright, but has been incredibly stupid, being so free with money is a thoughtless move. And, when will people realise that when children grow up, some will report their abuser, even years after their horrific ordeal? It seems his greed and ego have tripped him up. Let's hope it is his downfall because we must get him off the streets.'

'I agree, ma'am,' replies DS Winston.

'Less of the ma'am.' Caron looks across at her DS as he salutes. She rolls her eyes at him.

Boulter

I am becoming impatient. Everything I need is packed and in my white Nissan rental, apart from my laptop, which has remained undiscovered. When they dropped my car off, they confirmed it was hired under my alias.

My Range Rover is back on my drive. But honestly, a fucking Nissan! They're popular and won't draw attention, so it must do.

24

Bart

Caron answers her mobile phone as she pulls into Northumberland's HQ, 'DCI Dell.'

'Ma'am, you have had a visitor; he wouldn't leave his name or contact details. The gentleman left after he asked me not to inform anyone that he wanted to speak to you. What would you like me to do?'

'I don't think there is anything you can do. If it is important, he will come back.'

DS Winston looks inquisitively at his boss. 'Problem?'

'Someone has called into the station. He refused to leave his name.'

'Bart?'

'Possibly. Let's hope it is. I will park on the street, if he's still around, it might encourage him to approach me.'

Bart immediately recognises DCI Dell from her police photograph; he walks towards the pair and introduces himself.

Caron shakes Bart's hand, and Denny does the same. Surprisingly, he is immaculate; Caron chastises herself for her biased thinking.

Bart is taller than Caron, over six feet. He wears a long green army coat, which is in good condition. Underneath, he has a black jumper with a shirt collar peeking out from the top. His dark blue jeans and sturdy walking boots are pristine.

His dark hair recedes slightly, and his tanned face has a leathery appearance.

'How did you get here? Train?' Caron tries to build up a rapport without being too forceful.

'Yes, indeed, ma'am, it is a very straightforward journey from Leeds. My only issue with being here is that I may be putting others at risk. Would it be possible to speak with you both privately?'

'Of course. Let us go somewhere away from our HQ,' suggests Denny.

The three get in the car, and Caron drives towards a local country park. Even though it is a Sunday, it is quiet now as the daylight dims. They sit at a sturdy, forlorn picnic table, its green hue prominent against the sparse, grey, snowy background.

'Everything has to be off the record. I do not want anyone to know I have been to see you. No one should see me here because if Petra is alive, Boulter will think she has been speaking to me. There are a few of your police colleagues on the take from him, and I cannot risk sharing anything official. How you say you got your information is up to you.' Bart pauses as he chooses his words. 'To be straight with you, I will not provide any officer's names, simply because I have very little evidence, just some warning behaviour. You only need to dig down a little to unearth one or two names.' Bart waits for some acknowledgement before he continues. DCI Dell nods: she does not want to attract any further negative attention from Boulter.

'There have been events which will benefit your investigation.' Bart is extremely well-spoken, and his concerns for Petra and others are apparent.

'OK, Bart, you can take from our discussions whatever you want, but Petra Gould and Mary Cartwright could be vital witnesses. Their lives will not be put in jeopardy. Do we have an agreement?' Caron pushes Bart for an answer; he has something vital to say, or he would not have risked travelling to see her.

'Agreed. Boulter had a woman, Alina, who would do everything for him: he owned her. He is an animal, and I know for certain he killed her. I witnessed him bury Alina in the grounds of her cottage.' Bart repeats Boulter's words as he watched him put Alina's body into her freshly dug grave.

Caron sat with her poker face, staring at this articulate giant of a man before her, not daring to show emotion. Denny, meanwhile, sat with his mouth slightly open.

'Are there any more bodies in the grounds of Alina's cottage?'

'As I have stated, Boulter did say Alina was now with some of her flock as he looked down into the ground. But I cannot answer that question honestly, DCI Dell. I have no proof. I know no one from Yorkshire's force has even attended her home. I can only repeat what Boulter said. I daresay it will not be a pretty sight if more remains are found; I would not like to witness the outcome myself. A word of caution here: If you go and stomp around Alina's forest garden, Boulter will know that Petra is alive and well.'

'Why do you say that?'

'No one will ever break the seal of Alina's loyalty to Boulter, definitely not in Yorkshire. The only way you would know about Alina would be through Petra or me. But the only reason I would come to you would be to protect the homeless community. Usually, I would not give Alina another thought, now, however, I have witnessed her body being placed into the ground. Boulter's police contacts will never tell. Of that I am certain.'

'Who else would know of Alina?' asks Caron.

'Mary Cartwright won't know about her. Only his criminal contacts will. Unfortunately, DCI Dell, I fear the conundrum is yours to unravel. I will be happy to testify only if he is caught. While I worry about my life, the picture for me is much bigger. As you may imagine, I have often wanted to tackle Boulter, but cannot; there are far too many people with influence in his pocket. He has a lot of control, meaning you have a job on your hands with him. Innocent people will no doubt be caught in the crossfire.'

'So, you watched him dig a grave and place Alina in it?' clarifies DS Winston.

'Yes. And I do not doubt that there will be others; however, I have no evidence. A few younger people have gone missing. I didn't think they would be killed and buried so close to their place of safety: The viaduct. Murdered? Left of their own free will? Or, did they disappear by force? Who knows? However, ignoring the fact that they have vanished is not right. I can confirm, I do not know what happened to any of the others.'

Caron can see Bart has more to say. Remaining professional, she tries to push him for further information. 'Can you give me her address? I will ask my counterparts in Yorkshire the right questions, to the point they will have to provide Alina's address so no one will suspect you have been in touch.'

'Yes, I can provide that information. You know what you are doing; if someone in Yorkshire confirms where she lives, then I have done all I can to lower the risk of Petra or Mary being found.' Bart provides DCI Dell with the information, and DS Winston makes a note.

'Does Boulter have any family or other close friends?'

'His mother and father lived in the same cottage before Alina. I understand he arranged their move abroad, but the rumours are mixed - South America, Spain, and Japan were thrown into the pot of ideas. I am unsure if they moved away at all. Please understand that my conclusion here is based on my instincts, and nothing else. Don't be fooled, though. No one can stop him from doing what he wants.'

The three of them remain quiet in their own thoughts for a few minutes, digesting the possibilities of what could have befallen the parents of the elusive Tony Boulter.

'Where will you stay tonight? Do you have somewhere booked?' asks Caron as they stand up and walk towards the car.

'No, I will return to Leeds tonight. Sundays are generally the days I have to myself, so no one will be looking or expecting to see me. I am working tomorrow; suspicions will be raised if I don't attend. I have no doubt someone will watch my movements and report back to Boulter. There is a train in an hour, I will ensure I make it.'

'The station is only fifteen minutes away; we will drive you. It is the least we can do. If you remember anything further, please let me know. It will save you a journey if you call me.' Caron hands Bart her mobile number.

'You do see why I couldn't speak to you at the station, don't you? It would only take someone to hear one comment to make the connection that I had been in touch with you. And, if Petra is OK, I cannot risk anyone finding her because of a phone call.'

'I understand, but a call to my mobile won't be traced at the station. That is my number. Please use it if you need to.'

Caron is pleased she is not the only one who is paranoid, as she makes small talk and discovers more about Bart. He has been through a lot, makes sound decisions, and has done his utmost to protect Petra's vulnerability.

Bart goes into detail about the abuse and victimisation that homeless people encounter. 'It is disgusting. Making money when living rough comes with risks. A guy began washing cars, just a couple a week, to make a bit of money. A carwash owner broke his hand before robbing him of the small amount of cash he had made. Younger people are extremely vulnerable. I don't know of any youngster who has not received abuse of some sort.' Bart explained what he tries to do to help, acknowledging that his weekend shelter arrangements can only help a few.

As Bart exits the car, he turns. 'Give my best wishes to your witnesses, Detective Chief Inspector. It was good to meet you both today.' He says farewell to Denny with a slight wave of his hand. Caron hopes their paths cross again.

Boulter, in the meantime has ransacked Bart's place looking for anything to help locate Mary. He is unsure if the two know each other, but he can't ignore the fact that they might.

On his return home, Bart is satisfied Boulter has found nothing; he has taken the time to look in every nook and cranny, and Boulter might now give him a wide berth. Here's hoping he does. Bart sends a text to DCI Dell's mobile, keeping her updated whilst underpinning the fact that Boulter is still in Yorkshire.

Caron cannot sit on the information regarding Alina's murder. She calls DI Rustler.

'Hello, DI Rustler. My name is DCI Caron Dell. I am calling you to introduce myself before we meet face-to-face. How are you and DS Mosley getting along? Have you had time to digest the information and caseload in front of you?' Her direct call will hopefully catch him on the back foot.

DI Rustler is taken aback; he's unprepared for any interrogation so soon, and especially not on a Sunday! 'Well, it is early days and we are working through the data we have.' He hopes he sounds convincing.

'Is there anything specific coming to mind?'

'No, nothing has come up yet, ma'am. It is very early in the case.'

Caron has to bite her lip. She has some questions: Why does a DI in Yorkshire not have any concerns?

'OK, well, keep working through what you have. We can discuss your findings when we meet. Oh, something has just popped into my mind.'

DS Winston has to turn his head away from her.

'Is there anyone especially close to Boulter, family or friends, who could help us with our enquiries? I assume there must be others. He couldn't have just relied on Cartwright for his activities?'

Caron could almost hear DI Rustler's stomach lurch. He isn't ready at all to give away any details to his new DCI. It is obvious to Caron that there are others on Boulter's payroll, and it is clear to Caron that Rustler hasn't thought it through yet; he doesn't seem very forthcoming in releasing any information that might catch someone out. He must also know he can't hold onto evidence.

'Not that I can think of off-hand. I will contact nightclubs and bars where he is well known around the scene here in Leeds. As I said, it is very early in the case that I am unsure about any adult, but I will ask around.' He hopes that is enough for DCI Dell to think he does not know Boulter very well - in reality, he doesn't know him well at all, except for his threatening reputation.

Caron isn't buying any of it. 'OK, please pass any information onto me and do not contact anyone directly apart from the clubs. I don't want to set anyone off on a wild goose chase. Ring me as soon as you have any names.' She hangs up.

'Do you think you have DI Rustler on-side after your introduction?' Denny grins.

'Absolutely, he is crapping himself.'

DI Rustler tells DS Mosley to find Boulter's parents' addresses. He vaguely remembers they moved somewhere abroad and thinks Boulter could be in their home in Yorkshire - it's a long shot, but it may keep DCI Dell off his back.

Boulter
Text message received: *Dell's investigating your parents'*

properties.
Good work, glad I am ready to go.

25

Boulter And Box

Tony's father, Ed, was a proud and well-respected Polish man who relocated to the UK for work. Not long after he found employment, he met and married Susan Boulter. They both agreed on a double-barrelled surname: Jez-Boulter. Tony preferred his mother's name.

Ed Jez-Boulter was a grafter who worked all hours to support his family. He doted on Tony, his only child and sought a sporting activity to burn off some of his young son's energy, finally settling on taekwondo. Tony excelled in the world of martial arts except for one key component: discipline. Even at a young age he learnt how to hide his true nature. A few years later, he moved on to another element in the martial arts field, kickboxing. He fooled everyone for years. His commitment and discipline in respecting his sport were a well-hidden fraud on his part. Cage fighting eventually became his thing. His reputation on the club scene soared. Charm and the well-developed mask he created during the discipline lessons he attended all those years ago were a convincing pretence to hide behind. He was, and remains, a brutal, uncaring killer and the most believable influencer Mary has ever met. His recruiting ability is a testament to that.

'For the tape, fourteenth of December 2024, 12.30 pm. Detective Sergeant Dukefield and Detective Baker are present to interview Josh Holder concerning his arrest for breaking and entering a property within the Wakefield area. Mr Holder's legal representation is Ms Valerie Hindman.'

'Thank you, DS Dukefield. I have advised my client not to comment; he has provided a statement he would like me to read to you, ensuring the investigation continues.' Valerie Hindman pauses. 'Understand my request. You should release my client immediately. Mr Holder was assisting an elderly lady who lives at the address in question. He received a call from her whilst he was at home. Her boiler was broken, and she stated she was freezing. Mr Holder couldn't call her back once he got to the property because his mobile phone was out of charge.'

The two interviewing officers don't believe a single word of it. Their problem was that they had no evidence to the contrary.

'We will need the lady's contact details.'

'Certainly, we can arrange that.' Box is sitting tight-lipped as his solicitor manages the conversation. Furious that his fingerprints and DNA have been taken.

After speaking to CPS, it was clear there was no case to answer at this stage. The witness confirmed he had been in his car all night and was not violent. There is no record of anyone living at the rented property in Wakefield, but evidence demonstrates some form of occupation. The ruling was to release Josh Holder whilst the investigation was ongoing. Box is to attend the station weekly until their investigation is completed.

'Ridiculous,' responds Ms Hindman. She collects her things and instructs Box to collect his items from the desk sergeant. She will speak to him privately before he goes home.

Once outside, Valerie Hindman tells him to go home and to contact no one.

Box is still freezing, but at least he is out, even if further enquiries are pending. His car is still at the Wakefield address; he calls an Uber.

Box arrives home around ten pm, and whacks the

heating on full blast as he walks through the door into his luxurious apartment in a quiet suburb of Leeds. Whoever said crime didn't pay didn't know what they were talking about. Thick bastards, he smirks.

Just before midnight, his doorbell rings. Box beams as he checks his front door camera. That familiar frame he has been waiting to see for the last twenty-four hours is outside. His hood is up, and his head down, but Box recognises him immediately as he unlocks the door to let his visitor in.

A gun is pointed at his head. Box doesn't register what is about to happen until it is too late. Tony Boulter shoots Box between the eyes.

Box's hero walks away from the open doorway without a thought for his trusted sidekick, who is most definitely left out in the cold.

Boulter
Thick twat shouldn't have got caught. He can rot.

26

Northumberland & Yorkshire

Northumberland and Yorkshire Police issue details and a current photo of Tony Boulter for his immediate arrest across the UK.

Caron reads her witnesses' statements again and again. She understands why Petra, Emily and Jessie didn't want to attend school; adolescence is a difficult time. But they were vulnerable, and making risky decisions could lead anyone, God knows, where. In this case, the death of two friends.

Hundreds of people do it day in and day out, looking to escape from whatever their worries or fears are. Caron thanks her lucky stars for her home life, which was uneventful until she was eighteen.

Something Petra said bothers her: the smell, something about a scent, she still can't grasp that thread. Is it because her mental capacity is protecting her, still? She will unravel it one day.

Caron has plans to visit Macy in France after Christmas, probably New Year, but only if she can get Tony Boulter behind bars or six feet under. Christmas Day will be a subdued affair, with Léa and her husband Ross hosting and Caron as the third wheel again. She smiles as she thinks to herself, like they care. Caron loves a good Christmas feast with all the trimmings, and she won't have to lift a finger this time around. She doesn't usually drink much, but Christmas, New Year and birthdays are the exception for a tipple or two.

Caron makes a mental note: Christmas shopping.

16th December 2024

Jasmine Kapoor — Jaz, as she prefers to be known, is the most suspicious person in the world. Even more so when asked to discuss her data-gathering process with DS Winston. Caron clocks her body language and blank stare, showing her lack of buy-in. Caron knows she needs to nudge Jaz in the right direction and give her responsibility, so she follows the pair into the room.

'Jaz,' Denny says. 'Your process appears to be an exceptional data-gathering analytical system. Has it been tested?'

'Yes, it has,' she replies. Jaz moves her powered wheelchair to the only PC in the room. 'I can filter any information quickly.' Within a few minutes, she is logged into her current analytical data, and begins to demonstrate her explanation. 'It also helps with gap analysis, so if you are waiting for an update from a task, I can tell you immediately what the last entry was and who completed the task.' She eyes DS Winston suspiciously. 'Why do you ask?'

'I need you to join our investigation, but it isn't for the faint-hearted, Jaz. You will be responsible for all data analysis. As in all cases, it is essential to log and maintain a clear track record of who, when and why specific links and people are involved. Transparency enables CPS to accept our investigation as watertight and ready to progress – all data needs to be completely secure. I understand you have worked on a more efficient process to record all investigation data, and you are also a trained HOLMES disclosure officer.'

'Yes, of course I have tested my process, but you must be honest with me; what is your workload? Please don't say training.'

Caron watches and figures Jaz is just what she is looking for. She's bright and questions her concerns appropriately. She nods to Denny.

'Jaz, the Cartwright case has been given to DCI Dell for investigation. This will be an extremely fast-paced case with evidence, data, and facts paramount to ensure a conviction. Tony Boulter is not the only one we are looking for. With no evidence but strong suspicion that two or three of Yorkshire's officers are on Boulter's payroll. This case cannot be discussed with anyone. Your task is to head up all analyses and immediately highlight red flags for DCI Dell and me. Your natural curiosity and inquisitive mind are sharp, which will keep everyone on their toes as we move through the case.' He watches Jaz's excitement build and her hungry eyes demonstrate she is ready for the opportunity presented to her.

'Tell me who is on the team, and I will create a new programme to capture data, filters, et cetera. It won't take me long. DCI Dell, I will need authorisation to create an encrypted data file set. I can add and remove personnel as you instruct.'

With Jaz on board, Caron slips away. In agreement with Krubb, she FaceTime's DI Rustler, and she is aware that CC Gallows has also been briefed. Caron notes that Leeds's Chief Constable is closely monitoring this case. She will watch CC Gallows with her own scrutiny — two can play at that game.

'Hi Eric, I see Tim is not with you?' She can't give any details on how she knows Judge Hicks and the fact she was at the safehouse in Wakefield at the same time they were there. As far as they are concerned Caron was selected by Krubb and Gallows after Judge Hicks had spoken with them.

Rustler, Mosley and Gallows think Mary Cartwright is still in Wakefield. They are unaware of her ID and location switches. That's how it will remain.

'I was expecting another lead outside of our force, to be honest. I'm not going to lie, I'd have loved to step up to the challenge, but you will get my full support. Tim, on the other hand, well… a woman DCI that's a whole new world for him.'

'It is good to know you're committed to the cause. I appreciate your support; thank you. DS Denny Winston will be joining my team, and this case will require more personnel.' Caron lets that sink in and mentally notes his slightly grovelling acceptance. Mosley will be dealt with in due course.

'In preparation for our team's expansion, I can confirm the following have also been appointed.' Caron pauses again to ensure he is keeping up. 'So, undercover protection officers have been arranged. Nancy Dell, IT and Digital forensics specialist, will work on the data Mary Cartwright has supplied.' She explains that this information could not be shared until now. 'You need to be aware that Nancy is, in fact, my mother, and we have worked together on and off over the years. I have also appointed PC Jaz Kapoor, the best person to manage our analytics, a no-nonsense, committed constable who has been on the force for twelve years.'

'More importantly, Eric, I have recommended the UK's National Crime Agency to support my investigation. That was a conversation between Krubb and me. I will let you inform your DI.' She can tell he is not impressed with her decisions by his non-comment on everything she has said. It is almost like he doesn't care, and his unconvincing smile still rattles her; he has rolled over far too quickly.

'Léa Cochran is currently performing autopsies on the two dead girls. She has been in Leeds since this morning and will provide full reports. Should anything stand out immediately, she will inform me directly.' Another female for Mosley's prejudice. 'Your thoughts?'

'Is there a specific reason why you have brought her in?'

'I have my reasons. Let Léa do her job, and I expect you to provide support where necessary. No doubt she may get some resistance, but believe me, she won't be interested in anyone's opinion, not one bit. She might, however, need to be pointed in the right direction, location and colleague-wise. That is what I mean by support.'

'I'm sure she'll be welcome, ma'am, and Tim will be fine.

I will keep an eye on it, though.'

'He will have to adjust to changes more positively, and he should know that this case could help his career. Let's plan the basics, such as comms and meet-ups.'

'Of course, ma'am, I am more than happy to arrange the fundamentals. I don't think moving our witness is a good idea either.' Caron and Krubb agreed to keep Petra undisclosed for now. Krubb usually has a good instinct, and he also agrees that someone in Yorkshire is keeping Boulter informed. It was decided Petra's location was too much of a risk to share. Regarding Tim Mosley, Caron is not keen on him at all. Nevertheless, he could prove to be helpful with his local knowledge.

Caron has seen Mary's digital evidence. Her information has been securely downloaded and analysed from her USBs. DI Rustler is unaware of the evidence held within Northumberland's HQ. Recordings span several occasions during the last six months, where each time, Greg insisted on a break for Mary, or she should go and spend time with her mum. It hadn't dawned on her that something was up. She accepted his offer of a few days away, as he was always busy working. It transpires that Mary had no idea what her husband was doing at all.

With Greg, it is mostly fantasy sex. Tony's behaviour is just way off. Unfortunately for him, whatever happens during their investigation, he is in Caron's sights. It is just a matter of time before he is brought down. DCI Dell turns her focus back to her discussion with DI Rustler.

A communication plan is agreed upon, together with a rhythm of face-to-face collaborations. The first will be in less than twenty-four hours. Caron knows the pace of this investigation will increase, so in all fairness, their arrangements could be futile, but it's a start to see how her colleagues in Yorkshire operate. Tim Mosley will be in attendance. Denny Winston will also be there; seeing Mosley's reactions when they all meet will be interesting.

She will call the shots on location and let Eric know. Caron is unsure why Gallows has appointed Rustler and Mosley; it certainly wasn't because of their investigative skills.

'So, down to business. What's your initial thoughts on Greg Cartwright, Eric?'

'I don't see him as the instigator here. I've no evidence to support my statement, it's just a gut feeling.'

Caron smiles. 'Well, your gut feeling will need evidence. I agree that his wealth and everything that goes with it is a smoke screen. Something more sinister is at play. Whether it is trafficking, sex work, paedophilia, or drugs, I am none the wiser, but it is vile.' They both ponder their thoughts.

'Before we do anything further on your "gut feelings," is Greg Cartwright still recovering?'

'He is stable but critical, and it is still a touch-and-go situation. Chief Constable Gallows and I are happy with that. He is under armed guard protection, which will continue until the trial, if we can get our evidence into place. Personally, I'm unsure if Cartwright will make it. Boulter has gone to ground and could be anywhere near or far. He must have high-ranking players because they are protecting him. Who knows at this stage?' Caron doesn't move a muscle as she watches and listens to Rustler.

'Well, if that is the case, we have some work to do.'

'The case in hand still has public momentum on the face of it, although it does appear there is no evidence to bring anyone else in. I'd love to catch the evil bastard; we can't ignore the facts - no doubt someone is watching out for him, not necessarily the force. Let me have a go at interviewing him first. I want to see him crumble.'

I bet you would, thinks Caron, as she replies, 'Let me set Mosley on surveillance duties, we need to find out as much as he can about the three girls. Unless you have any update at all on the third girl?'

'I've had a sniff around the areas where they've slept and the local food banks and soup kitchens, but no one has seen the third girl. No one will give up a name either. Without a name we can't trace her home, parents or anything personal linked to her. However, one of our PC's has recognised the two dead teenagers. I have cross-referenced my intel within missing persons data, and I have names: Jessica Lowery and Emily Southern. No doubt Boulter will be looking for their friend. He will pay for any information and get to her first if we don't. We need to step it up.'

Caron thought how easy it is to manipulate two experienced officers to act as a decoy without any idea that their mission is pointless. She already has the two girls' identities confirmed by Petra and Léa. It is not the greatest of camaraderie, but the stakes are too high to disclose this to Rustler. If Boulter follows Rustler and Mosley, Caron and her team will have space to work on her investigation and arrest him. It is still possible that Rustler or Mosley is on his payroll. Having a police decoy in this case is a valuable investment, especially if the mole protecting Boulter is based in Yorkshire. However, they could be in any force.

Caron's suspicions have increased regarding Gallows; she questions why he sent DI Rustler and the incompetent DS Mosley to speak with Mary. Between the two of them, Caron hopes they will lead her to Boulter.

'OK, it seems we don't have much progress yet, Eric. Léa will provide an official cause of death for those two girls as soon as she can. There is no doubt in my mind those children were murdered because their use had come to an end, their deaths appear to be due to an overdose, but what with?'

'I also agree that we are looking towards a murder charge. A piece of thick plastic sheeting was found under the foot of a cabinet in Cartwright's dining room, ma'am, which also supports this theory. The victims were as good as dead when they were picked up that night. Once we have Boulter - it is clearly him on Mary's cameras - our evidence against him will be hard to disprove.'

'Describe the plastic in more detail for me, please?'

'Heavy duty, black, strong enough for damp-proofing, I'd say.'

'Where is it now?'

'I've logged it as evidence at the station, which is usual practice, ma'am.' Just realising he has cocked that up.

'You must take that from the evidence room and store it with Mary Cartwright's laptop as soon as possible. Where is the Cartwright's laptop actually?'

'Yes, ma'am. Mary Cartwright's laptop is held in the safe, where it should be. It is more secure than the evidence room.'

Caron was level-headed but had an *I don't believe it* moment. 'Who has access to the safe?'

'Just myself and three sergeants whose main appointment is to ensure evidence security is maintained, amongst their other duties, of course.'

How archaic, Caron thought. 'I need Mary Cartwright's laptop. My digital forensic team will want to analyse its contents. Take that, plus the plastic sheet evidence, and bring them with you on Tuesday. I want those two pieces of evidence out of Yorkshire.'

'Do you think that is necessary… ma'am?'

'I think it's vital. Would you question CC Gallows' orders?' Caron makes sure Rustler knows who he is addressing. It has been necessary for her to do this a few times during her career.

'No, sorry, ma'am, I will bring these with me.' DI Eric Rustler blushes at his stupidity. He should have known when to challenge; that was not the correct order to question.

'Glad that's cleared up.' Caron mentally notes his allegiance to Gallows.

'Sorry, ma'am, Gallows won't like that,' responds Rustler hopefully appropriately. 'He instructed the laptop to be logged and kept here securely.'

'Has Gallows instructed any forensic activity on it yet?'

'No, it is just to be kept here with myself as explained, no instructions to the contrary.'

'Does that not concern you at all?'

'No, not at all. Gallows is by the book.' Rustler states quite indignantly.

'All the same, bring it with you, Eric. I need to get a clear understanding of Greg and his home life. At this point, we don't know much.'

Gallows is involved in this somehow. That is a certainty. Rustler won't present that evidence, thinks DCI Dell as she ends her FaceTime call.

Boulter

Text message received: *Two girls have been identified, and autopsies are being carried out. PG has not been found. MC is still under guard in Yorkshire, but I don't know where yet. Your laptop was not found.*

So, it's just the Cartwrights to be obliterated, not long now. I need to access their whereabouts, then Mexico, here I come.

27

Macy – Eighteen Years Earlier

Caron

It was a bright Easter Saturday morning when it dawned on me that I could be pregnant. With my positive wee stick in my bag, I stayed with Beryl and Keith over the Easter holidays. It was the most emotional time I have ever spent with my sister.

Fury, sympathy, rage, and pity were just some of the emotions all three of us went through. Not one of us ever suggested abortion.

We played "Guess Who" for real because I had no idea who it could have been. He was heavy and smelled of cigars, a new handkerchief, belt (I think), and another smell - it enabled us to rule out some guests. But was it a guest at all? The handkerchief played a key role in our deduction. We scanned the wedding photos to see who had one in their top pocket, realising this was a useless process as it could have been a linen serviette. We got nowhere.

Then Keith almost whispered that he would love children; his pleading look towards Beryl melted my heart again. Beryl nodded, and they both looked at me. That was the solution, but not an adoption. I would pose as Beryl. And my lies continued to protect my rapist, but a bigger prize was at stake: my child. I never thought we could get away with it, but we did. I moved into their London flat, where Keith was picking up some commissions for his artwork and Beryl continued teaching pottery. I went to Uni.

My labour was swift, less than six hours. Thanks to my ante-natal appointments, presenting as Beryl in the delivery room was easy. Keith didn't like the idea of being my birthing partner, so I opted for my sister. Midwife Carina was brilliant, she didn't bat an eyelid at the change of husband to sister, 'It happens all the time when it comes down to the business side of childbirth,' she reassured us.

My daughter Macy was delivered safe and sound, a couple of weeks early on the first of November, weighing six pounds and nine ounces. A good weight, according to the midwife. Also, she was very long for being under seven pounds, apparently. I fell in love with her immediately. So did Beryl and Keith.

We both left the hospital the next day to plan for the arrival of the proud grandparents, who could only be put off visiting for so long.

Jim and Nancy Dell arrived late on the second of November. Saying how well Beryl looked.

I made myself scarce by blaming university commitments and I would be spending a couple of days with Léa Durand to let the grandparents dote on Macy and fuss about the whole new experience for Beryl.

Léa was the only person I ever confided in, apart from Beryl and Keith. Away from the fear of it all, Léa was fabulous. She never judged. Instead, she would offer suggestions when things got complicated, like how to hide my baby bump. She advised that I study from home, stating to my lecturers I had ongoing medical tests, which wasn't a total lie, but deceiving all the same. My GP was happy to provide a letter verifying my incapacity for a number of weeks, due to my pregnancy. We copied the letter, omitting the pregnancy reference and changing Beryl's name to mine. The lies continued to build up to protect the little life growing inside of me.

After a few weeks of helping Beryl and Keith with my adorable

Macy, I knew the time would come to move on. Léa and I rented a two-bedroom flat; we worked in bars and restaurants to make ends meet. This situation worked well for both of us. Even though we studied different vocations, we kept one night a week for relaxation. Every Thursday became our night, primarily because there were no lectures on a Friday until after lunch and that was just for a couple of hours.

We formed a team: The Hen Solos, for the local pub's weekly quiz, and an excellent name for an all-female contingent. Our team included Star Wars and Doctor Who experts, plus a devoted science fiction geek. The weekly quizzes usually got very heated, but the rivalry was soon forgotten after a few drinks. All in all, I completed my first year at university very successfully.

The following spring, Keith was offered a life-changing opportunity. Unfortunately for me, this meant a permanent move for the family of three to a French coastal village, Soulac-sur-Mer, eighty-five kilometres north-west of Bordeaux. Obviously, Macy would be going, too.

As an artist, Keith continued to develop his knowledge within the industry. They decided that working in one of the most beautifully situated artist studios in a foreign country, finding his niche in his art career, was an opportunity not to be missed. His contract would rely on commissions Keith was offered and a small wage to maintain the studio. Accommodation was provided. The owner was only to play a small part in the business as he sought semi-retirement. Beryl was able to work at one of the local bars and help with the village's summer events. She was in her element.

The area boasted seasonal camping sites and tourist accommodation, and in the height of summer, the community came together to provide a wealth of family entertainment. All of which brought the visitors in. Keith's paintings had started to sell, providing an opportunity for their contented approach to life.

I knew it had to be done, and the prospects it brought

were endless for all three of them. The tears I cried were for my own selfish reasons. They were less than three hours away by plane and a bit longer by train. Mam and Dad were extremely supportive. They had many tears too.

28

Task Force

16th December 2024

DCI Caron Dell and DS Denny Winston met DI Eric Rustler and DS Tim Mosley in a popular chain hotel just west of Harrogate, Yorkshire. All booked for one night, as she prepares for her task force's first meeting. An adequate conference room with interactive screens has been secured for their two-day conference. This morning, DCI Dell will inform the two officers from Yorkshire of the NCA's involvement. The rest of the team - including NCA's contingent - will arrive after lunch for a full briefing. That should keep everyone on their toes if they weren't already.

Introductions over and Mosley's nose well out of joint, Caron goes directly into their objectives for their twenty-four-hour stay. Working lunches and dinner if necessary.

'Can you download the USB footage which Mary Cartwright provided, please, Denny?' asks Caron, knowing all too well that DI Rustler could not provide those recordings. Beads of sweat were already forming on his forehead, and shock was written across his face - he had no idea of any other evidence. He can sweat a bit longer. Tim Mosley didn't register the turn of events at all.

Denny presents the footage across the interactive screens. Caron watches as Rustler turns puce, 'We have some questions about what we have seen. Tim, take notes of our findings for this morning, and please contribute.'

Tim Mosley is furious. Like a petulant child, he slowly opens his black notebook and ensures his pencil is sharp enough.

'I think you would be better putting your notes directly onto a Word document and sharing those with us,' Caron suggests in a supportive tone rather than critical reproach.

Mosley takes a painful six minutes to open his laptop before he starts typing. His cocky manner is plain to see, with one arm over the back of his chair as he swings on the two back legs. He tuts, coughs and clears his throat.

'Are you ready?' asks Caron encouragingly.

'Not quite, I need your email addresses so I can share my "typing",' he responds, putting virtual quote marks in the air as he states the word typing.

'Thanks, Tim. Denny and Eric, could you step outside for a minute?'

Denny gets up. Eric is about to say something until he catches Denny's eye. They leave without a word.

Caron smiles as she walks to Tim Mosley, kicking his swinging chair from under him.

Denny and Eric can hear his scream. 'What a prat,' says Denny.

'I agree,' replies Eric - neither laughs.

'If he knows what's good for him, he'll take notice and focus on the job at hand and not his own little world.' Eric shakes his head; he had told him to buck up.

Tim lies on the floor, squirming as he shouts at his superior, 'I'll sue you.'

Quietly and calmly, Caron replies, 'Please do, then you can fuck off my case. Two teenage girls are dead, possibly three, and you think you take precedence? You have one minute to change your ways and think yourself lucky I have given you that.'

'Think you've got that the wrong way round, DCI Dell; I will have your job off you.'

'Get out and stop wasting my time.' Caron responds

calmly. She holds eye contact with him.

'You'll be sorry.' Tim Mosley picks himself up and wipes his shoes. Caron thinks what the hell is he doing? He slowly gathers his papers and laptop, remembering now and then to yelp. Caron still has him in her sights, wondering not for the first time, how he even got past a police job interview, never mind becoming a DS.

Mosley begins to whimper.

Caron picks up her phone. 'Eric, can you both come in please?'

Denny and Eric are through the door in seconds. They stop in their tracks as Tim Mosley wipes his snot and tears away with his hand. Classy, thinks Caron.

'Christ, what happened?' asks Eric.

Tim looks at Caron. She doesn't know what he will say, she doesn't care. 'My chair tipped backwards. I think I've punctured a lung.'

Caron and Denny don't say a word as they watch. There is no smirking or reprimand. Together, they watch the wet blanket play to his audience.

Eric looks at him in disbelief. 'Punctured lung? You wouldn't be able to stand, breathe or walk. The only thing you've hurt here is your pride.'

Caron and Denny move towards the door. 'We'll leave you to it for a few minutes.' Caron says as they walk out.

'He needs to get a grip, boss,' says Denny. 'We cannot have that behaviour on our team.'

'He will Denny. He has no option.'

'How is the CCTV from The House going with Cerys?'

'Nothing yet. She will ring me as soon as she has something. But I do have some street CCTV. It would have been helpful if Cerys had remembered some dates.'

A few minutes later, Tim comes out of the small conference room. 'I'm sorry, ma'am. I don't know what came over me.' Denny walks away.

'Are you hurt physically?'

'No, just embarrassed.'

'You realise this case is a gift to you and your career. If you don't want to participate, I will happily find someone else. The difficulty is that you know too much, so you will be put on desk duties, probably Google searching or filing for however long this case takes. Why would you want to throw this opportunity away?'

'I can't help it sometimes.' He pauses and looks down at his feet. 'My father is very prejudiced and has brought us up the same way, too. He still doesn't know I'm a copper.'

'I would suggest you change your attitude. First and foremost, you are a Detective Sergeant, how I don't know, but here we are. With regards to your father, well, prejudice is prejudice. As an adult, you should make decisions and choices and carry that responsibility. Placing the blame on someone else for your childish actions is unacceptable. You are happy to take a policeman's salary, and that choice is easy for you - one more chance, Mosley, and I mean it. You respect every one of your colleagues, and I mean every person you come across during our time working together, or you're out of the force. What you do with your learning experience once our case has been resolved is up to you. Are we clear, DS Mosley?'

'Crystal.'

'It had better be. Go, sort yourself out, and come back with a positive focus, nothing less. If you want respect, Tim, you have to earn it. Don't blow this opportunity. I'll see you in there when you're ready.'

Caron makes a mental note to research Tim Mosley's family. Working within the police, you can't be too careful; a detailed note of Tim's prejudice and demonstration from today will be placed in his file. What an idiot. Caron goes back into the room, calm and collected. Not a hair out of place. Her professionalism is evident to the point where DI Rustler wonders if Tim's event had even occurred.

'The National Crime Agency are joining our investigation after lunch, along with further members of the

Northumberland Police.' She waits for a response, but nothing is forthcoming. Denny gives that 'told you so' look. She hopes her inward smile does not reach her lips. More work to be done on team building!

Caron Dell has studied the evidence they hold and is keen to drive their case forward. Three days have passed, and they are no nearer to locating Boulter.

Caron presents an overview of what the team will look like and notices the look of panic on Eric and Tim's faces. They are not prepared for this.

'This morning, we will recap what we know to allow me to present a detailed update to the wider team later today. Can I please have Mary Cartwright's laptop, Eric?'

He hands her the laptop. 'The evidence has been wiped, ma'am.'

'Really? How?'

Eric shuffles in his seat, 'I don't know, ma'am. There was no name on the sign-out book.'

'I arranged for one of your security sergeants to view the evidence and report his findings to me, Eric.' Caron said in a low voice, 'Mary's laptop had already been wiped. You had no idea that our main evidence had been destroyed within thirty minutes of ensuring it had been stored securely. CC Gallows has commissioned an investigation into the lack of safe-keeping measures within your headquarters; you will need to add your own version of events in due course.' Caron can see the fear in Rustler's face because he has been caught out - or is he afraid of something, or someone else?

'From now on, all evidence will be stored via Denny at Northumberland. It only takes one person to be lax about our security procedures. That's all, just one. If that device had fallen into the wrong hands, I have no doubt the press would have had a field day. And you both would be out of work.'

Mosley and Rustler give their superior their full attention before DCI Dell discusses the evidence she has. She most definitely will not be disclosing any of her witnesses' information.

29

National Crime Agency And Teamwork

Caron stands in front of her team. Thirteen personnel are assigned to this case, including herself. She is extremely pleased with the speed at which NCA has pulled in their unit. Impressive.

'Afternoon all. Formal introductions and who is working with who first, then we can get to work.' She provides a list of names to her team and clarifies who is leading the Cartwright case: DCI Caron Dell, Northumberland Police and Rakesh Patel, NCA.

'Jaz will head up and manage everything analytical. To be clear, Jaz is our report coordinator. If you need guidance, speak to her immediately - don't hang about. I cannot stress enough how important it is to update everything in real-time as much as practically possible. Our investigation will be based on a plethora of evidence and statements. The worst thing that can happen is the accused getting let off due to a technical error; everything is by the book. Jaz will ensure HOLMES is updated via Rakesh and me. I hope my direction to you all is crystal clear.' Mosley looks completely blank, 'To remind you, HOLMES is an acronym for: Home Office Large Major Enquiry System. Keeping abreast of major crimes and resources may assist in our planning.' Mosley's shoulders actually relax. Caron thinks he is a worry.

Silence. DCI Dell continues, 'Our team updates will require you to fully understand our actual evidence, risks, actions, confirmation of decisions made, et cetera. I will request more detail for each item of evidence, as necessary. This process is efficient and timesaving. Any questions?'

'Why is NCA involved?' asks DI Rustler.

'NCA has a wealth of knowledge and experts in the field. Rakesh and I have confirmed each of your skills across the team. They are also supporting our key witness. It is not unusual for NCA to support, which you should know. Remember, you are the investigator and must include NCA partners in what you do, uncover or resolve. And vice versa.'

'Next question?'

'Who has access to our documents?' This was from Mabel Newson, NCA, who has been assigned to work alongside DS Denny Winston.

'Should CC Gallows be kept up to date?' asks Mosley.

'Verbally, DS Mosley, with key information as previously agreed, but no specifics or finer details.'

Mosley pales.

'Answering your question, Mabel: the people currently in this room. Nothing is to be disclosed outside of our team. There is no doubt that this case will attract a lot of attention, and possibly other departments may become involved as we uncover further details and evidence. One exception, however, is that I will update Chief Superintendent Krubb in Northumberland. He will not have access to the finer details or our recorded information: he doesn't need to. Our investigation will be too fast for Krubb to keep abreast of all events. When we go to the CPS, accurate data will be crucial. We will present facts and evidence, and how they link to the case.

'Any further questions? No, OK. First and foremost, your health and well-being are key. You know your strengths, weaknesses, and limits; don't wait to be told to take breaks, ask if you need help, and offer up your resources if you have the capacity. Your health is your responsibility, and I am accountable for supporting you when needed. Let Rakesh or me know if you are overwhelmed or unsure. I don't expect anyone to work ridiculously long days, unless we need to. Working into the night can be counterproductive; be mindful of your capabilities. It is up to you to manage your workload to meet deadlines and chase, chase, chase urgent requests.' Caron waits for a response. None.

'Right, onto our case review – first slide, please, Jaz.'

The case is outlined to NCA, and details are added to provide understanding. With clear assignments cascaded, the team are eager to get to work.

'Thank you all for your attention. When you return after a short break, Léa Cochran will take you through her post-mortem findings. This can be a harrowing cascade of information to watch and listen to, so be prepared.'

Caron links in with Krubb, there is still no sightings of Boulter and no further incidents. With her team here, she needs to have every single one of them on board because once this afternoon's session is finished, they will hit the ground running.

Boulter
Another text from a different source: *I will provide info as it happens. Post-mortem reports this afternoon - no sign of the third girl or laptop. I'd seriously get out of the country as soon as you can.*

I need the Cartwrights dead. And my fucking laptop.

30

Post Mortem Reports

Léa Cochran places herself at the front of the group, with rows of tables running across the room. She has learned over the years, this set-up provides the most inclusive format, ensuring everyone can see at least one of the two screens.

Léa introduces herself as the case's forensic pathologist and explains her role, in which she will present her findings about the cause of death of the two girls. Léa encourages questions throughout her cascade.

Once her introduction is complete, Léa moves to the back of the room. Her French accent is confident and attractive, which has led some audiences to concentrate on her rather than the subject matter. Stepping out of their line of sight will encourage the group to give their full attention to her presentation as she walks them through her conclusions. Léa gives Jaz her cue.

Jaz uploads facial photographs of the two deceased girls on both screens:

- Jessica Lowery – 13 yrs. Known as Jessie.
- Emily Southern – 14 yrs.

Léa begins, 'Both girls' identities have been confirmed from missing person data, and their parents have also been through the agonising identification process. Both females had been heavily drugged with liquid morphine. The ratio of morphine to vodka in their system indicates they would have been unconscious within minutes and dead not long afterwards.' Léa pauses to ensure the facts are understood.

'Jessie and Emily's date of death is recorded as the thirteenth of December. Jessie's body was lying on top of Emily's arm when they were found lying face down.' More images make the situation horrifically real - as if it weren't already.

'Jessie Lowery was thirteen years old. Her clothing consisted of worn-down, flat, black ankle boots. Her denim jeans appear new but are at least two sizes too big, and she wore a black vest top. Jessie was not wearing underwear or socks. She wore a black, padded, slightly worn coat when her body was found. Some traces of makeup and dark lipstick have been identified. No nail varnish or false nails. Her nails were very brittle; I will discuss the reasons for this in a few minutes.'

Léa pauses for questions; there are none. She continues. 'Jessie was still growing and developing through puberty. Her alcohol level was relatively low. Weighing ninety-two pounds, she could not have survived the overdose. Jessie was average height for her age at 1.53 metres, with blue eyes and long, dark, blond, thinning natural hair. Signs show she was sexually active.' Léa indicates to Jaz that the pictures should be moved on.

'Here, you can see Jessie's small frame with her skeletal shape visible. You can see some of her bones quite clearly. Her hips and collarbone are obvious as they almost protrude through her skin. You can also identify bruising on her body, specifically on her wrists and some older bruising on her throat and neck area.' You could hear a pin drop. The image of Jessie is shocking and incredibly sad.

'There is scarring on both arms, which is approximately six to eight months old. Some difficulty here in identifying the exact timing of these scars due to the level of malnourishment. Her wounds appear to be from self-harming assaults. The scars on her left arm are wider than those on her right indicating more force was used in this area. The wound on her right arm

is not as wide as those on her left, leading to the conclusion that Jessie was right-handed. As the same hand could not scar both arms, the deduction of self-harming has been reached.'
Léa pauses and looks around the room; no questions, and each person is looking directly at the images on the screen. Some of her audience have paled at her narrative and the visuals in front of them.

'Jessie's hair had started to recede, and you can see small, bald patches that are clearly visible.' A different picture is displayed, 'This provides further evidence of malnourishment, which presents us with factual biological data resulting in her brittle nails. Jessie's body had started to decline during the last few weeks of her life. My hypothesis is that this is due to drug and alcohol misuse, together with evidence of malnutrition, as I have already explained.'

DS Winston raises his hand. 'Can you confirm what caused the bruising on her neck and wrists?'

'Current analysis shows that a natural rope had been used. The constitution mainly identifies jute, cotton and hemp. These ropes are more commonly used for light to moderate use. Generally suitable for crafting, decoration, garden, or farm use. The same rope was used for both Jessie and Emily. There is welt-type scarring on her wrists. However, those are not clear on her neck. Further examination is ongoing to identify the shape and depth.' Jaz zooms into the areas being discussed. 'As you can see here, a defined scar on her right wrist indicates some form of restraint has been used during her last few weeks. These scars are newer than those of her own wounds. Her neck, just under her left ear, has the heaviest evidence of bruising in that area. I have not been able to retrieve any fabric or evidence to confirm conclusively what was applied.'

Léa waits before asking Jaz to move to the autopsy photos of Emily.

'Emily was fourteen years old and weighed 105 pounds. Her height was 1.62 metres: heavier and taller than Jessie. Blue eyes, dark brown natural shoulder-length wavy hair. Black, mid-height, heeled, worn-down boots. She wore a long, green, woollen coat, which was in relatively good condition and a long, black, nylon dress. Black underwear with a sanitary pad inserted; however, no menstrual period was evident. Emily might have been using a pad to help with the pain and sores on her rectum. We will come onto that in a moment.' Léa pauses again.

'No makeup or nail varnish, but her nails were stronger than her friend's. Just to be aware, the level of morphine in both cases was the same. Emily would have taken just a few seconds longer before passing out, and the same timeline before her death. There is no evidence of self-harm scarring. There are signs of rope restraints; they are not as recent as Jessie's scars. Emily was sexually active and more developed through puberty than her age would suggest. She had almost reached her full adult form, so she was more advanced than an average fourteen-year-old. Emily's rectum was severely bruised and had been torn within the last three or four weeks prior to her death. There is also evidence of infection. You can see in the image here that remnants of oozing ulcers are visible. She would have been in some pain. I have deduced by the level of internal damage that she would have suffered from confusion due to the severity of the infection: lymphogranuloma venereum, a bacterial illness. This type of infection is not unusual for women, but uncommon all the same.' Léa waits for questions, but there are none.

'Emily had a high level of alcohol in her system. She was five times over the legal driving limit. There was also evidence of doxycycline, which is an antibiotic, so she was receiving treatment from someone.'

Caron notes that specific data. Was she in pain, so she drank more? Was she given more drink or drugs to perform anal sex? 'DI Rustler, can you find out who or what clinic would be used in this situation?'

Léa waits to allow DI Rustler to note his task before

she carries on, 'Both Jessie and Emily were taking oral contraceptives. Lab results show evidence of this, which would mean this particular drug had been ingested within the twelve hours leading up to their death. So again, these are prescription drugs.' DI Rustler notes that information, too.

'My team is forensically testing their clothes, and there are samples of their skin, nail, and hair follicles, as you'd expect. You will have noted there are no labels in any of the clothes either girl was wearing.' Tim Mosley hadn't noticed that at all. 'Results will be sent to DCI Dell once I sign off on each element. Instead of waiting for the full report, I will provide you with immediate updates as they happen. I know there is a lot of information, and there is a detailed report with DCI Dell. Any questions?'

The silence is deafening.

Caron looks across to Léa. She has delivered an excellent synopsis of the young teenager's autopsies. There is more detail to what has been divulged; in addition, Léa has pitched this brilliantly. Silence on this occasion demonstrates that her team's full attention has been given to the circumstances Léa placed in front of them. Caron wants to tap into the moment, to build more buy-in. She slowly walks to the front of the room before addressing her team.

'I know this is a sickening report, the horrific reality has hit home, and you want to give everything you can to resolve our investigation. The depraved state of these two girls and how their short lives came to an end should never happen again. It is vital you work together to crack this case.'

Firmly and quietly, DCI Dell continues. 'There is no room for error, nor is there any room for heroics or gut feelings. Facts and evidence will get us a conviction. Their use as young, underdeveloped girls had come to an end; they were both maturing, with Emily almost at her adult form. Whoever is behind this needs to be off the streets, because they will have moved onto another group of children to feed their demands.' Caron lets that thought sink in. 'There are many more people than Tony Boulter involved. Anyone in his paedophile circle may be of a high stature within their community. Do not rule anyone out. Somewhere, there is evidence. You need to find it.'

'OK, take a break, twenty minutes to get a coffee or whatever and ponder your thoughts. When we reconvene, we start documenting our evidence, actions, risks, and issues, and then we can make decisions. Based on fact.'

Caron

I know we need Boulter in custody; that's a screaming-out-loud detail! But I need to know who is helping such an evil excuse for a man. I am watching Rustler and Mosley; I know one or both are involved in protecting him somewhere along the way. I need to practice what I preach and find the proof.

Boulter

Text message received: *I'd start to leave, know girls' cause of death, one was treated for infection, know more about your activities than first thought.*

Shit! Time's up, Cartwright.

31

Greg Cartwright

16th December 2024

Tony Boulter knows exactly where Greg Cartwright is; he has known since his admission. He also knows, as his consultant confirmed today, that Cartwright is doing all right and has a good chance of recovery. Tony will make sure he won't.

Boulter waits for his moment outside the private hospital where Greg Cartwright is being treated. With Box now out of the picture, it is up to him to clear things up.

Armed officers protect Cartwright 24/7, with a static shift change every eight hours. The evening handover is at eight pm, the same time as the medical team - that is a risk to their patient. Thankfully for Boulter, rules are rules.

Tony is carrying his weapon of choice in his otherwise empty briefcase, and a hospital pass hangs around his neck - courtesy of his well-connected contacts. With his beard shaved off, flat cap pulled down, and his neck tattoos covered, he walks into the private hospital. His leather-gloved hand raises to show his pass to the night shift receptionist, who has been called in to cover the usual bloodhound's short-notice sickness absence. She smiles as she waves him in, and he nods. To be fair to her, she hasn't a clue what is going on. A friend of a friend's daughter was looking for work, and Boulter was more than happy to sort out a shift for her. He thinks for a split second about how lax we have become as a country. Tonight, he is extremely thankful for the lack of security. With his cashmere coat collar up, he walks into the lift and steps out on the floor below Greg Cartwright's room. He removes his coat, cap and leather gloves, leaving them in a storage cupboard; he won't have time to collect them later. Changing his appearance further, he puts on sheer gloves and a mask and wears a white medical jacket over his shirt. A stethoscope around his neck and a digital tablet in his hand complete his transformation. He climbs the last flight of stairs to the fourth floor and waits a few doors across from Cartwright in the empty hospitality room—eight o'clock approaches.

'Have security checks been completed?' asks the newly arrived armed guard.

'Yes, all quiet, no incidents,' replies his colleague. 'There is no one around but the medical team. His doctor has not performed their evening checks. There's a delay due to an emergency, but they should be here soon.' Cartwright's consultant has been sent on a wild goose chase courtesy of the new receptionist. Priceless planning, thinks Boulter.

'Evening, gents,' says Tony as he walks into the corridor, snapping his face mask in place. 'How are we tonight? All good?' Confidence, with a reasonably good, clipped English accent and a limited bit of knowledge, can get you anywhere.

'Evenin,' Doc,' Says the first guard, then goes back to the handover conversation.

Tony takes his time; medical checks usually take around fifteen minutes. He opens his tablet and appears to type in observation statistics. He can see the corridor's reflection on his screen and notices the second guard watching him.

Boulter continues. He remains silent and waits for his moment. It will only take seconds to administer a vial of liquid morphine. Death won't be immediate. It will take a few minutes, time enough to get out of the private clinic. Tony sees that Greg Cartwright has had a new saline drip administered.

Perfect! He leans over to check his patient's pupils, but he has no idea what he is looking for. He replaces his hand-held torch with a hypodermic syringe, aware of the second guard. Boulter continues to stand with his back to the glass door and pretends to key into his tablet. The guard is distracted by a nurse coming up the corridor. Shit! Tony swiftly empties the syringe into the third tap attached to the IV system; he has a limited understanding of what he is doing. This afternoon's YouTube instructions were extremely complex - well, they were for him. All done, now, he needs to get out before the nurse enters the room. It's a shame for his victim that the on-duty guard did not check tonight's consultant rota; he would have seen that Tony should be female; it's too late now. He needs to make his way out.

He continues to type into his tablet, but the guard is back on his scent. Tony places his torch back into his pocket, closes his screen, and folds his tablet cover while preparing to leave. The ward nurse talks to the second guard. 'Fancy a cuppa before you start? You don't mind hanging on a minute, do you?' she says to the first guard.

'No, that's fine.'

She enters their staff hospitality room while Tony steps back into the corridor. He smiles under his mask and says, 'All well, see you tomorrow.'

He reaches the stairs and hears the nurse come back into the corridor. 'Where is Ms Black? She is the consultant tonight.'

Heavy footfall is not too far behind him as he hears the emergency buzzer for the crash team; he thinks they're called. That is not important as he shifts down the stairs.

Tony legs it while keeping as close as he can to the wall. Armed guards are generally very fit, but they have equipment to carry - weapons, heavy protective gear, and the like. He has another floor to go. He launches himself down a set of stairs, ignores his ankle pain and continues to move. He reaches the ground floor and pushes himself through the fire exit as a gunshot whizzes past him.

His stolen car is parked less than fifty metres away. Within minutes, he is long gone, and so is Greg Cartwright. No amount of CPR will bring him back.

Boulter

One down, now to find the other bastard. Time to visit the judge.

32

Artists Retreat

17th December 2024

Caron reviewed Mary's recorded data with Jaz's help two days earlier. All documents were updated, and together, they take another look to make certain that their evidence is in line with expectations. She links up with Léa and Nancy (she never calls her 'Mam' at work; they both agreed to that), who confirm nothing unusual has shown up yet on any device they have in their possession.

Early Tuesday morning, Caron drives back to the safehouse from Leeds and arrives just before seven am. Callum has the door open before she reaches the garden gate. Freezing winds howl around the lone brick building, eerily forewarning the news Caron is about to deliver.

'Do you want me to wake them?' asks Callum.

No, let them rest. It won't make any difference. I'm assuming they don't know yet?'

'No, they tend not to listen to the news so early in the day, not that I think any information has been released yet. I only know from your call earlier.'

'Good. Is Cerys's support liaison here yet?'

'She is due any minute. She knows her stuff. One of the best in the business, I would say.'

'OK, we will wait. It is Avril, isn't it?'

'Yes, Avril Renwick.'

'Twenty-four-hour support will be provided from today

for Cerys and Janey. Your additional teammate will join us. So, your colleague, Uncle, should be here soon.'

Callum makes coffee and confirms that nothing has changed, with no odd happenings. 'Yes, already aware Uncle is on his way. Are you staying today?'

'We'll see. The team is focused and has clarity on our aim: apprehending the elusive Tony Boulter. More necessary than ever after recent events.'

'Here's Avril now.' Callum turns his screen so Caron can see her approaching the wooden bridge that crosses the narrow gorge to the North Sea and the rocks below.

Caron introduces herself and asks Avril how things are; she already knows, but it is good practice to let the experts lead, you never know if something has been missed.

'Cerys has some extremely dark memories of her time with Jessie and Emily. Horrific what they have endured, I am sure there are dozens more like them.'

'No doubt,' agrees Caron, thinking the number will be far higher.

Caron briefs Avril on Greg Cartwright's murder. Neither is sure how Cerys will react or digest the fact that Greg Cartwright is now dead. Avril reassures Caron that she will support Cerys as she delivers her news. Any adjustments for Cerys will be made.

'What adjustment would that be?' asks Janey as she walks into the kitchen. Caron is furious that she has not maintained her hair colour. Even though it's only been a few days, her red roots are poking through. That conversation is for another time.

Caron watches Janey pour herself some coffee before she turns to face her visitor. She acknowledges her sombre expression. 'What? What's happened now?'

'Have a seat, please, Janey,' Caron tells her softly.

'He's dead, isn't he?'

'Yes, it appears someone got to him last night.'

'Are. You. Fucking. Kidding. Me?'

'No.'

Janey glares at Caron, "He was safe," you said, "no one knows where he is," you said. "Twenty-four-hour armed guard," you said. Fucking hell, Caron. One guess - Tony Boulter, the undetectable "scarlet pimpernel." Does he have an invisibility cloak, or does he just use plain fucking pixie dust?' Janey was raging. Caron notes no tears, no sadness, just rage. 'What's your excuse this time?'

'None.'

'How?'

'Help from someone, we don't know who yet. With no challenge, Tony accessed a private clinic and went to Greg's hospital room. The on-duty nurse realised after a lethal dose of morphine had been administered by Tony, who was posing as a consultant.'

Janey scoffed.

'That consultant should have been a woman,' Caron continued, 'The appointed armed guard did not check the rota. He would not have been in any pain, Janey. It appears to be liquid morphine, which killed him.'

'Not in any pain! Is that supposed to comfort me? He should be alive, made to stand in court and look at me whilst the jury found him guilty. He should have suffered a long and hard sentence.' Janey paces the floor furiously. 'He wouldn't have lasted five minutes in prison before being attacked and God knows what else. My husband facilitated paedophilia! God's sake, Caron, his prison term was the only thing keeping me going!' Seething, she turns away, aware that her fiery temper is raising its head.

Far too outraged to keep calm, Janey faces Caron again, 'Christ. How fucking inept is *your* fucking team?' Janey storms out. Caron waits for the penny to drop when she realises that Tony will now be focusing his hunt on her.

'It's me next: I take it?' Janey puts her head back through the doorway. 'Thanks, Caron. When he finds me and no doubt learns Cerys is here? I want you to thank your team for me, please. Thank each and every one of them individually. Then, I want you to tell my mother and father that *your team* failed. Resulting in you killing me, by association, I should add. Oh no, don't worry, you won't have to get your hands dirty because you won't be doing any murdering, but you may as well do.'

Caron doesn't need that spelt out, but Janey is right; she is in Tony's sights, and so is Cerys.

No doubt Cerys has heard every screeching word out of Janey's mouth. Avril follows Janey upstairs to speak to Cerys.

Caron looks at Callum. He waits before he speaks. 'Who owns this property, Caron?'

'Why do you need to know that?' She tries to keep her defensive response in a more friendly tone.

'Do you know if there are any blueprints or architectural documents for this place?'

'None that I am aware of. Why?'

'There are nooks and crannies all over the place. Did you know there is an iron rung staircase inside the tower?'

'Well, yes, it leads down to the ground outside.'

'Not the outside rungs. I mean inside the building. Here I'll show you.'

They reach the art room in the tower, which is still relatively dark in keeping with winter's predictable long nights. Callum puts on the light and opens one of the many chests that would have been used for storing blankets, candles and binoculars when it was used as a watch tower. They now house cushions, soft wool throws, paints, easels and various art-related necessities. Callum lifts the lid of the easterly positioned chest, closest to the sea edge. He then pulls a heavy oak false bottom out of its resting place. Underneath that, you can see what looks like a wooden shelf.

'This was probably used as a place to hide someone or for smuggling contraband from the sea back in the day,' explains Callum, 'Smuggling was rife along the Northumberland coast.'

'Would a priest hole be usual within these types of

buildings?' enquires Caron.

'Not necessarily a priest hole, but possibly something similar. There is nothing to stop a priest or anyone out of favour using it, though.' He smiles, thinking how times have changed. 'What is more interesting is that the iron rung ladders are out of sight when you look down. I wondered why this chest was so deep, so I jumped in and looked. To my left is a gaping void where I can see iron rungs descending to the ground, leading to a flat stone jetty.'

'I can't see any iron rungs, Callum, standing here. Are you sure?'

'If you follow me in, I can show you.'

Callum easily fits into the four-foot-deep wooden box. Using a powerful torch, he lights up the small space as he steps onto the first iron rung, which is still secure after all this time. The steps are entirely out of view, and he is well hidden within the tower's thick stone wall. The downward tunnel, where the rungs are secured, is generous enough for anyone to fit through. There is plenty of room for contraband to be carried in large crates or barrels. Callum is exceptionally fit and has a slender build. He begins to climb down with ease. Caron is keen to learn more and follows.

Caron counts twenty-seven rungs down the uneven wall, making it difficult to judge the height of the stairwell. However, it still maintains a width wide enough to cater to large quantities of goods or a couple of people at any one time. Within a few seconds, Caron could hear the sea crashing against the cliffs. The noise increases as they step onto the final iron rung.

'Be careful as you step off that last rung.' Callum shouts. 'It is blowing a gale out here.' She can hardly hear Callum, but his swirling hand gestures assist her understanding.

They both stand on what would have been a makeshift jetty at one time, and now it's a weather-beaten flat-top rock, no bigger than two square metres. Clinging onto the bottom rung, the freezing north-east winter winds twist to and fro around their defenceless bodies. Callum indicates that Caron should climb back up into the tower room.

Once back inside, Caron asks how he found the steps.

'Just by nosing around the building, the age of this place piqued my curiosity. Each of the four chests is securely bolted to the walls and various places within the room. This one on the east of the tower has the only set of steps. The others have solid bases, and below those are the rooms downstairs. However, the eastern part of the tower extends outwards compared to the other parts of the building. You wouldn't know just by looking at it. If you look up to the ceiling, you can see the actual shape is not a perfect square; it has a bit of an odd extension on the eastern side.'

Caron looks up, and it certainly does have an anomaly in its shape.

'The room seems fairly straightforward,' continues Callum, 'Smuggling was a popular activity at the time when this was built in the late nineteenth century. I daresay it has many stories to tell.'

'Mmm… but the cut in the rocks, for the southern water inlet, was made after this building was erected.'

'Well, whoever used the building for whatever reason, probably found their way down to the sea via a different route. All the same, the rungs are here and I would be astounded if they are not on any architectural drawings.'

'I agree, Callum. I wonder if they were purposefully built for the Watch Tower and there's no secrecy at all as to why they're here. Maybe they were put in place to get access to the coastline quickly? I don't know, but they are intriguing. Do Janey and Cerys know these steps are here?'

'I haven't told them. I thought you might have known to be honest. You know Tony Boulter will find his way here; far too many people are searching for him in Yorkshire. That was the reason for my question. I cannot locate any drawings or blueprints online, and if Boulter finds his way here, the history might interest him. Knowing about this entrance would be useful. Anyway, I thought I would let you know.'

The pair are quiet for a few minutes until Callum says, 'One final thing. Janey needs hair dye. Can you get her some?' Callum goes downstairs and heads towards the aroma of a cooked breakfast.

Caron ponders. Boulter won't look at the history; he is far too arrogant to think of carrying out any research – by the sound of him, he knows everything.

Looking around the tower, she is perplexed as to why the stairwell has never been discovered. This particular building has belonged to her and her family for at least ten years. It forms part of Beryl and Keith's Artists Retreats portfolio, which is absolutely flourishing. It is doing so well; Beryl, Keith, Caron and her parents have an equal share in this particular holiday home. No one has ever mentioned the chests, nor the iron rungs. You can't see the access to the tower from the water either; the opening to the flat rock on which Caron stood less than fifteen minutes ago is within the cliff face. The entrance is concealed, even from the North Sea's narrow access. This is a possible hiding place to buy anyone some time, but it also allows someone to access the building: a double-edged sword. As risky as the stairwell is, seeing images of Tony Boulter and his well-trained physique, Caron does not doubt that he could climb up in seconds - after all, his life might depend on it!

Cerys comes into the kitchen just after Caron has made herself a coffee.

'What do we do now? Move again?' Cerys is worried about being found, and she knows there is an increased risk of Boulter locating their safe house.

'You are both to stay at this location. There is no reason for him to come here. Cerys, at this point, very few people know you are here. Léa, Connie and DS Denny Winston know you made it out of Yorkshire. Try to stop fretting and keep yourself busy. But you need to be on your guard, and I don't think you should leave this place at all.' Caron wonders if shipping the whole party out of the country would be safer. She knows Krubb would never agree. Neither would Judge Hicks.

'Callum, ensure none of you leave.' Caron instructs.

Cerys isn't going to be silenced that easily. 'Have you been to his home? Have you found anything? His laptop, he always had a laptop, have you found that?'

'A laptop? As far as I am aware, nothing has been recovered. Did he have it with him that night?' Caron rings DI Rustler. 'Eric, have we located any kind of digital device belonging to Boulter?'

'Nothing which belonged to him has been found. We do have Greg Cartwright's work laptops and phones.'

'Nothing of Boulter's was found? He always has a laptop with him.' Caron nearly let slip what Cerys had told her.

'How do you know?'

'Well, I remember he was carrying one at the Carwright's.' Caron has everything crossed as she lies through her teeth and is mad at herself for not spotting this. It was there on Janey's bloody USB. What else have they missed?

Cerys slips Caron a note. *Ask about Box.*

'Something else has come up. What do you know about Box?' Caron looks confused at Cerys.

Cerys has added to her original note. *He was the other bloke in the house that night. I had forgotten all about that twatting creep.*

Janey wanders back into the room, and she nods to Caron while adding a note of her own: *I never met him, but I heard a reference to 'Box.' I didn't know it was a person.*

'Box is potentially the third person in Greg's house that night. Have you heard of him?' presses Caron, realising how the hell would she know that name! She keeps everything crossed, again, he doesn't ask.

'I haven't, but I will dig around to see if I can get an address. Anything else, ma'am?' Caron notices his pause as he answers.

'Update our evidential documents so everyone can keep themselves informed. I know it's a pain, but it's much easier to have real-time information. No doubt, Jaz drummed that into you all. Also, ask Jaz to check out HOLMES to see if you get any names. Caron hears Eric's faint 'humph,' but she ignores it. 'Priority one remains the capture of Tony Boulter. Priority two: find Box and bring him in. The third priority is Tony Boulter's laptop, which is gold dust. Before you go, ask Mosley to review Mary Cartwright's data again. Make sure we are chasing every lead. Did you get any address for his parents?' She looks across to Janey and Cerys to see if they are forthcoming. They both shrug.

'Yes, I have two addresses, and I will get a search warrant for both,' answers DI Rustler.

Caron hangs up.

'Have you searched our private office?' Janey asks. 'The wooden slated panels form a wall at the back of the snooker room.'

'Boulter would often have a game of snooker after his fun,' interrupts Cerys. 'His fun, no one else's.'

Caron looks back at Janey. 'Go on.'

'Greg and I keep our papers in that room. I say room; it's not more than four feet wide but runs across the length of the double garage. Fire-proof and secure filing cabinets are along one side. That's where we store papers being worked on at home and our own passports, insurance documents, deeds, and the like.' Janey becomes worried. 'You must believe me when I say I don't trust anyone on this case but the people in this house right now. Not one person. You need to check this space out. It is very much concealed. If you inform your team, Tony Boulter will know what you are doing within minutes. He will know I have told you; it would be impossible to hide that fact. And for the record I would like to survive this shit storm. I genuinely don't know what you will find, but last week, I checked to see if anything had gone missing regarding our papers. Everything was as it should have been. You may find it useful to have a look, but you must keep this between us. If something is found, I will be happy to confirm what we've discussed on the witness stand. Not before. The whole lot of them need to be locked up first.'

Caron thinks, how many more secret passages and spaces are there? Who the hell built their house, the Tudors! Something else she worries about is how Janey does not know about Box. Has she set this whole charade up to get rid of Greg and Boulter herself? 'I understand your concerns. I will take extra precautions to investigate, which won't be straightforward, as we still have several forensic examinations to complete. As soon as it is safe to do so, I will take a look. Anything else?'

Cerys pipes up. 'Aw, come on, you're being far too paranoid. Just go and look, DCI Dell. You have every reason to do what you want; you're the boss.'

'Exactly the point, Cerys,' retorts Janey. 'If she goes looking, they - whoever they are - will know I am working with the police.' She turns to face Caron. 'Thanks, Caron. No, nothing else. I only found out about the other secreted storage as I watched Greg. I knew he intentionally hid the money from me, but I never had a camera set up in the snooker room; it was too risky. Our private office may not have been accessed at all. But if you or your team have not found it yet, it is because it does look like part of the furniture. At first, second and third look, you would only find racks of snooker equipment and paraphernalia. You can find your way in via the panel just a little to the left of the whiskey - Greg's idea.' She rolls her eyes. 'It's really not easy to locate.'

'Brilliant. Thanks, both of you. It doesn't matter when or what you remember. If any tiny piece of information comes to mind, ring me and let me know. No one knows you are here; let's keep it that way. I'm returning to Leeds, where our incident room has been set up.' She looks at Janey, 'I cannot wait now, your office room needs to be searched, Janey. That is exactly where Boulter's laptop is. No one will know I have been in your home.' Caron knows that's a risk, but it is worth taking to draw him out.

Caron changes her focus. 'Cerys, any leads from the CCTV yet?'

'It's not very clear. The screen strains my eyes to the point where I need to shut them.'

'Janey, you need to help out here, please. Both of you take shifts, but try to get through those digital images. The sooner we have something concrete, the sooner we can move.'

'Callum will have someone else join him, as will Avril. Twenty-four-hour care is in place. You need to rest, including Callum, Avril and their support. Callum has made some discoveries around the building, and he will update you all on them. Remember that you don't know about the hidden nooks and crannies this old building hides. Callum's information may come in handy. Also, remember the risks.' Caron sees Janey roll her eyes. 'We are doing everything we can to protect you. You need to be ready to move at a minute's notice. And don't wait for me to get your hair dye. I'm not your skivvy, so use your common sense and buy a few weeks' worth. Avril and Callum, whatever arrangement you have for food deliveries, ensure no hair dye is included. Boulter will know you will have changed your red hair, Janey.'

'Not a problem,' responds Janey, a little too smugly.

'Keep your heads down. No socials, no phones, nothing. I will be letting your father know of our current situation.'

Caron's phone rings, 'Yes, DI Rustler.'

'We can search Boulter's parents' properties as soon as you like. CC Gallows has arranged an urgent warrant for both addresses.'

'Don't wait for me; sort it out.' DCI Dell cringes

'I'm on it, ma'am.'

Boulter

Text message received: *search warrants approved; they're on their way.*

Well, let's see what happens.

33

Veronica Hicks

DCI Dell rings Judge Hicks as she drives back to Leeds and he answers quickly.

'Hi, how are you? It has been some time since I have seen you, my wonderful niece?' Asks Judge Hicks as he answers his mobile.

Shit! Boulters got to him. Caron's mind runs a million miles an hour, and she doesn't hesitate as she answers him, 'Aw, all is well with us. Thanks. Can I speak to Mary?'

'Oh, you know Mary is fine; she just needs some rest. I will tell her to call you some other time. Sorry, darling. I need to go and look after her now. Your auntie is a bit exhausted, but she is doing well, considering everything. Bye, darling.'

Fuck! Fuck! Fuck!

Caron sets the wheels in motion. Within minutes Krubb has authorised Caron's request for armed officers to attend Judge Hicks's home. She is on her way; it will take her a couple of hours to get there, and she can't trust Gallows or Rustler. She rings Rakesh, 'No time to explain, get your officers to Judge Hicks's home, Boulter is there.'

'Sorry, no can do. Taking any course of action would blow our cover; we can't get involved.'

'Thanks!' She hangs up the phone. Of course he can't, you bloody idiot, you've left yourself wide open there. But Rakesh is a fool to think Boulter won't already know about the

NCA. What a self-absorbed tossa. What is more intriguing is what the hell the NCA is actually investigating.

Her phone rings. 'Caron, it's me, Hicks, he's gone, he's taken Veronica. She's fine and no good to him dead, but...'

'I'm on my way.'

'No, you look after Mary, I will ring Gallows.'

'Gallows can't be trusted.'

'All the more reason to ring him. Keep Mary safe.' Hicks hangs up.

Caron rings Krubb.

Boulter

They don't know where their princess fucking Mary is, even their niece has no clue. Where the fuck is she? Time to rethink.

34

Caron

My friendship with Léa stood the test of university life. We worked hard, studied hard, and played harder. We had a blast. Partying every weekend after working at the pub. Thursdays remained our quiz night, a time to kick back and enjoy a few drinks with good friends. Happy times. Sunday afternoon was the time to recover from studying and working as many shifts as we could fit into our week. We vowed not to fail any of our exams – our careers were important to both of us.

During my university years, I combined my education with working a part-time position in the local library before I was successful in my application as a Special Police Constable. Perfect. My partying stopped, a small price to pay. Thankfully, our Thursday quiz nights continued - everyone needs some escape. Now I have my master's in criminology and criminal justice under my educational belt.

Léa's medical education would take a few more years to complete.

Beryl, Keith and Macy were happily settled into their French home and continued to be very content with their pace of life; it was perfect, even when Macy kept them on their toes. Once they had saved enough money, they bought a small property not far from the beautiful beaches of Soulac-sur-Mer. Their purchase had heaps of potential to develop. In reality, it was a run-down shack of a place. Their long-term plan was to create an artists retreat for their holiday rental business.

I visit France as often as my time permits, and even though their retreat idea was ambitious, I knew they would make it work. Beryl and Keith continued to live and work in the art gallery whilst they refurbished their investment. It was a hard slog, and once their one-bedroom house was in a fit enough state, their holiday rental plan took off! Soulac's beautiful beach was less than 50 metres away from their first Artists Retreat. Keith's artwork commissions increased, and his success was now providing a reasonable living in this beautiful part of the world. The locals gave the young family their full backing.

After a few prosperous years, they expanded their business. Their second Artist Retreat property, overlooking the rocky headland of France's west coast, has views across the seemingly never-ending beaches on the edge of the tempestuously wild Atlantic Ocean. It was considerably larger than their one-bedroom building less than a mile away.

Macy flourished; it was clear to everyone that she enjoyed her happy childhood. She spent her days at school or on the beach with her many friends, and the community spirit continued in the evening. Everyone looked after each other in Soulac-sur-Mer.

Macy had grown so much over the last few months, not just physically but in confidence. Her curiosity showed her thirst for knowledge as she absorbed new discoveries. Her personality was more aligned with mine than Beryl's - as it should be, in all honesty, but she was so content. I, however, still have many trust issues and keep my cards close to my chest.

It is a guaranteed bet that I will receive texts each February twenty-sixth, the first of November, and Christmas Eve, and I am no nearer to finding out who Macy's father is from that horrific night years earlier. Each text brings a memory from way back, a flashback to a time I want to forget.

It's teasing me, forcing me to think back to something I should remember. I don't know what it is, but it's there, that tiny important detail for just a second, and then it disappears, gone. I often look at Macy and wonder how such an incredible soul could be so innocent when her father was a rapist and her mother, well, a murderer.

Long may Macy's innocence continue.

Jim Dell, our dad, stayed with Beryl, Keith, and Macy whilst they got their second retreat up and running. He had qualified as an engineer draughtsman at the start of his career, which held him in good stead in the long run. Now, he only takes on work to suit himself and Nancy. But Nancy will not leave her job. Dad knows she will never give it up.

Dad and his best mate, Kenneth, grew up together, but had very different childhoods. Kenneth was an only child and had a comfortable life. His father started his career in the local bank, and with his confidence and drive, he became one of the youngest regional managers at that time – Kenneth still tells the tale. His ongoing success paid for his son's private education at the Newcastle Royal Grammar School. He revelled in the fact that his father was loaded, but his bragging rights were limited within such a distinguished community. The Royal Grammar held many of his peers in a much higher regard and a much stronger financial position.

Every Saturday, the two young friends, Jim Dell and Kenneth Hartford, would meet on the football field. If Kenneth's father knew, he would definitely have been grounded. But he was a cunning lad, studying through the week, which resulted in his grades being relatively good. No need for his parents to sweat, they still had bragging rites.

My grandparents were more of the norm within the North East at that time, with Grandad working in the shipyards whilst Grandma stayed home.

My dad, Jim, loved his time growing up. They had very little, but they were rich in other ways. A naturally happy personality made him popular, and he spent his days with his mates at school. Once tea was done, he went to play footy. He was highly competent at mathematics, and he sailed through his school years. Jim left school at sixteen and started his working life as a draughtsman's apprentice; he proved to be completely reliable, and his commitment to developing new skills was also evident.

My dad was very proud of his time at the Tyne shipyards. He often reminisced about the camaraderie, the noise at the end of each shift, when hundreds of men walked up the bank, was a memorable recollection. Happy times when the Esso tanker was being built in the dry dock. It was a massive order for the local shipyard, and as the terraced houses sloped down towards the Tyne, it looked like that great big ship was being constructed in the streets themselves. Living so close to the river held good memories. He met Nancy at one of the many shipyard socials, and once they hooked up, they were inseparable. Nancy was as bright as she was funny. She had many laughs working with her friends in the typing pool and was proud to be part of such a community. They still recall the merriment of the time.

Nancy and Jim are firm friends of Kenneth and his wife, Pamela - all four of them get on like a house on fire, and between them, they had three young children. Kenneth's career took a digital route. He worked in IT coding, bringing in a salary, which, in his mind, trumped Jim and Nancy's lifestyle. Nancy would soon wipe the floor with him. The difference between the two couples, Jim and Nancy, had never been driven by money or things; their working-class upbringing kept their feet firmly on the ground.

Nancy took an interest in IT after me and Beryl were born, and developed her skills through local courses before progressing to degree level, then onto digital forensics. She was happy with her lot, but Pamela and Kenneth always wanted more. They would have been better off spending time with their son, Richard, instead of packing him off at every opportunity.

Caron sat on the sand with Macy, building amazing sand sculptures, well, Caron thought, were amazing. She thinks of Richard and wonders what went wrong there. His father had no time for him, but boy, he let everyone know how well he had done. "That's private education for you. Top university to boot!" Kenneth would boast.

Pamela was very much like her husband when it came to things. A template for narcissism itself: happy in her own little bubble, and no one could burst it. If you had something Pamela didn't, she made sure everyone knew that she already had 'that.' When in fact, that was not the case at all. But she had to be seen to be the first to own anything or do anything. The sadness was that everyone could see straight through her selfish ego and didn't believe a word. Painful. She would 'bump' into people who were out for lunch just so she could brag about her designer shopping trip; sadly, for her, no one cared. Caron had never met anyone so self-centred, but her Mam and Dad often laughed with Pamela and Kenneth. So, no one interfered with the insufferable duo.

As the sun sets, I wonder what life has in store for Macy. One day, she will be told I am her mother, but not yet. Macy is much too young to understand. The old fire in Caron's belly starts to rise. Who is he? Is it Richard? He lives in London as some head barrister or similar. He has a small circle of friends, and that's great for him. Does he have a girlfriend or partner? I am not interested. Was it him, though?

I take my daughter's hand, and we walk home to Macy's safe place.

35

Ch -Supt Krubb And Rakesh Patel

18th December 2024

On Wednesday morning, DCI Dell is summoned to Krubb's office. Little did he know that she already was on her way to see him.

Caron's NCA counterpart, Rakesh Patel, sits opposite Krubb with his laptop open. Caron observes coloured graphs, and there is no doubt that Rakesh is highlighting various scenarios. There is a video link to a face she doesn't recognise. Caron immediately forms a few questions in her head. But the first is, why is Rakesh here in Northumberland's HQ? Krubb is sitting in his leather chair with an I-know-something-you-don't smirk. Caron groans inwardly. She cannot bear the preaching, which undoubtedly lies ahead.

'Sit down, DCI Dell,' Krubb instructs. She sits. 'You already know Rakesh, obviously, no need for introductions. Rakesh will take the lead here, but before we begin, let me introduce Jason.' Caron looks at the screen.

'Jason Woodman is NCA's lead and Interpol's point of contact…' That is as much as she learns about Jason: his name and rank. Krubb relishes that he is, again, the centre of attention and his audience of three allows him to ramble. If talking crap was a sport, there is no doubt he would win every gold medal. Eventually he stops nattering after a few minutes of spiel, which seems like an eternity. Ch -Supt Krubb, sitting in his leather chair, hands over to Rakesh.

'NCA has been building intelligence on a man named Ches Blain. He is sixty years old, a criminal mastermind and the head of a European crime network. Information has led us to understand he is Tony Boulter's commander.' An image of a tall, bald, reasonably fit man is displayed. Jason's image shrinks into the corner of the vast screen hung on the panelled wall of Krubb's office. 'Blain is extremely security conscious. Each visitor is vetted every time they visit - invited or not. His security is extortion; if he's caught, so is everyone else on his payroll.'

Rakesh pauses to allow his information to sink in. 'He will be looking for Tony Boulter so that he can remove him as soon as possible, that is, if he hasn't already done so. As an organisation, NCA is interested in the bigger picture, and we are working with agencies outside of the UK to bring ringleaders like Ches Blain down. He has other contacts across Europe, but if our intelligence is to be believed, which we have no reason not to at this stage, Ches Blain is responsible for people trafficking, sex workers, drugs and more. Tony Boulter's remit is Blain's lucrative money laundering element of his empire.'

Rakesh clicks through colour-coordinated charts, which mean more to him than his audience. 'Ches Blain has a plethora of portfolios, which are run by his recruits, but he is the key to the whole operation. Numerous agencies are working together and are liaising with Interpol to ensure their information is shared with the correct people. Our ultimate objective is to cease future recruitment and shut down Blain and his corrupt business.'

Caron feels completely blindsided. She isn't that naive; there was always a bigger picture here, and she is not surprised that a woman was omitted from their earlier discussions. Why would she have been included before now? The men didn't need her to be involved, but now, they want something from her. So here she is.

'What does that mean for us?' she asks.

'Well, we will continue to work together, you cannot inform any of your colleagues about our activities. Tony Boulter has had help from someone, and we will continue to try to identify any possible suspects from within Yorkshire Police. Another problem Tony has made for himself is that he has gone rogue. The paedophile ring he has created is purely for his greed and is not aligned with Blain's bigger picture. He has a platform on which he sells children's images; I cannot confirm whether the three girls who were at the Cartwrights are included. You can imagine the depravity of his photographs, Caron; I don't need to dwell on them. He is a wanted man. Not just by us, you understand, but by Blain himself.'

Caron understands perfectly.

Rakesh continues, 'Our suspect is CC Gallows with help from one of his team. They are, unfortunately for you and us, within our unit. We don't know who.'

Caron pipes up, 'I know CC Gallows is involved, and the background to it all. I instructed DS Denny Winston to look at his family to see how he got into this situation. Furthermore, he is getting help from DI Rustler, and there is no doubt about it. Again, Denny is investigating why they are important to Boulter.' It is good to play some cards close to your chest. Who has been omitted from her evidence now? Power crazy twats. NCA never wanted Gallows or anyone else, just Boulter. No wonder NCA had a unit ready within hours – Rakesh must have thought Christmas had come early when he was asked to support my case.

Ch -Supt Krubb is not impressed. 'Why have you not brought this to my attention, Dell?' He tries but fails to remain calm.

Caron thinks that's a bit rich, sitting in her boss's office as NCA ambushes her.

'Caron?' asks a soft Edinburgh accent. Caron turns to

look at the screen, and a dark-haired Jason with mesmerising, cobalt blue eyes stares back. 'You will have your day with Boulter, no doubt, but Ches Blain's impact on various criminal activities is vast. He is our key target. We need Boulter in custody, and any other information you hold could be vitally important to us.'

Caron hears what Jason is saying but continues with the conversation that Krubb started, because he is absolutely furious.

Caron opens her laptop and shows a first draft report on the subject Krubb is red with rage about, 'I need to make sure before I accuse anyone. With more facts, more evidence. It must be watertight. Sir.' She remains exceptionally professional. 'CC Gallows and DI Rustler are no threat to us, as they will lead us to Boulter. Of that, I am sure.' Now, who is smug, she thinks, but her body language says nothing of the sort.

'Why DI Rustler?' asks Rakesh.

'Quite straightforward, really. From day one, he tried to build a familiar working relationship with me, thinking I would easily be taken off track. He also has the highest regard for CC Gallows. What confirms his involvement further is his sidekick, DS Tim Mosley. He is bigoted with visible prejudices; Rustler has not addressed either. I have notified HR of Mosley's insubordination, and his file has been noted with details. DI Rustler should have had him under his wing, but, in my opinion, Rustler is distracted and has no interest in his DS. He has always appeared to be content with Mosley, happy that he is ignorant and sometimes a bit of trouble, which keeps everyone's attention off Rustler.'

Krubb was about to explode. Caron holds her poker face.

'Sir, as you can see, my report is gathering momentum, and it will recommend that nothing should be done with either CC Gallows or DI Rustler at this stage. They are too close to the epicentre, Tony Boulter: our remit is to take him off the streets. I don't know the depth and breadth of their involvement yet, but I will very soon.' She lets her information sink in.

'You will also recall, sir, that CC Gallows requested his detectives interview Mary Cartwright. His actions showed his hand.' Caron notes there is no mention of Judge Hicks. Why? 'We need Tony Boulter in custody as soon as possible. He's killed again. Greg Cartwright didn't stand a chance. His post-mortem shows liquid morphine was the drug which ended his life, the same as the two girls. I need to take every lead that I can.'

'Tell Rakesh and Jason about the third girl.' Demands Krubb.

Caron is fighting down her fury as Krubb's loathing for her spills over. Glancing at the screen on her left, before she turns to Rakesh on her right, she relays her information regarding Petra - now known as Cerys - stating she is with Mary Cartwright, in a safehouse with protection officers. 'There is no way you can inform the rest of the team. If you do, you will fall under my suspicion, and I will formally note that fact within our reporting structure. Frankly, your rank, NCA and any Interpol involvement will not influence me in any way.' Caron turns to Krubb. 'Update complete, sir.'

Rakesh looks at Caron and confirms he must inform the appropriate agencies of her suspect. 'She is paramount to our investigation and will influence the data we have to capture of one of the most notorious criminals in Europe.'

'No deal. Not a cat in hell's chance is that information leaving this room. That girl will make no difference to your evidence.'

Jason remains calm, 'Yes, she will. Because once we have Boulter looking for her, we can arrest him.'

'What you really mean is that Northumberland will pick him up, which I will ensure we do without divulging anything further regarding those key witnesses.'

Krubb knows his mistake.

'Caron, NCA task force agents will need to know.' That

soft Edinburgh accent again, overruling her.

'Just to clarify what you are saying, then. "*We*" are in this room, and Jason is here via our digital channel. Know that CC Gallows and DI Rustler are in Boulter's pocket. "*We*" all now know of Petra-slash-Cerys and how important she is to my investigation, and now NCA and Interpol. "*We*" know an armed guard allowed Tony Boulter into Greg Cartwright's medical room and killed him in plain sight. Do you honestly believe "*We*" can stop him from getting to Petra? Of course, "*We*" cannot prevent that. If Boulter does not know she exists, he can't go looking. Let's face it, if this information is shared, it is just a matter of time before the risk to her life is escalated. When that happens - because it will - the outcome will be at my investigation's door, not Rakesh's, NCA's, or Interpol's. Her details are not to be released.'

'I have no choice but to inform Interpol and my team, Caron, no choice whatsoever.' Interjects Jason.

Caron responds directly to Jason. 'Well, your lack of concern for Veronica Hicks is obvious. No mention of her has been made here. Why?'

'Veronica Hicks is home safe and well as of five minutes before you walked into my office,' says Krubb, 'Tony Boulter left her bound and gagged not far from the rear of their home. This was all a warning. Bravado. Boulter has tried to call out Judge Hicks to tell him where Mary is. Well, frankly, he couldn't because no one knows where she is. So that episode is over.'

'Sometimes I am rendered speechless at the lack of respect for our victims. "The episode is over," I will let Judge Hicks know your thoughts.' She concludes.

Caron looks at Krubb - he doesn't meet her stare. Like the bull-shitting attention seeker that he is, he has cocked up, cocked right fucking up. What a self-promoting prat. NCA wants Boulter, and they don't need to know about Cerys; he wants to strut in his top-brass position. Not for the first time, Caron thinks, all you need is confidence to get your career moving, not brains or ability, just bravado and a ton of bull-shitting confidence.

Caron picks up her laptop and stands. In the calmest manner she says, 'I will call a meeting for this afternoon in Leeds; not one word is to come from any of you. They will all receive my clear message at the same time. Do you understand? You might want to prepare an update to cascade back to your NCA and Interpol top dogs, Rakesh and Jason. By the way, all deals are off. My investigation is my priority. If you want data or information, look for it yourself, Rakesh; I am certainly not your administrator. I will not disclose the whereabouts of those witnesses. Is that understood?' She is halfway through the door before they know what has hit them – Caron's calm fury is not to be underestimated.

They can learn about the raids on Boulter's property from someone else. Because she knows he won't be found at any of them.

Caron
I've been played. How did I not see that going on right under my nose? No doubt, Rustler and Mosley will feel similar when they find out I have done the same to them. But … I need to check something out before I get to Leeds.

I call Jaz. 'Jaz, can you give me Jason Woodman's number? He's part of NCA – be discreet, please.'

Boulter
Larry and his partner, Neil, live opposite my mother and father, and after all these years, they foolishly think both of them are alive. Even now, they put notes through their door when they are going on holiday, hoping they may come and say hello. Alina had been acting as my parents' cleaner and keeping them at bay - she was not to tell them they had moved to Spain; she would have hated anyone to break in - or even worse, squatters. Why are people so fucking thick?

They fell hook, line and sinker for my story. Mother has dementia, and father can't bear to speak to anyone about it.

Together, they blissfully think both of my parents are now recluses living in their home. How very fucking sad.

Larry and Neil left a key with my parents years ago, and their latest holiday is an round-the-world cruise; they won't be back until Spring. Very accommodating for me. I watch the street through Larry and Neil's net curtains. Unmarked police cars and armed officers surround the place quietly. You really couldn't make this up.

No fucking wonder they don't get much done; they've been pissing about for ages organising their operation. They bust mother and father's front door open and shout the usual police thing in threatening voices. Several neighbours have their curtains twitching.

After a while, they leave empty-handed, and some neighbours provide information.

No answer from Larry and Neil's place. Fucking pricks.

36

Rustler And Gallows

Caron rings Jason as she drives down the A1 to Leeds just at lunchtime. 'It's DCI Dell.'

'Hello, Caron, how can I help?'

'Will CC Gallows' arrest impact your investigation or your case?'

'No. He has never been on our radar, we want Boulter and any evidence he has against Blain.'

'Thank you.' DCI Dell hangs up.

Next, she calls her DS, 'Denny, where are you?' Asks Caron as she continues to make her way to Leeds, 'Any update on Gallows or Rustler?'

'I'm in Leeds. Rustler has four daughters, the youngest is eight years old. There have been sightings of a man hanging around her school. Police have been notified, but they haven't located him yet. Possibly Boulter.'

'Right, that's enough to move him off the case. What about Gallows?'

'More than enough here, ma'am. As you know, his son Nicholas is a drug addict. CC Gallows is well aware of that fact. Further intelligence shows Boulter has provided him with drugs, no charge, of course. That will be Boulter's extortion move. Nicholas hasn't done very well in Gallows' books; he was homeless at one stage, but there is no record of this anywhere.

The only information available on Nicholas has been gleaned from witnesses across Yorkshire.'

'Brilliant. Jaz has already issued meeting invites for our face-to-face team update, which is planned for one pm in Leeds. I am about an hour away, and I need to see you before our meeting. I will give you a shout when I get there. Fabulous work, Denny. You have made me a very happy woman.'

Caron rings Ch -Supt Krubb and relays the information on Rustler, but keeps Gallows' details to herself. Krubb agrees to the arrest of Rustler and arranges for this to be done quickly and quietly, without fuss. He is to be transported to Northumberland HQ without any knowledge of his arrest being made public, mainly to protect his family from Boulter. Caron wants to get to Gallows before anyone else has a chance.

As soon as Rustler sees Denny walk towards him, he knows. He goes for his phone. Denny takes his phone from him. With no one around, Denny arrests the DI and takes him directly to Leeds headquarters car park, where a driver and a colleague are waiting. With no way to notify Boulter or his wife, Rustler's nerves are apparent as he starts sweating profusely. Before he reaches Northumberland HQ, his bowels will also let him down.

Caron goes directly to CC Gallows' office. She convinces his PA, Ruth, that she needs to see him as soon as possible. Ruth is unsure whether to stay or go, and she really makes a very good argument about taking her lunch. Her mother is waiting for her. Either way, her job comes first. She opens her CC's door so that DCI Dell can sit and wait. Ruth goes back to her desk. Caron knows Ruth will be interviewed shortly. That will be an action carried out well away from her superior's office.

Gallows breezes in and is taken aback when he sees Caron standing. 'Yes, what can I do for you?' he asks.

'We know.'

'Good for you. Know what exactly?'

Caron spelt it out. He reaches for his desk phone (how archaic, thinks Caron); dead, of course. He goes for his laptop whilst trying to remain calm. Caron has it out of his reach, ready to bag up. Next, he moves to pick up his mobile phone from his desk, where he had placed it minutes earlier. Caron beats him to it. He has no way to communicate, even as he goes to buzz Ruth to come in. Caron looks through the door to see that Ruth has left. She curses inwardly; she needs a witness.

Before his arrest, DCI Dell tells him precisely what she thinks of him.

'You're done, sir. We know about your involvement with Boulter and how Nicholas is attached to his inner circle of acquaintances.' Making it personal always bore more weight.

Gallows sits back in his chair.

'At least two young girls have died, no doubt many more. And you have done all you can to make that happen.' She puts her hand up to stop him from interrupting, whilst glancing over to Ruth's desk. She still hasn't returned. 'You are lower than the scum on the streets dealing drugs. You have the power to stop it, but your lack of action endorses Boulter's criminality. You are a piece of shit.'

Fury is written across his face.

Caron has to take her time as she needs Ruth back in her office. 'Does name-calling hurt your feelings?' Caron's silky, calm voice is pure agony to his ears. 'How would you feel if you were raped? What do you think gang rape would do to you? Because that is what will happen to you. I mean the cuts to prison guards' resources - they cannot be everywhere, can they?' DCI Dell lets that thought settle.

'What do you think drink, drugs and old men's dicks would do to you, hurt your feelings? Do you think young girls and boys don't have feelings, or that they wouldn't mind? After all, they do get a few quid here and there. That makes it all OK for you?'

'I had no choice.' He stands and looks across the city view from his window. 'He would have killed my wife, family and anyone else that came close.'

'Of course, he wasn't going to kill you or your family. You were all safe. The minute one of your family was injured or killed, his protection was finished.'

He looks at Caron, a broken man, and says, 'You don't know what he is capable of.'

She has to bite her tongue.

'Nicholas's friend disappeared, and we still don't know what happened. I couldn't report it; Boulter would have come after us next.'

'Make no mistake here. Men, women and children, not just in the UK but across Europe, are being targeted, and you're still protecting Tony Boulter and his followers. You have no idea of the bigger picture.'

Gallows looks confused.

'Interpol.'

His jaw drops open. 'Interpol?'

'No doubt many more agencies. People trust you. With your single vision, I don't think you will ever know the depth and breadth of your actions.'

'I had no choice but to do what he asked.' Gallows is strained but brazen all the same.

Caron's patience is wearing thin.

'No, poor you. How awful not to have a choice. How awful to pick up your over-inflated salary every month, to be protected by your status. But therein lies my issue with you. It is all about you preventing this sad sorry shitstorm. You had two choices, and you made sure your choice kept you safe. You facilitated rape, paedophile rings, money laundering and murder. That's just at the last count. Young men and women have disappeared. You should have stopped it all.' Still no sign of Ruth. 'You would have been protected, you would have been OK, you just had to say something. Your family would have been OK. You would have been safe. Everything you haven't done has caused more horror because you wanted to keep your status. You are a sad, sad man, and you're the common denominator here. CC Gallows, you don't have a fucking clue what you've done.'

'What happens now?'

'Names. Once you're arrested, your criminal friends will do a runner, possibly, sir!'

'I can't give you names, Caron.' He responds meekly. 'It would implicate me further.'

'Nothing could do that; you're in it up to your neck.'

She texts DS Winston. *'Get out of the station. It's time for arrests. Take back up with you, and be discreet. I will speak to Krubb.'*

CC Gallows begins to write, albeit very shakily:

> *Sir Hilary Ravelle, based in Nottingham.*
> *Actor Jonny Boston, lives alone in Hull.*
> *Samuel Morston, lives in Leeds.*
> *Nathan Olverton, Manchester businessperson*
> *Sonny Hock, Liverpool nightclub owner*

'Can you read out their names, please? Your hand is not very steady. And actually, who are these people?' Caron records his response.

'They fund Tony Boulter's sideline, but I'm unsure how. I know they are involved. Everything is in my notebooks.'

Caron stops recording.

'What, nothing is stored on your laptop?'

'No. You can destroy paper. You can't easily erase your digital footprint.' He scoffs. 'So, are you ready to arrest me?'

'That is up to you.' She glances over to the safe, which holds items that interest her.

Ruth returns to her desk. Gallows buzzes her in.

Caron presses the record button again.

'I am arresting you…'

Ruth walks into his office. Her face is priceless.

Caron continues, '…as an accessory to murder, money

laundering and paedophilia. You do not have to say anything. But it may harm your defence if you do not mention when questioned something which you later rely on in court. Anything you do say may be given as evidence.' She lets the words sink in.

'May I have a moment to change my shirt and tie?'

Caron assessed the situation. She knew fine well a change of clothes had nothing to do with him stalling for time. 'I am sorry, sir, I need you to follow me now.' She sees DS Tim Mosley standing outside Gallows' fish-bowl office and nods for him to enter. She does not see Gallows reach into the pedestal drawers beside him.

The noise is deafening.

She turns to look directly at Gallows; his brains are running down the window pane.

Job done, not technically murder. She didn't touch the safe or any part of his desk. She let her phone continue to record.

She had no idea what he would do and had no reason to think a loaded firearm was within his reach. There were no signs of risk to life within the minutes she was there. That would be her report. Together with her recording, there was nothing untoward.

Ruth screams, and Caron tells her not to enter the office, but she runs in screaming and refuses to leave. Caron slips the landline phone lead back into place and returns Gallow's mobile phone to his desk. Caron tries to pull his doting PA, Ruth, from his body. Distraught, his PA picks up his mobile phone to ring whoever she thinks can help. Caron takes it from her and passes it to DS Mosley, who is oblivious to Caron's previous discussion, to bag as evidence. Pandemonium erupts.

Another selfish bastard off the streets. No more extortion for Boulter here, and no protection for his sad crew of followers either.

Within minutes, senior police staff swarm the office.

Caron's face and clothes are spotted with flecks of her superior's blood. She walks out with his laptop, mobile phone, and notebooks, which are stored in his safe. Christ, a safe. Who do these fucking people think they are? She also spots another piece of equipment that is of no use to Gallows now, a second firearm. She leaves it where it is. He knew his time was up.

Boulter

Text message received: *Gallows dead, Rustler taken to Northumberland. Dell has called a meeting.*

I should have killed DCI Fucking Caron Dell first. No police here now, time to make a move.

37

Leeds Incident Room

Caron provides Krubb with her version of events.

'Bordering on insubordination, Dell,' he says furiously.

'I liaised with Interpol lead Jason Woodman before I arrested CC Gallows, sir.' Caron pauses to let that sink in; he will learn in time that their conversation lasted less than thirty seconds. 'Gallows information was vital to enable any arrests. Remember, earlier today, we established that whatever happens here on in, collectively, we established any failure would be down to me, so I saved you the bother. Sir.'

'Don't forget who you're talking to, Dell.' She visualises his bright red face as he reaches for his blood pressure medication.

'Never, sir. I have DS Winston on standby with addresses ready to move. The longer we wait, the more reputational damage we will cause.'

'Go, now, and I want every single one of them before the day is out. I will contact the necessary forces.'

Brilliant, she thinks, now we're moving, and pulling on his reputation, resulted in the reaction I was hoping for. Krubb is no different from other senior police officers she has worked with.

Caron speaks to DS Winston within seconds. 'Are you ready to go, Denny?'

DS Winston confirms two cars are ready and that he has one officer with him. She relays the nearest address, which is to be visited first. Krubb liaised with neighbouring forces across the Midlands to assist with their plans.

Usually, nothing urgent is planned on a Wednesday, not even a fire alarm test. Except this Wednesday is a week before Christmas, and the weather is vile.

All but one of DCI Dell's suspects are detained. Sonny Hock is nowhere to be found. It is just a matter of time.

Caron plans to meet with her task force to provide an update on events before interviewing any suspects if they are detained. Involving her team at this stage will also increase their buy-in, in case she misses something, which could be very embarrassing. She ensures Krubb is kept up to date.

'And you think your meeting with your team should go ahead?' he enquires with too much sarcasm for Caron's liking.

'Why? Do you think it shouldn't?'

'You really are pushing my buttons here. Their CC has just shot himself. Every single person in the station will need to be interviewed. Do not forget counselling is provided.'

Caron thinks, here we go; let us pretend Krubb cares. 'No, I disagree with cancelling our plans. It is good to talk to get those immediate thoughts out there instead of bottling them up. We need a community to discuss what happened. Our team will need some leadership right now and direction on going forward and some colleagues will not know whether working is the right thing to do. Once Boulter hears about this, who knows what he'll do? If anything, his arrest is more important than ever.'

'Go softly, Caron, and I mean it.' His tone is almost caring, knowing the show must go on.

'Absolutely, sir.'

Before she can even think of her cascade, Caron is grilled by every senior officer within NCA, the Chief Constable's office;

you name it, anyone who says they should interview her does. Some will brag they were "there when it happened, got the story from the horse's mouth – DCI Dell." It doesn't seem to cross anyone's mind that the clock is ticking regarding her suspects. Colleagues are also pulled into various interview rooms.

Acting quickly on the death of Chief Constable Gallows, local and national media swarm Leeds police station, hungry for information. Holding a press conference will prevent speculation, only if the situation is handled appropriately.

All personnel involved with the Cartwright case are on standby as they wait for DCI Dell's update. Rakesh has been instructed not to utter one word - he owes her that.

Food is shipped in with hot and cold drinks. Those who wish to go home after the shock of today's events can do so. No one leaves. Counselling is provided for anyone requiring support, and it is repeatedly encouraged. Without a doubt, some will need therapy at a later date; it's not every day your Chief Constable dies by suicide. The highly charged atmosphere continues.

It is after six pm when Caron walks into the room. Fully prepped, fresh as a daisy and raring to go. Rakesh's jaw drops. She doesn't even look his way.

As their leader, Caron must recover her team's confidence and ensure they and their NCA colleagues understand their contribution is vitally important. Every statement, phone call and follow-up will lead to the arrest of Tony Boulter.

'The dreadful news of CC Gallows will play on your mind again and again.' Caron pauses. 'It will be a long time before you forget this day. You have been offered a range of support. Please take it. If you are thinking you can cope, you clearly won't. I have used counselling in the past, and for me, it was instrumental in building my resilience and coping mechanisms. We are human, first and foremost. So, think about yourself. Your health must come first.' Caron pauses again.

'Let us just have a moment of silence in honour of CC Gallows and his bereaved family. This morning, he left for work as usual. His day did not pan out the way he had planned. So, let us have a minute of quiet.' A respectful hush shrouds the room.

Caron's reflection is one of sadness. At some point, CC Gallows was a good man, terrified by the fear Boulter had wrapped around him. What would she have done had it been Macy? Probably something very different, punishing Boulter way before he got too close. But Caron was a different breed: if only the force knew. Gallows allowed the vilest of crimes to carry on; he protected those who should have been behind bars.

DS Denny Winston is a sight for sore eyes as he walks into the room. He gives Caron a nod.

'Before we go any further, do not forget data protection endorsements, which you have agreed to - no exceptions. In brief, this means nothing goes out of this task force without Rakesh's or my approval. Jaz has encrypted our documents, which remain vital for prosecution needs. Once we have him, we must have proof. Any objections or questions?' Caron waits for a minute as she scans the room.

Rakesh stands, watching and listening, thinking, how the hell does she do that? Her body language openly includes everyone, making eye contact with each person in the room. Oh, and she is stunning, absolutely stunning, and incredibly clever. His wife would not approve of his thoughts, and neither would his superiors; his sexist judgements would not pass his lips. He made a mental note to try harder. Why shouldn't a woman be clever, stunning or not? Back in the room, Rakesh.

Caron cascades the turn of events, including the arrest of DI Rustler. It was Tim Mosley's jaw that dropped to the floor. Caron directs her comments to Mosley. 'We need additional support for Jaz, as this will be a wider and more complex case than we first anticipated. I have a recommendation from Tim for PC Barry Goodwin. Are there any objections or known conflicts if he joins our team? No room for any errors within our evidence; remember that.' Caron waits for a response.

DS Mosley raises his hand. 'I can vouch for Barry; he was with us for a couple of years before he recently transferred to Northumberland. He is good at organising, sometimes he might need direction, instead of taking the bull by the horns, so to speak.'

Caron rolls her eyes inwardly. Priceless. And she has never heard of Barry Goodwin.

'Any other comments or inputs about PC Barry Goodwin? No? OK. Jaz, can you please make sure Barry is contacted to get here and brought up to speed as soon as? Tim, keep a close eye on events as they develop and highlight anything to Rakesh and me if you spot anything requiring urgent attention.' Caron pauses to let that clear instruction filter through before she continues.

'You may be aware that Tony Boulter kidnaped Judge Hick's wife. This situation has now been resolved and Mrs Hicks is home. A scare, a warning, so be on your guard. Who was not aware?' A few hands go up. 'For the last time, if you are not up to speed when coming into our meetings, you are out; our information provides you with everything we have as a task force. It is up to you to read it; if you don't understand anything, ask!'

Caron turns away from her audience to collect her thoughts before cascading her update.

'I have some information that I need to share regarding our witness, or I should say witnesses. As you know, Mary Cartwright is currently housed in a safe location with an experienced protection officer. We also have the third girl.' There was some shuffling around the room. Mosley's jaw hit the floor again: he needs to work on his poker face.

'Petra Gould, fifteen, is also with Mary Cartwright. I will not disclose where they are staying. Petra has been through things at the age of fifteen that most people would never have even heard of. She has a child counsellor supporting her who is with her around the clock. The physical damage and mental impact are enormous. We should never underestimate the sickening levels Tony Boulter, his paedophile clients, drug runners and his money laundering scum will stoop to.'

'I want to make sure you are clear on your remit. Tony Boulter is key. We need him, his laptop, and his minions, of which there will be many. He walked into a private medical centre and killed Greg Cartwright; we cannot allow him that freedom any longer. CC Gallows' laptop is with IT forensics, as are his mobile and notebooks; we will receive information from the experts as soon as they have it.' Caron explains CC Gallows' involvement. She repeated her statement by providing the names of people given to her earlier in the day. She observes the room's reactions, looking for other rats on the ship, but none are identified. Caron goes on to discuss the bigger picture. Rakesh stands up to talk. Not a chance, dickhead, this is my investigation. DS Winston raises his hand.

'Yes, Denny?'

'We have four of the five suspects in custody, from the names Gallows provided earlier.'

'Excellent news, who is not in custody yet?'

'Sonny Hock.'

Caron remembers from digital evidence that Boulter had instructed Box to deal with Hock, which will need to be checked out. 'Thanks Denny.'

'Tony Boulter is a very small cog in a huge machine. Ches Blain is wanted by numerous agencies across Europe. Rakesh and his team are liaising with Interpol and feeding back our findings. He has also informed them of Mary and Petra.' You could hear a pin drop. Rakesh had the wrath of her calm rage ahead of him. 'NCA are just doing their job. It would have been helpful to have been aware of their prime objective on the day we joined forces, but we are where we are.' Caron despises that saying, but it seems appropriate.

She lets the atmosphere hang. A clear split in the room is forming; what did he expect? She is raging. No one notices. Outwardly, she is the ultimate professional. 'This should not impact our working relationships.' Highlighting the fact that it already has. 'Professionalism and integrity will win the race. Share your findings with the team via Jaz's data-gathering process. Rakesh and I will decide on our next steps and release information where necessary. Make no mistake, if you leak any data, your career is over.' Everyone sits up. Denny smiles inwardly; never underestimate her. Rakesh has clearly upset her, the fool. Rakesh stands up again, and again, he is ignored.

'OK, to summarise. We have murder, money laundering, and rent-a-family have been mentioned. For those unfamiliar with the term, this involves children, both male and female, being placed with adults posing as a family to transport laundered cash, in this case, across Europe. Also, we know that paedophilia and child prostitution, together with drug trafficking and extortion crimes, have been committed. Furthermore, we are fully aware of our late colleague's alleged involvement, and not forgetting the kidnap of Veronica Hicks. Tony Boulter is the UK's head honcho within Ches Blain's money laundering ring. Boulter has widened his criminal portfolio to include everything stated. He is ruthless. We need to reach him before Blain.' Caron assigns tasks across her team.

'One last thing before we break until tomorrow. Is there any update or information on Josh Holder, also known as Box?' There are many shakes of the head, but Mosley gingerly puts his hand up. 'Something to say, Tim?' Asks Caron gently; he still needs a kid-glove approach.

'He is one of Boulter's pals, I think, a bouncer somewhere, but I can't recall ever being in bother.'

'You sure of that?'

'No, ma'am, I will check.'

'Tim, update our evidential data. Paul, are there any outstanding tasks from Eric Rustler?'

'No, all up to date.'

'Great. Undoubtedly, our team will grow, but do not forget that our objectives remain the same. We need answers quickly. Chief-Superintendent Krubb's request for additional workforce has been approved.' Caron looks around the room and thinks CC Gallow's work is already irrelevant; within hours, a temporary CC has been appointed. She places the case objectives on the board as a reminder.

'OK, that was one hell of a day. Go home, rest, and talk to someone if you need to about CC Gallows' loss, but nothing else, absolutely nothing else. Look out for each other and work together. We must find Tony Boulter.'

'Everyone, please be back here tomorrow at eight-thirty sharp. Remember, all information must stay in this room. Most importantly, thank you.'

'Denny, Jaz, Tim, a word, please?' Caron motions to Jaz's desk.

Tim goes to push Jaz's wheelchair towards where Caron is standing.

'What do you think you are doing, Tim Mosley? Get your hands off my wheels!'

'Oh, I just thought I would help.' He is crestfallen.

'I have managed for the last eight years; I don't need your help in any way, shape or form when it comes to getting around. Back off!'

Caron watches Tim Mosley - he is trying to crawl his way into everyone's good books, and his latest attempt has just backfired. Jaz is one of the most logical, straightforward people she has on her team, and she tells it how it is. Good for her. Mosley, however, is still crawling, and his level of commitment fluctuates daily.

Rakesh walks towards her. 'What is it, Rakesh? Did I leave anything out?'

'No, but I thought we were jointly making the decisions?' he responds irritably.

'We did. You were in the room, weren't you? The team had to be told everything.' Caron detests public humiliation.

Just now, she dislikes Rakesh even more. 'Goodnight, see you tomorrow.' Caron wonders what name Emily would have given him.

'OK, Jaz, let us crack on and update everything. Denny and Tim, it is time to start interviewing our suspects.' It was already 9.15 pm.

Boulter

Text message received: *Petra Gould with Mary. Interpol is involved and knows links to Blain and several men arrested/questioned. You need to disappear.*

You've got to be fucking kidding me. Petra Gould is with Mary fucking Cartwright. Why did I not know? I message back: *Bring my laptop today and find the bitches, or you're next.*

38

Suspects

Caron and DS Winston have evidence against each of the named suspects, CC Gallows provided. His notebooks confirm his statement from earlier in the day, which now seems like a lifetime ago.

Every suspect, except for Sonny Hock, is arrested for sexual abuse of a child or children, in line with the Children Act 1989, and is taken to the nearest custody suite. Caron requests an extension to their custody time to thirty-six hours and will request additional time if necessary.

Just approaching midnight, with a long day ahead tomorrow and still no sign of Boulter, Caron calls it a night. She can feel her anxiety building, and she needs to be careful; sleep paralysis would render her useless. That cannot happen again.

Caron appoints DS Denny Winston and his NCA counterpart to lead interviews. The team's frustration is beginning to surface, primarily because Boulter could not be found.

All four suspects were interviewed and sang like canaries, dates and times, names and places; their information is invaluable. Each one of them pretty much fell to pieces and admitted their involvement in Boulter's vile paedophile ring. However, there is still no further information on names or addresses relating to Sonny Hock or Boulter. Caron wants all six in custody. Four will have to do for now.

Caron FaceTime's Cerys. 'Hi Cerys, how are you?'

'Yeah, OK, but I'm worried.'

'Try to keep focused, there are a lot of people protecting you both, and remaining indoors will help. I've spoken to Callum, and he is content that nothing untoward is happening; the security processes he has set up are still in place.'

'Is everything all right? Have you found his laptop?'

'No laptop yet. We do have four of the five men in custody.'

Cerys gives an audible gasp.

'Would you feel able to identify them if I show you their photographs now? Only if you're ready, Cerys?' Caron leads the conversation, and the sooner they have her confirmation, the further their case can progress. Cerys nods.

'I am showing some photos of four of the suspects. Let me know if these are the men who were at The House with you, Jessie and Emily.'

The photos flash up for Cerys to observe, and she confirms every one of them. Her nervousness is obvious as she begins to shake. As traumatised as Cerys is, she continues to keep a stiff upper lip.

'What about Sonny Hock?' she asks.

'He is a Liverpool nightclub owner, Cerys, and we don't know where he is just now, but his picture has been circulated. Can you confirm this is him?'

A fifth photo pops up. 'Yes, that's him. He's the biggest friggin' bastard out of the five of them, entitled twat.' Cerys asks for a minute as she leaves Caron's view. Avril can be seen sitting behind her. Good, her presence is necessary for formal interview and identification processes when we go to trial – if we ever get there.

'Avril, how is Cerys bearing up?'

'She has dark moments and nightmares, Caron, but her behaviour is to be expected. A detailed treatment programme is currently being discussed. I will keep you updated as it develops.'

Cerys returns.

'Are you OK to continue?' Caron asks.

'Yes,' Cerys' haunted eyes have not changed.

'So, do you know anything more about Sonny Hock that could help locate his whereabouts?'

'No, I don't; they didn't discuss anything, Emily came up with names so we could make up our own stories about them.'

'OK, let's not dwell on anything more now. If you remember any details, please let me know as soon as you can. I have to tell you that your name has been shared with the National Crime Agency. Don't be concerned, Cerys. There is a lot of protection here, as you know, but once word gets out that you are a witness, Tony Boulter will put two and two together and know you are around. NCA does not know where you are, and only a handful of people on my team have that information. As I said before, Callum and Uncle, who likes to be known as 'Uncle' for whatever reason, will keep you safe. Is Janey about?'

'Janey is here,' says Cerys. She is subdued as she speaks. 'And I know why he is called Uncle. Apparently, he looked like someone from a telly programme when he was younger: *The Man from U.N.C.L.E*. I don't know what this is.' Cerys shrugs her shoulders.

'Ah, I know who you mean. Before my time, but great TV. Thanks for clearing that up, Cerys.' His looks are irrelevant; he needs to keep everyone safe.

Janey buts in, 'I'm right here.' She steps into view. 'I've heard every word, and we will be careful, of course. We never go up to the tower. Callum moves the chairs, easels, et cetera, so we should not be spotted. But then again, a twenty-four-hour armed guard was with Greg …' She shrugs far too smugly.

'Yes, you are right to stay out of sight and away from the tower.' Caron doesn't rise to the bait. Arguing is not going to help.

'We know about the iron steps.' Janey continues as she rolls her eyes. 'Let me ask you, do you want us to be found?'

Again, Caron doesn't rise to the bait. 'Not at all. Keep safe and remember you could leave the building that way if needed.' Caron can see that Janey is becoming stir-crazy. She's probably never stayed indoors for so long in her life. Going outdoors would be even crazier.

'Will you be coming back soon?' asks Cerys.

'I don't know when I will be back, Cerys, but we will be in Leeds in the foreseeable future. If necessary, I can be there within a few hours, but don't forget that Northumberland HQ is less than fifteen minutes away. We can call them directly, and you have their number. If urgent, don't hesitate to use it. Remember that everyone is working on this case to protect you both.' Caron doesn't want to lead Tony Boulter to Artists Retreat. He knows she is the lead investigator and where she is located, but that doesn't mean she has to take him to their door. 'Very few people know where you are, plus Boulter doesn't have your location – he thinks you're still in Yorkshire.'

They sign off, and Caron promises to link in with them soon. Cerys is to inform Caron or Denny of any information that comes to mind.

Caron leaves her secure office in Leeds, not realising she is being watched. They are trying to listen to what was said and know she has more information than what is recorded on Jaz's system. Another plan comes to mind - getting access to her laptop and phone call log. Something has to be done. They must take risks; the fact that any IT interactions could generate red flags doesn't matter; they can't chance Tony Boulter's wrath. Being kicked out of the force and imprisoned if they are caught would be a far lesser charge than being wiped off the face of the earth.

Any action by Tony would be far more harrowing.

Boulter

Text message received: *Mary and Petra could be in Northumberland*

My reply: *Northumberland is a big fucking place. Where?*

39

Tony Boulter

19th December 2024

Every force across the UK is looking for me, I'm not worried. My informer keeps me in the picture. CC Gallow's death wasn't a shock; he knew he'd be dead soon – he saved me a job.

Living in one of my flats, away from prying eyes to avoid detection, is a sound move. My Range Rover remains in the driveway of my detached house on the edge of the Roundhay area of Leeds. Being the owner of several properties - not all in my name, of course, put me in a strong position to sell off my assets before that bitch of a girl ran. It was all going to plan until that night; Petra should have been finished off first. I knew she was bright, but Christ, escaping! No one does that to me. Petra Gould won't get far now, I know she is in Northumberland.

'Fuck-off, spirit, you can't harm me, man.' I snort another dose of coke, which feels fucking amazing. My father's ghost hanging around doesn't worry me because it's all in my head.

I'm glad I put Mother's house over the road from Larry and Neil in her name. It took much longer for the police to work it out than I thought, giving me some time to deal with Alina. A glass falls off the draining board and smashes. I put my two fingers up – there is no phantom, the glass could have fallen at any time.

I have checked DCI Caron Dell's background several times: a detective in Northumberland recently worked in Cumbria. She hasn't found me yet; that's something, at least. For the hundredth time, I curse at my stupid mistake of leaving my laptop at the Cartwrights, and everything is on that contraption. I have new identities, bank account details, and a new address - a luxury beach house in a quiet bay along the west coast of Mexico. I'm desperate to get my laptop before anyone finds it; up to now, it has not been located. Knowing I can access private documents via other means doesn't mean they'd be wiped off my fucking original device. But no one else has it. I am grateful for dozy coppers.

Mary has been watching me and her husband for months. She'll have information about my plans, and so will her bastard father – I might have to consider him after Mary. He'll keep quiet as long as his daughter is OK.

Sonny Hock left me a message, well, he can fuck off, no time for him now. The rest of them have probably caved. Luckily, they know nothing about me.

I look different. Brown contact lenses disguise my grey eyes. My short ginger hair and clean-shaven look doesn't resemble the photo shown on TV or in the press - no more tailored suits, leather shoes or cashmere overcoats. Once the loose ends are tied up, a flight from the nearest airport to anywhere, a fake passport and ID will do the job; both are tucked in my trouser pocket, with a few thousand pounds, just in case. My offshore banking arrangements are ready to access and will be activated once I arrive in Mexico.

I receive a message: '*House search and forensics are done, address freed up by 19th.*' Brilliant!

A second message a few minutes later. '*I'm tracing IP addresses for Northumberland.*' The messenger thinks evidence logs and saved documents were a goldmine for them.

I fling everything across the living room and message back, '*Get that address now.*' No way is a pointless homeless bitch ruining my plans. My tool bag is placed under the passenger seat, ready to go immediately.

'I'll fucking kill her and the Cartwright bitch.' He shouts out loud once he is safely back in the living room.

I crack open another Red Bull, the fourth of the day, then I'll lift some weights. I can't afford to lose my temper. I need to keep calm and think clearly. Where are those two bitches? No doubt under armed guard - again?

He turns on his mobile and searches for Caron Dell again:

DCI Caron Dell, Northumberland County Police – Profile:
Age: 38
Height:6'0"
Hair: Blonde
Eyes: Blue
Hobbies:
- Kickboxing
- HiTT
- Yoga
- Quizzing

There's not much info there, and it doesn't give much away. Kickboxing. What a joke! Looking at her photo, he could snap her in two.

Caron

I drive back to my hotel, tired from the day's events. I must keep up the pressure on those we have arrested; gleaning more information is vital. They've pleaded guilty, but I need more.

A gym session will relieve some of the tension building up. I swing into the twenty-four-hour gym car park, just five minutes from Leeds's incident room, and wonder, not for the first time, why we drive to a place of exercise.

I take my kit bag from the boot, which consists of a trusted pair of trainers, navy leggings, and a white t-shirt. It doesn't take up much room, although it should be used more.

After signing my health questionnaire, I collect a temporary pass before entering the gym. Cycle warm-up first, rowing, weights, and then a slow treadmill walk to cool down. It suits me fine.

After ninety minutes, I feel so much better, mentally and physically stronger. I head off for a hot shower and food.

Sitting in my hotel room with empty sushi cartons scattered on the desk, I feel content as I drink my hot tea. Now, fully refreshed, I can relax after the last few hectic days. And I let my mind drift to happy times.

40

Family And Friends

Macy is now eighteen years old. How did that happen? Eighteen years have gone by so quickly. I will undoubtedly receive another text on Christmas Eve and share it with her as I have done since she was thirteen.

During my last visit to Soulac, I sat on the windswept beach in winter with Macy. She asked me something which I'll never forget.

'Aunty Caron, can I ask you a question?' Without waiting for a yes or no, she went on, 'Are you my mum?'

We sat at our favourite spot on the beach, just up from the shoreline, and her question was not expected. 'Before I answer you, Macy,' I tell her, 'We should go home and be with your mum and dad.'

Time stood still, and everything felt off kilter. In November, wrapped up against the cold wind our lives had changed yet again due to my rapist. Our plans to discuss Christmas arrangements had gone right out the window.

Beryl and Keith were at home when we returned. 'You both need to sit down. Macy has a question.' Instinctively, they knew what was coming; all three of us wanted to wait until Macy reached sixteen. Not for one minute did any of us think she would have reason to ask. So, we planned on what to say in a few years, but...here we were.

Beryl was devastated. As I remember, she held Macy's

hands and answered her daughter honestly, 'Yes, Caron is your biological mother.' She waited for Macy's reaction.

'I've thought so for years, really.'

We were gobsmacked.

'Years?' exclaimed Keith.

'I look like Aunty Caron and have more of her personality, but it is much more than that.' Macy blushes as she looks at the floor.

'What? What is it, Macy?' I ask her. I recall her being very embarrassed.

'I know you can't have children, Dad.' Macy doesn't look up.

I was shocked, again!

'How do you know, Macy? Please look at me.' It was Keith's turn to take her hands.

Macy was still a little flushed talking about such a private matter, 'I saw a letter a few years ago. Because you had mumps when you were young, you are infertile, it said. It took me ages to work out what that meant.' She was uncomfortable discussing delicate areas of her parents' lives, but she needed to be honest.

Macy was right, and Keith was devastated. Emotions ran high. I remember Macy's face as she tried to apologise.

'I know you all love me, and I am sorry, but you must understand why I need to know. Would you have told me?'

I answered immediately. 'Yes, we planned to tell you when you were older. We were so worried about how you would feel and react.'

Macy couldn't look at Beryl or Keith when she asked, 'Who is my biological dad? Did he not want anything to do with me?' I didn't break eye contact with her.

I had to take over as she would be devastated at what she was about to learn. 'This is going to be difficult for you to hear, Macy.' I hugged her close as I spoke, wiping her tears, 'I was surprised to be pregnant when I was eighteen years old and I was terrified, Macy, but knew I wanted you.' I waited for her to register what I said. 'You were to be born, and we love you unconditionally, with no exceptions. I was selfish and scared, but I wanted you to have a happy home life with security and stability. We all knew I couldn't have provided you with such a promising lifestyle.'

'I only needed a mum and dad,' protested Macy, the hurt clearly visible.

I had to stop my selfish tears from spilling over. I desperately wanted the whole marriage and children set-up. I could never trust any man again. Without realising it at the time, my attacker turned me into a formidable DCI and a murderer. Bastard.

Holding my daughter close, I whispered, 'I love you. Macy, you needed more protection than I could give you. I am so very sorry.'

Beryl looked at Keith, who was crying and looking naively vulnerable, as they waited for Macy's reaction.

'I want to stay here with Mum and Dad,' said Macy, her guilty expression tugging violently at Caron's heartstrings.

'Of course, Macy, you should stay.' I was relieved by how Macy felt. Taking her home with me would have been difficult, but doable. She will have a better life if she remains here in this beautiful, safe place. Moving her would have been horrendous for all concerned. How could I explain the situation to Mum and Dad? Oh God, they were not to find out.

'Macy, you cannot let anyone know.'

'Know what? Who is my dad? I don't even know.'

And there it was, the first flash of a teenage rebel right before me.

'I don't know who your dad is, Macy.' I tried to make my voice sound caring, but telling your daughter you don't know who her dad is would never be a pleasant conversation.

'How not?' Macy folded her arms across her chest in defiance.

'Because someone took advantage of me when I was young, I didn't know who it was, then, I found I was pregnant.'

'Am I the result of rape?' Arms were now uncrossed, and I remember pure terror replacing Macy's rebellious state.

'Macy, the picture is much bigger than just us in this room. Many people could get hurt, especially your grannie and grandad.'

'Too late for that,' rebellion back in the room. 'I showed them your letter, Dad, as soon as I saw it. Grannie said she had known all along about your charade and not for me to worry; everything would sort itself out, in time.'

Another bombshell.

Carefully, Beryl asked, 'What did Grannie mean, do you think?'

'Well, she wasn't surprised. She told me to wait until I was older and speak to you, Aunty Caron. That is exactly what I've done.' Tears started to fall out of anger and hurt.

I was gentle when I told Macy who I thought her father could be. With a full, honest discussion, I told Macy nothing could be done unless we knew for certain who it was. Macy was not to contact him at any time.

It was a difficult day, and I extended my three-day break to a week. Truthfully, I was glad my child knew, but wished she had been a few years older before she found out. Staring puberty in the face at the same time as discovering your parents are not your biological parents was never going to be ideal.

We all knew we would now have to speak to Macy's grandparents. That was going to be a challenging conversation.

Today though, my vulnerability is poking its way back. Eighteen years ago, sleep paralysis took over most of my nights. With professional support and CBT treatment, I learned to channel my mindset and adapt my nighttime routine, resulting in me feeling protected during those episodes. It won't work for everyone, but it works for me as I drift into a deep sleep, feeling the protection of someone watching over me.

41

Leeds

20th December 2024

DCI Dell and DS Winston start early. They meet for a working breakfast at their hotel before driving to their incident room at Leeds Police Station.

'So, all hands-on deck to locate Boulter. Do you think he has done a bunk?' Caron asks Denny as she sips her tea.

'I think he might just do a runner unless Mary is holding something back from us.'

'Please call her Janey until we get her into the witness box at least.'

'Yes, of course.'

'We need him in custody, as do our NCA partners and Interpol. Ches Blain will be furious. Thankfully, he is not our concern-unless he finds him first.'

'How would we know if Ches Blain has got to him, Denny?' says Caron. 'His body would probably be in concrete somewhere, never to be found. His car hasn't moved, no cash withdrawals either, no evidence of him existing since we moved our witnesses.' Caron remembers, 'Someone was watching the house before when I was there. What happened to them?' Caron rang Judge Hicks.

'Caron, lovely to hear from you. I can tell it's urgent. What is it?'

'Nothing to worry about, but what happened to the person on the periphery at our last meeting?'

'Well, I understand, the local Neighbourhood Watch became involved. I don't have a name, sorry.' He is wise enough to say no more.

'Great, thanks so much.'

Caron and Denny walk into the station to overhear Jaz explaining things to Tim Mosley again, as she puts him in his place. 'No, it is not up to me to chase a suspect or anyone; that task is up to you, and then you update our documents. How can I complete your updates? I don't know what they are! I'm absolutely not your PA, so you have to do it yourself. Do you understand? It is your workload, DS Mosley, not mine.'

'Do you think he is as slow as he makes out, Denny?' asks Caron quietly.

'I don't think he is as daft as he appears.'

'Keep an eye on him. And Denny, have a quiet word with Jaz just in case she spots anything that's not quite right.'

'Er, yes, OK.' DS Mosley responds to Jaz's instructions as he begins his search, albeit slightly shocked by her driven nature. He uncovers details of Josh Holder's- aka Box's- arrest from a few days earlier. After speaking to the arresting officer in Wakefield, he learns that investigations are still ongoing. He also discovers that Box is due to attend Wakefield's Police HQ the following morning. After he updates their data logs, he heads over to see DCI Dell.

'Ma'am, here is an update on Josh Holder.' He stands proudly. 'He is due at Wakefield tomorrow morning in connection with breaking and entering at an address on the fourteenth of December.'

Caron can't believe her ears. 'What address was it?'

Mosley provides his superior with the address and adds, 'It's one of the terraces, ma'am; it seems the property was empty. According to the arrest report, he had equipment with him, but the reasons he gave the officers didn't satisfy their inquiry. According to our Wakefield colleagues, they had no option but to release him from custody, pending further enquiries.' Caron thinks, Mosley assumes I know what the terraces are, I do in this instance, but how would he know that?

'Excellent, let us get to his address. Remember, not a word outside of our team.'

'DS Winston, with me.'

'Barry, isn't it?' Caron asks a non-familiar face.

'Er, yes, yes, ma'am,' he responds. 'PC Barry Goodwin.'

'Get to work with Jaz and look for any information on Josh Holder that might help our enquiries.' Jeez, Goodwin is another wet blanket. Jaz has her hands full with these two.

Caron submitted a search warrant request for Box's home address. In the meantime, she and Denny make their way there.

She looks at Box's penthouse apartment, which is a section of Leeds's warehouse renovation project, that is currently being upgraded as part of the city's district development. The block itself houses four flats over four floors. Spacious, and not too pricey, but all the same, not bad for a club bouncer.

Caron and Denny walk into the foyer, which is clean, neat, and spacious. The unmistakable smell of rotting flesh is never pleasant. They put on face masks and protective gloves and noted the lack of people. Each apartment's mailbox is in the foyer, and all are very generous, which saves the need for a concierge. Box isn't quite in that league yet.

Denny calls the lift while Caron takes in the peaceful surroundings. She observes three empty apartments for sale. Box's apartment block overlooks the river Aire on the north side, whilst a building site, currently under further development, is visible on the south. With lots of potential and a great location, it is surprising that the other properties have not been snapped up. Box's address is not too far from the nightlife hub, but far enough for him to have a discreet existence.

Caron stops Denny from exiting the lift as soon as it reaches the fourth floor. Deathly silence: there is a hollow echoing feel and an aroma that only means one thing. Denny holds the lift doors open as they both scan the angled mirror suspended from the roof of the hallway, which includes the image of an open apartment door. The mirror yields no sign of life, just a square lump of reddish, black flesh jammed between the hall and Box's front door.

Tentatively, they walk towards the body. Denny tries not to gag. The fire escape behind them is firmly closed. Checking the peaceful corridor and armed only with tasers, they move closer. It is Box, according to the description they have—the stench of discoloured, mottled skin clashes against the cool, serene environment. Dark, almost black, dried blood under and around where his head lies is a disgusting spectacle.

'Police, make yourself known.' Caron shouts into the apartment doorway. Nothing. Each room is scanned. Empty.

Box has been dead for a few days, at least in Caron's reckoning. She makes a call as they both head outside. Within minutes, the place is crawling with police, and a logbook is implemented to record everyone's comings and goings—Caron wonders which one of the force will inform Boulter.

Forensics arrive, as DS Tim Mosley and PC Goodwin begin their door-to-door enquiries. A pointless exercise, as the new apartments are empty, only Box's address is occupied. Caron wonders why Tim has brought PC Goodwin, then thinks of Jaz and the penny drops. He is there to get out from under Jaz's feet, she laughs to herself.

Léa Cochran is forensically suited and booted as she begins her examination of the scene, and at first glance, it looks straightforward. If the bullet had gone through his forehead, death would have been instant.

All surfaces are scanned for evidence, fingerprints, footprints, plus any fibres. It's doubtful anything unusual will show up. A full search is carried out, and any evidence is safely stored. You never know what may be needed in the future; apart from that, if the surroundings are not processed appropriately, that technical error may cost them a conviction. Caron is completely paranoid – everything has to be right.

Inside Box's apartment, several digital devices are located, including a laptop, a tablet, and three mobile phones. 'Straight to Nancy Dell, please,' instructs Caron. Apart from that, nothing of interest, no written notes, receipts, tickets, zilch. The digital world proves convenient, but analysing the data will take many more hours than actual physical evidence.

'What are your thoughts, Léa?' asks Caron.

'Considering the cold temperatures, I estimate he has lain here for four to five days, maybe longer. It appears, as you can see, that black putrefaction has begun. I can identify one obvious bullet wound, but I need to get him on the slab for a more detailed report. Current freezing temperatures will have slowed down the body's decaying process; maggots or larvae will assist my timeline as usual.'

The smell of decomposing flesh has taken over the apartment block, and DS Winston is vomiting somewhere.

Caron is glad to get outside. Officers and our forensics team are the only people in sight as she looks at the other properties for sale. Good luck with selling those now. Some nights ago, Box's murderer - it has to be Tony Boulter - would have delighted in that fact. No one would have seen or heard him; Box was isolated. A shiver runs down Caron's back, another victim gift-wrapped.

Bastard. She will track him down.

Boulter

Text message received: *Box found murdered.*

Stupid fucking coppers, did no one check when he didn't show up at the station? I message back: *Address??? Laptop??? What the fuck am I paying you for?*

42

1 Fieldview, Leeds

20th December 2024

Caron states the obvious to DS Winston. 'We need to get ahead of Boulter. Where are we with his laptop? Do you have any thoughts?'

'More than thoughts, Denny. Both of us, together with Nancy, will be searching number 1 Fieldview, later tonight. It seems there is more evidence to be gleaned from our digital sources; that's our next focus. As well as keeping abreast of Boulter's location.' DCI Dell ponders before expressing her concerns. 'If that's what he does to one of his own, Janey and Cerys don't have a chance.'

Caron's phone pings with a message, *'Someone is logged in under Gallows sign-in to view statements and evidence logs. I have tried to locate the PC, but they know what they're doing. My search is pinging to each PC in the station, not just our team.'* Caron knows Nancy will be disappointed that she has not located the exact point where documents are being infiltrated.

'Speak of the devil, there is Nancy now,' Caron relays her message to Denny.

'It has to be tonight. We cannot put it off any longer.' She messages Nancy: *Meet me and Denny in 30 minutes to plan their access to number 1 Fieldview and tell Jaz to do what she needs to do to protect our data.*

Nancy knows it must be one of the team accessing data,

so she sends a private message to Jaz telling her of Caron's instructions. She picks up her belongings, reaches the door, and turns to see who is watching. Tim Mosley clocks her and smiles. No one else takes any interest, she notes Tim's actions.

Arriving at the popular pub just a ten-minute walk from Leeds police station, Nancy orders a sandwich and a cold drink. Caron and Denny are already there; they have both done the same. No one bats an eyelid as they order their lunch. The trio laughs and clinks glasses as the locals watch the never-ending sport on the enormous TV screens scattered around the popular bar.

'Tonight,' states Caron. 'We need to recover Boulter's laptop, which is probably sitting in the Cartwright's home. Nancy, can you gain access and download any data that we might find useful, then install a tracking device?'

'Can't we take the laptop with us?' asks Nancy.

'Usually, I would, but Boulter's plans will probably be hidden in there somewhere. He will have ordered someone to return that laptop to him before we find it, whoever is working for him. They must be part of our investigation.'

'When I crack his password, which can take some time. I can input a monitoring email, simultaneously cloning his laptop and placing a tracker onto it. Once I have done that, we can access his emails, inbound and outbound, digital trail, and any planned physical movements.'

'We can take all night, if need be,' chips in Denny. 'Although still a crime scene, there is no police presence on site.'

'Thanks Denny. Can you ensure we can access the Cartwright's address? Nancy, please bring everything you need. After what you disclosed earlier, I fear our rat is working very closely within our investigation. Do either of you have any idea who it could be?'

'My money is on Mosley.' Responds Denny.

'Hmm... I tend to agree,' Nancy answers. 'He was

watching me when I left the room earlier, and no one else took any notice. That lad's brain works differently from mine, so he might or might not be interested in me at all!'

'I'm unsure how involved Gallows was with anyone from NCA. I don't trust Rakesh, but I'm finding it difficult to point the finger towards NCA – they all seem focused and on the ball because of Ches Blain. It has to be someone within Yorkshire. Just because Mosley is an easy target, it doesn't mean that it is him. Whatever we discover must be kept away from the team; there is nothing about tonight which should be shared.' Caron clocks one of the bartenders taking an interest. 'So, we can agree on the cinema tonight then? I don't even know what is showing.'

Denny gets out his phone. 'Yep, I'll see what's on. It'll be good to chill out after a long day crunching numbers.' The bartender gets bored.

'Let's get back to the station. Nancy, get whatever you need. Denny, you do the same, obviously not together, and discreetly find access to number 1 Fieldview.'

'Mary's key safe has not been touched. I will contact her for the access number.'

'That's why I like you, Denny,' laughs Caron. 'You make life so much easier for me. Remember to be suited and booted; none of our DNA is to be left at the scene. I will collate some details for a report.' They finish their drinks and leave together.

'Actually, we will meet at the cinema. What's on around eight-ish, Denny?' asks Caron.

'No worries, I will find something.'

'Great, might do us all some good.' Nancy says she can see the strain forming on Caron's face, and she worries about how long she can keep these hours up. It's all well and good having a healthy diet, exercise, and the like, but only if you have the time to rest your mind and body. Working at this speed, adrenaline can be your downfall. Nancy makes a promise to herself to keep a check on Caron. If necessary, she will ask Léa to intervene.

With Krubb's agreement in place, Nancy's digital devices are held securely in Caron's bag, and the three of them have the front door access code to Number 1 Fieldview. With everything sorted, they take themselves off to the movies.

'*It's A Wonderful Life*, Denny?' smiles Caron.

'Well, we can watch Elf or a three-hour intense showing that probably wouldn't help. It would take up all our energy to keep up. The whole point is to relax.'

'OK, point taken.' The three walk into the cinema armed with sweet treats and coffee. None of them notices their colleague watching from afar.

Their phone pings, '*Update?*' They shake a bit at the thought that Boulter is never too far away.

'*Nothing changed.*' They don't want to admit they are stalking their DCI because they cannot retrieve any information.

'*Need laptop.*'

They start to shake a little bit more. '*I will have it by early morning.*' They intend to go to the Cartwright's house around 2am, the best time of day to breach an empty property.

'*Message me when done.*'

Their relief is overwhelming. Tears prick their eyes.

Elf kicks out first at 9.30 pm. As they watch the crowd disperse, Boulter's informer cannot see DCI Dell or her colleagues.

Fifteen minutes later, Caron, Denny and Nancy leave the building just before their chosen movie ends. Denny notices the car way down the other side of the road; the interior light is on, but the driver is not looking. Noting the number plate, he suggests they move quickly.

Their stalker has fallen asleep but wakes at the sound of the audience leaving a few minutes later. And still, they are unable to locate their foe. Christ, they're in it for the long haul, as they bunker down again. It was already a long night.

Denny Winston parks at the rear of the house, near the gate that Mary and Petra used a few days earlier. It is eerily quiet. The tall trees have protected the winter ice underfoot, making it slippery to walk upon. Careful not to fall, they climb into their protective gear. Even though there are no neighbours close enough to hear or see them, quietly and cautiously, the trio enters number 1 Fieldview.

Denny clicks the wooden panel behind the walnut bar, as Janey instructed. The concealed steel door is heavy, and he pulls it open. Once they enter the long, narrow room, Boulter's laptop is immediately located. Caron cannot believe the Cartwrights' office has gone undiscovered.

'Over to you, Nancy. We will take the device with us if it takes too long to access. I prefer to track it, though, and have no doubt our little rat will collect it soon.'

It is now eleven pm.

Caron remains in the private office with Nancy, trying not to touch her surroundings. Denny puts the front door key back in its original place. If someone else needs to access the house, they might also use the key. Using the same sanitised cloths as were used during the Cartwrights' home inspection, he dries their footprints and drips of ice off the floor and returns to the office. A change of dry shoe coverings has also been made. Everyone remains quiet while Nancy works. Denny emails his colleagues in Northumberland requesting the car owner's details from the registration he took earlier.

'This is more difficult to crack than I thought it would be. Some IT expertise has been employed to set this up for Boulter. I don't think he is involved in setting up this level of security; he is too busy making money.' Nancy, as always, remains calm under pressure. Little did they know their period of free time was ticking away. It's now after midnight.

'Just take your time, Nancy. We have all night.' Caron makes a mental note of the room for her report later and takes a couple of photos to ensure it is left the way they found it. The private office is around two metres wide, with a row of secure, fireproof cabinets and a small desk, which is more like a hall table, but it does the job. A folding chair finishes off the furnishings. Mary said it was for storing personal papers, and that it's not used as an all-day office. Intriguingly a portrait of Judge Hicks and his wife, Veronica, hangs above the small table. Mind games, thinks Caron and grins at the thought of Greg Cartwright's face when that was nailed onto the wall.

'How are we doing, Nancy?' inquires Denny, 'Can you use your IT kit to unlock it?'

'I may have to, Denny. Using additional software can be easily traced, but it is simpler than trying to identify the password.'

'It's 1.20 am. You'll be tired very soon, Nancy. Use your password software to gain access.' Caron can see her mam flagging, feeling the strain, and knowing they all have a full day tomorrow, and a couple of hours of rest will help.

Nancy cracks the password within seconds, but knows that her specific digital footprint cannot be erased. Caron notes the time of her instructions.

Nancy opens the files in chronological order and begins to download the data. 'There is a lot of information to transfer, Caron. I will need Kim from NCA to be on board with this analysis, she is red-hot in this particular area of IT.'

Denny checks his phone. Northumberland has confirmed the owner of the car: Mrs Bryony Watkins, aged sixty-seven, based in Leeds. Denny has never heard of her or her adult children: Bryn Watkins and Kaye Watson. He asks if any of the names sound familiar, and both Caron and Nancy shake their heads.

'OK, we will plan for Kim to assist tomorrow; just download the files. It's almost 1.45 am.' Caron's paranoia is settling on her again, and she needs to get everyone out as soon as she can.

All files are downloaded ten minutes later, and Nancy's

virus emails are accepted on two of Boulter's email accounts. 'OK, finally, I am installing tracking software, which is difficult to detect unless you look for it. Hopefully, if Boulter recovers his laptop, he will not have a clue how to access it. Done.'

'Right, we must leave everything as it was when we arrived.' Caron checks her camera image and returns the papers to their right place. Denny wipes down the cabinets that he leaned on, and Caron wipes the desktop, edges, underneath, the legs, then does the same with the chair. She pockets the used wipes.

'Light off, phone torches at the ready.' Caron opens the heavy steel door to the snooker room.

'Shush.' Denny instructs and holds Caron and Nancy back. 'There's a car outside. Torches off.'

A silent panic sets in for Nancy. Caron places her hand on her mother's shoulder to calm her down. They cannot afford to be caught now; their hard work is done. They must keep out of sight. If Tony Boulter walks through that door, Denny and Caron know precisely what they'll do. The group hold their breath. Denny has been in the house a few times, and there is no time to leave the expansive snooker room. Quietly, the three of them walk to the far side of the snooker table and crawl underneath. Just as well, Denny's hearing is perfect. Caron cannot believe what she is actually doing. She'd laugh if the situation weren't so severe.

The games room door opens quietly, then slams shut behind them. At that point, Caron knows this is not Boulter. All three have their eyes focused on the feet of whoever is walking in. Denny notes the shoe size of what could be a person of any gender or age walking toward the room they vacated less than a minute earlier: the Cartwright's private office. The door opens, and within seconds, Boulter's puppet walks back through the snooker room and out through the front door, silently, this time, closing the door behind them. Denny can hear whoever it is wipe the handle clean.

Within another minute, the purr of a car engine is heard

before they drive off. They all let out a long sigh.

Pausing another few minutes before moving back into the hallway, Caron says, 'That wasn't Boulter. Any idea who it could have been?'

'I noticed their trainers,' says Nancy. 'Black, flat soles, their feet didn't seem too large. They could have been anyone, even a child; who knows? Nancy always notices shoes, a trait she inherited from her friend Pamela. Good shoes, good breeding, she'd say. Nancy sometimes wonders how Pamela has ever gotten through the day and what a painful, boring life she has led.

'I also noticed the trainers, black jogging bottoms, again, unisex; no flesh was on show. Not sure what was on their head, some beanie, balaclava? Either way, I will instruct another search of the property and ask forensics to swab anything which shows up.' Caron is thrown off entirely, annoyed that she didn't even anticipate someone else having the same idea. She is slacking; she could blame tiredness and having too much to do, but she won't. However, it is time for some rest.

As they say in the movies: after all, tomorrow is another day!

Boulter
It's like watching fucking paint dry, waiting for an update. My little lady in Mexico will be worried.

43

Tracking Boulter's Laptop

21st December 2024

Tony Boulter receives a text at 3.14 am, *'Got it.'*

Boulter responds, *'McDonald's car park opposite Leeds Train Station, six am. Alone'*

After a quick device check, Boulter's informant is happy that no additional software has been installed. Completing a thorough scan will take too long. They trust their instinct, the investigation team hasn't even located the tiny room, never mind the laptop. They go to an all-night café and order a bacon roll and strong black coffee, content that a good job is complete.

At 5.50 am, Boulter's hire car sits opposite McDonald's car park. He watches the comings and goings of food deliveries. The council refuse truck also makes an appearance. Watching through the car's tinted windows, Boulter observes the vehicles that drive past. No one looks his way. Which is just the way he wants it.

He sees his pathetic servant drive into McDonald's just before six am Boulter watches, ensuring no one is following. He crosses the road in his puffa coat with his hood up and bangs on the driver's window, gesturing for it to be opened. Without a word spoken, the laptop is handed over. Boulter is back in his car before his servant turns on the engine.

Less than a minute later, Boulter texts, *'My car now, bring your work laptop.'*

They hold their breath and cross everything for luck, 'OK.'

Boulter presses open his window. 'Get in the back and keep your head down.'

In they pop.

'Search for Macy McAllister. Find where she is.'

'Who is she?' they ask as they start to key.

'Dell's niece.'

The silence in the vehicle is deafening. Boulter continues to watch the comings and goings of traffic. No one takes any interest. 'What comes up?'

'Not much. She lives in France?'

'I know that. Where is she now?'

His obedient minion accesses Caron's file, but finds nothing of note there. Then they access Nancy Dell's profile. Police headquarters haven't closed down CC Gallows software access. Fools. Next of kin is recorded as Jim Dell, then Caron. Bingo, Beryl McAllister is also listed as her emergency contact. 'I have a phone number for Macy's mother.'

'Find where Macy is.'

There is email traffic between her and various Edinburgh universities; it looks like she is heading there to study next year. Grinning, a call to Macy is made. They introduce themselves as a member of the university and offer a further appointment with her to discuss her course.

After a few minutes, they hang up and relay the information to Boulter, extremely pleased with themselves.

'Leave your laptop on the back seat and get in the boot. You're taking a trip.'

Like a lapdog, they climb into the boot with a secure click of the latch, knowing their days will be numbered if they do not do exactly as they are told.

After a few hours of rest, DCI Dell returns to her office at 7.45 am. Knowing Boulter's laptop is being traced takes some pressure off. An hour earlier, Nancy confirmed with Caron that his device was still in Leeds and hadn't moved far. So, the rat could still have it. Little did she realise that Tony Boulter is in Leeds and has not been too far away from Yorkshire Police at all.

Kim Turnbull was brought up to speed by Nancy, with Caron confirming that no one, including Rakesh, knew what they were doing in the early morning hours to snare Boulter. Once Rakesh learns of her actions, she knows he will play childish mind games, but she doesn't blame him - Caron won the last bout.

Caron contacts Ch -Supt Krubb and asks if she can privately discuss the case with him. As anticipated, Rakesh and his NCA superior were also invited.

'You have news?' asks a soft Edinburgh accent from a blank screen bolted to the wall.

Krubb looks directly at Caron from the same screen, but now his podgy moon face is displayed, 'Answer the man.'

It takes Caron all her effort not to laugh. What a fat lump of a twat. 'Yes, I do, er Jason, is it?'

'Yes, it is, er Caron.'

'Glad I am good with names, as you seem so detached. I mean, no face, no body, so no body language, just a voice.' She lets her comment hang just for a second. Krubb is furious, and his pink moon face is evidence of his temper.

'We have access to Tony Boulter's laptop. Data analysis is currently underway.'

'Why was I or my team not informed? Kim Turnbull has exceptional computer forensics skills.'

'It is a shame Kim hasn't informed you that she is working with Nancy Dell on this. Does she not keep you in the loop? Nancy also has exceptional skills and was with me this morning. All necessary precautions were taken to ensure the mole we have amongst us will not be aware of our actions.'

'MOLE!' screams Krubb.

'Yes, sir.' Caron divulges the events from earlier that morning, explaining why none of their actions were logged. She finishes her tale, stating, 'We have a mole. Had we not accessed this item before them, they would have handed Tony his laptop.'

'Why didn't you arrest them?' Krubb is beginning to calm down.

'Because we wouldn't be able to locate Boulter. Remember the bigger picture here,' states the blank screen. The intermittent change from a talking blank TV to a large disc of a reddening face is somewhat ridiculous.

'We are tracking him, digitally and physically. Currently, he is in Leeds.' Caron's phone rings, 'Sorry, sir, it's Nancy.'

'Nancy?'

'He's on the A1 heading north, Caron.'

'Fuck, sorry.' Caron hangs up.

'He knows.' She looks around the room at the blank screen. Krubb appears to be huffing and puffing; then, she looks directly at Rakesh and back to the TV screen. 'No doubt, due to your instructions for releasing details about Mary and Petra. Boulter now also knows their whereabouts.' She lets the door slam behind her as she leaves. She turns and opens the door again. DCI Dell orders Rakesh, 'Keep an eye on Boulter's laptop analysis. If there is anything that I should be aware of, ring me or DS Winston immediately. And your team member, Kim, can bring you up to speed.' She lets the door slam again.

Caron walks into their incident room. Denny knows instinctively that something is up.

'A minute, DS Winston, please.' Caron notes that very few staff are present. 'Jaz, and you too, please.'

As they walk, Denny drops into their conversation that Mosley, Goodwin and Mabel Newson, his counterpart, have called in sick, citing the winter vomiting bug for their absence. Caron stops in her tracks. 'Are you kidding me? Mabel, could it be her?'

'It could be anyone, ma'am. She is vigilant and knows the case inside out whilst being extremely professional. Possible smokescreen?'

'So, no red flags?'

'Not from me. You know that it could be anyone.'

All three of them move quickly to their secure space. 'Jaz, no time to explain; we have a mole. Most bets are on Mosley.'

'I know,' she replies. 'I wanted to flag an issue with you directly this morning.'

'Explain.'

'As you requested, I have been watching who is doing what within our recorded data. I think someone is trying to confuse the information we hold. I have set up an automatic backup for our documents, and some fundamental changes to our original data have been made. For example, I checked witness statements from the four men we arrested. Each statement has been altered; they now declare they don't know Tony Boulter. This fact has been redacted from their original interviews; I mean, totally blacked out, with confirmation from each witness that this is the case. But there is no evidence that our witnesses requested to change their original statements or that they were even present at the time. Whoever our mole is must have plans to speak to them at some point, instructing them to do just that: redact their crucial recorded account of events.' Jaz pauses, 'Regarding our digital records, I have reinstated the correct information. I will continue to do this when an attempt is made to alter the facts. Someone is trying to override my encryption and disarm our IT security, but our intelligence is secure; no one can infiltrate our protection, thankfully. This will be seen as a tech error when they speak to our witnesses. Nancy and I are discreetly liaising to ensure the correct action is being taken.'

'Fuck's sake,' exclaims Denny.

'Don't worry, Jaz, you're doing exactly as you should. All digital changes will have time stamps, so don't fret too much.'

'Whoever they are, they have a high level of IT knowledge.'

'How strong are their capabilities?' enquires Denny. 'Could they identify if an additional email address was added to a laptop?'

'Yes, very easily, if they check their email set-up, but they would need to know more about Boulter's personal information. If it were me, I would look for additional software being installed before email addresses.'

Caron brings Jaz up to speed in minutes. 'Do not disclose our intel; we don't know if our mole is Mosley or not.'

'Of course, but I am not sure they are even part of our team.'

'Hold that thought, don't repeat anything, and continue what you're doing. It's the only accurate record of what is happening across the case.'

Jaz leaves.

'Right, Boulter is going north, or his laptop is. We need to get going. Krubb knows, as does Rakesh.'

Caron gets into the passenger seat and presses one of her speed-dial digits. 'Callum?'

'How long do we have, or is he here?' he answers.

'About an hour if he comes directly to you. I am not sure he knows exactly where you are, but he's on his way north–batten down the hatches. Northumberland is on standby with no blue lights; I don't want to put him off! Let everyone in the house know, please.'

DCI Dell and DS Winston remain quiet for the remainder of their journey, gathering their thoughts whilst waiting for further updates.

Boulter

At last! My access to various internet cafes has paid off. Once the two bitches have copped it, I'm ready.

It's colder in Newcastle International Airport's open space, as I park my rental car in the long-stay section of the vastly overpriced car park. I laugh out loud because I won't be paying. My young thing waiting for me in Mexico has booked my flight. I am set once my business is complete here. I don't trust this weak, incompetent copper. They can remain in the boot. Live or die? That's not my problem. For now, I am one step ahead, at least.

My cabin bag and laptop are in secure storage lockers until I need them. I am set with my open ticket to Paris, ready to go, and my onward flight is also planned. Both trips under different names, obviously.

I won't be beaten. Arrogant, some may say. My new rental car is fast but not a show-off bollocks number. Clever Detective Chief Inspector Caron Dell won't know what's hit her.

44

Caron's Surprise

At four pm, like every transport hub across the country, Newcastle Airport is busy, and inbound flights are landing thick and fast. Outbound flights seem just as hectic. Northumberland Police and airport security staff have scanned the airport for Boulter, but no sightings yet. They reviewed the car park cameras but could not locate him. Nancy's laptop tracker shows he's here. No one has checked in under the name of Boulter; we all know he'll be using a different identity. They still check - there is no record of flights booked on his laptop, so there is no record of a new identity.

Caron and Denny received an update from Nancy that Boulter's laptop hadn't moved from the airport.

Denny points out the obvious. 'The downside of not having your laptop, ma'am, is you would be forced to use another one. Maybe even create a different email address. He could be anywhere. All we know is that his laptop, which he has not used for several days, is somewhere in this building. There is no indication that he is here; one of his lot could have brought it.'

'Yes, precisely, Denny. We have nothing but tracker software on a laptop, and we can't even find that. Nothing is booked under his name; he could be using any alias.'

'It has gone four-thirty now; his laptop got here midafternoon. Did he even come with it?'

'Denny, I will call into the Seafarers and contact Callum from there. Maybe I can lure Boulter to follow me.'

'Not sure that's the best idea you've ever had. Take some officers with you.'

'I will update Krubb and ensure we have armed officers on standby. If police are flooding the place, he will take his chances and get the next flight out if he hasn't already.'

'Callum, can you talk?'

'Yes. We've secured all doors and windows. So, everything is good here for now. Any update?'

'No sign of him. I hoped to lure him to follow me, but he could be anywhere. There's no sign of him at all. DS Winston has the airport covered, armed police are on standby, and there is nothing to note from your end; it will be a long night. Ring me immediately if anything changes. DS Winston knows where I am at all times.'

Caron

I am almost running on empty; a hot sandwich from the Seafarer's will do me good as I watch the comings and goings. If he is anywhere around, he might be tempted to follow me in. Minnie is the landlord and chats away about anything that pops into her head. But after some quizzing, it's obvious she has not seen anyone remotely like Boulter.

I reflect on how my stress presents itself, which takes many variants. Sleep paralysis still terrifies me. In my experience, the feeling of someone beside me as I sleep has to be the most soul-destroying state. My unsettled sleep pattern is on its way – my mind is sure of that. Even when I'm relaxed and feeling positive by the end of the day, it makes no difference: now, I know I'm heading for burnout. I pray I can block any forthcoming paralysis; so much for preaching to others to keep themselves well. My coping techniques help me to overcome these episodes, and I adapt my thoughts to a more realistic experience: the feeling that someone is watching me sleep is actually someone looking out for me. My mindset is reassuring. Thankfully, I see the signs, and as they say, prevention is better than the cure.

At almost 5.30 pm, a quick change and strong coffee will perk me up.

'Denny, I am heading home for a few minutes. There is nothing to note at Seafarers. Anything where you are?'

'Nothing here either. I will ring you if anything changes. He has no information about Artists Retreat; he has no reason to make his way there. Just take a break. It will heat up in due course.'

'OK. I can't take a break, but a strong coffee will perk me up. I have two plainclothes officers stationed across from the Seafarers. Remember to look after yourself.'

Boulter is too busy setting up his next move to follow DCI Dell. Her time will come. Keeping focused, he checks Newcastle's flight arrivals for later in the evening. All on time, perfect.

Caron feels Denny is right; she will not see Boulter in the Seafarers. After she devours her food, Caron drives home and switches on her kettle. She goes upstairs, pulls out a change of clothes and steps under the hot water jet. After a few minutes, she switches her shower to cold. Feeling much better, she makes a cup of strong coffee and heads back upstairs to change. It has taken her less than five minutes. Looking out of her bedroom window, she can see the lights on at Artists Retreat, unconsciously praying they keep safe. Caron sits on the bed, suddenly drained and exhausted. Feeling the comfort of her protector alongside her, she sleeps soundly.

Caron's phone pings. She knows she has to answer, but she is so relaxed that it seems to take an age for her to wake up. Checking the time, she can hardly believe she has slept for over two hours.

An image pops up as she opens her phone: Macy is

gagged and bound. Her blood runs cold. She didn't see that coming at all. Her head is fuzzy from sleep, resulting from working too hard and not being on top of her game. She has to think. She rings Léa.

'He's got Macy. Meet me at home, and tell no one.'

'Keep your head, Caron.'

Léa dresses in black, and she is content Boulter hasn't checked her out; his laptop activity proves that. Then she stops: Christ girl, he could've used any device, she leaves for Caron's home. A few minutes later, she pulls up at Caron's door and waits for her.

Caron gets into the driver's seat, and her mum rings. 'Hi, have you been home yet, Caron?'

'Not yet, Nancy,' she responds, wondering where this is going and praying it is work-related.

'I'm off the clock for now. Have you seen your surprise?' she asks.

Well, that's an understatement, thinks Caron. Very un-Christian-like, especially at this time of year. 'Surprise? No, I don't think so.'

'Right, Caron, go home. You've worked far too hard. Let the rest of the team collect Boulter. It's nearly nine o'clock. Try to get some rest.'

'Funny you should say that. I am on my way now. I just wanted to check in on our witnesses first, though.'

'OK, but don't be too long.' Nancy smiles as she hangs up. Never in a million years will she expect Boulter to have kidnapped her granddaughter.

Caron's phone pings again. A clear picture of her lying asleep on her bed, with Boulter's arm across her slim body. His message, *'Where's the bitches? You know I can take you anytime.'*

Her blood runs cold, taking her right back to Macy and how easy it is to be used and abused.

Caron

My thoughts are of Macy. If he touches her, he will suffer. My mind whirrs – I need to focus, but flashbacks of the shock our Mam and Dad suffered after discovering the fact that I am Macy's mother will not leave me. It was a harrowing time in all of our lives.

My parents' response impacted me the most. They had known it was me who was pregnant and not Beryl and had respected my reasons for not telling them; it was awful. Dad tried to reassure me, but it was apparent they didn't know the whole story, and my dread increased.

Mam and Dad thought Jack was Macy's father. Not once did it cross their minds that anything as distressing as rape had taken place. Mam and Dad's anger raged. Believe me, I knew how they felt. No one should be abused, ever. Telling the people you love about your disturbing event is heartbreaking.

Mam was inconsolable; she couldn't understand how I dealt with such a harrowing situation on my own. My strong, independent mother, Nancy Dell, aged ten years, right in front of me. I was devastated again by my rapist.

'It was going to take some time to comprehend,' I said more hopefully than I felt. But Dad, our reliable, resilient dad, kept his feelings pretty well guarded as he put his arm around my shoulders. I left the details of my physical attack out of the conversation, and I tried not to refer to Dad and Jack, but he would put the pieces together.

Whoever my rapist was, he could have done it anytime - if he wanted. The guilt I carry as to whether he condemned anyone else to a disgusting violation will never be erased: that is my doing. I tried again to put a positive spin on where we are now. I reminded Mam and Dad of a few facts: it was years ago, and we have Macy. Beautiful, kind, thoughtful Macy. Mam asked very quietly if Macy knew.

'Yes, no more secrets,' I said, 'I have told her the truth. Macy asked who her father was; I couldn't lie to her. As terrible as it is, she has the truth of her parentage, apart from the fact that I still don't know who her father is.'

Mam thought I was drunk before she sent me to bed that night; her guilt persists. She was utterly shocked after what she learned and would be for some time. Drunk or not, it was beside the point whether Mam sent me to bed. I explained I didn't know who it was then, and I still don't know.

Dad was beginning to get angry. He wanted answers.

I remember explaining that there was no evidence and clearly stating that no one could do anything about what happened. I thought it was Richard then, but there was no proof. None at all. I tell my Dad not to do anything drastic and that he can't ever confront Kenneth or that insufferable Pamela. Eventually, I asked how he would feel if it wasn't Richard. How could he ever put that right?

Dad put his head in his hands again. He was devastated.

Keeping as calm as possible in a room full of high-octane emotions, I continued, trying to influence the outcome. 'No one can accuse someone of a crime without proof. After my vile attack, I showered immediately and threw the bedsheets into the bath.' Emphasising the fact as much as possible by raising my voice, I state, 'I have NO PROOF, none.'

Dad asked how I could be certain it wasn't Jack. Mam added that we were both very close at the time.

I hoped they wouldn't press this point, knowing deep down that I would have to tell them. I said it wasn't Jack, reminding Dad that Jack was with him when it happened. I waited for the penny to drop. I remember Dad putting his face in his hands. By this time, I was over my anger and begged Dad to stop those thoughts.

Caron's phone rang, bringing her back into today's nightmare. If Boulter touches Macy, he will be the one bound and gagged by the time she's finished with him.

'Mam?'

'Just an update from Kim. Boulter received an email from a Newcastle estate agent stating his cash offer on a house has been accepted.' Nancy sends the address.

I was mentally and physically sick after Macy's traumatic week in Soulac, and it was something I never wanted to experience again. Here I am at the mercy of a fucking murdering paedophile - who has Macy. But I have an address, and that bastard will suffer.

45

The Seafarer's Inn

Boulter texts Caron: *Not so fucking smug now, are you, Dell? Tell me where those two bitches are and I won't kill your niece, she is very trusting, like putty in my hands earlier this evening.*

Macy's seven pm flight lands on time, and not long after she arrives at Caron's home, Boulter is waiting. As Macy's taxi drives away, he walks towards her and collapses at her feet. He stretches his hand up for help. Instinctively, Macy grabs it; she doesn't see the syringe he stabs into her upper left arm. She falls to the ground. He can't believe how easy it is to convince Macy to help an old, distressed man in the freezing night as he lingers beside her mother's home. Picking her up, he can't help but think how his good fortune is continuing; after all, he has earned it.

Macy is put into the boot of his rented car, convinced no one has seen him. He leaves her case in the middle of the pavement and drives to the empty property he agreed to buy just a couple of hours ago.

The estate agent was charmed into handing over the keys to him for a few days, 'Oh go on then, saying as you're buying the house. There's a lot of potential, so use the time to decide what you want to do with the blank canvas.' Her advice is disregarded, even though a deposit has cleared and is showing in their account, which will be as much as she gets. No doubt she'll lose her job. Boulter smiles at his controlling behaviour. They never let him down; women of all ages give him what he wants. The efficient estate agent emailed Boulter immediately, despite his request to delay any further contact until the New Year. She wanted to let him see how efficient she is. After all, it could be the start of a long working relationship - or more.

With Dell's niece unconscious, Boulter takes great satisfaction in texting another message: *Easy trade, your niece for the two bitches.*

'What's the plan, Caron?' asks Léa.

'We get Macy out, quietly, no fuss, Léa.'

'The address you gave, the house is empty, no lights, no car in the drive.'

'Let's keep our heads, do this properly. No heroics, just get Macy out.'

Léa parks at the rear of the property. Both women are in protective gear, including black shoe covers, and they make their way up the drive towards the garage. High, unkempt shrubs and trees form a natural barricade around the semi, almost out of view from the rest of the avenue. Léa is correct; no lights are burning in any of the rooms. Caron tests the garage door; locked. Boulter will have used the door keys – no doubt, he will have charmed the estate agent, and will have carried Macy through a door and not a window.

The side gate is unlocked. The wheelie bins are full, so a neighbour will be taking advantage of disposing their rubbish and putting the bins out for collection. We must keep vigilant; the last thing Caron wants is for the police to be involved. There is no way Macy is having her name or DNA recorded anywhere. She is a victim, not a criminal.

Walking silently around the back of the unloved building, neither can see any sign of life. Patio doors have been opened at some point. Caron is slightly puzzled as to why they are unlocked: potential thieves?

They both step into the dark dining room, aware that Boulter could be lurking, watching their every move. A quick flash of Léa's phone torch shows a room full of cheap ornaments and corn dolls propped against worn-down furniture but empty of any human form. Even with masks on, they can smell the stench of an old, unoccupied, dirty house, which used to be someone's home - no sign of Macy.

Staying together, they move into the passage. Worn carpets are lit up as Léa keeps her torch low. The empty hallway has no furniture or ornaments, and is a stark contrast to the dining room. A quick flick of light into the tiny kitchen shows orange units and cracked floor tiles. All of the rooms downstairs have their curtains drawn; Caron knows Boulter would have done that.

A noise, a squeak. Did it come from upstairs? Léa turns off her torch. They stand still in the kitchen doorway, listening whilst they adjust their eyes, looking for anything that moves in the pitch-dark house. Silence. Red eyes stare at them. Rats. Caron's blood turns cold. A dozen or so rats scurry past. Caron heads for the stairs, and Léa follows.

Each step groans as they run up them, two at a time. Caron is confident Boulter isn't here; he would have kept the rats away. She tries the first door she comes to and discovers a room filled with old furniture and a mattress laid out on the floor. Hypodermic needles have been discarded and are scattered across the bare floorboards. Léa moves quickly to the next room. The contorted door scrapes the bare floor as she opens it. Macy is lying on a scruffy mattress, still in the same position as in Boulter's photo.

Léa takes over. Pulse is low, and Macy is extremely cold. Together, they carry Caron's daughter downstairs. Léa stays with her as Caron brazenly parks on the drive, and her daughter is placed in the back seat within minutes. Caron notes the next-door neighbour's curtains twitching. With no car lights on, they'll struggle to see number plates or even the car's make or type, but they need to move. Luckily, the overgrown garden hedging and trees are blocking most of their view, and Caron knows they will be dialling three nines right now. She gently puts her foot down.

Léa removes Macy's gag and bindings before she wraps a throw around her freezing body. Caron drives to the end of the street, turns towards home and puts the car's lights on. Boulter could be anywhere, watching. Caron doesn't want him to know she has Macy, his bargaining tool. For the first time, she is controlling the situation and Boulter's plans, who continues to cause destruction and misery. Now, Macy, just as innocent as the rest of his victims, has been affected by his vile mind.

'Léa, how is she?'

'She will be OK, Caron. We need to get her home and warmed up. A visit to the hospital would be helpful, though?' She knows her suggestion is futile.

'No, only if absolutely necessary.'

Arriving at Caron's home, the cold rain begins to pour down. Icy spikes sting their faces. Macy remains unconscious. They carry her into the house, and Caron whacks the central heating up, switches her fire on and brings blankets into the living room. Macy is lying on the sofa. Léa confirms she is warming up.

'He left her to die.'

Léa looks at her friend, where she can see her raging fury. She comforts Caron and tells her truthfully, 'You need to keep your head now. Macy will be fine, Caron. She is young and will bounce back.'

'We don't know what he used to drug her. It could be anything.'

'My bet is liquid morphine, enough to knock her out. Caron, Macy was no good to him, dead. She was his bait to get to you, far too valuable.'

Caron stands up and looks out of her bay window. She watches the grey shadows of the sea popping in and out from under intermittent clouds as the rain begins to ease. How easily things change. 'How did we get here, Léa? My own daughter's life is in danger from a monster of a man, who was lying beside me on my own bed! Christ's sake.'

'Because of who you are, Caron, Boulter knows nothing about how your brain works or mine.'

Caron turns to her friend, smiles a weak, unconvincing smile and returns to look at the raging sea. 'I know, but why do we go one step further? Why do we have to put everything right?'

Settled in his car for now, Boulter sends his second photo to Caron Dell. This image shows him lying beside Caron on her bed just a few hours earlier. *'You've got until 6 am, you give me the two bitches then I'll let you know where she is.'* Let her sweat; he sleeps.

Caron can't believe how stupid she has been. Exhausted or not, how did that happen? She passes her phone to Léa. 'How the hell did he get in? That's the second image he has sent of him lying next to me.'

'I have no idea how he got in. No sign of any break-in. He drugged me and lay on my bed! He is a dead man walking, Léa.' Caron checks all doors and windows but finds nothing. 'The garage, he got in through the garage. Why do we think a fire door with a mortice lock from the garage will keep us safe? It is always the weakest spot in any property and the last thing we check.'

'We need to keep calm and think carefully.' Léa ensures Macy is warm, with pillows under her head and her body rolled onto her side. She marches Caron out of the living room and takes her directly into the kitchen. She switches the lights on, then the kettle. Caron stops her.

'The kettle, he put something in the kettle.'

Léa boils fresh water in a saucepan, makes camomile tea, and places the kettle in the bin. She hands the steaming cup to Caron. 'You know why we do it, to stop it happening again.' She collects her thoughts before she speaks again. 'We are of the same kind, Caron, made from the same cut of cloth. We don't look at it as murder. We both agreed to prevent further rape, killings, and serious crime when the justice system lets victims down. There is too much focus on criminals, how they feel, and how their human rights are impacted. Most victims are provided with family liaison officers until the trial. Then, not much after that, unless they change their names and uplift their whole lives to somewhere they know nothing about. Criminals are offered support and sometimes compensation for wrongful imprisonment if they choose to sue. The victim gets very little in comparison.' Léa stops and takes a deep breath to calm her fury.

'Caron, Tony Boulter is frighteningly powerful. You only know what is going on in his world now. How many have suffered at his hands alone? We don't know and cannot change history, but we can stop him now. No more killings. Interpol is all over Ches Blain. If he reaches Boulter, who is to say he will kill him? They may start up again. We're not proud of what we do; we know something has to be done to finish him. If we sit back and let such atrocities happen, I won't sleep at night.'

Caron looks at her friend and knows she is right. Léa continues and focuses their conversation on what's important, 'Those images of the young and old I forensically examined early in my career have not left me. The tangled, mutilated body of an older man killed by a drunk, drugged-up driver, I can never forget. Numerous suicide victims I have had to examine and report on died because they were unable to process the trauma they had suffered as victims of crime. The bigger picture, Caron; there is no such thing as a victimless crime. It stays with you all your life. Yes, some people can move on. You have moved on, had a successful career, a couple of relationships, and never took any seriously, but would you have anyway?'

Caron shakes her head. 'You know, Léa, I don't know if

I would have married and settled down; I often think that's what I want, but once this job gets its claws into you and you see the level of injustice...' She shakes her head. 'I don't think I could have done anything else. But my rapist is still free. Why didn't I do anything at the time? Has he done it again? How hypocritical of me, I try to prevent more heinous crimes from being committed when I didn't report my own. What else is he responsible for?'

Léa walks back into the living room. Caron follows this time like a sheep. Wallowing in self-pity isn't good for anyone, especially not for Caron.

Macy sleeps, her pulse almost normal. Pink patches flush her cream cheeks, and not for the first time, Léa thinks she is a carbon copy of her friend. They have the same looks, build and determination. Léa hopes Macy keeps her relaxed personality and acute, sharp memory. Léa wants nothing more than for this beautiful young woman to stay just like Macy; she has a promising career ahead of her. But she can't help but wonder how she could change, just like her mother did, once she recovers.

'She's OK, Caron. Still, we will keep her warm and let her sleep. She will be fine.' Léa hopes Macy will be the same as she always was, but how can she be? How can anyone be the same after an abduction? Both women are thankful she wasn't touched. For God's sake, Macy has been drugged and abducted; where's the need for thanks in that?

They both return to the kitchen. 'You're right, Léa. You're absolutely right. We do it because we can't let delinquents escape. We've removed four of the worst people we have known. How many more would have been hurt by those four alone? Maybe dozens. I can't change now. Boulter is a dead man; it's just a case of who gets to him first.'

Once Boulter had Macy in his newly acquired home, he rested to keep his mind sharp. After his reboot, he moves his car to the Seafarers Inn car park. The taxi driver said it had good food and a warm fire. He thought the Inn's location was precarious, not too far from the cliff edge. It'll be in the sea within fifty years.

The Seafarers Inn had stood for over 100 years beside what Boulter thought was a rickety bridge to a tiny island, where an old lighthouse-type building stands. Happy with his seat in the bar, he can see Caron Dell's house in the distance. Good, no police, nothing unusual. She'll cough up the address of those bitches soon enough.

The police officers outside watch for Boulter, but don't recognise him as he closely follows two ladies into the building, appearing to be with them. Charm is at its best as he chats away while opening the door.

Boulter concentrates on the outside of the building and doesn't bat an eyelid as a door to the bar opens. A woman with a faux fur hat covering her black bob is accompanied by a slender, fit man who now stands beside her.

She had forced Callum to let her collect some food. A ridiculous decision, and he knows the danger. She has gone out on her own many times before without a thought for anyone else; he has kept that fact from DCI Dell. Janey is a very scary woman. So, this time, before Janey does precisely what she wants, he agrees to go with her. Even though Boulter is on his way here and it's against his better judgment, a few minutes out of the house together will reduce her anxiety. His colleague, Uncle, is on watch; no one is around the tiny island, and he still feels nervous. But Janey is one hell of a woman to say no to. He could have made the biggest mistake of his life.

He requests their takeaway order from the bartender. Mary Cartwright looks longingly at the gin bottles against the mirrored wall, stored securely on the back shelf of the bar. Can't she have just one? She freezes. She will never forget his profile. A sickening feeling in her stomach threatens to rise. She carefully raises her scarf above her mouth and squeezes

Callum's arm. He looks towards where Janey is pointing. Not to attract attention, he collects their food order and pays. They leave quietly.

Tony Boulter turns to see the door silently close behind the exiting customers, then turns to watch the road outside. A few minutes later, his hot food is placed before him. Minnie takes some time to get to know him. She doesn't like seeing anyone on their own, especially at Christmas. With a terrible Welsh accent, he explains that he is investing in property in this area. He wants to tell the nosy bitch to fuck off, but that would cause problems for obvious reasons and he needs to provide an excuse for visiting the place. Her distraction is interrupting Boulter's surveillance of Caron's home.

Caron's phone pings. 'He's in the Seafarers Inn, Christ, Léa. He's at the other end of the bay.'

'Well, do what you do best, Caron, no heroics. Remember, keep to the book.'

Caron looks desperately at Macy.

'She's fine, honestly,' says Léa. I would tell you if I was worried. Go.'

46

Death And Despair

21st December 2024

Caron messages Denny, *'He's at Seafarers Inn, need back up, no lights, quiet approach.'*

'He's practically on our doorstep!' He replies. He makes the call.

Caron rings Krubb; everything is to be by the book. 'We need armed officers; Boulter is almost at the safe house. Can you authorise?'

'Consider it done. I will inform NCA.' Caron hangs up. Unbelievable, he's still crawling to those twats.

Boulter continues to look out of the window. No movement, no texts, not even an acknowledgement. He decides to return to his car a few streets away as he goes to pay his bill. Usually, he wouldn't bother and walk out, but he didn't want to attract any attention.

'Don't suppose you have any rooms left?' he asks the manager in his awful Welsh accent, but she seems to have fallen for it.

'No, sorry, pet, fully booked. Everything will be full now. It's a popular little seaside fishing village, you know. You probably already know if you're buying property in the area. Even Artists Retreat has been booked for six months, which is a long-term booking, I understand. Usually only for four weeks at a time.' Boulter's interest is piqued.

'Never mind, I just don't fancy the trek back to my hotel in Newcastle. Just out of curiosity, what is Artists Retreat?'

'What it says on the tin, people book it for a painting holiday. But between you and me, I don't think any artists are staying there just now. She, I mean Janey, dyes her hair black, trying to look younger, but she doesn't. I should think that flaming red hair pops through every couple of days. That's the only painting she does – her roots!' She laughs, thinking she is hilarious. Boulter loves her for that as he laughs with her.

'Well, that's just a funny situation. How do you get there? Is it far? I may want to book it for myself sometime.'

'Oh, you'd love the views from the tower; you can see for miles along the coast. Mind, it's just been done out again, so this is the first booking they've had. Goodness knows what they charge now. You cross the wooden bridge, pet. It might not look very safe, but it has a full service, or whatever they call it, every autumn without fail. It's as safe as you can get. There's a stairway hidden inside the tower, and you can reach it from the rocks if you know where to look. I'll tell you something: if you believe in folklore, it would have been used for smuggling, I bet, but not anymore.' She chuckles again. 'You'd never get near those steps now, though, the sea is far too rough. Even on a summer's day with the water flat calm, I wouldn't fancy my chances. Still, it's just a stone's throw away.' She turns away from her Welsh customer and asks, 'Yes, love?' to her next punter.

Boulter doesn't see the cars or vans which pull up alongside the pub. 'Oh aye, something up, maybe someone in the water. Poor soul, hope they're OK.' Minnie goes on to pull her beer orders.

Boulter looks around. Fucks sake you must be kidding.

He sends another text: *'Your niece won't survive now.'*

Boulter walks out through the rear exit of the Inn. He looks over the cliff edge and decides to take his chances. Walking and running, but mainly falling towards the narrow cliff path to the harbour, he hides below the tiny walled jetty. Keeping out of sight is his immediate plan.

Caron resists the temptation to text back; desperately, she must remain professional. And she will need his phone.

Caron walks into the Seafarers and says, 'Hello, Minnie, have you seen this man? I know I asked you earlier.' She's known the manager for years.

'No, sorry, pet, I haven't. While you're here, I've just had a Welsh chap ask about renting your Artists Retreat next year. Sounds like a potential customer.'

Caron turns to walk away.

Minnie continues, 'He's buying property here. He might invest heavily, so maybe consider that when he books. I didn't get his name, sorry, my bad.'

'Describe him, please, Minnie. Height, build, et cetera.'

Minnie provides an excellent description of her earlier encounter, telling her he was staying in Newcastle. Caron circulated this across the team. 'This is Boulter's current description. He will be armed.'

Caron knows he won't be far. Minnie has told him about the current occupants staying at Artists Retreat, and any numbskull would work out it was Mary and Petra.

Callum and Janey update their little throng, who know the direct danger they're all in now: Cerys's support workers, undercover protection officers, and everyone involved are targets.

Callum remains vigilant, watching his cameras feeding back meaningless images from the perimeter fence and across the island. Artists Retreat has cameras in every doorway, covering the entire room and window access. He watches closely; he can't see anyone apart from the group on the other side of the bridge. Once the Seafarers Inn was searched, its occupants were told to stay indoors, away from the windows. Consequently, curious faces could be seen peering out. Caron doesn't have the time or resources to prevent selfish, idiotic behaviour; no one does.

Armed officers form a line around the Inn's rear car park, highlighting the fact that Boulter is nowhere near the building. Callum's job is frustratingly difficult, and far too many people are milling around.

The north-easterly wind begins its usual moan as it whirls around the estuary. Heavy clouds start to gather, threatening a winter storm with snow on its way, no doubt. No drone would last longer than a few minutes: a pointless exercise. The RNLI from the River Tyne has been called out to help locate any boats which foolishly go into the North Sea from the island.

Callum moves one of his cameras onto the sea and rocks below. Nothing, he wouldn't survive a minute in that water. Darkness and weather hinder his view, and he increasingly relies on infrared images. Various types of boats are safely moored to the wooden jetty below the Seafarers Inn, and some smaller boats are stored further upstream in the quieter waters of the estuary for the winter season. Callum keeps searching; his armed toolkit is now open and on show. Cerys feels the strain of the situation as the party of six scans the screens in front of them.

Boulter can see the stone jetty on the opposite side of the inlet; he knows he can get across and back. Various iron ladders are obvious, and he can see several of them bolted into the tiny rock. Because he is close to reaching Mary and Petra, he has to try. He crawls from his dark space behind the brick life buoy store and remains crouched behind the boats on the jetty. Removing his long puffa coat, Boulter watches the police and the RNLI join the party. Re-thinking his approach, he can make out the rock jetty on the other side of the estuary, but there is no way he can get across without being seen. Lights sweep the black water, which is no more than ten feet away from him. Mary has to die, or it's not worth it. She will know of his plans;

he is sure of it. Boulter places his coat in the raging sea and gets soaked as he does so. Then he heads towards the Seafarers Inn and keeps himself just above the water's reach. The waters drag his coat out, and powerful light beams from the lifeboat pick it out.

Caron receives a message.

'Ma'am, he is in the water.'

'Denny, light up the water just below the jetty on the south side of the estuary.'

Within minutes, powerful searchlights are scouring the area. Nothing can be seen.

47

A Will To Survive

Back at Artists Retreat, all eyes watch the sea crash against the rocks as they strain to locate Boulter in the sea. Callum trains his infrared on the water and picks out various images on the jetty; all are police officers. He still can't pick out Boulter.

Boulter's distraction appears to be working, but he needs to be smart; he might need a miracle. He has been in worse situations. Crawling on his belly behind the boats, Boulter keeps himself hidden. Infrared cameras would pick him out in minutes, and he needs to move quickly. Armed police above him and officers walking around the bridge area will draw attention to him. Waiting behind an original stone wall which supports the wooden bridge beside the Inn's car park, he pauses, gathering his thoughts before he moves again.

Using the bridge as cover, Boulter silently swings underneath the walkway using the wooden slats, confident his strength training will get him across swiftly, without being seen. The sea and rocks below are about a ten-metre drop; the wind has picked up, and he is swaying more than he would like to. In his conceited mind, the possibility of him falling is ridiculous; it just isn't going to happen.

Safely on the island, with winds howling around him, he scrambles to the west side of the garden. The focus is still on the east as everyone watches his coat floating out to sea.

Boulter unpacks his gun and six bullets. 'Shit, what a cock-up,' realising his limited amount of ammunition. He squats down as he silently moves further away from the bridge. Knowing everyone's interest will turn from the sea in minutes, with nowhere else to run to, he places himself in front of the hundred-year garden stone wall and faces north. Nothing is between him and the island's edge, some fifty metres away. He plots his escape route because he must get off this piece of rock once Mary and Petra are obliterated. Obsessed with his need for killing and survival, he does not consider any threat from armed police or the coastguard. Overthinking the risks will hinder his plan; he has never been shot in his life.

At midnight, his coat is rescued from the water. 'Christ man, he's fooled us again,' shouts DCI Dell. 'He won't be in the water,' she tells her team, 'He's moved away from the sea. More security on the island now!'

Armed officers cross the bridge to the safe house.

Uncle sees the colour drain from Cery's face and stands before her as he speaks. 'He won't get to you, Cerys, or you, Janey. The best thing he could do is escape from the sorry situation.'

'Is that right?' One shot blows Uncle off his feet. Everyone dives towards the hallway except Callum.

Callum grabs his gun, but it is too late. Boulter stands in the garden doorway leading directly into the dining room. His second shot misses Callum's chest but catches his left arm. Boulter, in his haste, thinks it is another direct hit. Four bodies escape through the double doors into the hallway. The solid oak front door is locked, and there's no time to unlock it. Artists' Retreat is now their prison. Cerys and Janey run up the stairs. Boulter follows the group of women out of the room. Unsure of who went off in what direction, he chases Avril and Connie. Connie shouldn't be there. She has built a good rapport with Cerys and called in with Christmas gifts. What a poor decision that was.

Boulter knows he has a limited amount of ammunition. He face-kicks Avril, immediately knocking her out. Connie stares in horror as she watches his foot reach out and do the same to her. Boulter thinks both women are fortunate. He has an excellent strike rate in less than two minutes; that is good going. Now, he must finish what he has planned. He climbs the stairs, not stopping for a second.

Cerys and Janey know precisely where they are going. They shake under the wooden floor, which forms the base of the most easterly oak chest in the tower, silently, huddled up to each other, as terror engulfs them. They planned their escape and hiding place, with Callum coaching them both on survival techniques. The most important one now is bearing their weight onto the rope handles underneath the oak base of the chest, to prevent Boulter from lifting it. Their life depends on keeping a firm hold and not letting go.

Boulter is on the chase and hears armed officers burst through the garden door, which he had used minutes earlier. Their instruction is to disarm with reasonable force. Each armed officer knows they will decide whether to shoot or not. Lives are in danger; they will shoot to kill.

Caron says to Denny, 'He's a first-class illusionist. How does he do it? A step ahead all the time.'
Caron is prevented from going across the bridge, as is Denny. Boulter doesn't have a chance.
'How did he get across?' Denny wonders, looking through binoculars.
'Nothing surprises me concerning Boulter. He's bloody invincible.' Caron knows there is no way he will walk out of there alive. The problem she has now is protecting everyone else.

Boulter slams doors and checks each room, but he can't find

either of them. Armed officers race upstairs. He makes a split-second decision and barricades himself inside the tower room. His priorities have changed, and he needs to get out to survive. It is not impossible. He remembers Minnie's conversation and the steps outside. Looking up, he spots the odd-shaped ceiling, which shows the room protruding on the east side. The door will be down within minutes. Lifting the lid from the most easterly chest, he reaches down to the solid floor and tries to pull it up, unaware of his quarry holding onto the handles on the other side. He can't understand; he looks for a latch or catch and rattles the floor. Nothing.

The barricade is almost through. Out of pure frustration, he slams his foot on the chest floor again. It moves. Did he hear a noise? No! Surely, they are not underneath. He smiles his arrogant smile and gets his gun ready. He heaves again; it moves a couple of centimetres.

Janey and Cerys descend the iron-rung stairs with spectacular speed. They plan to hold onto the last rung and attempt to keep out of sight. Reaching the freezing stone jetty, the north-east wind howls around them, and icicles thrash their faces. Their lives depend on holding on.

Boulter pulls at the wooden floor so hard that it releases and whacks him in the face, forcing him to reel backwards. After rocking on the floor for a few seconds, he pulls himself together. 'Fucking bitches,' he shouts. Picking up his gun, he fires it down into an empty void. 'Are you fucking joking?' he shouts. The barricade is almost through. 'Where the fuck did you go?'

Janey and Cerys hang onto the last iron rung of the tower steps for dear life. They can't speak; the storm takes their breath as soon as they open their mouths. Cerys is petrified, and Janey doesn't feel much better. Bitter, freezing waves and driving sleet soak them to the skin—their grip slips. Janey is clinging to Cerys, keeping the frail child from entering the dark water. Boulter investigates the chasm; he can't understand it. Did he imagine it? He checks the other chests. Are they connected? Nothing.

He goes back to the first chest and jumps down. He locates the small opening running downwards, under the floor. 'I'm coming for you. There's nowhere to hide.' He's glad he accessed the island; he can release the small rowing boat, take cover, and still get away. In his mind's eye, the RNLI will follow the boat. He is so wrapped up in his own world that he knows he can escape. Boulter's unstoppable in his mission. If his mind were clear, he'd realise he doesn't stand a chance. A familiar voice in his head makes him prick up his ears.

'Leave it, son, no more, you're done.'

'Never.' Adrenaline pumps around his body; he is not giving in that easily.

DCI Caron Dell crosses the bridge, putting her life in danger. She has to do it. Uncle lies dead, a bullet in the back of his head. He didn't stand a chance. A team of armed guards couldn't protect him. There was no sign of Callum, just a trail of blood. God, what a mess. Denny yells at her to get out; she isn't going anywhere. How many fucking officers does it take to stop him? Caron can hear the attempts to break into the tower, and the solid doors throughout the building make it a challenging task. Life or death depends on breaking that door down.

Boulter scrambles down the iron steps. Violent winds are howling up the sheltered stairwell, suffocating his screaming threats. He tries to locate his target with a gun in one hand and a rung in the other. Nothing, no one in sight. He screams again.

The tower room barricade smashes through. Armed police go directly to the open chest. Empty. Searching the remaining chests in the room, they don't understand how or where

Boulter has gone. All of the upstairs rooms are empty, and the armed officers are astonished as to where he has disappeared to.

Callum knows precisely where they are. He forges ahead with his left arm, bleeding freely. One of the officers shouted for him to stop. He doesn't; on he goes. These two women rely on him to survive. He jumps down into the space leading to the iron steps. Two armed officers follow.

Callum points his gun down the stairwell; he sees Boulter just below him. Boulter doesn't see him. The noise from the raging sea and the winter storm is deafening. For once, Callum Brown is pleased he is in such a freezing place in the middle of winter.

Outside, terror and screams are lost on the wind, carried away into the chilling black night. Cerys can't hang on any longer; her will is spent as her fingertips slip away from the last iron rung.

Janey uses all her strength and grabs her, every muscle burning underneath her cold skin. Cerys and Janey are sliced from sharp rocks as the storm pushes and pulls them around the jetty. Both are screaming with pain as the salty waves batter the tiny jetty, pounding everything in their way.

The lifeboat cannot reach them; it is too broad to get through the narrow gorge. They throw life buoys out towards the flat stone jetty. Cerys sees them and hopes she can reach one if she goes into the sea.

A search and rescue helicopter had been scrambled from the Humber 40 minutes earlier, and the faint sound of its rotors can be heard - they liaise with RNLI. If it comes too close, the winds generated by the helicopter rotor blades will place Cerys and Janey in further danger.

Janey is clinging onto the last iron rung with all she has. It is the difference between life and death for both of them. Her efforts torture her body as she continues to muster all of her strength to hold on.

Callum hears Boulter shout out to the women. 'Not a chance of escape now, bitches.' He cocks his gun and fires. He misses Janey by a fraction of an inch. He aims again. Janey and Cerys pray to a God they haven't stopped praying to these last few days. Another shot.

Boulter comes down the chute as quickly as gravity would pull him, his face inches from Janey's as his dead body becomes wedged in between the entrance of the steps. Janey can't believe it: shock, horror, and relief. Cerys clings onto her arm. Janey doesn't know how long she can cling to the step herself. Her adrenaline is spent. She isn't going to make it.

An officer's hand reaches down and pulls at her wrist. With newfound energy, she is determined to make it. She hauls Cerys in front of her. Cerys's screams are lost in the wind; the shock of a dead body is bad enough, but the dead, haunting eyes of Boulter staring up at her nearly sees her off.

Cerys slips back onto the jetty, the shock forcing her to let go of Janey. She stumbles as she tries to survive. Lying flat on the rock surface, she crawls towards the opening where Janey is holding on with both hands. She sees her mouth move but hears nothing. Janey disappears as she is hauled up the stairwell. Cerys knows the next wave will sweep her into the sea.

The RNLI searchlight provides much-needed help as Cerys' mind sways, and she cannot focus. Her world is slowing down as she feels herself floating upwards. She cannot see. Her world is dark and silent. Her time is up.

Cerys is seconds from the crash of the next wave. Powerful lights shine directly onto the small female; the lighting loses her as she is swept from the jetty.

The helicopter is directly above the terrifying situation. A coastguard officer is winched down, and they battle against the wild winds. All lights focus on the area around the jetty.

Without warning, the helicopter crew winches their

trained officer further down near the wild water. He pulls Cerys from the sea.

The coastguard officer's focus was on getting the child back to safety.

Mary is wrapped in blankets from one of the chests, she is spent, near to unconsciousness as you can be. Ravaged by sea and rocks, there is very little left of her clothing. Her skin has been destroyed by the rocks and sea; some deep gashes need immediate attention. But her will to survive is strong.

She knows she will make it.

Back in the tower, Callum is broken. His weak and damaged body is going into shock from the sheer exhaustion of the last hour. Callum's duty is done. He slips into unconsciousness.

Cerys is receiving CPR, and the trained officers working to resuscitate her are counting, then breathing into her mouth. They switch places to give her the best possible chance.

Nothing.

They keep going.

Her legs, arms and torso have been violently whipped, and wide welts of flesh ooze through the girl's damaged skin.

Medics are ushered across the bridge whilst officers prepare to dislodge the bulk of Tony Boulter. It is no easy task to hoist him back into the building. Caron's instructions are clear. 'We need his body; do not let him go into the water.'

As she waits for the wounded to be cared for, she watches with utter dismay as the body of Uncle is taken away by a private ambulance. A second vehicle is waiting for Boulter.

'I need to see Boulter's body.' Caron walks straight past the SIO, appointed immediately by Krubb. Caron knows he is doing his best to keep her out of any further decisions. She won't be quiet, and neither will she be blocked out.

Léa can't be contacted due to an urgent family matter, she tells DS Winston. Another pathologist is in attendance.

Caron looks into the face of pure evil. His eyes are half closed; his arrogant bastard persona remains with him even in death. Her long coat covers the bottom part of his body. She peers into his face, waiting for the SIO to turn away, but he doesn't. She needs Boulter's phone.

'Does he have any other weapons?' she asks.

'I haven't searched his body, DCI Dell; I know who he is. His gun was found at the bottom of the outside staircase, I understand. I will ensure that if I find any items of interest, I will pass them to you?' he says, slightly exasperated.

'Yes, OK, I just want to ensure it was him. Are you OK? You seem frustrated.'

'Well,' he removes his glasses and rubs his eyes. He turns to sit down. That is all the time she needs to retrieve Boulter's phone. 'I am exhausted, but I'll be fine.'

'OK, I am sorry to hold you up. I will get out of your hair.'

Caron relaxes her shoulders.

Several NHS ambulances and one helicopter took five people to the hospital that night.

Two were touch-and-go, and three would survive.

Two left the Seafarer's Inn car park in private black ambulances.

48

Debrief

22nd December 2024

A few minutes before eight am, Caron eventually sits down in her superior's office and speaks to Krubb. Rakesh is on screen. The latter is fuming because Boulter is dead.

'Do you know how much we needed him? We cannot find Blain without his input.' Rakesh has been taking too many lousy behaviour lessons from Krubb. His attitude is a disgrace. 'He was key to finding Blain. What an absolute shambles.'

DCI Dell is the consummate professional, but sometimes, she must directly instruct fat-headed twats criticising her. 'Firstly, don't ever speak to me like that, remember you were brought in to support my team. Secondly, what shambles? Where were you and your specialist squad when the chips were down?' Caron wants an answer.

'Leeds, you know that.'

'Well, I've travelled to and from Leeds for many days now, and I can confirm it's not that far away.' Caron is seething, but she doesn't show it. 'And I take it you cannot locate Blain by your tone of voice?'

'No, we've lost sight of Blain. He has disappeared from his sprawling mansion!' Rakesh is raging.

'Where is Jason in all of this?' Caron thinks of those blue eyes and that soft Edinburgh accent.

'He's taking some compassionate leave. That's all I

know.' Rakesh has shown his cards; he is livid at being left at the helm when the chips are down.

'Ah, so you're carrying the can then, Rakesh?'

'Enough!' shouts Krubb. 'How many body bags, Caron? Are you still counting?'

Immediately, she responds, 'It certainly is a sorrowful day to have lost an exceptional officer in these circumstances. No one should ever have been under that pressure. Boulter was a loose cannon. The details of my witnesses should never have been released. My report will point out that NCA released vital high-level security information across their team after I specifically requested that no one outside of my group should know.' Caron turns to Rakesh on screen. 'NCA knew this was a risk to life. I was never told of NCA's mitigating actions to prevent these facts from falling into the wrong hands because you did not have plans to protect this data. You went ahead anyway. Your irresponsible act forced me to reveal the fact that Petra Gould was safe, but not in Yorkshire. You know that particular safehouse is not on our books. Who did you tell? When you look at the facts clearly, you will realise that information contributed to Boulter's death – your star witness.' Caron was incredibly calm on the outside. Inside, she feels like a failure; she's let people down who had protected the very essence of her case. Uncle should not have been killed. Boulter should never have been told about Petra.

'I didn't release any address; I just said Northumberland. Also, it is now the twenty-second of December, so by my reckoning, it is Christmas in a couple of days, and you have a knock to do, Caron.' Rakesh is saying that it is her fault and that she should be punished.

'No, Rakesh,' says Krubb. 'That will be your job today. You organise yourself and get to Newcastle. Caron has far too many reports to do.' Krubb pauses, 'My DCI has just told you not to speak to her in that manner! You have absolutely no authority over any of my staff; barking orders out is not your remit. How dare you take the moral high ground in my station.'

Caron hopes her mouth isn't wide open. She should be the one to deliver such dreadful news. 'I will go with Rakesh if that is OK, sir? Working so closely with them all, I should really be there.'

Krubb looks at Rakesh. 'Caron's response is exactly what I expect from any of my DCIs, Rakesh. Caron has put her colleague's family front and centre as she prepares to deliver the devastating news of Uncle's death. I am unsure what happens in NCA, but you will attend with Caron. You are jointly responsible for the outcomes. If the result had been different, you would be basking in the glory.' Rakesh stands up and goes to dial out of the Zoom call. 'Sit down! Several of my DCIs choose to lead from their desk, too. Caron doesn't; she engages with people and gets results, and she found Boulter. He could have been off. He planned to leave the UK for Mexico. Make no mistake, we would have located him, but he didn't get out of the country. The number of lives saved may be immeasurable. Never underestimate my DCI again. Is that clear?'

'Crystal.' Rakesh hmphed.

'Still no apology to Caron?'

Rakesh looks across at Caron, and she can see the pain he has brought on himself. 'Please don't, Rakesh. If you need to be told to apologise, it doesn't count. Once you arrive in Newcastle, I will drive us both to Uncle's address.' Caron's soothing voice calms the heated exchange. Rakesh's unprofessionalism has eventually been called out. She's happy with that.

'Caron and Rakesh, you must wait for further instructions. Uncle's department may want to deliver this news themselves. Do not delay your plans to travel north, Rakesh.'

'Thanks, Sir.' Caron responds with an inward smug expression.

'Keep me updated on our injured colleagues, please. What about our witnesses? I understand Mrs Cartwright is recovering well?'

'Yes, sir, and they have reverted to Mary and Petra, so there is no more confusion when discussing or updating information.' Caron waits to find the right words for her update on Petra.

'Petra Gould is in critical care and will be there for several days, depending on her recovery. She is still unconscious but alive, and where there's life, there's hope. The officer at the scene who pulled her from the sea has given her a chance. She is not out of the woods yet, but her medical team are hopeful at this stage.'

'That is good news; let us hope she returns to normal in a few days.'

Caron despairs. What is normal for an abused fifteen-year-old? Krubb is another prat with no fucking clue.

'One last question, DCI Dell,' says Krubb. What now, she thinks.

'Did we find our mole yet?'

'We have three names: DS Mosley, PC Goodwin and Mabel Newson.'

'Mabel?' Rakesh is astonished.

'She may be our mole. Rakesh, you have shown little respect to me or the team by keeping your discoveries confidential. That is why I have not mentioned it, just in case you were wondering.' Caron walks out of Krubb's office. There is no slamming of doors and no drama, just a sense of sadness and failure. She makes her way home. It's more than Uncle will do.

Sometimes, the reality of the job is complete injustice; Boulter would have died, either at the hands of officers, Callum Brown or herself. As soon as he touched Macy, he didn't stand a chance. She drives home, knowing she has much more to do.

Macy has been awake for a few hours, bathed and changed. She bursts into tears as Caron walks into the living room. Léa is curled up on her chair and turns away from the pair as they hug each other.

Macy tells Caron what she remembers.

Caron tells her daughter, 'Well, he won't return. You're safe here.'

'You don't understand how stupid I feel, not hurt nor a victim.' That's my girl, thinks Caron, but doesn't say it. 'No one is to know, not Mum, Dad, Grannie or Granda, and certainly not Grandma Peg, no one.'

'Only if you promise you will never bottle up what you've been through. Even when you are away from here, call me immediately if you need to talk or it gets too much to bear.' Caron remembers she has Boulter's phone.

'You know you can also call me, don't you?' says Léa.

'Yes, thank you, Léa. How could I have been so idiotic - it could have been so different.'

There was a knock on the front door, Mrs Chambers from a few doors down. 'Is everything alright, dear?' she asks Caron, placing Macy's suitcase over the threshold.

'Ah, yes, we wondered what happened to my niece's case. She forgot to bring it into the house when she arrived. You know, Christmas spirit and all that.' Caron hopes she sounds convincing.

'Thank the Lord for that; I was worried she might have been kidnapped. Merry Christmas.' She totters down the steps, putting her hood back up against the unrelenting weather.

Caron walks back into her living room, 'She doesn't know how right her thoughts are, does she?' She looks at Macy and Léa, grateful they are both OK.

'Right, ladies, I am off home.' Says Léa as she hugs them both.

Macy turns to Caron, 'I really don't know what you'd do without her.' She waves as Léa pulls off.

'Neither do I.'

Caron is back in the office before eleven am, freshened up and ready. Today is going to be a difficult one for many people.

Her team wanders in early for her 11:30 am debrief. She watches for Mosley, Goodwin and Mabel.

DS Denny Winston joins her. 'Penny for your thoughts, ma'am?'

'Mole?'

'Well, Mosley has called in again today, and he plans to return tomorrow. NHS guidance advises that he should isolate for at least forty-eight hours. He will do his shift starting at midnight tonight. Sensible really.'

'Agreed.' She picks up the phone. 'Nancy, can you review any digital correspondence between Mabel Newson NCA and PC Barry Goodwin? They could be connected. Get Kim involved, if necessary, please, it's urgent.'

The rest of Caron's team and the NCA staff are present, and Rakesh has also made an effort. He sits at the back of the room, a wise move.

Caron requests a few minutes to reflect on the previous twenty-four hours and the life lost to protect vital witnesses. 'We still have work to do. As you are aware, there is a mole, or as I prefer to say, a rat amongst us.' DCI Dell gave her task force time to digest her statement, 'With that in mind, if any of you have information, let me know. You can tell me in confidence. Remember, they played a key part in the murder and attack of our colleagues.' Caron looks at each person individually but sees nothing.

'OK, Rakesh and I are going to see Avril and Connie today, and depending on Uncle's instructions, we may also visit his next of kin. They probably won't want to see us, but our colleagues would respect our visit.'

'Your task today is to ensure your case information is accurately logged. Jaz will provide support, and please take heed of her requests.' Jaz places her powered wheelchair in front of her workstation and begins her task.

'DS Winston and Rakesh are working together with me

as we need to tie up some loose ends; you may or may not be called upon. So, no early finishes or long lunches. Keep yourself available. As always, I am genuinely grateful for your dedication and continued commitment to our case.' Caron dismisses the group as her phone rings.

'Nancy.'

'You will not believe this: Mabel Newson is Barry Goodwin's mother.' Caron looks at Denny. 'Do you have their addresses, Nancy?'

'Oh yes, Mabel is just outside Leeds, and Goodwin is less than twenty minutes from Northumberland's HQ.'

Christ, they were recruited to infiltrate our data and update Boulter. Bastard Gallows again. 'Great thanks, Nancy.'

'Change of plans for us. Rakesh, we need to do our visits, then it's back to Leeds for us both. Denny, make your way to Leeds. Do not give anyone a reason to question why you are there, and keep an eye on Mabel Newson's address. I'll forward you the info, and we'll be there as soon as we can.'

The three of them leave the building.

49

Aftermath

Caron gets into the driver's seat of their unmarked police car. Rakesh asks, 'Why are we not visiting Uncle's family?'

'Well, it turns out he has no family, not that we can locate. His job was everything he lived and breathed for - to protect others and ensure justice was delivered.' Caron thinks, justice? There's no justice here. Even the force and the NCA have proved that. At least four officers, one very senior, have let them down.

'Where are we with DI Rustler?'

'Thrown the book at him, and apparently, he is relieved. Rustler's family have moved out of their home, and won't be going back, that's for sure. But they're safe; Rustler was worried about Boulter getting to his wife and kids. Thanks to Callum, he can't touch anyone anymore. Eric Rustler has given a factual and honest statement, and apparently, he is on suicide watch. The lives one man has ruined are incredible. Just one copper had to speak up.'

'What will happen to Mabel? I didn't think she was involved with Boulter or involved with any of it.'

'Are you sure? How can you be so certain?'

Rakesh looks out the window. Snow flurries start forming around the countryside as they tear down the A1. 'You can never be sure, can you? I mean, not really.' He pauses. 'Can I talk to you openly, Caron, not as a DCI or colleague, but never to be spoken about again?'

Caron glances across at him, 'Yes of course,' she says, simultaneously thinking, "*tossa*."

'How well do you really get along with Chief Superintendent Krubb?'

'Workwise, yes, we generally get on ok, in the main. In all honesty, I'm not his biggest fan.'

'Would he normally praise you in front of others?'

'Praise me? Hell no, he'd rather pull me down. So, his comments earlier today were surprising.'

'I thought so.'

'What? Spit it out, man.'

'Well, it's just Jason.'

'Who the hell is Jason?'

'The Edinburgh blank screen, Jason.'

'Ah, yes, I'd just about forgotten him.' No way has she forgotten his accent or the mesmerising blue eyes she'd seen on their first encounter, but she isn't going to tell Rakesh that.'

Rakesh looks at her, surprised. 'You forgot about him? Not many people do, especially women.'

'Wow, there's a statement.' Caron grins.

'No, sorry, it's just that Jason asked Krubb if he could approach you to transfer to his department. You'd be an excellent role model, apparently. Well, for his team's DCI counterparts, he thinks they would benefit greatly if you were to join his team and share your experience.' He puts his head down.

Caron's mind whirls. 'Interesting. What was Krubb's response?'

'Krubb completely changed his attitude about you. He isn't keen on you; that is pretty obvious. Once he knew another agency was interested, you weren't going anywhere. He told Jason and anyone who would listen, for that matter, how much of an asset you were.'

'Our earlier conversation now makes sense. He won't do it again, though; it was because you were on the call. He likes to brag about how well his department works. No one can recall his last day's work. Thanks for that, though, Rakesh. It has cleared up some confusion.' Unbelievable how arrogant that fat, lazy twat is.

They arrive at Leeds headquarters early in the afternoon and meet DS Winston. The roads are OK, but the weather is closing in slightly. Caron thinks if the gritters continue throughout the evening and night, she will get home, as will everyone else.

When she opens her front door, Mabel Newson looks like she hasn't slept for weeks. She is taken to Elland Road Police Station, where there will be an internal investigation, and criminal charges in due course.

Mabel is clearly frightened and aware that Boulter has been killed; she is also sensitive to the fate of her colleagues, a shame she will never shake. But Mabel's fear for her son Barry Goodwin is her overriding emotion. Where is he?

Caron, Denny and Rakesh remain professional as they talk to her. Before she is taken into custody, they want as much information as they can possibly glean, from her case and her son's.

'We haven't seen PC Goodwin for a few days. He rang the station, citing his illness as the winter vomiting bug, so I didn't expect to see him. How did you know Tony Boulter?'

'He was controlling me and Barry. Barry's dad, my ex, was thousands in debt. Tony sorted it out with another loan.' Mabel pauses and looks up sheepishly, 'He had a few moneylenders after him. We divorced years ago because he was a gambler. He started on the horses every Saturday, just a quid here and there. Looking back, it's amazing how quickly his addiction took hold. Barry and me would never have had any life if we'd stayed with him.'

She puts her head in her hands. 'He's dead now. He fell from a balcony in Vegas just last year. He was probably killed because he owed far too much money. Boulter had me and

Barry on his payroll by then. With Gallows, protecting him and his vile mates. Had we squealed, we'd have been six feet under; we both knew it couldn't continue. We were euphoric when Boulter said he was calling it quits at the end of the year. We'd be off the hook and never need to see him again. He planned to move away, I don't know where to, but out of Leeds, possibly out of the country. We just had to bide our time.'

'Off the hook? Interesting statement, Mabel. Do you know what he has done for a living?' Caron remains calm and professional as her fire rages inside.

'Yes, to my shame. If it's a certainty that you're going to die because you don't do as Boulter tells you, what would you do?'

'That's an excellent question,' says Denny. 'Where do you think Barry is?'

'I don't know, I have no idea. He was due here on Friday. We always do drinks late on a Friday, just one or two, sometimes none, depending on work commitments. And if he can get away from Newcastle.'

Caron can't believe her ears, work commitments! 'What work commitments are you referring to?'

'NCA for me, PC work for Barry,' she replies defensively.

Caron's opinion changes. Mabel, the woman who sits in front of her, chose to be on Boulter's payroll. Another criminal turned victim, and it sickens her to the stomach.

'What car did Boulter drive?' Caron asks.

'The last one was a rental, four-by-four, white. It was a Nissan of some sort.'

At last, we seem to be getting somewhere. 'Who would he rent it from?' Caron presses on.

'One of the main dealers, under a different name. He'd use the one near the airport, away from his home address. That's where Barry hired ours from.'

'What name did you use?'

'It was always in my ex-husband's and his mother's name: Bryn and Bryony Watkins.'

'So, Barry's surname is not his Dad's?' asks Caron.

'No, he changed his name to Goodwin by deed poll.'

Caron thinks that is why they didn't show up as mother and son on our records. It should have flagged somewhere, though – a thought for another day.

'You will remain here, in Leeds, while an investigation into your conduct is carried out. You may also face criminal charges. You will not be granted release because of your alleged involvement with Boulter. Our priority now is to try to locate Barry as soon as possible.' The three investigators leave while Mabel Newson remains at the station. Rakesh will return as soon as possible, for more details, but he needs to continue with their ongoing investigation: finding PC Barry Goodwin.

'Rakesh,' says Caron, 'Denny and I will drive back to Newcastle. His rental will be at the airport where his laptop was last located. Can you investigate what car Boulter was driving? Time is tight if we want to find Goodwin.' Caron instructs.

'I will get onto it now.'

Caron and Denny discuss the case in depth as they head home. If Barry Goodwin is dead, he is no use to Boulter. Thankfully, Boulter is of no use to anyone.

Caron's phone rings, and Denny answers.

'A white Nissan X-Trail, NV61 XXB, thanks Rakesh.' He hangs up.

Denny contacts Newcastle Airport's car park authority, explaining that he needs to track down the vehicle. Hoping they will have located it by the time they arrive. Being one of the busiest times of the year, car park attendants have far more to worry about than searching for a vehicle for the cops. However, they said they would try their best. Caron calls for officers to attend the airport to work with their security employees.

It's around 9.30 pm when Caron and Denny arrive at Newcastle

Airport. The car park staff are just too preoccupied. The two officers sent to look for the vehicle are still trawling the car park. The two detectives begin searching the vast area of parked cars, thankful it's not Heathrow. They'll have the car open in a jiffy once they find what they are looking for. After a freezing thirty minutes, the vehicle is located. The rear lights have been damaged, but that is all which can be seen from the outside, and there is no evidence of anyone around. They need access to the boot; Denny opens it within seconds, no alarm screeches; Boulter has deactivated it.

Barry Goodwin's frozen, stiff body is curled up in a ball. There are claw marks everywhere. He would have suffered hypothermia, no doubt, before passing away. No coat, just a shirt, trousers, socks and shoes. He was purposefully left to die, screaming the place down and terrified. He would have known he was in an airport, but maybe not the location. Barry Goodwin had kicked the rear lights out, but there was no one around; nobody would have seen his hand, foot, or whatever, nor would they have heard him. The back seats are tied down with seatbelts. So cruel. The inside boot release tag has also been snapped off. What a vile piece Boulter was. Goodwin didn't have a cat in hell's chance of getting out.

Léa receives a call-out, and Rakesh will need to have another difficult conversation with his colleague, Mabel, who is still being questioned in Leeds.

With the team and Krubb updated, there is nothing much left for Caron or Denny to do. Léa will carry out a preliminary examination, and a full autopsy will be completed the next day. Nothing will change over the next few hours for the young man's body lying on the metal forensics table. Caron agrees that his killer was more than likely Boulter, also in a fridge in the morgue. Alongside is one of their brave, courageous serving officers: Uncle, a senseless waste.

'DCI Dell,' Caron says as she answers her mobile.

'This is Petra Gould's consultant. Can you talk?'

'Yes.' Her body freezes; please let her live. Denny watches her with concern.

'Petra has gained consciousness, and her vitals are improving. Our patient will remain on our high dependency ward for now. One of her leg wounds has a serious infection, which is our priority. It is positive news, DCI Dell. However, a word of caution: Petra may relapse into unconsciousness, and her wound infection needs to be under control. I thought you would appreciate an update.'

'Thank you. That is positive, and I understand your concerns, so still a bit of a watch-and-wait situation?'

'Yes, I would say that is a fair assumption. I or one of my team will keep you updated.'

'Thank you.' Caron hangs up

With a sigh of relief, Caron relays the conversation to Denny. 'We know Mary is OK and is still receiving treatment. Petra has suffered enough, and I hope she pulls through. God knows what will be going around in her parents' minds.'

Caron makes it home just before midnight. She walks into a warm, loving home, where her Mam and Dad are with Macy and Grandma Peg, who is looking very annoyed. Standing alongside them are Beryl and Keith. 'Of course, you would be here,' she says, smiling the most welcoming smile, hugging everyone, and giving thought to those families who aren't so lucky.

Léa texts, *'Just home. I hope you can now enjoy your surprise Christmas. Goodnight. x.'*

50

Reports And Factual Findings

The next few days are spent ensuring all evidence is accurately collated. This takes some time, given the number of people involved, not just victims and perpetrators, but for the vast amount of data provided by the police and NCA.

Caron was happy in the main; digital data was time-stamped and matched the series of events. Thank God for Jaz.

Christmas Eve:
DCI Dell has kept in touch with Petra's medical team, who confirmed she is recovering and responding well to all treatments - long may it continue. Mary has been discharged and has booked into a hotel near the hospital. She insisted Petra's parents are also catered for within the five-star establishment. Mary wouldn't take no for an answer. Petra might just let her off with her show of luxury this time. Mary's parents were told to stay away and do something useful over Christmas, making it quite clear that things would have to change in that regard. Petra's comment about ticking boxes concerning donating to charity was not enough, and Mary knows she is right.

Once Caron's reports are complete, Krubb tells her to go home and rest. That is kind of him; it's Christmas Eve and nearing three pm. Most of her team has left for home already, and those in Leeds would have done the same. Anything else can wait until the twenty-seventh unless something urgent comes up.

'Merry Christmas to my two favourite women. I love you both, X.'

And there it is, my Christmas Eve text from the modern-day Grinch, my rapist, trying to steal Christmas. No chance of that.

51

Christmas Day

On Christmas morning, everyone is cheery; Caron especially counts her blessings while keeping an eye on Macy. It is early days, and she could still react from her ordeal. After breakfast, gifts are exchanged, and they agree to keep at least one gift each to open with Léa and Ross later that afternoon.

'I can't believe Léa has enough time to do everything,' says Caron. 'I swear she is some kind of superwoman.'

'Both cut from the same cloth, you two mind. But I am sure it's Ross doing the cooking,' her dad laughs. They have both thought that many times, and she nods in agreement.

Caron wonders about those who died, those who have survived and those who are under investigation. Their families' lives are dramatically different from last Christmas.

Petra remains under medical supervision, but is no longer classed as critical. Her mental health and well-being are still being observed. Mary stays close by as she takes the time to rest and recover, her terror of imprisonment felt very real as they hid from Boulter. Although freedom beckons, it is too early to appreciate it.

Petra speaks to her mum and dad and promises to go home for a few days once she's well.

Mary and Petra agree to be near each other while they process recent weeks and start looking towards the future. Phillip Hicks and his wife Veronica understand their daughter's decision to stay with Petra, thinking it is the right action for her just now, which will naturally allow her grief to take its course.

Christmas is always busy in the Hicks' household. The judge and his wife, Veronica, host a Christmas supper for charity volunteers each year. This year, they recruited their wider family to help with homelessness, but only if they wanted help. It's a humbling experience, and they know their effort doesn't scratch the surface. With a different mindset, they commit to doing something more meaningful to help all year round, not just at Christmas.

Back home, Caron tells her visitors she will see Mary and Petra this morning to ensure they are OK. She usually takes gifts when visiting on Christmas Day, but she feels it may compromise the investigation if she is seen as too friendly. Ridiculous but appropriate.

Caron arrives at the hospital, and Mary sits with Petra. They all hug. Both victims are slowly coming to terms with the fact that they are free. Caron dismisses their thoughts on blaming the NCA for allowing Boulter to reach them.

'No, no, we were a team, all in it together. Everything happened so fast we didn't see what was in front of our eyes,' Caron says. Once she's satisfied that they are both doing as well as they can, 'I'm calling in to see Callum later this morning. It is still touch and go, but my last update is that he is doing as well as he can be.' Petra winks at Caron and nods to Mary with a knowing look.

'No way! You two are an item?' Caron is shocked - pleasantly shocked.

'Well, nothing serious, we just clicked,' said Mary sheepishly.

'Good for you. Remember, there are still people who may want your story. Say nothing until everything is complete; it may compromise ongoing investigations into the other four and anyone else who comes out of the woodwork.' She doesn't want to dwell on the fact that police officers are also guilty. Thankfully, Mary and Petra are well aware of that.

'What happened to Tony's boss?' asks Petra.

'NCA and Interpol are still working on it; I am not involved. I hope for an outcome soon. The risk to you both on that count is minimal. You had no idea of the bigger picture, so neither of you would have witnessed any of Ches Blain's activity. Your knowledge of people trafficking is limited, plus you have no factual evidence, Petra. Don't fret about that at all. Just recover, take your time and use the support offered.' Caron doesn't see the point in telling them that neither Interpol nor the NCA locate him. Blain left his home on Christmas Eve with his driver. He and his car have not been seen since. Strange, thinks Caron, his vehicle, apparently a stretch limo, is a statement you can hardly miss. Anyway, that is for Interpol's Jason to deal with.

Petra interrupts her thoughts, 'I will use the help and support, and then maybe I will go home with Mum and Dad to decide what is next for me. I'm not worried unless Boulter's mates come after me.'

'Doubt it. They are just as relieved as you, I think. Cold-blooded killer comes to mind when I look back. He was pure evil. Anyway, let us try and look forward and ring me anytime you need to.'

Caron leaves two very relieved women and thinks again of Callum Brown. She smiles.

Christmas lunch is impressive, and the cat is let out of the bag. 'I cheated,' Ross admits. He volunteered to do the main shopping and cooking, but it proved too much. 'I hired a chef yesterday.'

'On Christmas Eve?' everyone screamed.

'I know it would take me longer than I thought, but

I couldn't deal with the overwhelming tasks ahead when I found out you were all coming. Regarding the cost, I need a loan just for the Christmas Pudding!' Laughter fills the room.

'Let's face it Ross, you could not have cooked this on your own,' says Léa. 'It has everything, bells and whistles.'

Caron and Léa have promised not to reveal Macy's ordeal to anyone. More secrets, but it is for the best. Caron thinks her daughter is coping well; let's hope she continues to do so. They both start clearing the table as everyone else plays immature but excellent board games.

'That was a hell of a few weeks Caron. It could have ended so very differently.'

'It's not over yet. We can talk tomorrow. I'll come to your office. Let me know when you've finished your reports.' She scrapes the leftovers into the bin. 'Mam and Dad will want to spend time with Macy. She won't mind me being out of the way for a while.'

52

Caron And Léa

With the family Boxing Day walk complete, it is time for lunch. Ross joins Caron and her family today, as Léa has left them to it, and she heads to the mortuary to carry out her duties.

There were plenty of leftovers from the extravagant amount of food on Christmas Day, which was extraordinarily out of character for them. Ross had overcompensated for what he felt was his lack of skills. He had decided that a feast prepared and cooked by a professional chef was what he should do. It was agreed on Christmas night that when Léa drops off their festive hamper donation to their local foodbank, they could donate a few lunches too. Both families recognise their luck to have such luxuries as good food with close family and friends. Of course, nothing had come easily for any of them, but at the same time, they were grateful for studying and working long hours to earn their keep.

Léa contacts Caron to let her know she has finished her reports and asks if she wants to join her in her office. Caron takes her some lunch and keeps to her zero-alcohol fizz. She will upgrade to a vodka tonic later if she fancies it.

'What is left to do, Caron?'

'We need to plan our next steps carefully, Léa. I have done some searching online, and Nancy has unlocked Boulter's phone; she doesn't know it is his mobile or what I am looking for. But we're off to Alnmouth on Sunday. Both of us are off work. Denny has everything covered, and we need a break. One night will do us both good. Train tickets are first class; look at it as a mini break. The downside is that the train is at 7.50 am. We will need your chemi....' She doesn't get the chance to finish what she was saying as Léa holds up her hand.

'The penny's dropped, Caron.' She puts her finger to her lips and writes a note; *walls have ears.*

Caron nods, then writes, *We need some of your samples. Is it possible?*

Léa nods as she burns their notes after she wrote the last one: you see, our plans may not be suspicious now. In the future they might be if we leave evidence. Their paranoid minds have protected them so far.

Caron agrees wholeheartedly that every precaution must be taken. They head home to enjoy what is left of Boxing Day.

Opening her front door, Caron hears the unmistakable voice of the insufferable Pamela Hartford. She rolls her eyes at Léa, and they grin as they walk into the living room. Caron stands still. Richard is right in front of her, standing beside his parents. He walks towards her and kisses her cheek; she is transported back to that night years earlier. The scent of his aftershave has been the loose thread all these years. How could she forget that? The overpowering smell of his fragrance. Caron doesn't hear the introduction to his wife, Daisy or his son, Julien. Caron's mind is whirring. Pamela and Kenneth walk across to kiss Caron on her cheek, too.

'Are you OK, Caron?' asks her mam, poker-faced. 'You look like you've seen a ghost.'

Léa nips Caron on the back to nudge her back into the conversation. Caron snaps out of her thoughts; a smell has brought back those horrific memories. She needs to get a grip.

'Er, I am so sorry. Such a surprise. God knows how long it's been since I saw you, Richard.'

'I know exactly when that was, says Richard. 'Beryl and

Keith's wedding all those years ago. And Macy, a honeymoon baby. What a perfect outcome.' Caron can't believe the brass neck of the obnoxious bastard standing before her. He had that look again - arrogance! Her father is seething.

Léa stands by her friend and looks at her, encouraging her to say something.

'Yes, really? Was it that long ago? Goodness me? How are you? So lovely to meet your wife and son. I didn't think you'd ever settle down.'

'Oh, didn't you? The best thing I have ever done is get married and have children. I understand you're married to the job.' Still that confident face. Bastard!

'Very happily married to the job, yes. Best decision I made.' She knows she is being defensive, but she can't help it. 'Goodness, where are my manners?' She takes his glass. 'Another drink?' Caron waltzes off to the kitchen. Léa makes small talk with the others before bringing empty glasses to the kitchen for a refill.

'Are you OK?' Léa asks, knowing it is one of her most ridiculous questions ever.

'Caron passes Richard's used glass to Léa. 'Can you arrange a DNA sample, please?'

'Leave it with me. Now collect yourself, get back in there and host! Do not let anyone suspect what you are thinking. Macy is here. It's not the time or place, Caron.'

Caron walks back into the living room with a tray of fresh glasses and a smile. She opens a bottle of champagne. 'Let us celebrate properly. It has been a while.' Now, she will find out if Richard is Macy's father, and then she can act. In her mind, he is a dead man walking.

Pamela continues bragging - off to Italy, skiing with family and friends they have made while travelling. Caron would rather poke pins in her eyes. She's happy they are away for the New Year, so there's no chance of catching up with them again.

She feels for Macy; is Richard her father? Looking at

them as a family, they appear to be an odd lot. Something makes her sit up as she discreetly studies Richard, who has almost jet-black hair and a more Mediterranean skin tone than his parents. With her strawberry blonde hair, Pamela would no doubt be descended from some Viking chief or someone of equal importance; she is not brunette. Kenneth's hair is more brown but not very dark at all. She has never noticed that they are so unalike. The next hour or so goes past in a haze for Caron. The Hartford's thank Caron for her hospitality and express Happy New Year wishes and goodbyes as they leave. She is relieved as she closes her front door behind them.

Nothing is said about Macy's potential father tonight. No one will let Richard spoil their Christmas, even though a considerably large elephant has been left in the room.

Boxing Day draws to a close; everyone is full of food and wine, and they are gamed out to the point that Monopoly will end up on the open fire. The group begins to look ahead to the New Year.

'Léa and I are having a night away on Sunday,' says Caron, 'You did say it was OK for me to plan Ross, so it was a bit of a late Christmas gift for Léa.'

Macy pipes up. 'Oh yes, you should both have a night away at a spa or something to treat yourselves.'

'Agreed,' says Nancy, 'You both work far too many long hours. You know it is not good for you.'

'That is all sorted then. The train and hotel are booked.'

Beryl says, 'Well, we'll be here until the New Year, so it gives us time to look at Artists Retreat from the outside.' She rolls her eyes.

'It will be returned to its previous lovely self in no time. Forensics aren't finished yet, though. It will take at least a few weeks to get inside.' Caron hopes.

'I've no intention of going inside, Caron. That is for you to sort out.' She grins.

'When did you discover hidden passageways, stairwells

and jetties?' asks Macy, eyes wide - she can show a delightful innocence sometimes.

'One set of steps under one of the chests in the tower. We should have known they were there, but there's no evidence recorded anywhere that they exist. The Seafarers Inn has something similar, like many old buildings on Northumberland's coast, including castles and mansions across the vast county. Just so that you know, Callum scoured the place and found the steps. I thought it was a joke, but according to Callum, it was not unusual for the time. I am very pleased he did, too. I don't know what would have happened if Mary and Petra hadn't gotten themselves hidden; even if they were there for just a few minutes, it probably saved their lives. I can't help wondering if they were purposely built for the watch tower, you know, to allow their crew to reach the sea quickly. It seems strange they're not recorded anywhere, though.'

'How is Callum?' asks Nancy, as her voice remains upbeat.

'He should be OK, Mam. Boulter must have thought he had shot him in the chest; He'd never have let him survive, but his mistake proved to be his downfall. Callum thinks he turned, and the shot hit his left arm. Exhaustion and blood loss nearly killed him. I didn't know until yesterday that he is over fifty! I know that's no age before you all have a go. Genuinely, I thought he was so much younger. It just shows if you look after yourself...'

'Well, you look ten years younger, as well. How anyone takes you seriously, I'll never know.'

'Typical Dad comment,' responds Beryl. 'Glad I caught the same genes.'

The twenty-seventh of December was also a nice, easy day with walks, TV and more food. Caron and Léa returned to work to squirrel themselves away in Caron's office at Northumberland HQ. There are plenty of staff around, but thankfully, no Detective Superintendent Krubb. They set out their plan.

53

A Night Away

29th December 2024

Waiting for their train, the two friends walk onto the platform from the first-class lounge. Caron holds her hot tea as the train doors open. Their 7.50 am train is due to leave in a few minutes. Both women board, and settle into their seats. They talk absolute drivel until they arrive at their destination.

With their overnight bags checked in early at their Alnmouth hotel on the Northumberland coast, they make their way towards the beach for a brisk walk in the chilly winds, then a hot cuppa at the golf course. After a few hours, they return to their hotel for lunch, ending a wonderful morning.

Early afternoon, Léa heads to the train station. She looks different from this morning; her natural hair is gelled and pulled into a plait, then hidden under a patterned woollen hat. A mid-length brown coat is a change from her usual style. Caron leaves the hotel an hour later, wearing a hooded green coat, which does not resemble her usual dark attire. Her umbrella shields her face from the icy rain.

Their plans are now coming to fruition. They have a bit more travelling to do before they complete their objective.

Going further up the East Coast Main Line to Edinburgh, they plan to visit a residential address currently rented by Marcus Towns. With meticulous coordination, Léa and Caron are lone travellers, and once in the bustling city, Caron sits at a table in an exclusive hotel bar. Léa is already comfortable at another table. Sitting separately, their strategically placed high-backed chairs ensure they can see Marcus Town's front door from their viewing points.

Watching, they wait for him to leave. Caron sits with a couple of books, and Léa is a few tables away, keying absolute rubbish into her laptop. Their working cover story puts off any potential interruptions.

The hotel owner enters the bar and stops in his tracks just as Caron leans forward to take a drink of her tea. *'What is she doing here?'* he thinks to himself and steps back into the doorway. Intrigued, he watches to see what she does next. He has seen a flash of her fury and decides to remain out of her line of sight. He makes a call and then speaks discreetly to the head bartender.

Caron and Léa continue to watch their selected doorway. A police car pulls up outside the address. Caron watches intently, but the officers remain in their vehicle, and after ten minutes, they move on.

The hotel owner realises she is watching an address. He also notices an equally fascinating second woman doing the same. Well, this is entertaining, he thinks.

Marcus Towns leaves his home just after seven pm.

Caron puts on her coat and gloves, picks up her small backpack and leaves her cash payment on the table. Once outside, she makes her way through the busy streets, ensuring her hair is tucked under her hood. Arriving at Town's address, Caron lets herself in. Léa watches from her vantage point in the window seat of the same pub, with her phone and a small case beside her.

The hotel owner looks on from afar.

Caron

Calmly, I top the cognac bottle up with liquid morphine, which only seems right. In less than five minutes, I'm done. Keep focused, I tell myself.

I walk along the unlit hallway towards the front door, confident that my task is complete.

My phone vibrates. The message reads: "*HIDE*."

Returning to the dining room is not an option; there is no escape route. With doors on either side of me, I have a fifty-fifty choice where to go – I go left. A masculine scent is overpowering as I enter the expansive living room. A wide Georgian window lets the streetlight stream onto the large monochrome sofas and furnishings which decorate the space. The light also shines on me. I should have gone right.

The doorbell rings. Seconds later, the front door to the spacious ground-floor apartment opens.

Standing six feet tall, I wouldn't be hard to miss if someone were to come into the room. I quickly move behind a black leather Chesterfield sofa set off the wall. The living room door has settled against its armrest, concealing me further. I thank the yoga gods for my flexibility as I lie face down on the floor, listening.

My stomach lurches as I hear two young females talking. Inevitably, I want to know more. I crawl forward and peer through the crack in the door to watch. My reaction is foolish, as my foot rattles a side table.

A girl's voice said, 'Hang on, someone's here.' She storms into the living room.

I hadn't planned on murdering again tonight, but life-changing memories remind me of that frightening night when I promised never to let anyone destroy me again. So, I will kill again, if necessary.

Two young girls enter the room where I am holed up. One girl switches the lights on, and I can't do anything but remain still, not daring to look.

A second voice says, 'He's not here. Let's rob the bastard; his money is in the freezer.' They turn back around, giggling, and step back into the hallway.

My mind is whirring. Those young girls will be arrested if they are seen. I have to stop it and pour the drink away. Then my blood runs cold as one girl suggests, 'Come on, let's drink his favourite. He'd have a fucking fit if we took that as well as his money. There's a wad of cash here, Trisha. Or we could piss him right off, pour it down the sink? He shouldn't have it; he's a wicked bastard.'

The first girl is right behind her. 'Are you for fucking real, man? We need to get out, take the money and fucking leg it. We can buy plenty of our own fucking brandy.' They flick the living room lights off as they walk past my hiding place. The front door quietly closes behind them. I let out a long breath.

That was too close. I wipe down everything that I have touched, before I do the same in the kitchen and hallway – I can't let those girls take the blame for this. My research has shown that Marcus Towns has had no visitors over the last couple of weeks. Any other fingerprints will raise suspicion. At the same time, I swear I am being watched, but there is no one around and no cameras: paranoia, total paranoia, setting in, I must leave. Silently, with my head down and umbrella up, I close the solid front door behind me.

Both women walk separately as they head to Edinburgh's Waverley train station and catch the next LNER service heading to King's Cross.

Disembarking at Alnmouth, Caron heads for the rear of the hotel, which is on a poorly lit street. She makes her way to her room and changes her clothes. Léa waits a few minutes, reading a map before leaving the station. She turns the opposite way from her friend and takes a longer route. She removes her hat and coat before entering the hotel.

Léa and Caron are ready to fully unwind and spend a

couple of hours relaxing in the restaurant of a different hotel. Unaware that someone has followed them from Edinburgh, they drink their glass of champagne. Neither woman glance at the man watching from the bar. Alcohol has lessened Caron's suspicion.

Their stalker is trying to fathom out what they have been up to. He plans to follow the duo the next morning, for now, though he heads for his parents' home, where his father died a few days earlier. Many happy memories pass through his mind. His father was a hard taskmaster; now, as grown men, he and his brother are thankful for his firm and supportive upbringing.

The two women make the 6.30 am train back to Newcastle the following morning. Their pursuer is furious that he has missed them. Never mind; he knows about DCI Caron Dell, so it'll wait.

54

New Years Day

The New Year began with the case of a missing twenty-one-year-old woman. DCI Dell convinces DS Winston to lead, and Krubb wholeheartedly approves. Caron focuses her time and effort on work as she waits nervously for the DNA results.

There has been no mention of Marcus Towns. Caron and Léa agree that it was pure luck that they weren't caught. Their usual MO was never to leave it to chance. It should always be 100 per cent secure. Now, they hope their foe will be the only one drinking drugged brandy at some point. Their plan had been far too risky, but that episode is over, never to be spoken of again.

Léa texts Caron; *DNA results are here.* Caron nervously makes her way to the mortuary. Her giggle tells Léa to be careful when delivering her message. Caron tries to hold back tears of fear or relief, she can't decide which. They move out to the car park, and Léa reminds her that whatever she finds out today, she should not do anything rash.

'Anything rash? I've been waiting nearly nineteen years for this.' Caron is keen to see confirmation at last, in black and white. 'You open it, Léa, and just tell me, please.' She paces.

'No match.'

'Don't joke Léa.'

Léa shakes her head, 'Caron, there is no DNA match between Macy and Richard. Results from the sample quality are high, meaning it is cut and dry. I am so sorry, but it's not what you want to hear. It definitely is not what I expected.'

Caron sits on a cold, damp bench, 'After all these years, it isn't Richard, well that's going to take some time to get used to.' She stares at the wall opposite, unsure what to do or think.

'Are you OK?' asks Léa.

'Totally shocked. I expected it to be him, Christ, all this time, and I have had the wrong man. Could you imagine if I'd done something?' Her mind is whirling at the discovery. How do I identify who it was, Léa? Where do I go from here?'

'Take some time, go home, try to process all of this.' She hands Caron the results.

Caron reads them again and again. 'Jeez, Léa, I could have murdered him.'

55

Bart

Caron cannot shake the feeling of being watched, as she looks out of her bedroom window and sees a familiar figure on the opposite side of the road, watching the North Sea. It's ten pm, she needs to understand what he is looking for.

'Bart,' she shouts as she crosses the quiet road, wrapping her woollen coat around her. 'What are you doing here?'

'I am visiting the crime scene, ma'am. Not literally, just walking. I have been home for a couple of days and just wanted to be somewhere no one knew me, to walk off the suffocation of my father. I sound ungrateful, but I needed to get away.'

'I understand completely. Would you like to come in for a warm drink?'

'No, but thank you. Did you know they are still digging in Alina's garden and the surrounding area?

'Yes, I do know. Unfortunately, you were right. There are more bodies there.'

'Tsk, those kids. Just youngsters with their lives ahead of them. One thing I have learned is that nothing stays the same forever. Things change; people change. Not always for the better. I am incredibly sorry for those whom he employed. I have never met such an evil soul.'

Caron couldn't tell Bart much more. Seven bodies and skeletal remains have been found after his tip-off.

Identification is ongoing.

'Are you sure you won't come in?'

'No, thank you. I am off the Seafarers for a pint, and then I will get my head down.'

'Keep in touch, Bart, and thank you.'

'Anytime. And I will keep in touch if you don't mind.'

'Not at all. Goodnight, Bart.'

Caron returns home and shuts the cold out as her door closes. Bart is a fascinating man, and she wonders if he has been looking out for her over the last few weeks. She feels more secure in that knowledge.

Bart walks towards the Seafarers but stops beside a parked car less than 100 metres from Caron Dell's address. He signals to the driver to wind his window down.

'I don't know who you are, but do not hurt a hair on that woman's head, do you hear me? And don't think she does not know you are watching her for one minute - or stalking may be a better phrase.' He turns to continue his journey.

'Just a minute,' said a man with a soft Edinburgh accent. 'I intend to watch out for that woman, nothing more.'

'That makes two of us. Except I'll be watching you as well. Goodnight, Edinburgh.' Bart is content with his mild threat.

56

New Beginnings

3rd January 2024

Macy, Beryl, and Keith are now back in France. Caron has a new energy now, with the weight of her last case lifted from her shoulders. After the DNA results, Caron has a different worry: who the hell raped her? She knows if she were well in her mind, she'd process her findings more objectively. It is time to repair herself. Back at the gym each morning and yoga each night would mend her body and soul.

After just a few days, she starts to feel the benefits. Caron's reflection on the Cartwright case begins to show a positive assessment. Her new workload is well covered, and DS Winston is leading the case of the missing twenty-one-year-old, allowing him to step up the ranks. Caron acts as an official mentor, so she is still very much involved; she is just not leading.

Tying up the Cartwright case was a good feeling. Evidence against the four men - Hilary Ravelle, with his knighthood now stripped from him, Jonny Boston, Samuel Morton and Nathan Oliver - was solid. On top of that, they have all pleaded guilty. Hopefully, they'll never see the light of day again, and Petra will never need to face them.

DS Winston wonders what happened to Sonny Hock and airs his frustrations out loud, 'We should have found him, investigated more. He is probably the worst of the five men.'

'My money is on Boulter getting to him, remember he

ordered Box to see to him when they were in the Cartwrights. Hock was the biggest creep and Boulter wanted him dead,' replies Caron Dell, the murderer. 'I just hope his body is found someday to give everyone peace of mind. We must let it go, Denny. There are many cases which need our attention. Sammy Hock is not one of them.'

News bulletin from Chief Superintendent Krubb:

The body of Sonny Hock has been found at his home in an affluent area of Edinburgh. It seems he was murdered by ingesting liquid morphine - Tony Boulter's go-to murder weapon, as well as firearms. Hundreds of child porn images were stored on his laptop. It has also become known that Hock was on CID's radar, suspected of running his paedophile ring. However, he had a different identity: Marcus Towns, hence why we, nor any force, were not informed of their investigation.

It was anticipated that a substantial amount of cash would be found in his property. No significant amounts of money were ever recovered. Police and CPS have now confirmed they are not looking for anyone else; the traces of morphine provided enough evidence to link his murder to Boulter. Liquid morphine has been there for at least a few days, possibly weeks. No one else's DNA or fingerprints were identified. That fact alone would be highly improbable due to his ongoing criminal activities. Staff at the nightclub he owned have confirmed that he worked each night during Christmas. No one could confirm Hock had received any visitors at his flat in the lead-up to the festive season. Boulter went off the radar, and we now know where he was. Again, it appears Boulter has got away with murder.

Caron looks at DI Winston, 'Wow, that's spooky, that, Denny. Do you think you have a sixth sense?' Caron laughs a nervous laugh, hoping no one picks up on it.

'Honestly, ma'am, I didn't think he'd be found in a million years. Boulter was always belt and braces, mind you.'

'Absolutely. Done everyone a favour there, I think.' Inwardly, she is relieved. But she is a murderer all the same. She'd be judged at the pearly gates if she ever reaches them.

All known paedophile clients of Boulter's were sentenced to life in prison, with two of them on suicide watch. The evidence against them allowed the judge to issue the harshest sentences possible. They are a danger to society, so life it is. DI Rustler was also sent down; he came off the worst. Another inmate bit off his tongue, the culprit's reasoning: 'If he wasn't prepared to speak up to protect kids, he shouldn't be allowed to speak at all.' God help the others. No one else will.

Mabel Newman was also found guilty of numerous crimes, and they threw the book at her as well, twenty-three years without parole. She'd need divine intervention, too, if she were to survive her prison term.

Caron, Denny, and Léa received an invite to spend a weekend at Judge Hicks's place - a rambling house located in the fabulous Yorkshire countryside. The invite was extremely vague, which raised their interest. 'Yes, definitely going,' says Denny.

'Agreed. I think all three of us should attend. Sounds like it could be a bit of a celebration.'

57

Judge's Quarters - Yorkshire

They arrive as planned for dinner on a lovely Friday evening in spring. Marking the beginning of summer, Mother Nature was just on the cusp of displaying her colourful show of flowers, plants and blossom trees. Caron drives the three of them through the twists and turns of the country roads. Relaxed and excited to see the judge and his lovely wife Veronica again, she looks forward to a chilled-out couple of days.

On arrival, Caron observes four cars in the drive, two of which belong to the owners. Caron wonders who else is there.

Petra flings the front door open and runs towards Caron, 'So pleased you all made it, we're delighted you're here.' Caron notices a slight change in Petra's demeanour, and her rough-edged personality seems to have been smoothed down.

Caron goes over to her host who is waiting in the doorway, 'Judge Hicks,' she extends her hand for him to shake. He brushes it away and hugs her so tightly she struggles to breathe.

'It's Phillip, Caron; just call me Phillip unless we're in court,' he winks.

Everyone moves into the living room. Mary is there, grinning the widest of grins. Callum is sitting beside her; his grin isn't that much different.

Another couple are sitting in the room. Caron has never met them but instinctively knows they are Petra's parents. She waits to be introduced. Both parents are in tears and repeatedly thank Caron, Denny, and Léa for their intervention. They continue to thank everyone during the weekend until Mary tells them they have to stop! They are thankful for that, too.

Caron relaxes in bliss once settled into their home for the next two days. Friday evening is an informal affair, and dinner is a casual event. They share laughs and some tears, with tales reminiscing of times spent with family: blood family, or street family. The night ends with Petra revealing she and Mary have an announcement for the three of them the next day. Caron, Denny, and Léa are intrigued and look forward to seeing what the following day will bring.

Saturday arrives with Petra and Mary's presentation at the front and centre of the room. It is delivered before lunch. Neither Caron, Denny, nor Léa saw this coming.

Both families and Callum have their new venture approved in principle by the appropriate governing bodies: their young women's enterprise is declared. Before they progress, Petra especially wanted Caron, Denny, and Léa to know. As the forerunner of their innovative charity programme, this was just the beginning. Implemented to support the changes that adolescence can bring. Youngsters who wish to escape from it all will have a safe opportunity to see what it is like living and fending for themselves. The stipulation, Mary explains, is that the programme has limited red tape. Experts would be employed; however, it is not government or council owned. Mary concludes her part of the presentation with more technical information on how their venture will be funded and sustained, and how they will network with established children's charities. It is a long-term plan, and there is much to organise and work through, despite the considerable challenges ahead.

Caron can't believe what she is hearing, and Petra, of all people has come so far. Six months ago, she was down and out and hated everything about her life, and now, after she has been through so much, she has a positive future. In her words, her wicked experience has made her stronger. Growing up and constantly battling with herself, led to a horrific set of circumstances, crossing paths with one of the vilest men to walk this earth: Tony Boulter.

Petra's ongoing therapy is improving her well-being. In the future, Petra plans to finish school and then university, but for now, she is working with Mary and the Hicks family to provide help to those who are as lost as she was. Everything will come to fruition in due course.

It was only eighteen months ago that Petra walked out of her family home; she still has some way to go before she fully recovers, if she ever does. But in front of them today is a teen qualified to understand some of the issues numerous adolescents experience. She is far more knowledgeable in this field than many adults.

Once their presentation is complete, the room erupts in applause and whistles. Everyone is delighted with what's been accomplished in such a short period of time.

Caron takes Mary to one side. 'Whose idea is this?'

'Petra's, to the very last detail. I think she has found her niche, and so have I. She's been great to be around this last year or so; her newfound energy is contagious. Out of all the horrendous pain, heartbreak and death, she has a determination, a clear focus, to help others. Petra has so much to give, she was suffocated and protected for far too long, she chose to become homeless.' Mary looks at Petra with so much pride, you'd think she was her mother.

'A year or so ago?' enquires Caron.

Mary could have bitten her tongue off. 'Petra came to find me sometime during the summer of last year. When Greg became involved with Boulter's paedophile clients, she didn't know whether I would believe her and neither did I. Dad was the only person I trusted at that time, and I turned to him for help.'

'You should have contacted the police.'

'You mean those in Yorkshire? Remember, nothing untoward had happened at that time. I didn't realise, nor did Petra, that she and her friends were being groomed. This was before The House and the vile atrocities those children were subjected to. Petra came to warn me; she knew who Greg was and knew he would never get out of Boulter's grip. Petra took the initiative to do something. She couldn't risk going to the police; Boulter was involved with a number of officers, and she'd have been dead in days. Coming to me was, in Petra's eyes, her way of doing something; she had to try to get away from Boulter's manipulation. That's when I decided to monitor Greg and set up my surveillance cameras. I didn't see her again until that night in December last year. That is the truth.'

Phillip Hicks joins the conversation, 'You must know, Caron, I would not have let Greg, or anyone, continue to do what they were doing, had either of us had known.'

'I do believe you. It would have been useful to know at the time. You realise we could have prevented the nightmare for Petra and her friends.' Caron's statement cools the friendly atmosphere, leaving an awkward silence. But Caron always felt Mary was involved somewhere along the line.

'I disagree, Caron, remember Northumberland, nor you, were involved until those girls died. This is down to Boulter.' Mary knows she and her father could have done more; she doesn't need that pointed out. And the thought of those two dead girls will be on her mind until the day she dies. How could any of them have trusted Gallows?

Caron lets the dust settle for a minute; no one in this room is responsible for Tony Boulter or Greg Cartwright's actions. Mary most definitely could not have gone to anyone local, and she didn't know the extent of the damage.

'Don't get me wrong, the guilty parties are the only people to blame here. Boulter was one terrifying man. It's just frustrating that he caused so much destruction. Not one person in this room is to blame for any of the choices they made. Let's be absolutely clear on that.' The three of them nod in agreement; Caron changes the conversation to a lighter subject. She does not want any of the previous year's corruption and wrongdoing to damage their friendship; Boulter is not getting away with that.

EPILOGUE

Caron

It could have ended so differently. I know I'm a hypocrite, and I should have left it to the police to capture Sonny Hock and deal with him. With further investigations halted, it would never have happened. He had set up his paedophile clientele; children were being constantly abused. We all have choices, and that was his, young girls and although I cannot say for definite, probably murder later on down the line. I couldn't live with myself if another child suffered before he was caught.

Petra and Mary are trying to move on from their dreadful experience. Whatever happens, I must applaud them for it. Petra has found her way, but at the cost of the lives of her two friends and her traumatic past. Too many grieving families will continue to suffer. I have no time for the choices those officers made, but what about their families as well? The ripple effect is far and wide. Boulter and Sonny Hock had to be stopped, through conviction or death.

I know perfectly well how difficult it can be to move on from the deaths of friends and colleagues. Staring terror and confusion in the face whilst grieving is emotionally exhausting. It can take over your life and bring you down, mentally and physically.

Full investigations have been completed for each of the unnecessary deaths, but that doesn't change the outcome; what a needless waste. Lives were lost by protecting the innocent or because Boulter's corrupt police officers let it happen, neither of which will be easily forgotten.

Chief Superintendent Krubb led a memorial service for Uncle; it was highly respectful. I certainly won't forget his sacrifice. I understand Barry Goodwin's funeral was a low-key affair, the sad reality of his father dragging him into Boulter's scummy world. The lad didn't stand a chance, and neither did his mum. But they had choices.

Two girls, Emily and Jessie, wanted to hold onto their youth. They thought being away from thier homes would provide that opportunity. Harmless children who, in their own words, wanted to stay young, tried to experience a lifestyle different from what they were facing as they were growing up. Petra, Emily, and Jessie were raped, abused, drugged. Emily and Jessie were killed. We will never know the depth and breadth of the atrocities they faced. How many others are out there? Boulter had to die.

My team in Northumberland and Yorkshire, who worked with me on such a fast-paced case, hopes Petra succeeds. She's been to hell and back. No one should knock anyone's incredible achievement. And who would have ever thought about Mary and Callum? I do smile at that; it's very lovely.

So, my day is just about done. All data is secure, and my laptop is closed. Leaving my office, I head to the car park. I still reflect on the Cartwright case as I start my twenty-minute drive home.

Seven was the final count of bodies buried in Alina's garden; two of them were Boulter's parents, and one was Alina. The remaining four await identification; one may be CC Gallows' son's friend. The impact on those families will be enormous.

I enjoy where I live, my safe place, and I have a more secure door between my garage and house. Carrying a cup of hot tea as I climb the stairs, I have mixed feelings when I look out of my bedroom window towards Artists Retreat. From a business point of view, the family is pleased that the historic building is back in our hands. Our holiday home has been in high demand since reopening. We fully refurbished the property, leaving no trace whatsoever of what had happened. Outside, the iron rung steps are now well sealed off and firmly out of reach of all inhabitants.

Many rumours have been concocted, which I disapprove of. Haunting stories idolising the monster Tony Boulter, I will never be rid of him. I'd prefer not to have his name on anyone's lips, though; he was pure evil with a dirty black heart.

As I continue to look across the bay, I still cannot shake the feeling of being watched. Paranoia? Or is it, Bart? If it is my rapist, I will track him down someday.

I climb into bed, and I just want to say a final word on my own behaviour. Léa and I have the same principles and ideals, and I am forever thankful for my partner in crime. To be clear on one point, I'm not proud of my murdering personality, and neither is Léa.

However, my work is essential; victims are important, and monsters must be stopped. Just as well murder is something I am exceptionally good at.

Acknowledgements

Special thanks go to my adult children and husband; their patience has been exemplary as I squirrelled away in my writing world. Their feedback and points of view gave me a different perspective, which I might never have considered. Although *Dying to Stay Young* is a work of fiction, it is a reminder of how challenging life can be. *Stay Young*, written and performed by Beth Robinson, took me back to my teenage years and many memories, some of which I had completely forgotten.

I also wish to thank close family, especially my sister, for her eagle-eyed review, and cousins for their unwavering encouragement, as I created and developed my debut novel, along with the unfaltering support of close friends. Your patience is very much appreciated.

From an editorial point of view, I wish to acknowledge the support and guidance provided by Gareth Watkins at Watkins Editorial Services. Without his expertise, I would still be ploughing through numerous edits!

New Writing North should also be mentioned. I first shared my writing with our tutor group, and was encouraged to continue on my creative journey. Thank you for your professional critique and direction.

As a member of Alex's book club at sarahs-star.org, we give a firm but fair review of our reading material. I am thankful to those who have encouraged my writing journey, and especially grateful to Sarah for providing such an exhilarating group! I hope for favourable feedback from my straight-talking, critical friends - I have everything crossed!

Last but definitely not least, I thank my Mam and Dad for a happy home life. I was lucky to have such supportive parents, and if they were here now, I would apologise for the worry I caused them as a fifteen-year-old! Unconditionally, they continued to love and guide me. Thank you both.

ABOUT THE AUTHOR

Glynis Drew

I was born and raised in a small coastal town, which at the time formed part of the county of Northumberland. Now, just a few miles away, I spend most of my time writing and enjoying the area where I live, with family and friends, all of which I am grateful for.

Dying to Stay Young is my debut novel, which introduces DCI Caron Dell, and is the first publication of my written work. I am currently in the process of forming my second story involving Caron and her colleagues:

>   Where is January Blue?

My second book in the series is planned to be released in early 2026.

Thank you for reading Dying to Stay Young.

Printed in Dunstable, United Kingdom